A Royalty Crew Novel

RUTHLESS NOBLE

RUTHLESS NOBLE

A Royalty Crew Duet Book 2

ALLEY CIZ

HOUSE OF CRAZY
PUBLISHING

Also by Alley Ciz

The Royalty Crew (A #UofJ Spin-Off)

Savage Queen

Ruthless Noble

#UofJ Series

Cut Above The Rest (Prequel) Freebie

Looking To Score

Game Changer

Playing For Keeps

Off The Bench- #UofJ4 Preorder, Releasing December 2021

BTU Alumni Series

Power Play (Jake and Jordan)

Musical Mayhem (Sammy and Jamie) BTU Novella

Tap Out (Gage and Rocky)

Sweet Victory (Vince and Holly)

Puck Performance (Jase and Melody)

Writing Dirty (Maddey and Dex)

Scoring Beauty- BTU6 Preorder, Releasing September 2021

I was the epitome of control.

Cocky.
Powerful.
Ruthless.

Until the day Savvy King swaggered into our world.

She defied me at every turn, refusing to yield to my command.

Her insolence infuriated me as much as it captivated me, until the battle *consumed* us.

She's the perfect counterpart to my reign. Except…the ring on her finger belongs to another.

People want to play politics with my life—with *our* lives. That is a mistake.

Don't underestimate what I'll do to claim her as mine and secure my queen.

RUTHLESS NOBLE is book 2 in The Royalty Crew Duet and cannot be read as a stand-alone. It picks up right where the cliff of SAVAGE QUEEN left you breathless. The secrets and lies are piling up around them. This Queen needs someone ruthless enough to stand by her side.

Ruthless Noble (A Royalty Crew Duet)

Alley Ciz

Paperback ISBN: 978-1-950884-23-0

Ebook ISBN: 978-1-950884-22-3

Cover Designer: Julia Cabrera at Jersey Girl Designs

Cover Photographer: Wander Book Club Photography

Cover Models: Joey Lagrua and Kennedy Moran

Editing: Jessica Snyder Edits, C. Marie

Proofreading: Dawn Black; My Brother's Editor

❀ Created with Vellum

To Julia Wolf and Laura Lee, for without you both I...don't even know.
#BestiesForLife

Author Note

Dear Reader,
RUTHLESS NOBLE IS BOOK 2 in the Royalty Crew Duet.
You must read book 1, SAVAGE QUEEN, prior to this
installment to follow the story properly.

It is a #UofJ Series Spin-off. You do not need to read them to
understand the story, you just get to know them a bit more.

All are available in Kindle Unlimited.

The Royalty Crew

1. Savage Queen
2. Ruthless Noble

#UofJ Series

1. Cut Above The Rest (Prequel) Freebie
2. Looking To Score
3. Game Changer
4. Playing For Keeps

5. *Off The Bench*- #UofJ4 Preorder, Releasing
   December 2021

If I'm new to you and you haven't read my #UofJ books
you're fine.
If you have met my this crazy cast, this duet takes place the
school year after PLAYING FOR KEEPS.
XOXO
Alley

Playlist

- "Trust Fund Baby"- Why Don't We
- "Up & Down"- Dana Dentata
- "Hot girl bummer"- blackbear
- "Human"- Rag'n'Bone Man
- "Juicy"- Notorious BIG
- "Youngblood"- 5 Seconds of Summer
- "Why Don't You Love Me"- Hot Chelle Rae Feat Demi Lovato
- "Easier"- 5 Seconds of Summer
- "Woman Like Me"- Little Mix Feat Nicki Minaj
- "Freak"- Little Mix
- "I'll Be Missing You"- Diddy, Faith Evans, 112
- "Not Your Barbie Girl"- Ava Max
- "Queen"- Loren Gray
- "F.F.F." Bebe Rexha Feat G-Eazy
- "Say My Name"- Destiny's Child
- "Distraction"- Kehlani
- "Break Up With Your Girlfriend"- Ariana Grande
- "Pray For You"- Jaron And The Long Road To Love
- "Teenagers"- My Chemical Romance
- "Royals"- Lorde

- "She Hates Me"- Puddle Of Mud
- "Shameless"- Sofia Karlberg
- "Hate (I Really Don't Like You)- Plain White T's
- "Do re mi"- blackbear
- "Play With Fire"- Sam Tinnesz Feat Yacht Money
- "How To Start A War"- Simon Curtis
- "Games"- Demi Lovato
- "Suffer"- Charlie Puth
- "Sorry Not Sorry"- Demi Lovato
- "Hallucinate"- Dua Lipa
- "Bad guy"- Billie Eilish Feat Justin Bieber
- "…Baby One More Time"- Britney Spears
- "Latch"- Disclosure and Sam Smith
- "I'm Not The Only One"- Sam Smith
- "Mama Who Bore Me"- Lea Michele
- "I Won't Give Up"- Christina Grimmie
- "Faking It"- Calvin Harris Feat Kehlani & Lil Yachty)
- "Keep On"- Kehlani
- "All About The Benjamins"- Diddy, Lil' Kim, The LOX, The Notorious BIG
- "Breakin' Dishes"- Rihanna
- "Unlove You"- Star Cast
- "I Don't Care"- Fall Out Boy
- "Watch Me Burn"- Michele Morrone
- "Ten Duel Commandments"- Hamilton Cast
- "Mama's house"-push baby
- "Treat You Better"- Shawn Mendes
- "The Kill"- Thirty Seconds To Mars
- "Savage Remix"- Megan Thee Stallion Feat Beyonce
- "Miss Me More"- Kelsea Ballerina
- "The Fighter"- Keith Urban Feat Carrie Underwood
- "Fall In Line"- Christina Aguilera Feat Demi Lovato
- "River"- Bishop Briggs

- "Dive"- Guitar Tribute Players
- "Monster"- Michael Jackson Fest 50 Cent
- "Castle"- Halsey
- "Give 'em Hell"- Everybody Loves an Outlaw
- "I See Red"- Everybody Loves an Outlaw
- "Crazy In Love"- Beyonce
- "High Heels"- JoJo
- "Come Little Children"- Myuu
- "Piece by Piece"- Kelly Clarkson
- "You should see me in a crown"- Billie Eilish
- "Bury a friend"- Billie Eilish
- "Porn Star Dancing"- My Darkest Days, Zakk Wylde
- "Crown"- Camila Cabello and Grey
- "Fuckboi"- Gianni & kyle
- "A Decade Under The Influence"- Taking Back Sunday
- "Into You"- Ariana Grande
- "You Don't Own Me"- SAYGRACE Feat G-Eazy
- "Danger Zone"- Kenny Loggins
- "Princessess Don't Cry"- CARYS
- "Gorilla"- Bruno Mars"
- "New Girl"- FINNEAS
- "Creep"- Kelly Clarkson
- "Jealous Remix"- Nick Jonas Feat Tinashe
- "Amen"- Halestorm
- "Woman"- Kesha Fest The Dap-Kings Horns
- "Best Friend"- Saweetie Feat Doja Cat

FIND PLAYLIST on Spotify.

CHAPTER 1

MARRIAGE?

Really?

Fucking MARRIAGE?

What. In. The. ACTUAL. Fuck?

Behind me, Jasper's body turns to stone. I swear to all things holy, if muscles could speak, the ones in the leg pressed along the length of mine would be echoing the thoughts currently blaring in my brain.

Let's not bring up the fact that I actively sought him out for comfort during Natalie's entire brain-melting diatribe. I'm currently struggling with basic biological human functions like breathing; I can't be expected to work out the convoluted dynamic that is…well…Jasper and me.

I can't handle…

ALL THIS!

My pulse is erratic, the adrenaline pumping through me wreaking havoc on my system. I've already used my inhaler more in the last hour than I should in such a short amount of time, and doing so again could have adverse effects.

You can do this. Breathe, Savvy. Just breathe.

I close my eyes, shutting out the world, and look internally for a calm I sure as shit don't feel but desperately need to find before I spiral entirely.

Natalie is busy muttering apologies and trying her best to cover up her faux pas of blurting out details that were meant to be disclosed in a more official capacity.

Yeah, because telling your teenage children you're arranging their marriage is just another basic contract to slide across the boardroom table.

Behind me, Jasper shifts, and I instinctively step with him, moving until my whole body is leaning against his. A hand snakes its way around my waist and anchors itself on my hip, fingers tightening with a slight pinch when he notices the daggers Natalie glares at his touch.

Jasper doesn't move.

I do…but not out of his hold. Instead, my shoulders brush his muscular chest as I roll them forward and back in an effort to open up my lungs as much as physically possible.

"*Breathe.*" The deep cadence of the softly whispered word barely registers enough for me to realize it's Jasper joining in on my inner coaching. "Just breathe, Princess." His thumb rubs back and forth and back and forth over my hip bone, the repetitive motion adding a sense of calm I'm in dire need of.

It also helps that Natalie keeps sliding looks toward the Nobles and Delacourtes, trying to gauge their reactions to Jasper touching me instead of Duke. If I wasn't dealing with my own shit, I would smile at how she's subtly suggesting we reschedule our evening.

Also…

Did she *really* bring up Carter, or was that some sort of weird hallucination brought on by lack of oxygen and too much albuterol?

Sure, she didn't say his name, but that was the *first* time she's acknowledged she gave birth to another human since she added St. James as her surname. And…what was with her mentioning it so casually?

Hell…

I probably shouldn't be surprised that it was a passing comment when she spoke of pending nuptials like it was common knowledge.

"What—" I clear my throat, the action painful against the rawness inside it, and press a hand to it in counterpressure. "In—the—*actual*—fuck?!" I struggle to get out the question I asked myself only moments ago. "Wait…" A sudden, probably inaccurate thought hits me. I whirl around, Jasper's touch falling from my body as I step back on wobbly legs to hunt down Duke with an accusatory gaze. "Did you know about this?"

"What?" Duke's eyes are wide, and if I were thinking rationally, I would likely notice he's paler than usual and seems to be as confused as I am. But I'm not—rational, that is.

"This." I stab a finger at Natalie. "This Medieval marriage bullshit. Did you know about it?"

"Umm…"

When he stutters, I whip my attention over to a broody Jasper. "What about you?" With each labored breath that fails to reach the bottom of my lungs, my fury grows. "Was this last week all an act? Playing nice so I lower my guard and then, BAM"—I smack my hands together—"sit back while I'm hit with this?"

I start to laugh, the sound ugly and dark, doing nothing for me except triggering an uncontrollable coughing fit. Plus side? It makes some of the adults start to back away as if I'm contagious or something.

I'm spiraling, and if I don't get my emotions in check, I'm going to be in a full-blown attack. Ask me if I care.

Spurred on by stubborn righteousness, I continue. "I gotta say…" I start to slow clap when more coughing steals my speech. "You *really* upped your game, Noble." His eyes narrow at his name, and I circle a finger in the direction of my bedroom while puffing my breaths like I'm in a Lamaze class. "That whole possessive *mine* thing you did was pretty convincing. I would have never guessed you were only taking me for a test drive before passing me off to your friend."

"The fuck?" The black dots dancing into my vision make it hard to see, but there's no mistaking the blind rage twisting Jasper's features.

An arm snaps out and he grips me by the nape, but when I expect him to drag me to him like I'm some doll for him to maneuver the way he typically would, he doesn't. It's not a punishing hold; it's...supportive. It's proprietary.

Tears burn at the backs of my eyes and I blink them away, doing everything in my power to focus on the face I shouldn't but can't help but think is handsome when he steps in closer.

"I have no idea what you're playing at, but that shit stops *now*." He's not outright denying the accusations, but that doesn't stop relief from flooding my system. Why? Why do I need him to not be involved in this...this...*insanity*.

"No, no, no. Please don't apologize." Jasper's gaze flits over my head, his eyes following Natalie as she starts to guide his parents and Duke's around our small cluster. "It's my fault for letting it slip out like that. We can reschedule after the kids have time to get used to the idea."

Yeah, oh-kay.

"It'll never happen, Savvy." As a unit, Jasper and I turn to acknowledge Chuck's attempt at reassurance. I see how he eyes me warily as I continue to struggle to regulate my breathing and heart rate into less dangerous territory. Jasper? He sees a threat he tried to warn me away from.

"Don't call her *that*," Natalie snaps, whirling around as Mitchell continues to walk their other guests out.

"Why doesn't it surprise me that you're focusing on *that*?" There's a snark to Chuck's tone that's reminiscent of Tessa. "Real mother of the year," he mutters, stepping around and dismissing her by giving her his back. I'd smile if it wouldn't take too much effort at the moment.

Jasper and Duke wear matching furrowed brows as Duke mouths, "*Savvy?*" and Jasper answers with an *I have no idea* shoulder shrug.

Chuck runs a hand down my back and Jasper growls, like legit growls like some kind of feral animal. It's hot, and if my body wasn't currently melting down, my girlie parts would be going haywire over it.

Yes, yes I know there is something wrong with me.

If I weren't having yet another coughing fit, I would woman up and tell Jasper there's no threat here, tell him Chuck's touch is not at all what he thinks it is. He's practically my uncle, and I don't mean in the creepy sense.

"Savvy..." Jasper lets out another growl, his fingers flexing behind my neck at my nickname rolling off Chuck's tongue while he does another up-and-down pass along my spine.

I meet Jasper's angry gaze with a slow, pleading blink, holding it until the sound of Chuck's voice brings my attention back to him.

"I mean it," he says. Again I have to force a swallow at the dark energy surrounding him; it reminds me of the Royals. "It. Will. *Never*. Happen."

Distantly I register the sound of other voices talking, but it's muffled. Over the roar of my blood pumping through my veins, only bits and pieces of the conversation make it through to me as they say their goodbyes.

I shake my head, trying to clear it.

With the only witnesses she would care about now gone, Natalie leans in, her nose practically touching mine as she hisses, "I don't care what Charles thinks—he's wrong." She shifts closer, her lips skimming the shell of my ear as her voice drops until it's barely above a whisper. "This engagement is very much real, and you'll do well to remember *that* if you don't want others to suffer the consequences."

A chill chases down my spine, the sensation only growing in intensity when I catch the malevolent gleam in her eye as she straightens.

When Natalie first demanded I live with her, I didn't tell Carter about the threats she made against him. First, it was a petty thing. He's keeping something from me, so I figured it was only fair I keep something from him. But the truth of the matter is, my brother has spent a good chunk of his life protecting me; it was time for me to protect him.

Playing into Natalie's perfect mother act seemed like a small price to pay in the grand scheme of things. But this? I think the *only* person who might have been able to dream this scenario up would be Tessa, because this shit is straight-up fiction. Natalie thinks she can trade me like I'm some kind of baseball card? Offering up a betrothal to further her own agenda?

I don't think so.

This is a clusterfuck beyond anything imaginable. Carter is going to lose his fucking mind when he hears about this. *Shit!* Chuck already has his phone out.

"Savvy, you need to relax before you make yourself sick," Chuck commands, ignoring Natalie entirely.

A crushing weight settles on my chest, and I think, *I really should listen to him because...*

My symptoms aren't getting better. They're...getting worse.

CHAPTER 2

HOLY FUCK.

Married?

Samantha's—

Wait! Hold up. Savvy? Her name is Savvy? Why is that name so familiar to me?

Shit!

Whatever the fuck her name is isn't the point. The detail I need to focus all my attention on is that her mother wants her to get *married*?

TO. DUKE?

Yeah…not gonna happen.

Why do you care?

I ignore the question from my subconscious. I don't…*care.* It's just…

…

…

Fuck! I don't know! But it's *not* going to happen.

My heart is pounding, and there's a thundering between my ears.

Duke's eyes are double their normal size, his eyebrows winged up his forehead, his hands extended out by his sides like *I had no idea, man.*

Some may say the decision I made earlier to go against the Royals to claim Samantha—*shit! I guess she's Savvy?*—as mine was a death wish. Whatever…I could handle that.

Going against my parents? That's an *entirely* different scenario. Make no mistake, doing *anything* that could negatively affect Governor Delacourte's political career would be considered an insult to my own parents. The business relationship Walter Noble has with Frank Delacourte is valued above anything else—a fact the side-eye he sends my way as they all take their leave tells me I need to remember.

Complicated just took on a whole new meaning.

Then I remember what other new piece of information I learned tonight.

Oh, fuck me sideways.

She has asthma.

Shit! Shit! Shit!

"Savvy, you need to relax before you make yourself sick," Chuck commands. Every ounce of possessive, caveman-like rage drains out of me in an instant.

How long has it been since she needed to use her inhaler because of what we did in the bathroom? Ten minutes? Twenty? Can she use it again this soon?

Panic slams into me hard and fast. "Where's your inhaler?"

"You know she has asthma?"

"She has asthma?"

"Must you make a scene?"

Chuck and Duke's questions trip over each other, both shockingly confused on different ends of the spectrum. It's the third one that really gets me, though, the one asked in a haughty tone I can't believe anyone would voice, if not for the simple fact of *Why would you?* when a person is in the midst of a major medical episode, let alone for the asker to be the person's mother. Is this woman for real?

For the first time…ever, I meet Chuck's gaze over Samantha's shaking shoulders without any of the derisive ridicule that generally simmers in my blood for him.

Sam—Savvy—fuck, I'm not sure *what* to call her—wobbles, my hold on her nape the only thing keeping her upright. I curl her into my chest, coasting my free hand down the length of her torso, fumbling with the soft material of her dress to find the opening of her pocket in search of her inhaler.

"Fuck this," Chuck curses and pulls his phone out.

Duke moves in close for support. I slide him a thankful glance. I can't even imagine what he might be feeling being the other half of this marriage equation we knew nothing about, but still, he manages to focus on what's important. Unlike Natalie St. James, whose—

You know what? It doesn't matter.

Chuck has his phone on speaker, and the tinny ringtone of the call he's making cuts off with an amused, deep voice asking, "I can't believe the bitch didn't make you check your phone at her pretentious penthouse door."

"Carter." There's a tinge of panic lacing Chuck's tone, but that's not what has me finally ripping my gaze from Sam —*aaa*vvy to him.

Carter? As in Carter King?

"Why yes, let's just add to the dramatics." Natalie rolls her eyes, feeling free to be her true, terrible self now that most of her adult audience is gone.

"What's wrong?" The abrupt change to Carter King's speech could give a person whiplash.

"Tell me what to do when Savvy's having an asthma attack."

Puzzle pieces start to come together, but it's not enough to form a clear picture. It's like trying to put it together without having the box to look at for reference.

"Shit," Carter curses, his voice fading slightly as he shouts, "Wes! Call Tessa. She's at the St. James and knows what to do. Tell her she needs to get upstairs to the penthouse right *fucking* now."

Tessa? The redhead? Why would he want her here? And why the *hell* did Chuck call King in the first place?

She's not a race rat, my mind whispers, the thought floating right out as I *finally* feel the smooth cylindrical plastic of the inhaler.

"Natalie." The boom of Carter's voice as he returns his attention to the phone call has everyone—including a heavily breathing Savvy—looking toward the pinch-faced woman. "I don't give a shit about any of your other failings as a parent—"

I swallow, darting my gaze from Natalie to Savvy to the phone lying on the flat of Chuck's palm, to the man himself, and lastly to Duke, his eyebrows lifted the way mine are. We've heard the stories about Carter King. Most seem like general rumblings or overblown rumors that, while perhaps not believed by most, still end up having the power to cause people to heed them.

This? The dark danger simmering beneath the surface as he speaks? Maybe there's more to his reputation than I ever gave him, or the Royals, credit for.

That might mean—

I shake that thought off before it can finish forming.

"—but so. Help. Me. *God*, if you don't move your ass and make it possible for Tessa to get upstairs in the next two minutes, I will make you *rue* the day you ever gave birth to me."

WHAT?!

HOLD ON.

FULL STOP.

Carter King is Natalie's son?

That would mean…

"Oh fuck," Duke whispers next to me, and I shit you not, even in these dire circumstances, the asshole chuckles the tiniest bit.

Sonofabitch.

She's. His. Sister.

That's why I thought I recognized her. I must have seen her at one of the races before this year. Carter and his crew typically congregate around the bonfire at the Royal Balls, and with her asthma, Saman—Savvy wouldn't. Add in the age gap and the fact that I've only known her as Samantha St. James—*how do you get Savvy from Samantha anyway?*—and it was easy for me to not make the connection.

All those times people have cut themselves off when saying her name start to make sense. Samantha must be a fake name.

Her knowledge of how the hierarchy worked at Blackwell Public didn't come from being a student there.

The Royals don't care about her because she's their favorite race rat.

She's one *of* them.

Fuck my life.

JASPER NOBLE

CHAPTER 3

"THE BEST THING you can do for her is to stay calm," King coaches through the phone.

Savvy may be his sister, and I take it he has experience with her having asthma attacks, but does he not remember how scary it is to see the tendons in her neck pop out in stark relief or the skin on her chest pull tight around the thin bones of her clavicle?

Stay calm?

Yeah, oh-kay.

"Who the fuck was that?" King barks, and I guess I said that part out loud. "It doesn't matter." He dismisses his own question just as quickly as a ring beeps through.

Another glance down shows Carter's switching to a video call, and again Duke cuts me a look warning me to keep myself in check.

Chuck stretches his arm out, his hand hitting my chin as he angles the phone so Savvy can blink hazy eyes at her brother on the screen.

Shit!

Carter King is her brother. That means *she's* a King. That makes her connected. Which means…Governor Delacourte will only want Duke to pursue her more. *Double shit.*

"Cart," Savvy wheezes, her cheek pillowing against my chest, more of her weight falling into me. I shift to better support her, now able to see the screen while my face stays out of view of the camera.

"Oh, baby girl." The harsh line of Carter's brow softens as his gaze bounces over his sister's face. If I had any doubts about how important Savvy is to him, that simple and automatic change to his facial features would erase them. Things are only growing more complicated by the second.

Mitchell returns during another coughing fit from Savvy, and it's clear this is far more than an anxiety attack brought on by unexpected news. Uncertainty flashes across his features and his gaze bounces from Savvy in the center of our small cluster to his silent wife, looking for direction.

Thankfully Duke has enough presence of mind to ask Mitchell to have the hotel's staff allow for elevator access to the penthouse for anyone getting on at the seventh floor.

Mitchell does so immediately, his phone at his ear at the same time Carter asks Savvy where her inhaler is.

Having freed it from her pocket, I hold it up for her. I don't get the chance to appreciate the way her lips tip into the tiniest hint of a smile—at me—because the tremble in her fingers as they curl around the inhaler is more than concerning.

"Can she use it if she only did an hour ago?" Chuck asks, but his timeline is off, and I'm smacked with the realization of how dangerous fucking the shit out of Savvy could have been.

I'm not a fan of the slimy sense of guilt coiling in my gut. It pisses me off. It's probably why there's more attitude riddling my words when I inform them that Savvy used her inhaler less than *thirty*—not sixty—minutes ago.

Without having to be told, Chuck spins the phone, and now I'm face to face with Carter King. If looks could kill, I'd be roadkill behind his Corvette.

His eyes are more gray than the purple of his sister's, but I'd recognize that defiant, challenging gleam anywhere. I see it every time I attempt to exert my dominance over Savvy. Except…Carter's has a lethal edge. It's not a threat; it's a promise—of punishment and pain.

His glare is steady, but the video is not as the details in the background seem to fly by to the soundtrack of male shouts and orders being called out.

"Yeah, baby," Duke coos while I continue my stare down with Carter King. I don't get the chance to give him shit for sounding like an outdated Austin Powers impersonation. The sound of shoes slapping the ground at a run is the only warning I get before a body is throwing my arm up by the elbow and shoving its way between Savvy and me.

Red and gold fill my vision as hair goes up my nose, causing me to sneeze, all while I wonder what the hell just happened. *It's the friend.*

With a confidence that matches the surprising strength that was able to move me, she liberates Chuck's phone from his hold. "I'm hanging up." King goes to interrupt, but she cuts him off. "Don't argue. You can't drive the way you want if you're on the phone. I already called the ambulance, they're on their way. Meet us at the hospital." She pauses, waiting until she has his full attention again. "I got this, Carter." Another pause. "Promise." She holds out a crooked pinkie, black I can't make out scrawled across the inner skin.

The finality and utter conviction she infuses in that one word immediately calms the worst of the panic brewing inside me, and the slight nod I catch Carter give before she disconnects the call proves he feels the same.

The phone gets passed off to Chuck.

There's an eye roll given to Natalie.

A hair flip dismisses Duke and his cocksure grin.

An elbow nudges me back farther.

Hands cup Savvy's face, and that possessive instinct floods my veins. It doesn't matter in the least that it's a female doing the touching this time. It should be me.

"Breathe, Savs, just breathe," Tessa coaches. Tears dot Savvy's lower lash line, one falling free and coasting down her now ruddy cheeks as she meets her friend's eyes. "I got you. I'm here. It's going to be okay," Tessa continues, and like Carter advised us to do, she keeps her entire demeanor calm, her words steady and even.

Savvy's own mother is in the room, yet it's a high school senior who is in command of the situation.

Savvy's gasping now and swaying on her feet. I tighten my hold and wonder if I should make her sit down or not.

"Where's your inhaler?" Savvy answers Tessa's question by holding up the device in question. Tessa grabs it, thumbing open the cap and shaking it.

"She's already used it twice in the last hour," Chuck cautions.

Tessa's face screws up in contemplation, but I look away as something brushes along my abdominals. I glance down, purple fingertips ghosting over the black of my vest before clutching at it, however weakly.

She's bent forward, her forehead dropping to Tessa's shoulder while she rubs at her back. Her best friend is here, right in front of her, and she's reaching for *me*.

"Tessa Marie Taylor, you don't just order someone to call 911 then run off on your own," an unfamiliar voice calls out from the foyer as four more people come rushing in. Holy *shit* —I'm pretty sure Eric Dennings from the Baltimore Crabs is among them.

"Yell at me later," Tessa answers, keeping her focus on Savvy instead of the super-tiny blonde scolding her.

Having made the BA varsity hockey team as a freshman—

thanks mostly to my exceptional skating skills—I've spent years facing down opponents larger than me. Tessa may be tall for a girl at around five six or five seven, but she shouldn't have the ability to intimidate me. Yet, when she turns her attention to me, eyes assessing, lips flattening as she takes my measure, that's precisely what I am—intimidated. I don't like it, and I lash out.

"Are you going to help her or not?" The strangled whimper Savvy expels only ratchets up my temper, and I take it out on Tessa. "You told her brother you *got this*, but from where I'm standing"—I do a quick scan up and down her body—"it doesn't seem like you do."

Tension and animosity crackle around the room. I don't give a shit. Every other person can go fuck themselves. A few hurt feelings are the least of my concerns.

Tessa shifts her eyes to check on the other new arrivals and holds a hand up as if to stop them from intervening. She wraps an arm behind Savvy's back and dips her shoulder to act as a crutch on the side not pressed against me.

Behind me, Duke moves until he's at my back between the newcomers and me.

Tessa steps into my space, getting all up in my face and poking a finger into my sternum. I don't know this chick from Eve, but in this moment, it's clear to see how she became friends with Savvy. "*Oooh*, like *you're* one to talk." Another poke to my chest. "Just because you played nice all week doesn't mean you aren't still a dipshit."

Someone snorts while somebody else shushes them, and this whole thing is unraveling faster than the rolls of toilet paper we used to teepee the BP locker room.

"Pretend all you want, *Noble*." Tessa says my last name with the same derision as Savvy, the only noticeable difference being that it doesn't make my dick perk up. "But I'd bet good money this *current* attack could be added to the column of ones you've been the cause of."

Wait…

Hold up.

I've given Savvy asthma attacks before? How? When?

"Now…" Tessa moves to take more of Savvy's weight from me, which I reluctantly allow. "If you want to continue acting like you're my girl's white knight—"

I get the impression she selected those specific words with purpose. I can see it in the challenge issued by the arch of one eyebrow. For once, I'm smart enough to ignore it and wait for the rest of her directive.

"—you need to help manage her symptoms as best we can *without* her using her inhaler."

Fear hits. "Why?" Mitchell and I ask in unison.

"Isn't that what her inhaler is for?" Duke asks, echoing the exact thought that came to my mind.

"It is, but an overdose on albuterol could be just as dangerous, if not deadly."

Did I say fear? No, now I'm…I don't know what; it's unfamiliar and wholly uncomfortable. "What can I do?" Is that my voice coming out all garbled?

Tessa pauses a beat. Then with a nod more to herself than me, she eases Savvy toward me more. Once she's sure I am fully supporting her friend and she doesn't need to worry I'll drop her, she spins around, searching the room for god knows what.

It hasn't been all that long, but Savvy goes from her body having physical reactions to weakly sagging against me. It only reinforces my dismay, and I watch Tessa like a hawk, waiting for a cue, despising how utterly helpless I am.

She stops in front of the St. Jameses, and I find it interesting that it's Mitchell she asks to turn up the thermostat. Natalie looks close to stomping her foot when Mitchell removes his arm to follow through on the directive. Tessa keeps walking, perking up at the sight of the lit fireplace, even if I do catch an eye roll.

With a snap of her fingers, Tessa calls me to bring Savvy over. I take a step but feel the way Savvy wobbles. "I got you, Princess," I promise and scoop her up from underneath her knees.

Tessa pats the floor in front of the hearth. "Put her down here."

I clench my jaw, annoyed by her ordering me around like I'm some lapdog. "Were the aesthetics not to your liking over there?"

"Untwist the panties from around your balls, douchewaffle," she snaps back.

There's another pattern of a snort and shushing from the random arrivals, this one capped off with a "Told you she didn't need you."

"The cold makes it harder to breathe. Keeping her warm will help keep her airways from contracting more."

People move around us, each asking questions and voicing concerns, but it's mostly ignored as I watch the way Tessa crouches in front of Savvy, once again cupping her face in assessment.

We're all on edge as emotions run high. Constantly snapping at each other isn't getting us anywhere. Instead, I take a breath—something I'm all too conscious of Savvy struggling to do—then ask, "What can I do?"

There's the slightest softening around Tessa's eyes when she glances my way again. "Give her your coat." I shrug my shoulder and already have it halfway off before she calls out, "Yours too, sidekick."

"I'll show you my sidekick, baby."

"Bro." I give him the *Keep it in your pants* eyeball.

"What?" Duke mutters, his voice pitched low. "Not appropriate now that I have a fiancée?"

His comment sets Savvy off on another wave of coughing, and Tessa snaps her gaze between the two.

Me? I'm going to pretend I didn't hear it, because if I

don't, I'll only get pissed at my best friend, and he didn't do anything wrong. Instead, I concentrate on draping my suit jacket then Duke's around Savvy.

Again at Tessa's instruction, I plop down behind Savvy, positioning a leg on either side of her, using my front as a backboard to help her sit up. Pressed against me the way she is, I can *feel* the way her chest rattles every time she inhales.

Where the fuck is that ambulance?

CHAPTER 4

THE IMAGES of the last few hours play across my memory like a nightmare that refuses to leave you alone no matter how many times you force yourself awake.

For the first time ever, seeing the way Savvy's mouth needed to open wide didn't inspire fantasies of what my cock would look like sliding in and out of it because I was exceedingly aware of her doing it in an effort to breathe.

The edges around Savvy's lips starting to take on a tint of blue.

The paramedics arriving and being forced to relinquish my hold so they could lay Savvy flat on her back.

The sudden silence that became deafening in a room full of people when Savvy succumbed to her attack and stopped breathing.

One of the paramedics kneeling at Savvy's side to fit an oxygen mask over her mouth, his hand squeezing the blue bubble thing that would force the oxygen into her lungs while the other checked her other vitals.

And the worst, the thing I see clearer than all the others, is how Savvy's arm flopped over the edge of the gurney, practically lifeless as the paramedics lifted it into position.

Needless to say, the previous plans for the evening were canceled in the wake of such serious events and left me to pace inside my dorm suite.

It wouldn't be so bad if I wasn't here by myself. Unfortunately, Duke went to find his parents to talk about the whole *engagement* situation, and I have no clue where the other guys are. Probably at a party, if I had to guess.

I should text them to meet up, but instead, I'm here stewing in the things I learned, the revelations that were made, and the simple frustration over both people's actions and their *in*actions throughout the night.

Natalie St. James is a cuntbag of the highest order. I don't even think Savvy is aware, and, yes, I couldn't hear every word, but I heard enough to know she threatened her daughter about the engagement.

Natalie hides behind an intricate mask, but I saw the complete lack of maternal concern over her daughter being taken away by paramedics beneath the surface. How is that possible? Am I the only one who found it weird that it was Savvy's friend Tessa who rushed behind them stating that she was riding along in the ambulance? Honestly, if you ask me, I don't think Natalie would have even gone to the hospital if it wasn't for Mitchell calling his driver to bring the car around.

I may have been the only one to hear it, but I can recall Natalie muttering something about "such dramatics" while we waited for the elevator to return to the penthouse floor.

I seriously question if the woman is delusional. If it weren't for Savvy's friend showing up and taking control of the situation, things would have dissolved into chaos.

As I round the end of the couch in the center of the room for the millionth time, I finally snap. I need to know what's going on and if Savvy is okay.

I don't stop to question if it's a good idea. It's not—I know it.

I'm not family and will most likely be denied any information about her condition. It's even less likely that I'll be allowed to see her because it's closing in on the middle of the night and well after visiting hours. Plus…if I *am* able to sweet-talk my way into finding out her room number, there's the chance Carter King, or any of the other Royals, could be there.

Ignoring all the obstacles that could be waiting for me and the uneasiness stemming from caring for someone who isn't my family or Duke, I'm out the door and sliding into the bucket seat of my Ferrari in minutes.

I don't feel bad in the least having listened to Mitchell confirm—with *Chuck*—which hospital they would be taking Savvy to.

Driving like I do when I'm racing, it's not long before I'm pulling into the parking garage closest to the emergency room. There's a chance Savvy has been admitted by now, but I figure this is as good a place to start as any.

Unfortunately, I don't see any familiar faces in the waiting room, but I am able to charm the nurse working the administration desk into divulging what floor they took Savvy to.

I hear them before I see them, their raised voices carrying and echoing down the mostly empty hallways when I make it up to the sixth-floor waiting room.

"If all you're going to do is complain, why are you even here, Natalie?" Carter King stands with his arms crossed and legs spread as he stares down at a bored-looking Natalie.

"How many times do I have to tell you not to call me Natalie?" Even seated, this woman manages to look down her nose at him. It's a skill more than one chick at BA would kill to master. "I am your mother. You will show me some respect when you address me."

King scoffs. "You stopped being more than the person

who incubated Savvy and me the day our dad was put into the ground."

Even I suck in a breath at the harsh bluntness of that statement. It seems the tension I was picking up on earlier tonight was mild compared to the resentment that really exists in the King family.

"Don't call her that," Natalie snaps. "Her. Name. Is. Samantha. You and your hoodlums bastardized her name, and it stops *now*."

"You're delusional." King scoffs again, the sound of disgust rolling around in the back of his throat. He backs away from his mother and stepfather. "*You*," he growls when he sees me lurking around the corner.

I figured the chance of finding Savvy's room without being spotted was slim to none. I straighten the suit jacket I never changed out of after getting it back from the paramedics, grab hold of the lapels, and push off the wall to enter the waiting room.

"Is Savvy all right?" I ask, both as an opening to soften King toward me and because, deep down, I have a burning need to know the answer.

"Why the fuck do you care?" he snaps, closing the distance between us until the tips of his Jordans bump against the tips of my Chucks.

"Just tell me if she's okay." I give a quick check to the other four Royalty Crew members moving into position behind him.

"It's funny…" He chuckles, but there's zero hint of amusement to it.

Like an idiot, I take the bait. "What is?"

"Since *my sister's*"—I don't miss the emphasis he puts on the relational phrase—"first day at BA, you and your fellow BAssholes have been hell-bent on causing her stress. Yet here you are…" He waves a hand up and down in front of me.

"All of a sudden caring about the consequences of your actions."

"Look." I slide a hand through my hair. "I'm not sure what Savvy has told you—"

A bark of a laugh has me cutting my gaze to where Wesley Prince stands to the left of King. His dark eyes are somehow filled with both mirth and danger.

Carter raises a hand as if to hold Prince back, my spine straightening at the perceived threat. "See...that's the thing." He pauses, and I swallow down the urge to ask *What thing?* "She didn't."

Huh?

A wave of laughter rolls through the Royals, and I get the impression I'm the only person not in on the joke.

Golden red flashes, and once again, Tessa is pushing herself between a King sibling and me. "He doesn't understand how powerful your reign is, *Your Majesty*." There's too much sarcasm for any person to take the title seriously as she pats King on the chest.

"Always with the dramatics, Tessa." Natalie crosses one leg over the other, her detestation for the perky redhead coming across clear as day. "You're as bad an influence on Samantha as my unfortunate first attempt at procreation."

Fuck, this woman is harsh.

"Yeah...because an All-American, World, and National Champion, future valedictorian, daughter of the fire chief is *so* not the type of person you would want being friends with *your*...daughter."

Color stains Natalie's cheeks as a snort brings our attention to the sarcastic commentator standing with Emma Logan. And yes, before you ask, thanks to my dad's profession, I am able to instantly recognize the daughter of a senator.

"And *that* is why you are my favorite sister," Tessa cheers.

"I want to say it's because Kay is your only sister, but the lack of blood relation makes even that not quite true," Prince comments.

"Shut it, Charming," Tessa counters.

"Can you two not start?" King cuts off their bickering, and they fall silent immediately. "You both can argue the Taylor-Dennings family dynamics when we don't have a BAsshole to school."

Now is not the appropriate time for recognition to dawn, but it does anyway as the name clicks. I knew she looked familiar when their entourage showed up at the penthouse earlier. Eric Dennings was easy to place, and it's almost embarrassing that I didn't realize the tiny blonde was his sister Kayla. I should have. There was this whole to-do about her that went viral last year when she started dating Mason Nova, one of the U of J's top football players.

Since my attempts to get information out of King were a bust, I decide to try my luck with the best friend. She seemed to like me earlier. We bonded and shit over caring for Savvy during her asthma attack.

"Tessa, how's Savvy?"

"*Ooo*"—she bounces on the balls of her feet—"I kind of *love* that you use her real name now."

"Don't answer him, Tess." King wraps an arm around her middle and shifts her into Prince's hold.

"Why the fuck *shouldn't* she?" I step forward, the lack of information pissing me off.

"Why the fuck *should* she?" he counters, bringing both hands to my chest and shoving me back.

"It's a simple question." I give him a shove of my own.

"One you have no *goddamn* right to the answer to." Another shove, this one causing me to stumble, and I ball my hands into fists, preparing to swing.

"Whoa," a voice calls out, and this time it's the hot brunette jumping into the fray and casting a look around to make sure we haven't drawn unnecessary attention. Thankfully the wall behind me hides us from view of the nurses' station.

"God. *Damn*. It, Emma," King growls, his arm falling from his fight stance to hook around her and tuck her in tight to his side. "I thought you girls learned your lesson about jumping into the middle of a fight?"

"Don't try to tell me what to do." She rounds on him, sticking a finger in his face, and *damn*, it's impressive as hell how she holds her ground against the glower King gives her. No idea what this chick did to piss him off, but it's even more intense than the one he was giving me seconds ago.

Carter curls his hands over Emma's shoulders and tries to shift her out of the way, but she's having none of it. *Looks like the king Royal isn't as formidable as people think.* "What the fuck are you smirking at?" he snaps at me.

Whoops. Except instead of dialing back my amusement, I hitch my lips higher, letting them part until my teeth are visible with my smile. I roll my shoulders back and hold his stare.

He may come from a founding family of Blackwell. He may be older. He may have ruled at Blackwell Public years ago and garnered a reputation that is both feared as much as it is revered, but it only extends so far inside the walls of Blackwell Academy. BA is my domain. *I'm* the king there. *I'm* the one people fear and kowtow to. He may have his crew with him and my boys might not be with me, but I'm not backing down. Not in this.

My teeth clench as he shakes his head, dismissing me. These Kings need to learn to not underestimate me.

"And you…" Again his attention goes to the brunette. "Unlike when I asked you that question, *I'm*"—Carter punches a thumb at his chest—"*not* the one in the hospital."

"True." It's Kay who responds instead of Emma. "But you're the one who needs the reminder that *your. Sister* is."

"*Trust* me, Dennings…" He scowls at the blonde. "I

haven't forgotten *that*. And…" That peel-my-skin-from-my-bones glare is back on me. "I *also* haven't forgotten that *he's*—"

I stumble back, not expecting the shove this time. I scramble for footing and instantly get in his face. Shouts, curses, rogue limbs, and two brave females entering the fray have me dropping back, hands held in the air signaling that I'm backing off.

"—the cause of her needing to be here in the first place."

I'm about done with being blamed for Savvy's asthma attack.

Did I know about her asthma? No.

Did I fuck her tonight? Hell yeah I did. I fucked her so good I had her coming all over my dick, melting for me despite how she tried to claim she hated me and refused to say my name.

I won't lie though—seeing her pull out her inhaler shortly after I tried to fuck her into submission was enough of a reality check to ruin my postorgasmic high.

But…

She was *fine* after she used it. She wasn't outwardly struggling to breathe. She let me…hold her.

Besides…Carter can try to place the blame on me all he wants. It's not like he *knows* I fucked his sister. Forget about how *weird* it would be for a brother and sister to locker-room-talk their sexual conquests; there wasn't any time for Savvy to divulge such information.

We fucked.

Savvy used her inhaler.

Duke came to find us to…

Holy shit.

I cut a glare to where Natalie picks at her nails like she has more important places to be than a waiting room while her daughter is hospitalized.

Savvy's asthma didn't spiral out of control until Natalie dropped the marriage bomb. It was *Natalie*—not me.

"You can try to blame me for this all you want, but *maybe* you should look a little *closer* to home." I barely manage to get the words out as that it's-never-going-to-happen-Savvy-is-mine urge strangles me. She can't marry Duke. It's ludicrous, ill-conceived, straight-up unbelievable.

Except…is it?

History is filled with marriages of convenience. American democracy is built and maintained by political power couples, with the strongest being those who have advantageous legacy pairings. I wouldn't be surprised if this insanity was my father's brainchild.

I can't even count on the revelation about Carter King and his questionable business dealings being a part of the family tree Mitchell St. James inherited to put a stop to the union. Politicians and businessmen like St. James have been known to employ all kinds of "fixers" and experts who would be able to spin the facts into a story they want people to believe. Hell, Dad has a few of them on his speed dial.

"What the fuck is that supposed to mean?" King puffs out his chest, and I'm not sure how much longer the others will be able to rein him in. I didn't come here to fight. I will if I have to, but that wasn't my intention for being here.

"You know what?" He shakes his head, ripping off the beanie he's wearing with a jerk. "It. Doesn't. Fucking. Matter."

"You keep growling like that, Cart, and I'm going to think you're part werewolf…*epp*—"

A chuckle rolls through the Royals when Prince cuts Tessa off with a hand clamped over her mouth. "Cut back on the shifter romances, Buttercup."

There's another wave of laughter from all the Royals except King. He's still the growly werewolf Tessa accused him of acting like. Lord help us if she and Duke ever spent any time together. One person with a penchant for smartass comments at inappropriate times is more than enough.

Prince wipes his hand on his jeans, causing me to believe Tessa licked it before stepping out of reach. "I don't need to stand here and take this kind of disrespect." The way she can't quite smother her smile makes me think this is an old dance for them.

I'm confused, to say the least. This glimpse into the Royalty Crew reveals a dynamic I would not have suspected existed. Where's the exertion of power within the ranks?

"I'm going to check to see if the doctors are done with Savs." I turn, shifting to see around the wall as Tessa starts to walk away. If I'm lucky, I'll be able to see what room she goes to.

King's furious voice has me redirecting my attention to him just as Tessa disappears into a room at the opposite end of the long hallway. "This is the second—if not third—asthma attack I can trace back to you." He tries to push me again, but Emma wraps her arms around the one he lifts toward me.

"What the hell are you talking about? I've never given her an asthma attack." *Have I?*

A sinister smile spreads across his face as he starts to tick things off on his fingers. "The time you gatecrashed a Royal Ball. This one I'm not positive about, but I am pretty sure you are responsible for the night of the BA Alumni Gala. And now tonight." He wiggles three fingers in my face before folding them over in a fist. "As they say in baseball, three strikes and you're out."

I know I'm not responsible for tonight's, but I think back to the others. Nothing stood out to me at the time, but now that I know about Savvy's asthma, I see our every interaction in a new light.

How many times have I watched her rub at her chest?

How many times did it seem like she was struggling to breathe?

How many times did I attribute the hitch in her breathing to her being turned on by me? And how many of those were really because...she. Couldn't. Breathe?

Anger at myself, at being accused of something I didn't do, at the fact that Savvy has asthma in the first place, at the beyond-complicated situation we've found ourselves in has heat moving through my veins. A beast beats inside my chest, roaring for me to lash out.

"Look at you with your cute turn of phrase." I make a show of straightening my cuffs as my fists clench. "Well, I have one for you. How about...*too little too late.*" He remains silent, only lifting one of his blond brows. "That's what this is, right?" I quirk my own brow. "You're coming at me because of *your* misplaced guilt."

"Guilt? Oh, do enlighten me as to what I have to feel guilty about." The way King rocks back on his heels says *This should be good.*

"You're Carter King. Your reputation precedes you. If people don't know you, they know *of* you." I pause and let my gaze run over each one of the Royals. "Yet, your own sister transfers to a school without using your family name. And then you stand here"—my wrist breaks as I exaggeratedly flounce a hand up and down in front of him—"claiming you know the things that happen inside the halls of BA, and *you* do *nothing* to put a stop to it?"

I let another smirk form as I watch King's jaw pop out to the side before shifting to meet the dark glare of Wesley Prince.

"You would think your little guard dog here"—I jerk a chin at Prince—"would have at least confronted me. It *is* his pussy piece I've been moving in on."

My body hits the wall before the pain in my face registers. My jaw aches, and when I drag the back of my hand across my mouth, it comes away with a streak of blood.

The nostrils flaring, chest heaving, and fingers of his left hand flexing as Lance Bennett and Cisco Cruz hold him back tell me it was Prince, not King, who punched me.

Fuck me, that hurt. The coppery taste of blood coats my tongue as I straighten away from the wall and play off the hit as if it were like any other I would take out on the ice.

"Tell me, Prince—how did it make you feel to see my mark on her?"

"Fuck you." He bucks in his friends' hold.

"No thanks." I shrug. "Though I wouldn't rule out another round with your little race rat, because the way her cunt squeezed my cock tonight was what wet dreams are made of." I give a chef's kiss and shift my gaze to an eerily stoic King. "For as much as you want me to be the reason we are here tonight, that honor gets to stay in the family. Because while *you*"—I point at Carter—"were too busy to be around, your *mother*"—I hook a thumb back at Natalie, Mitchell the only one paying us any attention—"had a *little* announcement to make."

"What—announcement?" The deadly menace in his tone has the hairs on the back of my neck standing on end.

Projecting a calm I certainly don't feel, all while acting as if I'm not rage-y at the prospect, I say, "Congratulations... your sister is officially engaged to be married."

CHAPTER 5

THE SLACK-JAWED, just-been-told-aliens-stole-his-Corvette expression on Carter King's face would have been amusing if the reasoning behind it didn't make me want to beat the shit out of my best friend. It's unfair. Duke isn't the one responsible, just like I'm not the one responsible for Savvy's asthma attack, no matter what King says.

You sure about that?

I hate the doubt that's creeping into my thoughts because of this asshole.

Same as when Natalie first dropped the marriage bomb, all hell broke loose. This time, instead of an asthma attack, it was in the form of Carter epically losing his shit on Natalie. Things got so heated I thought security was going to be called. The only thing that prevented that from happening was Emma Logan forcing Carter to take a walk.

I was completely forgotten in the melee, and now I'm walking down the hallway leading toward Savvy's hospital room undetected.

With one last glance over my shoulder to confirm the coast

is still clear of Royals, I push the handle on the door and step inside the room.

The lighting is dim, only the ones around the perimeter lit as the TV mounted on the wall plays one of the *Harry Potter* movies without any sound.

My gut tumbles at the sight of Savvy in a hospital bed. It's not like I was expecting her to be sitting in a chair or anything, but seeing her hooked up to machines is jarring.

A clear, egg-shaped oxygen mask covers her nose and mouth, the steady flow of air a quiet hiss in the room.

Her eyes are closed, lashes resting on the curves of her cheeks, which, thankfully, have lost their deathly pallor.

A blue and yellow hospital gown has replaced the ball-tightening dress from earlier. This time when I look at her chest, it isn't to check out her phenomenal rack but to make sure it's moving up and down without issue.

A blue blanket with a white sheet folded over the top is tucked in tightly around her middle. I hope the lack of tension in the arms lying on top of the covers means she's sleeping and not still unconscious.

There's a blood pressure cuff wrapped around one arm and an IV inserted in the other, with one of those little plastic clips attached to her forefinger.

There's a portable console at the head of the bed, but outside of knowing the wavy line in the middle is tracking the rhythm of her heartbeat, I'm clueless about the other numbers. My hospital experience has been limited to the treatment of hockey-related injuries, nothing long term or requiring admission.

That also has to be the reason why my heart trips as I take another pass over Savvy's prone body. Yeah, that's it. It's not like I have…feelings for her.

Possessiveness? Sure. I don't like to share my toys; it's nothing more than that.

"I can't decide if you're ballsy or stupid." The comment

has my gaze snapping to the left, where Tessa sits at Savvy's bedside. I didn't even notice her there, my focus on Savvy was so acute. A contemplative frown tugs at the edges of her mouth, and a little V forms between her brows as she studies me. "It's stupid." She nods, answering herself. "Definitely stupid."

I shake my head. "I thought the Royals were against bullying." I move to the opposite side and stare at her from across the bed. "Doesn't calling a person stupid fall into that category?"

Tessa lifts the collar of her sweatshirt and buries her face in it to smother any sound, but I see the laughter dancing in her eyes. I get the impression it's more at my expense than because she thinks I'm funny.

Once she composes herself, she straightens her hoodie, running both hands down the front before stretching an arm out to me. "Hi, Pot. I'm Kettle." I shake her hand on instinct before the words get a chance to register, her grip tightening as she adds, "I'd say it's nice to meet you, but that would be a lie."

"You're nothing at all like Savvy described," I muse.

"Let me guess..." Tessa shifts, leaning to slouch in the sizable padded chair with her arms crossed. "You heard how I'm *sweet as apple pie*?" I nod, which makes her smirk, except the way she arches one of her red brows gives me pause. "That's true...until you mess with someone I love." She points to Savvy. "That's my *best* friend." She bends and extends her finger with each word. "The only apple pie you'll get from me is the one made with the Evil Queen's poisoned apples."

I widen my stance and fold my arms over my chest, not missing how she gives my body a quick scan.

"I *hate* having to correct you..." Fucking hell, the sarcasm from this chick. "But I'm not what you would call a 'real'

Royal." She uses air quotes, nodding to Savvy as if to say *Like she is.*

It's been hours since I learned that Samantha St. James is really Samantha—or Savvy—King. I'm still not entirely sure how you get Savvy as a nickname for Samantha, but that's not as important as the surname. I can't believe she *is* a Royal.

Tessa sits up suddenly, spinning in her seat to look toward the door, gaze pinballing from it to me to Savvy and back before finally settling on me again. "Speaking of the Royals… how are you here? In one piece? *Alive*?"

Yeah, it's confirmed. She definitely can't spend time with Duke.

But won't she? Her best friend is now engaged to him. Don't you think they'll be around each other now?

I drop my arms, wrapping my hands around the plastic side rail of Savvy's hospital bed as if to strangle away the traitorous thoughts. One thing at a time.

"I slipped away while they were distracted."

Tessa's mouth presses into a flat line. "What did the Momster do now?"

"Momster?" I bark out a laugh, startled by the good humor bubbling up in contrast with my earlier anger, while at the same time double-checking that the burst of sound didn't disturb Savvy.

"She's fine." Tessa strokes a hand down Savvy's arm and links their pinkies together. "She'll be in and out of it all night."

The surge of relief the confirmation brings on is as confusing as the insatiable need I had to get it.

"Is she really okay?" I've already been in here a few minutes; I doubt I'll get much longer before my luck runs out.

"Yeah." I don't miss the way Tessa's voice softens. "She responded to the medicine they gave her almost immediately."

I wave a hand at the monitor I still can't interpret. "What's with all this?" Would they need to track all those numbers if she were fine?

"It's pretty standard monitoring for asthma patients."

I give her a *How can you be so sure?* brow scrunch, and she verbally answers, "I've been friends with Savvy for as long as I can remember. Unfortunately, this isn't our first trip to the emergency room because of an asthma attack."

Why do I get a fluttery jolt of panic hearing this?

"The first number is her heart rate." Tessa jerks a chin at the console, and I look at the ninety-two on top. "It's a little high for a resting rate but still within the healthy range."

"And the others?" I think the one with the slash is for blood pressure, but that's the only one I can guess about.

"Her blood pressure," Tessa confirms my assumption, but I appreciate the added insights she gives. "It's also elevated, but that's common given all the adrenaline dumps her body went through. It's the next two numbers the doctors are most concerned about."

"Are they for her breathing?"

"Yeah. Her respirations—the bottom of the two—is back into what is considered normal."

"And the other?" I look at the blinking eighty-nine.

"That's her oxygen saturation. The goal is to get it back up over ninety-five."

Fuck that sounds serious.

The plastic rail groans in my grip. I hate...*this*. It's foreign territory, and with each step deeper, things only become less stable.

Fuck this. I need to get back to the place where I don't give a shit.

I've seen her. She's...fine. I have *nothing* to feel guilty about—time to move on.

Still...

As I look down at Savvy lying there...that familiar draw tugs at my center.

A lock of hair hangs partially over one eye, and I shuffle closer, brushing it away and tucking it behind her ear. Letting my touch linger, I slide a thumb over the skin of her cheek.

Unable to resist—no matter how out of character it is—I lean over and place a kiss on her forehead, her familiar lime scent lingering underneath the harsh hospital antiseptic.

Tessa sighs, and I think she mumbles something about Romeo and Juliet, but I'm not quite sure. I'm straightening and about to ask when Savvy's lashes twitch and her eyes slowly blink open.

Those purple pools are hazy, and it takes a few seconds and a couple more blinks before they focus.

Overwhelming relief slams into me, and the itch that forms underneath my skin urges me to get out of here and to do it fast.

A crinkle forms in the space between Savvy's brows as her eyes bounce between mine, seeing me but not *really* seeing me.

Something hard brushes against my arm, and when a hand covers the oxygen mask to lower it, I realize it was the clip on her finger. "Jasper?"

Why doesn't it fucking surprise me that it takes her lying in a hospital bed for her to say my name without a fight? The soft yet raspy sound of her voice scrapes across every one of my nerves. How many times have I heard her sound like this? It *should* be sexy, but I'm starting to realize it's most likely a side effect of her asthma flaring up.

King might have a point, and I want to punch him for it.

I cover her hand with one of my own, ignoring the tingles that shoot up my arm at such a simple touch.

What the fuck is that?

Bracing myself with a hand by her head, the cheap down of the pillow flattening in an instant, I shift the mask back into place. "Leave this on, Princess." I cut a glance at her oxygen saturation level.

Of course, she doesn't listen, knocking my hand away. "What are you doing here?"

"Checking on you." The *duh* is implied.

The furrow of her brow deepens, sheets rustling as she starts to shift to look around, only to settle for flopping her head to the side when her limited energy supply is depleted.

"I'm the only other one here." Tessa giggles after the two make eye contact. "Now, will you stop being stubborn and listen to the man?" She mimes putting on a mask.

Savvy doesn't, her mouth working side to side as she brings her attention back to me.

"You came with Duke?"

I rear back as if slapped, my foot catching on the edge of something with a clang. Not once has she shown an interest in my best friend. Why now? She could have asked about any number of people. Her brother. Prince. Hell, I would even accept the *fucking* mayor at this point. But Duke? FUCKING DUKE?

Oh hell no.

"No, *Savvy*." I exaggerate the name, just in case she forgot I'm *well aware* of it given everything that happened. It's not like she lied about her name—so why does it feel like it? And why does it feel like she lied to me specifically? "Your *fiancé* isn't here."

Her eyes squeeze shut, a choked gasp causing her to cough harshly.

Her motherfucking fiancé. What a joke.

That's your best friend.

I tell myself to shut the hell up because who the hell gets engaged when they're still in high school?

"Her WHAT?" Tessa screeches as the monitor starts to beep.

I stare at the jumping numbers without really seeing them, the roaring in my head as the blood rushes through my veins making me blind to everything except the rage that particular factoid brings on.

"Oh…she didn't tell you?" I mock. "Maybe she wanted to wait, make it real *special*." I spit out the last word with a sneer. "I mean"—I wave my hand—"you are her best friend after all. I guess there's a chance she wanted to do it in some *cutesy*"—I add a shoulder shimmy to be a jerk—"girly way when she asked you to be her maid of honor, as I'm assuming she would."

Shit! If this actually happens, it would mean I would be Duke's best man. How the hell am I supposed to stand up with him and watch him marry *her* when all I'll be thinking about is the quickest way to get her alone and bent over something to fuck her?

"Listen, BAsshole." Tessa shoves out of her chair, bracing both arms on the mattress and leveling me with a glare. "I have no idea what the *hell* you're talking about." She averts her attention to Savvy, forcing the mask back into place and leaving her hand to hold it there. "And…honestly, it doesn't matter. Your jackass, jockhole, douchebully ways might fly most of the time, but not *now*." She throws an arm toward the door. "Get the fuck out."

Finished dismissing me, she leans over Savvy, coaching her to breathe as she did earlier.

I watch, hands clenching and unclenching as I take in the scene.

Without looking at me, Tessa threatens, "If you're not out that door in five seconds, I'll call Carter to tell him you're in here."

You know what? Fuck this. I don't need this shit.

CHAPTER 6

"YO, MINI ROYAL, *VÁMONOS*," Cisco shouts from downstairs.

I double-check my bag, flipping the flap closed, and slide my inhaler into the inside pocket of my uniform blazer, almost annoyed I have to keep it on my person.

I would have said a week away from the BA world with Tinsley as my only connection to avoid falling behind on coursework sounded like heaven. Too bad the reality didn't live up to the expectations.

For the past six days, I've thought, I've mused, I've straight up asked how the hell Carter managed to get permission for me to stay with him after I was discharged from the hospital. Did I get any answers? Nope.

Actually…

If I stop and *really* consider things, his behavior has been… weird. More so than when he insisted I not fight Natalie on enrolling me as a St. James at BA. We've always been close, more friends than siblings despite our age gap, but it almost feels like he's avoiding me.

We've had a grand total of *one* full conversation, and that centered around me telling him how Natalie was all "This engagement is real, act like it or else." Even without knowing exactly what Natalie is threatening me with, Carter still suggested it might be best for me to play along.

I think it's a legit possibility I've seen him *less* now than after I moved out.

Sure, there was some hovering and constant—borderline annoyingly so—wellness checks to see how I was feeling and making sure I was doing everything the doctors said to do. And yes, he was the one to go with me to my appointment with my pulmonologist to see if my medications needed to be adjusted. But I swear, all the time in between, he was just... not there.

Ugh! I don't have time for...all this. Not for thoughts of my weirdly distant brother or my psychotic mother.

Flipping the light off, I grab my lapels, tugging and straightening as I trudge down the stairs, only stopping when I meet Cisco at the bottom. There's a playful smirk dancing on his lips as his teeth fiddle with the ring pierced through the corner of the bottom one. I give him my best scowl and *Do I really have to go to school?* nose scrunch.

"Come on, *guera*." He takes my bag from me and hooks an arm over my shoulders, tucking me close and leading me stomping begrudgingly toward the door.

"Don't you have to open the garage?" I ask, the door beeping as we exit the residence section of the building. Unlike the private bays—three cars wide and about five cars deep—we're currently crossing, there's a full-service body shop / auto garage located at the back of the lot.

"I did," Cisco assures me, keeping his steps slower, stride shorter than it would have been a week ago. "I left one of *Papa's* old guys in charge while I see you off to school."

Unlike Lance, the other non–founding family Royal, Cisco

hails from Blackwell. Whereas Lance earned his place by defending my brother, Cisco found his when his father decided to take Carter under his wing instead of calling the cops when he caught him trying to boost cars from him.

Sixteen-year-old Carter King wasn't necessarily the crown jewel he is today, but desperation doesn't necessarily breed the smartest solutions. If Nonna Falco ever found out about how he tried to handle things, she would whoop his ass with her slipper…or a wooden spoon.

But who did he need to make those questionable decisions for, hmm?

I ignore the guilt-inducing question from my conscience and remind myself how well things worked out. Cisco joined the Royals. He and Carter mentored with and eventually took over Marco Cruz's auto garage and exotic car rental business. While Cisco is the one who primarily runs it, it's the same artistic talent that brings people from all over for tattoos from Carter that made them expand into the custom bodywork side of the business.

See? I say to that annoying inner voice. *It all worked out.*

It isn't until we pass Cisco's Hellcat that how he phrased things clicks inside my brain.

"Wait…" I stop walking, Cisco stumbling as my body weight holds him back. "*See* me off to school?" I point over to the Hellcat, its matte black paint pristine under the fluorescent lights. "You're not driving me?"

He's the only one still around. Tessa's on her way to school, Lance is at morning skate, Carter and Wes have class, and Leo is working at city hall with Chuck. Is Daniel picking me up? Guess that means it really is back to reality.

Cisco holds the door open for me, and I step out into the slightly chilly morning. Reflecting sunlight causes me to squint and pull my Ray-Bans from the top of my head and over my eyes. Once I can see without being blinded, I continue toward the waiting car, only to come to another halt.

The color is right, the silver paint job damn near reflective with its high-gloss shine. Except…

The vehicle is wrong—all wrong.

Instead of a Bentley, a gleaming G Wagon with spinning 22s idles a few feet away.

"What's *he* doing here?" If it were possible to glare from your fingertip, that's exactly what my finger would be doing; my point is that aggressive.

Cisco fiddles with his lip ring again, the black metal spinning in a slow circle around his lip. I narrow my eyes, envisioning pinching the piercing between my fingers and tugging like one would a misbehaving child's ear.

These assholes *knew* about this. It's yet another time the Royals cut me out of the conversation—one that involves *me* —and made decisions. Without. *Me*.

Jesus Christ. Is this why Carter treated me like I was contagious and not recovering from an asthma attack? He didn't want to be the one to tell me *how* I would have to play into this charade?

"You needed a ride, *reyna*." He shrugs like it's no big deal when it's anything but.

"*Don't* you *dare* pull that queen shit with me right now." His nose smooshes down as I poke him. "You don't get to act like I'm one of you when you *clearly* don't believe it."

Anger pulses inside me, and I pull a concentrated breath in through my nose and push it out through my mouth. I will not be triggered this early in the morning, goddammit.

Remorse sobers Cisco's expression as he stares down at me, and I swear to god, if that's pity in his gaze, I'm going to knee him in the balls. He takes me by the shoulders, pulling me around until we're face to face, his hands curling over me, fingers fiddling with the collar of my blazer.

"You are one of us, Savs." I scoff, and his mouth presses into a flat line. "You *are*."

"Uh-huh. Whatever you say, Francisco." My lips twitch at

the way his eyes go flat. He hates his full name as much as I do mine. My chin brushes against his knuckles as I glance back at the Mercedes.

"Stop being a brat," he scolds, lifting a finger to tap my chin and bring my focus back to him. "You know how your brother worries." *Yeah, too much.* "You needed a ride, and we need to find ways to make the Momster think you—*we*—are playing her little marriage game so she doesn't stop you from being allowed to hang out."

The thought alone makes me nauseous.

"Besides…" Cisco jerks his chin behind me. "It could have been worse."

"How's that?" I ask in a droll monotone.

"You could be forced to ride to school with the asshat who bragged about riding you."

I suck in a startled breath, the blood in my veins turning to ice as the rest of me flushes hot, my hair standing on end, my skin itching in indignation.

"What did you just say?" I growl.

"Aw, how cute." Cisco boops me on the nose. "Being all growly must be a King trait." I smack his hand away, not at all in the mood for his jokes when I need clarification.

"No, no." My chest grows tight, and I rub at it, closing my eyes and breathing through it. After a beat, I peel them open and meet his gaze. "Explain."

Cisco grips the back of his neck, glancing to the left, no longer meeting my eye. I let out another sound of frustration, and the center of Cisco's cheek indents as if he's biting it before he releases his neck to pat me on the head as if I'm a growling puppy.

We stand there, me doing my best to hold on to a mad I don't quite feel and him trying to hide how amusing he finds me. It's one of the downfalls of people knowing you from your carried-a-stuffed-dragon-around-everywhere phase in life.

The sound of a car door slamming reminds us we aren't alone, that this isn't another "brother/sister" quarrel we're familiar with. Once again, an arm drops around my shoulders, and I'm tucked back against Cisco's side.

I could be annoyed that he's going all "big brother protector" on me, and while all the Royals—except for Wes—are guilty of doing so, that's not what this is. This is a show of solidarity. A display of Royalty unity. A reminder that you mess with one Royal, you mess with *all* of the Royals.

Duke swaggers around the front of his six-figure vehicle, his familiar playboy flirt smirk tilting his lips, hands casually shoved into the pockets of his uniform slacks. He doesn't approach us, instead opening the passenger side door, hand curling over the top of the frame as he leans against it.

"You ready to go…" Duke pauses, licking his lips and full-on smiling, his baby blues twinkling in amusement before finishing with, "Babe?"

My hackles rise. Yeah, that shit is *not* gonna fly.

"I need your tire iron," I mumble to Cisco, who drops his head to mine to smother his laughter.

"No dice, Savage." Cisco grips one of my lapels and fluffs it. "It'll be a nightmare trying to get blood out of cashmere."

I snort, smashing my lips to the side like I'm contemplating if it would be worth the effort. Probably not.

"Fine." I sigh.

"Good girl." Cisco lifts my bag from his shoulder and settles the strap on my own while I battle with the urge to smack him. His deep chuckle tells me he knows exactly where my thoughts went again. I'm sure he said that on purpose to distract me.

"Now go to school." With a hand pressed to my back, he guides me forward a step or two. "Learn all the things and try not to maim any BAssholes."

"I make no promises," I mutter as I start toward Duke.

"Of course not." There's another deep chuckle and a "Bye, Savs" before I catch sight of Cisco heading for the garage.

The flirt factor from Duke only intensifies as I get closer, and he drags a hand through the air in a semicircle like a game show host. "Your chariot awaits, Princess."

I stop just outside of touching distance, frowning at the use of that particular nickname.

"What?" Duke steps into the opening of the door. "I think the nickname fits you even more now that we know you're a King." He arches a brow and levels me with a look. "Don't you think…Savvy?"

"You're annoying, you know that?" I huff, still not moving closer.

He gives me a *Whatcha gonna do?* shrug. "You'll get used to it. We are betrothed after all."

I ball my hands into fists, my nails making my palms sting. "Don't tell me you're on board with this plan."

It'll be exponentially harder to fight Natalie's apparent insanity if I'm the only one trying to do so. As much as I don't want to "make nice," Duke could be a formidable ally. *Dammit.* Now I'll have to admit Carter and Cisco might have had a point about playing along.

"I mean…" Duke rocks back on his heels. "At least you're hot."

"Thanks," I deadpan. Of course he's thinking with his dick.

"Don't act like you wouldn't enjoy having a piece of this." He waves his hands down the length of his body, a body we both know is in shape and makes the other girls at school drool with the way his uniform fits. "I would rock your world, baby."

I roll my eyes. So cocky. "Not interested."

"Shame." He winks and hooks a thumb at the open door behind him. "You getting in or what?"

I purse my lips, giving an *I'm still debating* face scrunch.

"What if—" He reaches an arm into the cab, body stretching, uniform shirt tugging tight against his muscular back as if to say *See? I'm hot. Look at all these muscles you could lick.* I don't know how he does it, but I get the impression only Duke Delacourte is capable of having his body project cocky charm for him.

I hear him shuffling around with something before he straightens, a familiar paper cup in hand when he does. "—I offer you a bribe."

I bounce my gaze between him and the cartoon rendition of Harry Potter. "You're giving off creepy *man with a van* vibes."

Duke palms the cup in his hands, swinging it side to side. "Hey there, little girl…" His tone takes on a lascivious quality that has creepy-crawlies dancing down my spine while at the same time making me choke on a laugh. "Wanna go for a ride?" He adds an exaggerated eyebrow waggle. "I have *candy*," he singsongs.

That does it, and I give in to the urge to laugh. Duke is ridiculous, and while I feel like I'll never be able to admit it, in the week before engagement-gate, I actually had fun eating lunch with him.

There are two more seconds of stubborn hesitation before the draw of Lyle's java goodness is too great to ignore, and I'm reaching for the cup. "You didn't poison it, did you?" I ask as the nutty aroma of pecan hits my senses.

Duke barks out a laugh, dropping a hand to my back and guiding me to get in the car. "No." He backs away as soon as I'm settled into the seat. "I value my life too much."

Ah, yes, the Carter King effect. The girl capable of tricking you into eating rat as revenge isn't a threat at all. But, *oh no*, find out that girl is related to *the* Carter King— yeah, now she's off-limits. Yes, I know it doesn't make sense that I'm annoyed, but *come on*. Jasper may call me Princess, but I don't need saving. I'm a queen. I've got this shit. It shouldn't take my connection to a man to make me a formidable opponent.

With a huff, I click my seat belt in and wait for Duke to make his way back to the driver's seat while Billie Eilish sings about burying a friend.

Blowing across the lid, I take a cautious sip. I get another wink from Duke after he catches sight of the surprise written across my face when I discover it's made to my exact specifications.

"I told the barista who it was for, and after *he* had the good sense to flirt with me"—his implied *unlike some people* as clear as day—"he assured me he knew your order."

I take another sip to hide my smile at the image of Lyle flirting with Duke, disappointed I missed out on it. I bet that was something to witness given Lyle's shameless nature. I don't know if Duke is eighteen yet or not, but I need to remember to have Tessa tease Lyle for his cradle-robbing, jail-bait-flirting ways.

Snapping a quick pic of my cup, I shoot off a text to my brother.

ME: If this BAsshole didn't show up with my favorite coffee, I would be taking a detour to BTU to kick your ass.

As if he was waiting for me to reach out, my phone pings with a text almost immediately.

BRO KING: It was a tactical move, and you can't be kicking anyone's ass right now, remember? You're supposed to be TAKING IT EASY! So chill. Drink your coffee, go to school, USE your inhaler BEFORE you HAVE to use it, and relax. We'll figure this shit out, promise.

ME: *GIF of Anna Kendrick saluting* But you don't have to yell. I can HEAR your tone from here.

BRO KING: Good. Now, if only you'd LISTEN.

ME: 50/50.

BRO KING: Those odds seem a little high, but I'll take it.
Love you.

With a message confirming I love his overprotective, bossy ass back, I click my phone locked and slide it into the side of my knee-high boot.

"Were you talking to Red?" Duke jerks his chin at my phone, asking about Tessa while keeping his eyes on the road.

I shake my head. "My brother."

"Oooo." Hands draped over the steering wheel at the wrists, Duke dances in his seat. "And what did Daddy King say this morning?"

My face scrunches in disgust. "Eww. Can you *not* call him that?" I mime gagging. *Gross.*

"Spoilsport."

I take another sip of coffee and lean against the door. "You have issues."

"You're just not used to all this awesomeness." He shimmies his shoulders, that easy camaraderie growing between us and confusing the hell out of me.

"Why'd you want to know if I was talking to Tess?" I ask as he slows to a stop behind a school bus.

"I was going to have you tell her hi for me if you were."

This guy doesn't get it. No matter how many times I try to warn him away from her, it doesn't stick. "Why would I do that?"

Still waiting for the students to finish boarding the bus, Duke turns to face me, a big, brilliant, all-the-ladies-love-me smile on his face. "We"—he bounces a finger between us— "may be betrothed." Now it's his eyebrows doing the bouncing up and down. "But since you're smashing my best friend, I figured yours is fair game."

That earlier frisson of anger when Cisco made a similar insinuation works its way through my system. What the fuck? Jasper's just going around telling people? Oh hell no.

CHAPTER 7

"LOOKING GOOD LATELY, NOBLE." Coach claps me on the shoulder as I make my way out of the locker room.

I nod, not acknowledging that I've been using these morning workouts and subsequent practices in the afternoon as a distraction technique. Without them, I would have spent the last week stewing in conflicting…*feelings* brought on by Savvy's absence.

Feelings. Blah, fucking *feelings*. If that's not like taking a skate to the nut sack, I don't know what is. I'm damn near turning into a chick with all these…*emotions*.

If we weren't so close to the start of the season and more at risk for random drug testing, I would smoke a J and just be done with it, ride the wave of Mary Jane bliss to where there are no females tempting me with their defiance and pussy that can squeeze my cock in a choke hold, specifically a pussy that's now forbidden because it's engaged to my best fucking friend.

Speaking of which…

Where the fuck is Duke? When it was time to leave the

dorm this morning, he told me he would catch up with me later, but I didn't think it meant he was skipping the team's morning workout.

I meet up with Banks in the hall and fall into step with him. He's probably going to find Tinsley since the dude is obsessed, and Little Miss Scholarship should be able to provide me with some information. Thanks to our network of minions around the school, I know she was tasked with making sure Savvy kept up with any schoolwork she missed while absent.

Tinsley isn't at her locker as we walk through the senior hallway, but when Banks starts to softly whistle, I know he's spotted her somewhere. I follow his gaze toward the main entrance, and sure enough, there's Tinsley hovering near the double doors, phone to her ear as she periodically looks through windows to outside.

"What do you mean she'll be pissed when she gets here?" I hear her ask whoever she's on the phone with when we get closer. "There's nothing on her locker. I checked."

She's talking about Savvy. Interesting.

Tinsley leans to look out the glass again, shaking her head no, even though the person she's talking to can't see her. "I told you...they seem to have been leaving her alone since before the dinner. Though I wonder if—" Her eyes flair wide enough to reveal a full ring of white around them when she turns and spots us closing in. She visibly swallows but continues her sentence. "I wonder if it'll get worse now that the Royal cat is out of the bag."

Tinsley holds my gaze as she listens, nodding along as she does. "That's one way to put it," she says with a soft smile when all I want to do is rip the phone away and demand to know exactly who she's talking to and what they're talking about.

"Look, T, I gotta go." Well, that answers one question—it's

Tessa. "I know, I know. You gave me a crash course. I'll watch her, promise. I'll see you tonight at The Barracks."

"Who you talking to, Tins?" Banks asks when she ends the call, yanking the phone from her hand, holding it overhead out of reach, and pinning her tight to his body by wrapping an arm around her.

She doesn't answer, too busy trying to climb Banks's body to retrieve her phone without much success.

"Savvy's best friend," I answer for her.

"Who's Savvy?" Banks asks as Tinsley drops down from her toes, eyes now cartoon character wide.

"Samantha," I explain. Banks nods without questioning the correction. "The real question is"—I move to the opposite door and peer out like Tinsley has been doing—"*why* were you and Tessa talking about her so early in the morning?"

The hesitation and side glance toward the doors have me straightening and folding my arms across my chest in an assertion of dominance. If Tinsley thinks she's getting away without answering the question, she has another thing coming.

"Tinsley," I warn, sandwiching her between Banks and me.

"It's nothing, Jasper." Her color-changing eyes plead with me to drop it. Yeah, that's not going to happen.

"You're lying." My voice lowers an octave, and Banks gives me a *What the fuck, bro?* look. Yes, I'm a dick, but except for one very notable exception, I don't actively try to intimidate the female student body into bending to my will.

"Jasper…" Tinsley actually moves closer to Banks, and now I'm getting a death glare from my friend.

I don't care. I want answers.

"Tinsley." I bend and move my mouth next to her ear. "I *hate* it when people lie to me. Don't do it."

"Bruh…" comes from Banks as if to warn me away. I only straighten enough for Tinsley to see just how serious I am.

"You'll be able to see for yourself any minute," she says instead.

Fine. That's how she wants to play it?

Without a word of apology or goodbye, I turn on my heel and stalk outside, the heaviness of the entrance door the only thing keeping it from banging back against the wall.

I toss my bag on the ground, not giving one thought or fuck to the iPad inside. I strip off my uniform jacket next, adding it to the pile of my belongings. It's not the temperature causing me to strip. We're a few weeks into fall, my weather app telling me we're comfortably hovering in the upper sixties. No, it's the frustration pulsing through my veins, burning me from the inside out that necessitates the jerky roll of my shirtsleeves until they're folded near my elbows.

I'm pacing, or more like stalking like a panther, across the top step when Duke's Mercedes speeds into the lot.

Fucking finally.

That's one missing person found. Plus, he can back me up when we confront his…*fiancée*. Just the thought of the word makes me want to throw up in my mouth while simultaneously wanting to punch a wall.

Except…

Ex-*motherfucking*-cept the passenger side door opens and out steps Savvy.

What. In. The. Actual. Fuck?

I'm off the steps, clearing them in a single jump instead of wasting time walking down them individually, and at the G Wagon before either of them makes it past the rear bumper.

"Well, if it isn't the happy couple." I shoot my supposed best friend an *Et tu, Brute?* sneer.

Duke shuffles back, holding up his hands to proclaim his innocence. "It's not what you're thinking, brother."

"Oh no?" I get in his face, my chest bumping against his, knuckles cracking in an effort to not connect my fist with his jaw. "Then how about *you* tell me what *I'm* thinking, *brother*." I spit out the title like a joke. "Because from where I stand, it sure as shit looks like you're more than happy to slide into my sloppy seconds."

I'm shoved to the side, but not by Duke. Nope, that honor goes to his little fiancée. I wheel around, a raging bull ready to explode, and she's a china shop.

One, two, three steps is all it takes. She's backed against the rear hatch of the Mercedes, her silver hair fanning out along the matching paint when she's forced to tilt her chin up in order to maintain eye contact.

It's a miracle I don't dent the back panel as I slam my hand against it, trapping her between my arm and the chrome wheel cover hanging in the middle.

I step my feet between hers, taking in the tall boots from their flat soles and up over the slouched material and two wide buckles, following them until they end and the black socks take over at mid-thigh. I want to bite the few inches of leg visible between the socks and her plaid skirt.

My hand is on her thigh, my fingers gripping her hard enough that the skin blanches around my hold.

There's a whistling sound, and not until a *crack* splits the air and a burn blooms across my cheek does it register that I missed the warnings. Savvy slapped me.

Slow and with purpose, I lift my chin, rotating my face until I'm staring at her sunglasses-covered, nostrils-flaring, lips-parted, seething-but-hot-as-fuck face. My gaze drops to where her chest heaves up and down in rushed inhalations.

Thanks to my height, I can just make out her eyes hidden behind her purple framed Wayfarers, but I slide them up to sit on top of her head and out of the way.

Her hand rises again, but not to slap me. Instead, she snakes it inside her blazer and pulls out her inhaler.

Her eyes never leave mine as she shakes it and thumbs off the cap, bringing the mouthpiece to her lips, all while her *How fucking dare you?* glare is equal parts pissed off and hurt.

The *whoosh* of her medicine being dispensed combined with the hurt edge of her glower extinguishes the bulk of my ire.

I shift back to create a little bit of space but maintain my position, not willing to risk her being able to run away from me.

"Fuck—you—" Savvy pauses, eyes falling closed, the long line of her throat moving with a swallow, and inhales a single deep breath. "Noble," she finishes, her voice stronger and steadier than seconds ago.

"Told you once wouldn't be enough." I smirk, feigning a sense of unaffectedness the growing pressure in my groin mocks me for.

"You're delusional if you think that's *ever* going to happen again after you've been spreading it around town like an old biddy."

What? Is that what she thinks?

"And to think…" She shoves at my chest, growling when I don't move an inch and pushing a second time, hands balling in the material of my dress shirt when it yields the same result.

I crook a finger under her chin and bring her gaze back to mine when it gets stuck on how she's wrinkling the shit out of my shirt. "To think what, Princess?"

Her eyes fall closed, and a pained whine escapes at the endearment. I don't need harsh words to break her.

The *I hate you* glare is back when she opens her eyes again, and I meet it with a *No you don't, baby* smirk.

Her focus goes to the dimple in my chin as she holds off for a few more seconds. "That up until half an hour ago, I… wanted to see you."

She did? Well, that's…unexpected.

"Oh yeah?" My smile is too big, too self-satisfied, but like everything else, I don't give a fuck.

The way Savvy sucks air in through her teeth tells me she does. That only makes me grin harder.

"You're an asshole."

I nod, manacling a hand around her wrists and loosening her hold on me, stretching her arms overhead and lacing my fingers with hers. Her back arches, her tits and hard nipples brushing my chest with each inhalation. Conscious of her asthma, I pause to take stock of her breathing, but despite her using her inhaler, it seems steady, and she hasn't coughed once, which from the research I've done can be one of the symptoms.

"Let me go, Noble."

I bury my face in her neck, savoring the sweet lime scent I didn't realize until this moment I missed for the last week. "No."

"Grrr."

I smile against her skin because she grrr-ed at me. She didn't growl, not like how her brother did with pretty much every sentence he spoke to me, but grrr-ed. I'd never say it to her face or admit it to anyone else, but that was kind of adorable.

"Your growl needs work, baby." I kiss the soft spot behind her ear, enjoying very much when her head falls to the side, granting me better access. "You should have your brother teach you. From what I experienced, he's an *excellent* growler."

Savvy bucks against me, her knee connecting with the outside of my thigh as if she went to knee me in the balls only to have my body serve as its own shield.

"Is this the part where you want me to feel guilty? Where I should be *apologizing* for my overprotective big brother and telling you I don't care what he has to say because I'm my own person and I make my own decisions?"

I'm practically giddy at the prospect but urge that part of me to cool its jets and not get ahead of itself. I may know her by a different name, but this is still the same woman who could earn a varsity letter in challenging me.

"Never gonna happen, Noble." I don't know if it's due to her being back to continually using my last name or the slow, satisfied curl of her shiny lips, but something in me snaps.

"Why do you have to be the most *stubborn* female on the planet?" I shout.

"Why did *you* have to be the type of guy to run and brag to the *world* every time you get between a girl's legs?" she shouts back.

"What?" That's the second time she's said as much, and it still doesn't make sense.

She releases a sharp, short laugh. "Guess I should be *grateful* you only deem the times your dick gets wet as boast-worthy." She looks toward the school. "Otherwise, who knows what I would have been subjected to after the gala, hmm?"

The *Yeah, I know your tricks* hum grates on every one of my nerves.

"I didn't tell *any*one about *any* of the times we hooked up."

I get a *Yeah, right* lip purse. "Duke." She says it with such finality it's laughable, because she's wrong.

"Sorry to disappoint you, Princess, but Duke figured it out all on his own. Right, man?" I turn for confirmation, but Duke isn't there. He's actually not in the parking lot at all. I was the one who went after him, and yet he gave us this moment alone.

"Fine." Savvy huffs. "I'll give you that one. Tess is scarily the same way." After meeting her best friend in person, I can believe that.

"Good." I shift forward, our fronts touching again. "I'll take that apology now."

"Fuck that and fuck you." She bucks again, her back slamming against the metal of the SUV behind her in a way that would have Duke sweating if he were still here. "Duke figuring it out doesn't explain why you told Carter— and *every other* Royal—that you *wham bam thank you ma'am*-ed me."

What?

What is she…

Then it clicks—the hospital.

Carter and everyone else refusing to tell me if she was okay.

Being blamed for her being in the hospital in the first place.

All the events of the night—Natalie's disdainful attitude, witnessing the closeness between Chuck and Savvy, the arguing and fucking Savvy in her bathroom, learning about the asthma, the engagement announcement—created small fractures in my self-control until it splintered apart into nothingness.

"It wasn't like that." I barely remember what I said to anybody. It certainly wasn't the intentional brag she's characterizing it as.

"Uh-huh." Her tongue runs across the front of her teeth. "If you were hoping smashing me would earn you a place with the Royals, you're going to be sorely disappointed."

My fingers flex, my knuckles skimming along hers where we're linked. "What the hell are you talking about?"

"The only thing showing interest in me will get you is an invitation into the ring with Wes for an ass-kicking."

It doesn't escape my notice that it's Prince she claims will deliver the ass-kicking. Common sense assures me it's because of his reputation as both a fighter and enforcer for the Royalty Crew, but the deeper, jealous side of me reminds me of all the times I've seen Savvy's hands on him, her lips kissing him in ways that were anything but platonic.

You can't have her, my inner voice whispers. *Yes I can*, I counter.

She's not yours, it challenges. *The fuck she isn't.*

The beast is back, beating inside my chest, roaring and clawing at me to claim what's mine. Not Wes's, not Duke's, not *any*body else's—MINE.

Releasing one of her hands, I bring my own to her face, pinching her chin between my fingers and tilting it up to me. I pause for one beat and one beat only, to catalog her breathing and slam my mouth onto hers.

A startled gasp has her lips parting under mine. I instantly take advantage of the opening and slip my tongue inside, stroking along hers and teasing her with the barbell pierced through mine.

Fingers comb through my hair, their tips skimming the side of my face before her hand falls to rest on my neck.

I release her chin, snaking my hand inside her blazer, caressing Savvy's side, squeezing the soft spot where her waist indents. Her body rocks forward, rolling against mine like a wave, her center cradling the hard-on trying to break free from my slacks.

Down, down, down I travel the length of her body. The soft material of her skirt bunches in my palm, and I smile against her parted lips at the needy whimper that escapes when I knead the rounded muscles of her ass.

I abandon her mouth, noting how she sucks in a deep breath as I kiss along her jaw and down to her neck. I listen for a wheeze or any sign that Savvy's struggling to breathe, but all I hear are breathy sighs of pleasure.

Smooth skin meets the callouses years of wearing hockey gloves have formed on my palms, and I clutch at the toned muscles of her thigh. I widen my stance, hitching Savvy's leg over my hip, my hand slipping under the hem of her skirt and grinding against her exposed panties.

"Fuck, Savvy." She mewls as I breathe her name against

her skin, latching onto her neck, flicking the ball of my piercing intermittently as I suck harder.

Satisfaction fills me at the sight of the reddish-brown mark marring her creamy skin, the center a deep purple of broken capillaries that will take days to fade.

Releasing her other hand, I cup her nape, run a thumb over the hickey, and press down. "You look *damn* good wearing my mark."

Eyes darkened by blown-out pupils blink dazedly at me. "Guess it's a shame this will be the last time you'll ever get to see it."

That's what she thinks. She'll wear my mark every day if I have anything to say about it.

Even when she's wearing your best friend's ring?

The taunt from my subconscious shoves me to the edge of my limits. It's not going to take much to push me over the proverbial cliff.

I bring my hand around to the front, gripping Savvy's throat for control and forcing her to hold my gaze, pressing on the underside of her jaw when she tries to look away.

Beneath my touch, I can feel...everything: the speed of her pulse as the blood rushes through her veins, the contractions as she swallows, and the subtle way her throat expands with each inhalation. It's a conscious effort on my part to not press hard enough to restrict her airflow, but I manage.

We're a clash of wills as we stare each other down. Deny it as much as she likes, she wants me. I see it every time she lets her guard fall the briefest bit. It's in the way her eyes get caught on me, her gaze lingering when she thinks I'm distracted by other things. I feel it in all the brief moments she moves toward me, her body seeking the comfort of my touch.

And the way she kisses me? It's ardent. It's only happened twice, but the passion released when it does is enough to rival any sexual experience of my life.

Then there's the sex itself—the animalistic way she unravels, her pussy clenching around me like it refuses to let me go.

In the distance, the bell rings, but neither of us makes a move to get to class.

With the foot still planted on the ground, Savvy pushes onto her toes, and our torsos connect. Taking advantage of the better alignment, I rock into her only to have something hard poke me in the stomach.

Fuck, her inhaler.

I've tried to be conscious of her asthma. After experiencing the utter helplessness of witnessing one of her attacks, I want to do everything I can to limit the chances of a repeat.

Why is your hand around her throat then?

"Shit, Savvy." I drop my hand as if burned, running it over my hair with a muttered curse. This is a mess. *I'm* a mess.

"What?" Her eyes dart all over my face, trying to decipher the sudden shift.

This time I'm the one reaching inside her jacket, feeling around for the inner pocket, and pulling out the inhaler when I find it. "Do you need this?"

"What?" she questions again, gaze dropping to the plastic device pinched between my knuckles.

"Your asthma…"

Her eyes narrow as my words trail off, that hardened edge from earlier returning as she goes rigid. "…is under control," she finishes for me.

"Yeah…but—"

"Jesus Christ." She slaps open palms to my chest.

"The fuck?"

Her palms press flat, fingers splayed as she pushes, back arching against the Mercedes, hair flying around her flushed face as she shakes her head. "At least you kept your word and aren't using it against me."

The admission is a concession a part of me didn't think she would ever give freely.

"But…fuck, Noble"—angrily, her hands swipe the hair away from her face—"finding out I have asthma sure has turned you into a pussy."

A pussy? She can't be serious.

What the hell does she want from me?

Since when does showing another person compassion make you a pussy?

What do you know about being compassionate?

"I'm a pussy because I don't want to see you carted away in an ambulance again?" I ask incredulously.

She rolls her eyes, making me want to claw them out just so they can't do that anymore.

"No, it's being *scared* that I don't know my own body enough not to put a stop to things if they get out of control that makes you a pussy."

"Like you did last weekend?" I shout.

"That was different." Her jaw hardens, defiant as ever.

My nostrils flare, my shoulders rising to my ears as I breathe through the absolute exasperation this woman ignites. "I don't believe you."

"Whatever you say, Noble."

My last name falling from her lips…*again*—that's it, I'm done.

I hook an arm underneath her ass and hoist her against me, the foot of the leg not already trapped over my hip dragging along the asphalt as I round the car and yank open the thankfully unlocked rear passenger side door then toss Savvy onto the back seat. She bounces once when she lands, scrambling around, hands searching for purchase on the leather interior, legs akimbo, one falling to the floorboard, the other stuck in an awkward bend from the seat back.

The hem of her skirt flips up from all the movement, and I have a clear view of her panties—white and virginal, tempting me to take her in all the dirtiest of ways.

She attempts to sit up, but I'm on her, slamming the door

behind me, the bulk of my body forcing her legs to remain open as I settle myself between them and grind.

"Noble."

Her moan is music to my ears. When her hands press against my shoulders, I expect her to push me away, but she curls them around the sides, clutching at where my triceps pop from holding myself propped above her.

There's a faint thud as her inhaler bounces around under the seat, but it's all but forgotten as I crush my mouth down on hers. I nip and suck at her lips, Savvy returning the favor with equal fervor. There's nothing sweet about our kisses. Every time, it's like a clash of Titans—thunderous explosions of need and lust in the hunt for dominance.

I have her underwear pulled to the side and two fingers thrust inside her without a hint of warning, warm wet heat hugging my digits.

Savvy mewls, head falling back, neck arching, my lips falling to her chin, my teeth scraping along the cut of her jawline.

The leg not pinned between the seat and my body kicks out, the cramped space allowing it to connect with the door.

She whimpers at the loss when I remove my fingers from her cunt, her wetness dragging along the back of her leg as I grip her thigh and bend her knee, trapping the limb over my upper arm.

Her center is spread open for me, the stretched-out lace of her ruined panties sitting on the outside of her bare pussy lips, the black metal of her VCH piercing standing out in hard contrast to the pink skin glistening with her arousal. Her pelvis is angled up just enough to allow me full access as I swipe my fingers through her slit, scissoring my fingers, driving one into her ass, the other into her cunt, and my thumb straight to her piercing, working it into her clit with the intention of making her come as quickly as humanly possible.

She wiggles her hips against the leather seats as if running away while at the same time chasing the fullness of my touch.

In and out, I work her, the plunge of my fingers punishing, as is the way I thrust my tongue into her mouth as I swallow down her moans.

My cheek drags along hers as I move my mouth to her ear, flicking the black diamond stud in her earlobe with my tongue ring. "Say my name, baby."

Her heel kicks my back as her leg twitches in my hold. "Why?"

I bite her. "So damn stubborn."

Her hands thread into my hair, and she yanks as she does a full-body roll beneath me.

"You know the deal." I bring my fingers as close together as her body allows, feeling them rub against each other through the thin membrane of skin separating them. "No cheating this time. You say my name, and you get to come." I flick over the skinny barbell pierced through her clit. "Give it to me, Savvy."

She cries out, tugging on my hair and guiding me back to her mouth. She kisses me long and deep and says, "Jasper."

Victory fills me as the first flutters of her impending orgasm dance on my fingers.

She cries out again, this time in loss as I rip them out of her body.

I slap a hand to the seat back and use it as leverage as I fumble around for the button that opens the center console. Diving my hand inside as the doors on it wing open, I toss the contents until I find one of the condoms I know are there.

As soon as I have the foil packet in hand, I have it ripped open, my zipper lowered only enough to free my dick, covering it and plunging inside Savvy.

We groan in unison, and I hiss as I work through the fist-like resistance.

I've only managed to get half my length inside her tight sheath, and she's coming, the rush of wetness easing the last of my entry. There's no orgasmic reprieve for my girl as I continue to pound in and out of her.

Sweat coats my skin, my uniform shirt clinging to my body uncomfortably but not slowing me down.

The tension disappears from her leg, and it falls to the crook of my elbow. I hitch it higher and drive myself deeper. Pressure building at the base of my spine is my only warning, and I swivel my hips so I graze along her swollen clit with each thrust.

My orgasm breaks free, my release filling the condom a second before Savvy's walls grip me again as I hold myself inside her.

Two more lazy pumps of my hips and I smirk at the disgruntled sound she expels when I shift away to tie off the condom and straighten my pants.

The windows are fogged. If anybody came patrolling through the parking lot, it would be blatantly obvious what's going on inside the vehicle. Not giving a damn about that or the fact that I'm sure first period is close to over, I hook an arm under Savvy's limp form and reverse our positions.

Unlike Savvy, my entire lower half has to bend to fit on the seats, but it doesn't prevent me from having her draped over me. She's got a leg thrown across me and an arm flopped over me, fingers hanging toward the floor.

Her sated state is probably the only reason she's being so docile, but I'll take all I can get if she's going to allow her cheek to rest on my chest, her eyes closed in contentment.

I run my fingers through her hair, watching how the light hits the different shades of silver, and tuck it behind her ear.

She sighs, her lips parting the tiniest bit, and she nuzzles into me more.

This is an entirely different aftermath than what I've experienced before, and there's no chance I'm rushing it. The longer she's on me, the more my scent will imprint itself on her. The thought makes me smile as I match my breathing to hers, a sure way to tell if hers is in a normal range.

It hits me that this—the cuddliness—isn't just new for Savvy and me; it's new for me…in general.

Except…

The longer we lie here together, the more it starts to feel like this is just a stolen moment in time.

CHAPTER 8

BY THE TIME I climb out of Duke's Mercedes for the second time today, first period is long over. Jasper doesn't seem to be in any rush to get to class as he straightens his rolled shirt cuffs, his forearms twisting as he does, the sinew and strength displayed in them sending a bolt of heat to my core.

You're turning into a hussy, Savvy.

I just came twice while having car sex—and on campus, no less; my body should be sated and not getting turned on by the sight of Jasper smoothing his now wrinkled shirt over his washboard stomach and tucking it back into his pants.

Shaking myself out of my lust-induced stupor, I take stock of myself. My breaths are a little bit fast and my heart rate is slightly elevated, but neither is cause for concern.

My shirt didn't fare much better than Jasper's, the bottom almost stuck bent up where it hangs over my skirt, though thankfully that's an easy fix. My underwear, however, is a lost cause, so I slip them down my legs. Jasper's eyes turn stormy at the sight of the white lace, and I don't even get the chance to straighten before they are being snatched away and shoved into the pocket of his pants.

"Those are mine," I complain, but there's a distinct lack of heat to the words.

That maddening smirk makes an appearance, the action only exponentially sexier given the puffiness all the kissing caused on his lips. "When are you going to learn, Princess…"

The nickname is meant to provoke, so why am I starting to like it?

He moves in closer, caging me in next to the car door. "Everything about you is mine." His mouth grazes the shell of my ear, my head tilting to the side. He cups the side of my neck, his thumb pressing onto the spot he marked earlier, my knees turning to jelly against my better instincts.

There's a part of me—albeit a small one—that wants to be his, wants to give in to the push and pull between us.

It'll never happen. There's too much baggage to unpack, not to mention the fact that I'm technically supposed to be engaged to his best friend.

That's a problem for future Savvy. I need to make it through this day first.

Jasper straightens, peering down at me as he steps back. The way he's looking at me, his gaze studying and cataloging everything he sees, makes my breath catch for an entirely different reason than I'm used to. Gone is the usual malevolence that simmers beneath the surface. There's almost…dare I say…care.

"Are you sure you're good?" He grips my lapel but doesn't reach inside my blazer like he did earlier. I want to be annoyed, to lash out again about being perfectly capable of taking care of myself—except he seems too damn genuine.

I get it. An asthma attack is a scary thing to experience for both myself and those around to witness it. When it's your first, and especially when it's as severe as the one from last Saturday, it can be downright terrifying.

The details surrounding the event are always a bit hazy, but the few pieces I am able to recall all feature Jasper.

Not once did he let me go as I succumbed further to my symptoms. He didn't let Chuck take over or shy away when confronted with my brother—as both Carter King himself and as our true relation to each other. Not even the commanding I'm-in-charge-here side of Tessa could push him away.

I remember leaning against him, seeking comfort where I had only experienced peril.

I remember being wrapped in him—not just in his coat to keep me warm, but in his presence. He held me, cradled me against him, reassuring me despite the fear tingeing his words and coaching me through the worst of my symptoms by following Tessa's lead.

"I'm fine." I slide a hand up the hard plane of his chest, fiddling with the silk tie hanging between us. "It's not…" I bite my lip, coyly watching him from beneath my lashes. "… physical exertions that triggers me the worst."

Jasper's lips twitch in amusement, his eyes crinkling at the corners. I can hear the entendre he wants to let out about *physical exertions* without him having to say it.

"So you're saying I can fuck you any time I want without having to worry?"

I laugh, ducking beneath his arm, and start for the school. "In your dreams, Noble." His disgruntled curse about using his last name has me giggling before I let out a startled squeal as I'm lifted from the ground and pinned to the stone wall of Blackwell Academy.

"One of these days, Princess…" Jasper skims a hand along my side, his palm splaying across the center of my chest, his fingers angling over my throat. He's never squeezed hard enough to restrict airflow, but a frisson of something forbidden still sparks inside me. "You're going to say my name without your orgasm being held hostage."

"You really are living in dreamland, huh?" I taunt, the tip

of my tongue pinched between my teeth to restrain a full smile.

Trading barbs is how we communicate, so I don't know how to respond or even react when he ghosts his thumb across my bottom lip, eyes locked on my mouth as he does. "I like it when you giggle like that. It makes you seem…softer, sweet even."

Stunned speechless, my head thunks against the wall while I process the statement. I don't think *anyone* has described me that way before. I mean…you don't earn the nickname Savage by being sweet. Why does it feel like he sees parts of me nobody else does? And why does it feel like that thought could trigger an asthma attack?

Engagement Announcement

CHAPTER 9

Two powerful families will be united most romantically.

"GOVERNOR AND MRS. DELACOURTE are happy to announce the engagement of their son, Duke Dashall Delacourte, to Miss Samantha St. James, stepdaughter to hotelier Mitchell St. James and his recently wed bride, Mrs. Natalie St. James," the governor's office said in a statement.

The union of Mitchell St. James to his wife, Natalie, took most of the socialite community by surprise this past summer, and to this reporter, it looks like love blooms swift and strong for this family.

Natalie St. James and her daughter Samantha hail from Blackwell, New Jersey. The town is known for Royal Enterprises and the slew of players its academic establishments turn out in professional sports.

The town is also home to the prestigious Blackwell Academy, the famed preparatory school that boasts some of the brightest and most influential young minds in the country, including the happy couple.

The two female members of the St. James family have a long-standing history in town, as Natalie's late husband descended from one of Blackwell's notable founding families.

The governor and his wife confirmed that while their son fell hard and fast for the beautiful Miss St. James (pictures of each attached), the two are in no rush to set a date. However, sources close to the Delacourtes suspect we could hear wedding bells shortly after the youngsters hear "Pomp and Circumstance."

CHAPTER 10

I SLAM the door to my locker with more force than necessary.

Two weeks. It has been two weeks since the night none of us talk about, and they have been spent blissfully living in denial.

Well…blissful might be a stretch. I've more been living on a sliding scale of extreme emotions that seem to have been triggered by Savvy returning to school eight days ago.

After spending a week waffling between trying not to think about her and worrying about if she was truly okay after being in the hospital, seeing her get out of Duke's Mercedes had me raging.

I took most of my frustrations out on Savvy. We fought—no surprise there—and we fucked—that was kind of a surprise—but it's been the moments where she lets her guard down and opens herself up to me that have shocked me the most.

The…friendship we started to establish before the night that took years off my life when I thought she might lose hers has picked right back up, with us carrying on like nothing changed. I don't see how that is going to be possible now.

It's official—the whole world knows Duke Delacourte is set to marry Samantha St. James.

They also know Samantha St. James was Samantha King prior to her mother's marriage to Mitchell. It didn't take much for the guys—and I'm sure the rest of the school—to make the connection to Savvy King.

None of that, however, is what has me damn near ripping the locker door from its hinges.

No, that honor goes to dear old Dad. Thank Christ I had hockey practice before his surprise visit. If it weren't for those hours out on the ice to exhaust me, I don't know what I would have been liable to do, though I know enough to be sure it wouldn't have been good.

For the last twelve hours, I've gone back and forth between wanting to hunt down the motherfucker who thought they could take pictures of Savvy and me and being pissed at my father for issuing an ultimatum because of them.

How fucking dare he threaten to cut me off and renege on our agreement about hockey if I so much as hold Savvy's hand, let alone do anything else with her. Even now, all it makes me want to do is find her and reassert my claim on her, which in and of itself is a problem.

The fact that the pictures were sent to my parents, not the press, or even the Delacourtes, makes me suspect whoever was dumb enough to think they'll get away with taking pictures is someone with a vindictive agenda. But who? The only person brave enough to stand up to the kings at BA is Savvy, but…she was in the pictures.

Unless…

Could she have arranged for Tinsley to take the pictures? She was waiting for Savvy at the front of the school that day. Could it maybe be an attempt to break off the engagement?

Except…

Duke seemed utterly clueless about the images when I practically tore our dorm apart after Dad left. If it *was* Savvy and they *were* sent in an attempt to end the engagement, wouldn't the pictures have been sent to his parents?

It's a complete mind-fuck.

Here is what I do know: the person responsible for putting my hockey career in jeopardy by playing paparazzo better fucking run, because if I get my hands on them…I'm going to destroy them—*whoever* they are.

A buzz fills the halls, and there's a crowd gathered near the school's entrance. More than one person nods toward Duke beside me as they all whisper amongst themselves.

Arabella and her posse hover on the outskirts, a smug entitlement twisting the Queen B's lips as her gaze takes in the commotion.

The whispers grow louder, and there's a surge toward the door, with a few brave enough to actually open them and step outside while the others settle for trying to see out the windows bracketing them.

The thrum in my bloodstream is all I need to know; Savvy has arrived, that cluster of students parting like the Red Sea as she strides inside.

Her typical I-don't-give-a-fuck attitude radiates off of her in full force as she basically ignores everything and everybody.

I don't know if it's the forbidden stamp on her or what, but she looks extra fine this morning. She has on those same boots and thigh-highs as when I fucked her in Duke's car, but instead of the blazer, she's rocking the girls' long-sleeved button-up and black vest cinched tight over it. The combo shows off her figure perfectly. The only thing that would have made it better is if the hickey I marked her with hadn't faded, because the way she has half her hair tied back in a high ponytail would have shown it off perfectly.

"We need to talk, Princess." I snag her wrist before she can pass by.

Pressure builds in my groin at the challenge she issues with a simple flick of her eyes to where my fingers overlap around the fragile joint. I'm shifting on my heels when that defiant gaze rises to me. Yes, I can hear people whispering about her being related to *the* Carter King, but she's never needed that connection. Chick has balls bigger than most guys on the hockey team, and we have some big-balled moth-erpuckers. I would know; I've seen them in the locker room.

"Careful, Noble…" Midas shoulder-checks me as he strides past, flipping around to walk backward. "Isn't she supposed to be engaged to Delacourte now?"

"Fuck you, Abbot," I toss out, not releasing my hold on Savvy when she jerks her arm.

Brad and a few others from the football team are close behind, the former stretching out a fist for us to bump, adding, "Eh, you know our boys are used to tag-teaming bitches. Duke's people are French." He stretches his arms up at a forty-five-degree angle and thrusts his hips in the air. "Eiffel Tower those sluts."

Savvy kicks out a foot, tripping Brad as he passes, which has Duke dishing out the knuckle bump he denied the jock-hole moments ago.

"Check yourself, Manning," I warn Brad.

He scoffs. The idiot. "Shouldn't it be Delacourte warning me away? Bitch is his fiancée."

"I love that you call me a bitch like it's an insult," Savvy says dryly. "I'll have you know I'm an *expert* at bitchcraft."

Some of the students who formed a small circle around us start to snicker at Brad's blatant confusion and lack of comeback.

"Is that a course I can take?" Duke slings an arm over Savvy's shoulder. "Where do I sign up, and what do they teach?"

"You're too happy-go-lucky to pass it, playboy." Savvy pats Duke's chest sympathetically. "You need to be serious to excel at the art of pissing people off by telling them the truth."

This girl. How am I supposed to quit her?

CHAPTER 11

I'VE FIELDED as many questions about Carter being my brother as I have about being engaged to Duke.

Here I thought nobody would believe the arrangement our parents came up with, only to learn it's more common than I thought. Hell, Tessa's *I told you so* GIF is mocking me from my phone right now. She followed it with picture after picture of all her favorite books that fall into the "trope" my life is turning into.

I hate her. Okay, I don't actually hate her, but let me pretend.

The whispers hidden behind hands and the less-than-covert glances being sent my way are starting to get annoying. I mean, sure, I'm used to them on some level—you don't spend weeks being the target of bullying without experiencing them—but now it's…different.

By the time lunch rolls around and Tinsley and I retreat to our usual table outside, I'm regretting not going out to eat. I could have used the reprieve from the attention, if only for an hour.

Tessa isn't the only person blowing up my phone; the Royalty group chat is close to bursting. Carter is still being all kinds of weird, so I've actually been spending less time at his place than ever. I tried hanging out with the guys twice, but all it did was make this growing distance between their leader and me even more glaringly obvious. Honestly, it hurts too much.

With the engagement announcement hitting the news yesterday afternoon, it's clear it's not just going to go away like I had hoped.

Who knew the entire trajectory of your life could feel like it got knocked off course in less than three hundred words. The pen really is mightier than the sword.

Though I wouldn't mind having a sword right now because there are more than a few heads I would like to chop off.

The time has certainly come for me to clue my brother in on Natalie's actual threats, but knowing how poorly he handled the engagement announcement—by yelling, cursing, and breaking a chair, according to Wes—has me reevaluating that idea.

It speaks volumes regarding how things have changed for me at BA that Tinsley and I don't bother pausing our conversation when we hear the guys set their trays down. It isn't until someone rudely snaps their fingers in front of my face that I notice we seem to have inherited some of the football set.

Fantastic—not. Dealing with Jasper is one thing; Midas and the others take douchebaggery to another level. Case in point: the finger snap and the shit-don't-stink lip curl he's sporting.

As I shift back in my seat, I feel the weight of Jasper's arm stretched across the back of it, his familiar sandalwood scent enveloping me. I glance at him out of my peripheral, expecting him to say something to his jockhole friends. He doesn't. Instead, he seems content toying with the ends of my hair.

He doesn't even say anything when one of them comments about how it seems more like I'm engaged to Jasper than Duke. A glance at my *fiancé*—yes, that was sarcasm you heard—shows him eating up the drama the same way he's digging into the delicious risotto that's on special today.

"Was there something you wanted?" I ask Midas. Not that I care.

"Yup." Midas shifts forward, his forearms stretching across the table and his eyes falling to ogle my cleavage. Classy. "Seeing as you're the little King," he says to my boobs, "you must have the inside information."

"Little King?" *Ugh.* It's funny…Carter was all worried these BAssholes would try to show how tough they are by going after me since I'm his sister, yet they went after me because essentially they are bullies—*yes, I include you in this assessment, Jasper Noble*—and it was finding out my Royal relation that made them all want to be my…friend. Yeah, not happening.

"You know what? Let me stop you there." I put a hand up. "The correct term is Mini Royal, but that's beside the point." I shake my head. "I don't know what kind of *inside information* you think I have, but even if I *did* have it, I wouldn't give it to you."

A throat clearing has us all looking toward the head of the table to where Headmaster Woodbridge stands with a man whose polo declares him to be the BA football coach.

"Glad to see you back, Miss St. James."

"Thank you, Headmaster Woodbridge," I say even though I've been back for over a week. Whatever.

There's a beat of silence as his gaze drops to where Jasper's arm is draped across the back of my chair, his fingers still playing with the ends of my hair. I've given up trying to fight off his casual touches. We're going to pretend I'm not actually starting to like them, mm-kay?

There's another throat clearing from Headmaster Woodbridge, this time with the addition of the straightening of his tie before he meets my eye again. "Ah, yes…as you are aware, it is homecoming weekend for both schools here in Blackwell."

I nod because I am. I'm not sure how many years ago it was that Blackwell Public moved the week they used for their own homecoming to coincide with Blackwell Academy's. All I know is it was an attempt to "stick it" to the prep school with the one area they hold more prestige in.

Around the table, football jocks straighten in their seats. Ah, is this what they wanted inside information about?

Not only is it homecoming, it's also one of the biggest prank weeks between the two schools. Last year we released five bearded dragons—you know, because we're the Blackwell Public Dragons and the fire-breathing variety sadly don't exist in real life—into the Blackwell Academy halls. This on its own was good, but our chef's kiss of the scheme was Tessa's suggestion to label them 1, 2, 3, 4, and 6. It took them two weeks before they figured out they weren't missing one.

"Is this the part where you're asking for my RSVP?" I ask, barely managing to choke down the sarcasm in front of an authority figure. "Because if it is, you might be disappointed." I can already hear Natalie's bitching.

The slow blink and furrow that forms between Headmaster Woodbridge's brows almost make me laugh. I don't necessarily have an issue with authority, but there have been too many adults trying to make decisions about my life when they know nothing about me.

Again he glances at the football coach, who gives a subtle nod of encouragement. "Actually…we were wondering if you wouldn't mind asking Eric Dennings if he would come to speak with the football team here in addition to BP's when he visits this weekend."

"What?" I bark out a laugh, not at all expecting that to be his question. "Why in the world would you think I have enough pull with E to ask that of him?"

"You did just call him E," Duke whispers.

I hiss at Duke to be quiet and return my attention to Headmaster Woodbridge. I know what brought this on. Tessa's "family" has a closeness that rivals the Royals. I'm sure when they played golf this past weekend, Mitchell told him about how they all followed Tessa when she rushed to be there in my time of need. I try to explain how it may have seemed like Eric Dennings showed up for me, but it was more to support his sister.

"Even if I could…" I offer to soften the denial. "E won't be home long enough. The Crabs don't have a bye this week. As far as I know, he's driving up for the game—and to see his family—then driving back to Baltimore the same day."

Disappointed but understanding, the two men leave. Unfortunately, it sets off our new dining companions.

Questions fly at me left and right about Eric Dennings. How do I know him? How close am I to him? Have I met any of the other players on the Crabs? Am I close with his sister too? Have I met Mason Nova or Travis McQueen? Do I know what really went down with Liam Parker?

The details they know are almost too much to handle. It's insanity. I could answer yes to all of them, but I won't. It's bad enough they know as much as they do, thanks to the UofJ411 gossip account. I honestly don't know how Kay deals. If this is the result when I'm only loosely connected, I can kind of understand why she tried to avoid the spotlight all those years.

Once they finally realize they aren't going to get any information—on the BP prank or top-tier NFL player-wise—the football jocks leave. I never thought I'd be grateful to be left alone with the puck heads.

Tinsley and I fall back into our earlier conversation about the special stunt clinic she and Tessa will have this week at The Barracks then Duke raps on the table.

"I'm not introducing you to E either," I tell him. He leans in close, resting on his elbows and flashing his baby blues at me. I shake my head.

"That wasn't my question," he counters.

"Oh *really*?" I mirror his position, giving a *Do go on* eyebrow arch.

"I was gonna ask…what's goodie with Tessa?" Now it's his brows on the move, bouncing up and down on his forehead like a jumping bean.

"And, that"—I stretch a hand out to poke him in the nose —"is *why* you won't be meeting E. Big brother does *not* play when it comes to his little sisters."

"Can the same be said about—"

He flicks his gaze to Jasper, who's watching us closely from beside me. I don't know if the cat-that-ate-the-canary grin is for my benefit or Jasper's.

"—*your* big brother?"

CHAPTER 12

IT'S a good thing I'm used to balancing on three millimeters worth of steel when I'm on the ice because this past week has felt like exactly that—a balancing act.

On the one hand, I have Dad's threat forever looming over my head. On the other, I want Savvy despite what he has to say.

Then there's the fact that Duke is Savvy's fiancé. On the flip, *he* isn't taking it seriously, so why should I?

Have I touched her more than I should? Sure. Sorry not sorry, Dad. But can you blame me? She smells so good, and the skin on her upper thigh is so soft. At least I haven't marked her again. Plus, I feel like I should get credit for not dragging Savvy into the nearest empty room with a lock and fucking her until we're both blind.

"You sure you're cool?" Duke asks in a surprising display of empathy. We haven't really discussed the whole he's engaged to my girl thing. At school and at practice, it doesn't factor much into play.

No new pictures have surfaced either, not even the time I

couldn't help myself when I caught Savvy in the library. I had her pinned to the stacks, her ass cradled against my hard-as-fuck dick, my mouth licking along her neck as I pretended to reach for a book on a shelf above her.

I've chosen to ignore the niggling voice in the back of my mind that wonders if that particular moment not being documented was because Savvy realized the first attempt didn't succeed in getting the engagement called off, or if she's not the one responsible and the one who is just wasn't around. While smashing in Duke's Mercedes sort of just happened, me going outside was witnessed by others, so it wasn't as spur of the moment as the library.

I've tried to feel Savvy out, tried to see if she's treating me any different, if she's trying to lure me into a false sense of security. She isn't. She still gives me the same attitude she always has; the only change I've noticed is it has a slightly less hostile edge to it, but the argument could be made that it's because I stopped nailing dead rats to her locker.

There's also the fact that she has no idea what's at stake for me if we get caught messing around, so is it really believable to think that's her motivation?

"How bad could it possibly be?" I hold the door open for Duke, and we exit the locker room. "The last dinner we attended with our families ended up with a trip to the emergency room. The bar is set *low* for this one."

Because of the close relationship—personally and in business—of our fathers and Duke's future stepfather-in-law, my family was invited to this weekend's celebratory engagement dinner.

"Truth." Duke holds out a fist for me to bump. Like the engagement, we've avoided all talk of Savvy and her asthma. I don't know about Duke, but I hate how even the memory makes me feel helpless.

"Just be grateful they are doing it at home and not Drumthwacket." He mentions the "official" governor's mansion with a shudder. "I always feel like I'm going to break shit when I'm there."

"Could you imagine how much your mom would freak if you did?" It's my turn to shudder. Like the White House in DC, the New Jersey governor's mansion is known as "The People's House." They offer tours to the public and often rotate out priceless art exhibits. Duke's not exaggerating. The last time we attended a state dinner there, he almost took out a bust of George Washington on loan from an art museum in Princeton.

"Hopefully, it goes by quick. And who knows"—he pops a shoulder—"maybe being with Savvy could open up a spot in one of the more exclusive of her brother's races. He typically has them on Saturdays."

The possibility of a race is like an injection of gasoline into my system. *Fuck yeah.* Now that's a plan I can get behind.

"Oh shit!"

"No way!"

"How did they do that?"

"Is that Savvy King sitting on…"

"*Daaayum*, they had an inside man."

The excited comments and shouts echo down the hallway as students rush toward the front of the school. It's the mention of Savvy that has Duke's feet and mine moving a little bit faster to follow.

The volume and severity of the curses being spewed increase as we step outside to see that the parking lot that was once filled with the cars of the athletes who had morning workouts is now mostly empty.

"Is that my *fucking* car?" Midas roars, and sure enough, the missing cars have been shifted to the manicured front lawn. Headmaster Woodbridge is going to pass a stone.

The vehicles' seemingly sporadic placement makes me suspect they were used to spell something out, but I can't quite make it out from this vantage point. There's also a small box with large purple bows placed on the hood of each.

Front and center is my Ferrari. A smug-looking silver-haired devil sits nestled in the S-duct carved out of the front hood, phone in hand, gaze trained our way.

Duke cracks up, arms folded across his middle and bent over while he does his best impression of a stoner told the world's lamest dad joke. Dude is lost in his own little world while Midas and Brad are ready to rip heads off bodies. It's only the fact that most of the faculty are now outside that keeps them from storming over and doing just that.

Duke takes off toward Savvy, bellowing her name, tapping the side of his G Wagon parked two spots down from my F8 on the way.

I head in their direction, arriving at the same time Duke scoops her off my car and into a spinning hug. "How did you pull this off?"

"Because we're awesome, and you BAssholes are amateurs when it comes to pranks," a voice calls out from Savvy's phone.

"Hell yeah! You only have my girl on loan. Doesn't mean she switched loyalties," adds someone else, I assume Tessa with the *my girl* reference.

Duke and I move behind Savvy to see those on the screen, and Savvy flips the camera so it's showing us and not the guys currently losing their shit around us.

"Tasty Tessa!" Duke winks.

"You *wish* you knew if I was *tasty* or not." Tessa rolls her eyes.

"You got that right, baby." Duke shamelessly licks his lips. "Name the time and place, and I'll make it happen."

"You *do* realize you're *supposed* to be engaged to my bestie, right?" She calls him out for flirting. She's got that same ballsy, call-me-a-liar delivery as Savvy.

Thankfully the only people within hearing distance aren't

paying our little group any mind, and those around Tessa don't seem to be able to hear us all that well. Unsurprisingly, people took the news of the engagement at face value. Arranged marriages are not uncommon among powerful families. Duke and Savvy aren't the first alliance and won't be the last set up for those attending Blackwell Academy. It was a fact I had to accept after the shock wore off.

The dynamics at school have changed. The shift in the social hierarchy was cuttingly swift. Duke and I have managed to keep our top spot as kings of the school, but Arabella and the rest of the Unholy Trinity have seen a loss of their influence.

"Tessa, you ready to go?" A male voice calls out, and as he moves into view of the camera, I get a jolt of *What the fuck is he doing there?*

I take a step forward as if I can reach the asshat who put his hands on Savvy when I drove her to BP. Same as that day, Savvy stops me from intervening. It's not necessary. It's not like I can grab him through the screen.

I glance at the hand pressed to my lower belly, matte purple fingernails playing along my muscles, before lifting my eyes to silently ask her the same question I did myself.

"Yup." From the shake of the video, you can tell Tessa bounces on the balls of her feet, a perky ball of energy I would have never paired with Savvy's stoic nature. She blows a kiss. "Love you, and your Royal reign."

"You're a nut, T." Again, I'm taken off guard by the open affection, though it turns off like somebody flipped a switch when she focuses on the football douche. "You got the aerial shot I sent?"

"Received and posted. Nice to see you haven't lost your touch going to school with those jackoffs."

The smile that curls Savvy's lips—lips I want to kiss, bite, suck on until she's squirming against me, *shit!*—is anything but sweet. It's the one she's reserved for the times she's sparred with me, the times she wouldn't back down no matter how much I pushed—the same one that makes my dick harder than my hockey stick.

"It would do you well not to forget that fact again, Gunderson."

That's my girl. Fierce as hell.

Yeah, yeah, I know—not my girl, but whatever, I'm proud.

She hangs up and flips through her apps until she pulls up an Instagram account showcasing a picture of an aerial view of cars spelling out BA SUCKS—twenty-eight familiar, I'm standing right in front of them cars.

Wow!

"How'd you do it?" I ask, only to get a maddening smirk in return.

"Did you bring in the"—Duke drops his voice to a stage whisper—"*Royals*? You know"—he waggles his eyebrows—"to help hot-wire or whatever."

"No." Savvy rolls her eyes with a headshake. "We used your keys, of course."

She turns to face my Ferrari. My gaze drops to watch the way the hem of her uniform skirt rides up the backs of her thighs as she stretches across the hood. My dick chooses that moment to perk up and point out that we haven't fucked her bent over a car yet. If it wouldn't cost me my starting position on the hockey team, I would be making plans to rectify that immediately.

I'm still too busy getting lost in my fantasies of riding Savvy from behind to notice she's now standing in front of me, hands holding a small black box with a giant purple bow I can see is printed with miniature versions of the Blackwell Public dragon mascot.

She stares up at me, a hint of vulnerability peeking out from beneath her lashes while she does her best to cover it with a mischievous glint. She's pure temptation in every way. From her attitude and confidence to the way she wears her uniform with an I-don't-give-a-fuck lack of conformity, there's not one thing about her I don't want to own.

She presents the box to me much like I suspect Eve presented the apple that damned humanity to Adam. She's the definition of forbidden fruit, and I long to sink my teeth into her.

CHAPTER 13

THE ENDLESS STREAM of text messages from Tessa teasingly quizzing me about *What is this fork used for?* or *How about this tiny spoon?* has helped put an entertaining spin on tonight's dinner at the Delacourtes. I can't even with this chick, but it's one of the reasons I love her the way I do.

That said, I could do without all the colorful commentary she tosses in about the whole me being engaged thing. If I get one more picture about a bridesmaid dress she likes, I'm going to officially excommunicate her from being my maid of honor when I'm engaged for real in the future.

When I'm not texting with Tessa, I'm talking to Mitchell.

It's probably petty, but I do enjoy how it seems to rankle Natalie whenever Mitchell actually shows interest in my life. Even now, as Daniel drives us in Mitchell's custom Becker Cadillac Escalade ESV to the celebratory engagement dinner the Delacourtes invited us to (you bet your ass I'll be mentally rolling my eyes all night), he peppers me with questions about yesterday.

I ended up keeping my word and attended the BP home-coming game while Mitchell went to cheer on his alma mater.

My whole night was spent with a giggling Tessa who was all, *"This is a first. Normally people want to use you for the connection to* your *brother, not mine."*

So while my football-watching experience was sprinkled with calls to JT Taylor to tease him about his place in their crazy family's hierarchy, Mitchell's was filled with all kinds of stories about the mass automobile relocation prank.

"I can't believe you participated in such *childish* antics, Samantha." Natalie doesn't bother to look at me while she issues her opinion. Her focus remains on the flat-screen above my head.

Yeah, you heard that right. There's a freaking thirty-two-inch flat-screen hanging on the back wall. The whole vehicle is money, and if Mitchell didn't need it for when he travels for work, I'd ask if Daniel could drive me to school in it.

The interior is done in snow white leather with polished black accents. The four chairs are configured to face each other, with Mitchell and Natalie's able to fully recline and footrests that rise out of the floorboards.

There's a glass-doored mini fridge and more amenities than should be in something on four wheels.

Natalie is living her best life in the lap of luxury, and this one time, we can agree. It's almost, *almost* enough to make me forget about where we're being driven to.

"It's a rite of passage, dear." Mitchell gives Natalie's hand a squeeze while sending me an affectionate smile. "Though maybe we can work on Savvy using her powers to help BA plan their next one instead." The fact that Mitchell has switched over to calling me Savvy when Natalie still vehemently refuses to do so has me close to agreeing.

"I wouldn't bet on it." What? I said it has me *close to agreeing*, not that I actually would.

I may have told Mitchell how much I appreciated that he helped arrange for me to stay at Carter's for the week after my major asthma attack, but I certainly didn't tell him the truth about *why* it benefited me the most. I let him believe it was being surrounded by the familiarity that would help keep my symptoms from flaring. Plus, I pointed out that I wouldn't be alone much since all the Royals have rooms there.

In the long run, it feels more like using a Band-Aid to treat a bullet wound, but any reprieve from Natalie is well worth grasping hold of. That right there is where the lie comes into play. For some god-awful reason, Mitchell seems to actually love the Momster. I don't think he would like to hear how his bride can spike my anxiety in ways no one else manages to do.

At first, it didn't make sense to me. I'm not saying we've spent our time having grand stepfather/stepdaughter bonding sessions, but how can a man who seems genuinely kind be married to Satan's mistress?

I wanted to chalk it up to him being pussy-whipped, but the more time I've spent with Natalie while in Mitchell's presence, the more I've understood. The way Natalie can portray herself as not only a good mother but a decent human being is eerie. Poor Mitchell doesn't know that his bride is more black widow spider than *Homo sapiens*.

As much as I want to warn him, I have my own battles to fight with his wife. I'll have to trust he can take care of himself.

"Oh, Mitchell, don't encourage her." Natalie slides a hand over his knee, and I look away before the water I've been drinking makes a reappearance. I don't need to witness the gold digger at work, thank you very much. "Carter's *influence* is bad enough."

I ignore the dig against my brother. It helps that I'm annoyed with him for abandoning me tonight. It's time for us to have it out. We're well overdue for a little sibling heart-to-heart, and if he tries to avoid it like every other attempt I've made to talk to him alone, he has another thing coming. I'm not afraid of a little Royal Rumble.

"Nonsense, sweetheart." Mitchell links his fingers with Natalie's to soften the blow of his disagreement while keeping his focus on me. "Tell me…how did you pull it off?"

"You mean…you want me to give away all my secrets?"

After a quick glance at the television to check the score of the U of J football game, Mitchell leans forward, his elbows resting on his knees and—I kid you not—a twinkle of mischief in his eyes. It's moments like these where I get a peek at the playful side hidden beneath the hotel titan that make me seriously question how he ended up married to Natalie of all people.

"Maybe not *all*…just this one?" He holds up a single finger. "We are family—can't I cash in on that to get a peek into the brilliance I'm sure it took to orchestrate a prank of this magnitude?"

My heart gives an unfamiliar squeeze. He's playing the family card? Sure there's something he wants, but he didn't use it as a guilt trip. No…it was more like a…claim. Plus, the compliment he threw in at the end doesn't hurt.

"Fine." I shift so I'm mirroring his position across the short space between us. "But…if I tell you…" I pause, letting the silence build both the anticipation and the…seriousness of my own question.

"Yes?" There's this almost giddy excitement I'm only used to experiencing with adults like Chuck and his older brother Anthony.

"You have to *promise* not to spill the beans to Headmaster Woodbridge the next time you guys play a round of golf."

Could the prank get me expelled? Maybe. It's sort of a gray area. We didn't *technically* break any rules. And let's be real—even if I did get expelled, it's not like I would actually care. I didn't want to be at BA to begin with.

But you wouldn't get to see Jasper every day if you went back to BP, my conscience points out.

Like I care, I think in an attempt to convince myself I don't. Spoiler alert: it doesn't work.

"Deal." Mitchell stretches a hand out for me to shake, full businessman mode. Except I can't imagine the tilt to his lips helps him much in the boardroom.

"Well…" I stall, considering how much to divulge about my part in the prank. The disapproving sneer painted on Natalie's face as she studies us out of the corner of her eye confirms that yes, yes I will tell.

"So this year, things were a *little bit* different because BP had someone on the inside." I bounce my eyebrows up and down like I'm my favorite Charlie Chaplin GIF.

"I'll be sure to check the mail for my *thank you* card for making that happen."

Oh, he's got jokes. Seriously, how did he end up married to my Momster?

"I ordered specialty stationery and everything," I say with complete confidence.

I do my best to keep some of the details vague to protect the innocent—aka our motley crew of BP pranksters—while I tell him how we snuck into the athletes-only locker room and helped ourselves to any car keys we could find. Until I started at BA, I, one, didn't know they have a locker room that is specific for their jocks, and two, didn't know the football team and hockey team work out together for an hour and a half every morning before school starts.

I always assumed Jasper beat me to school because he lived in the dorms, but that's not the case. And let me tell you…the eye roll Duke gave me when I questioned how he was able to pick me up my first day back would have made Kay proud with its intensity. Guess it's a perk of being the governor's son.

I go as far as to pull my phone out to show Mitchell the

aerial shot I took from the school's roof that showed off the large BA SUCKS to perfection.

Natalie scoffs as Mitchell laughs while also confirming he saw the post at the game last night. Neither of us acknowledges the mini tantrum she's having in the back seat.

The car ride is such an unexpected experience—in all the best ways—that when Daniel pulls to a stop and rolls down his window, it feels like someone tossed a bucket of cold water on me.

I scoot over in my seat, peering out the window at a set of tall iron gates as Daniel converses with a gentleman stationed at the small guard shack in front of them.

Security lets us pass, and Daniel follows along a driveway that feels like it's a mile long until he parks in front of a gorgeous mansion. The size denotes its value, but the multi-hued stone facade gives it a cozy, homey feel. It's welcoming.

Daniel opens Natalie's door first, extending a hand to her and helping her out before rounding the car and doing the same for me after stepping aside for Mitchell to exit.

The cool autumn breeze has my recent shave at risk as it blows across the skin of my bare legs. I shove my hands into my pockets and snuggle into the wool peacoat wrapped around me.

Arm in arm, Mitchell and Natalie head for the front door held open by a waiting Mrs. Delacourte, but I remain rooted to the spot, staring up at the house like it's about to eat me alive.

The tight band forming around my lungs warns me that might be a more accurate descriptor than I realize.

CHAPTER 14

RYAN DONNELLY FLIES DOWN the ice, handling the puck with the blade of his stick like it's an extension of himself. That—that is what I want to be when I grow up. Yeah, sure, that's a childish notion, but fuck me if he's not one of, if not *the* best hockey player of a generation. He's America's answer to the Great One, Wayne Gretzky.

I've been a die-hard New Jersey Blizzards fan all my life. Most of the better memories I have with Dad are tagging along with him to his suite at The Ice Box, the arena where the Blizzards play.

The NHL MVP may not know it, but Ryan Donnelly has been one of the examples I consistently use in my arguments with Dad about being able to go pro. He's a hometown hero, born and raised in Jersey, and he attended BTU, where I hope to go before turning pro myself.

My acceptance letter to Blackwell Academy was penned before I was even conceived. Thank Christ they have a stellar hockey team; otherwise the opportunity to be scouted by such a prestigious Division 1 program like the BTU Titans wouldn't be more than a pipe dream.

Ryan dekes, and it's only because Jase Donnelly, his brother and another BTU alum, somehow blocks the shot by practically snipping it out of thin air that it doesn't go in.

"Holy fuck!" Duke jumps out of his seat. "Did you see that shit?" He gets all up in the television, obscuring my view of the Blizzard/Storm rivalry game.

I nod. "Sit the fuck down, bro." Duke's a true blue Blizzards fan too, but as a defender, he's got a hard-on for the younger Donnelly sibling.

Duke flops back onto the couch just in time for me to see Jase Donnelly dump the puck to his teammate, skate around a Blizzards defender, and get into position for a slap shot that has won Donnelly the title of hardest shot at the All-Star challenges.

Along with Duke and me watching from home, the arena collectively releases a breath as the Blizzards' goalie, Jake Donovan, executes an inhuman glove save.

"That's going to be us next year." Duke gestures to the TV, where Donovan slides his helmet up to taunt his brother-in-law while Ryan skates over and they share a gloved knuckle bump.

It isn't until I don't respond that Duke's jovial attitude fades, his forehead creasing with a frown as he gives me all of his attention. "Brother?"

I hate the hesitation I hear in his tone. This entire situation is fucked.

For years, Duke and I have had a plan.

Kick ass in hockey. Help the Knights win as many state titles as we could in four years. Play for the same Division 1 team in college. Repeat our championship run in the Frozen Four. The theme: doing it together.

Now all that is in jeopardy.

Why?

Because I want a girl I can't have, and the reason I can't have her is because my best friend's parents want her for him. It doesn't matter that he doesn't want her, and I'm sure she doesn't want him.

You don't know if she actually wants you though.

I slide a hand through my hair. *Fuck!* I'm letting pussy put my plans at risk. I'm a chump.

Before I get the chance to suck it the fuck up and finally talk to Duke about...*everything*, a beaming Mrs. Delacourte walks through the large archway leading into the den, the cause of my internal discord on her arm.

Holy shit!

I don't know why this continues to be my reaction to seeing Savvy outside of school. Maybe it's because she so rarely wears makeup or that the uniform helps when I try to pretend she's just like every other bitch who roams the halls.

The why doesn't fucking matter. What does is how the sight of her in a white, crocheted, long-sleeved minidress makes me rage for multiple reasons. The color is a slap in the face with what this evening is supposed to represent. It also makes my dick harder than should be allowed in mixed company because I have firsthand, dick-wetting knowledge of how *un-virginal* this bride would be on her wedding day.

"Duke, sweetheart, look who's here." This union may have been politically motivated, but Mrs. Delacourte is all heart-eyed happiness.

Duke, never one to disappoint his mother, stands up to meet her and his...*fiancée* halfway. "What's up, Grand Theft Auto," he says, pulling Savvy into a hug that she unfortunately returns.

"Can you not?" Savvy giggles. She. Fucking. Giggles. At Duke. I hate him. "You're going to give your mom the wrong impression of me." She gives a glance to Mrs. Delacourte, but she's all smiles as she watches this disgusting display of playfulness. "And no cars were actually stolen in the making of that prank. They were just—"

Because I'm a fucking stalker, I notice every little detail of Savvy's playful transformation that happens in the next second: the little twitch to her nose, the slight scrunch around her eyes, and the sliver of white as she bites the corner of her lip.

"—relocated," she finishes.

Duke guffaws, and his mom's eyes light up as he hooks an arm around Savvy's shoulders and tucks her against him.

Aww…look how cute. I'm not at all thinking of ripping his arm off her.

Liar.

Duke starts to regale his mom with a colorful account of yesterday's prank from BP, going as far as pulling out his phone and showing her the picture that went viral thanks to Eric Dennings sharing it on his Insta.

"I still wanna know how you pulled it off," Duke says, and Savvy makes a zipping motion across her lips as the rest of the parentals filter into the room.

Duke pouts when he learns that Savvy told Mitchell the details. The clown even drops to his knees to beg. I'd laugh at him making a fool of himself, but Savvy's giggling again makes my blood boil. Not the sound of it—that's magical music; it's how Duke is the one to inspire it, not once, but twice now. Tessa is the only one I've witnessed who can bring out this side of Savvy. What does it mean that Duke is joining such selective company?

"We're supposed to be getting married, Princess." My hands curl into fists at Duke using *my* name for her. "Doesn't that entitle me to some liberties?"

Fuck that. I'll take his liberties and shove them up his ass sans lube before I let them anywhere near Savvy.

CHAPTER 15

IT AMAZES me that two of the biggest assholes I've had the misfortune of having to deal with on a daily basis are the spawn of such lovely mothers. I know I can be a bitch, but it's more a defense mechanism than anything else. I swear, if anyone had to pair a child with their parent based on their narcissistic personalities, Duke and Jasper would get first pick as Natalie's offspring before me.

That said, the more time I've been spending with them, the deeper I've gotten to see beneath the shells they project to the world, the more I'm learning it's mostly that—a facade to hide behind.

Duke is still on his knees, looking like Kay's Labrador Herkie when we're eating something he wants but shouldn't have. The more I think about it, comparing Duke to an overactive puppy begging for attention is pretty accurate.

"Nice try." I pat him on the head, smothering my amusement at how it fits with the internal comparison.

"Speaking of…" Mrs. Delacourte starts, moving toward

her husband and extending the flat of her palm to him. With a smile that has a hint of patronizing to it, he reaches inside his suit jacket and pulls a small box from his pocket before handing it off to his beaming wife.

My heart jumps into my throat, and I pat along the couch for the small clutch I packed for myself, settling my nerves with the knowledge that my inhaler is close by.

"Duke, sweetheart." Mrs. Delacourte motions for him.

The goofy joy slips from Duke's face, and that clogged-throat feeling only intensifies for me when a furrow forms between his brows as he slides his gaze from me to his mom and back again.

Slowly he pushes to stand. When his eyes fall to me again, he smiles, but this time it seems false. Unease shoots up my spine and has me shifting in my seat.

Around the room, the six parents watch the scene with various expressions while I work on not throwing up. I have no idea where this sudden bout of nerves is coming from or why it's coming at all, but I can't deny the sense of foreboding hanging above me like a piano suspended from fraying ropes.

Duke's footsteps are slow and heavy, the drag of his shined dress shoes audible along the floor's aged hardwood.

"I thought we agreed this would be private." His hands are too large for me to make out what he takes from his mom before he's standing in front of me again.

"We did, but seize the moment, sweetheart."

Tingles race down my arms, goose bumps springing up despite the warm sweater material of my dress.

A creak of leather has me searching for the source of the sound, my gaze landing on a broody Jasper. His brows are drawn in a harsh line, his eyes churning with an intensity that only seems to emphasize their unique pearly color. His knees are spread, his elbows resting on his thighs, his hands clasped together.

He should be the picture of casual observance—except I can see how his knuckles are turning white because he's squeezing his hands together, and the deepening of that chin dimple tells me he's clenching his jaw. That weird pang stabs at my heart.

"Do it right, Duke," Mrs. Delacourte instructs with a subtle nod, widening eyes, and a slight hitch to her brows. Duke stares at her a second longer, his throat moving with a hard swallow as his mom curls a hand around his dad's upper arm, tucking herself in close and reaching to link her free hand with his.

"I really don't think now's the right time."

"Nonsense, Duke. We're here." She gestures to herself and Governor Delacourte. "Samantha's parents are here." She points to Natalie and Mitchell. "Your best friend is here." She nods to Jasper. "What better time is there than right now?"

Expectation settles like a heavy weight on my chest, and I fiddle with the clasp of my bag, debating if I need my inhaler or not. I've been doing better managing my anxiety, but that feeling like everyone else knows what's going on except me has it flaring as that itchy uncertainty forms beneath my skin.

The sound of Duke clearing his throat—twice—has my attention snapping back to him, his mouth pinched to the side, a hand raking through his hair and mussing up the styled strands. He mutters a curse under his breath when he realizes his mistake.

It's so minute I'm not sure if anyone else picks up on it, but this close, I catch the way Duke dips his chin just so and uses his peripherals to chance a glance at Jasper. What the hell could his mom want that would have him checking on Jasper?

With a breath deep enough to lift his shoulders and strain against the fine material of his custom-tailored suit jacket, Duke steps a foot behind him and lowers himself down to one knee. There's a grace to his movements I attribute to his athleticism that's distracting enough for it to take a second longer before the meaning behind his position hits.

He's down…on one knee.

Blue eyes rise to mine, but I can't focus on them. Instead, I concentrate on how his tie is now off-center, that tiny space between the knotted blue silk and starched white collar my salvation, my island in the turbulent sea my reality continues to be.

Duke remains silent, his hand rising between us. The bumps of his knuckles jut out as if they're millimeters from bursting through his skin as he clutches the object in his hand.

Rubbing my hands over the tops of my thighs, I focus on how the weave of the crocheted detailing of my dress tickles my palms and not my mounting panic or the sweat I'm wiping off with each pass.

Long, tan fingers gradually unfurl, and there's a distinct possibility that Tessa and I watch too many movies with how I feel like something is going to spring out at me.

Nothing does. There's no creature waiting for its chance at freedom to attach itself to my face and suck out my soul.

No. The thing cradled in Duke's palm is worse…much, much worse.

I think I'd rather face the hairy, prickly scales of some newly discovered mythical beast than the smooth black velvet of a ring box.

Shit just got real.

The ornate, handcrafted silver clasp sitting in the center shines like an omen. The rock forming in my gut directly correlates to the rock I'm sure is hidden inside. Except the longer I stare, the more it feels like it's Pandora's box rather than a jeweler's box.

I think a part of me was hoping this was all a bad joke, that despite the engagement announcement hitting the papers, the lack of any other discussion meant maybe we could treat it as fake news.

Hell, even the bulk of my interactions with Duke haven't changed. Jasper treats me more like a fiancé would their betrothed…sorta.

Movement out of the corner of my eye has my attention once again going to the Delacourtes. Governor Delacourte is patting a close to bursting Mrs. Delacourte's arm.

Trepidation pulses off of Duke, and though I would say the friendship we've formed is tenuous at best, I scoot to the end of the couch and place my hand under his. Unless he went to his parents with the idea of our betrothal, we're on the same side here.

With the slightest nod from me, Duke slips his thumbnail under the thin scalloped edge of the clasp and flips it open.

I swallow, anticipating the opening of the box to be loud and ominous like a door in a horror movie. It's not. Just a distinct *snick*, and I'm nearly blinded by the bling nestled inside.

"It's a family heirloom," Mrs. Delacourte cries out, unable to contain herself anymore.

I drop my gaze to the ring again. It's gorgeous. The design has a distinct vintage feel that makes it easy to believe it's most likely several generations old.

"Do you like it?" Mrs. Delacourte asks in a squeaky rush.

"Of course she likes it," Natalie jumps to answer, and I don't bother correcting her or informing her I can speak for myself. Not that she would care if I did. She is the architect behind this insanity.

Duke adjusts his stance in front of me, his knee bumping my foot as he does. One would assume it's because kneeling on a hard floor is hurting his knee, but the new angle allows him to keep Jasper in his sightline.

"Samantha, don't be rude," Natalie scolds, shifting to hover over my shoulder. "Give Duke your hand."

Why does this feel so final?

I lift my left arm, curling my fingers into a tight fist then flexing them to their limits when I notice how my hand shakes. I wish I could blame it on a symptom of my asthma, but it's not. It's nerves, plain and simple. This entire situation is breaking me down in a way that's making me lose parts of myself.

The fact that I can feel a similar tremble in Duke's as he takes me by the wrist with one hand and positions the ring in front of my fourth finger with the other does nothing to assuage my consternation.

The rose gold band slides effortlessly to the base of my finger, the fit perfect, as if it's been sized specifically for me.

I can't deny the ring itself is breathtaking. The marquise diamond has to be close to three carats and is housed in a setting that lends a delicate elegance. The prongs at each point look almost heart-like, and the small diamonds spaced between the other rose gold balled prongs give the overall impression of a flower. Two half-carat teardrop diamonds bracket the center stone, and the piece is finished off with a row of diamonds down each side of the band.

I wiggle my fingers, watching the way the prisms of light dance off the gems. It's exquisite but not me in the slightest.

"It's perfect." Mrs. Delacourte sighs. The adults in the room are all quick to agree. None of them notice the complete lack of excitement coming from the teenagers.

It isn't until the thud of heavy footsteps beat a hasty retreat as Jasper storms out of the room that there's any kind of less-than-pleased reaction from them, and that mostly comes from Mr. Noble.

"I—" I start only to stop. I what? What the hell am I supposed to say? It's been made clear my opinion on the topic doesn't matter.

"Are you okay, Savvy?" Mitchell asks when I start to rub at my chest.

"I'm fine," I assure him. On the other hand, Duke looks a

bit green as he rises and plops down beside me, both of us at a loss for words.

A part of me feels compelled to thank Duke for not actually asking me if I would marry him. Lord knows what I would have done if he did.

CHAPTER 16

DO NOT PUNCH your best friend.

Do not punch your best friend.

Do not punch your best friend.

The mantra continues to play on repeat as it did throughout the whole ring spectacle.

Christ.

That whole thing felt like a car wreck I couldn't look away from, all while being repeatedly kicked in the balls as I watched.

I'm pissed, and I'm sure my father will have something to say about my abrupt departure during the *happy moment*.

I don't give a fuck. I may be playing along, letting him believe I'm following his *hands off* directive, but if he thinks I can sit silently by while they insist on playing out this farce, he has another thing coming.

I'm pissed beyond measure. Not even the chilly night air is enough to cool me down as I stalk through the gardens at the back of the Delacourte property.

The beast inside my chest roars like never before.

I knew coming tonight was a mistake. It was going to be hard enough to keep my hands to myself when every instinct inside me demands the opposite. I convinced myself I could handle it. I'm a man. I'm not a slave to my urges or my dick.

That was before there was a ring. Without it, I was able to pretend the engagement wasn't real.

Now? Having to look at a physical reminder that Savvy is promised to somebody else when she belongs with me? Fucking hell, I don't know if I can do it.

I'm nearing my breaking point.

I don't know how long I've been outside, but I complete a full lap through the flower beds and around the greenhouse before I feel calm enough to return without losing my shit and costing me my future.

I feel like a creep slinking around corners and hugging the wall as I approach the arc of light streaming out from the den through the French doors.

I keep my steps quiet, sure the security staff is getting a good laugh at how I'm peering through the glass.

The first thing I notice is the absence of adults. *Good.*

Then my blood turns hot, and my vision tinges with red.

Well, isn't that precious.

When I left, neither Savvy nor Duke seemed to be faring any better than me. Now? They look like the picture-perfect couple, a regular Barbie and Ken, if Barbie dyed her hair silver and Ken was a backstabbing motherfucker.

How is it Savvy can laugh with Duke after what happened? She was so distraught over the idea of being engaged to Duke she had a fucking asthma attack when she was first told. You're trying to tell me she's okay with it now? Have I read her completely wrong? Is she just like all the other bitches at BA, easily distracted by trinkets and baubles? A childhood engagement is fine as long as there's a huge-ass rock that comes with it?

No way. I refuse to believe any of that is true.

Except…

Why is it that she can laugh with Duke and not me? She's never been that…carefree with me. Though…I don't know if I can necessarily classify anything she does as carefree, but that's the best description I can come up with.

Duke says something that makes Savvy laugh, and she backhands him lightly on the chest. Savvy shifts around on the couch, tucking one leg underneath her while letting the other swing, the toe of her suede bootie skimming the floor with each back-and-forth motion.

When she holds her hand out to inspect the ring before propping her arm on the back of the couch and resting her chin in her hand, I snap.

Am *I* so easy to forget? Does she think she can cancel me? She'll learn I'm the most relevant thing in her life.

I banish all thoughts of my father and his threats. It's time to claim my girl back.

Savvy and Duke jump as I barrel into the room from the outside door.

I don't pause. There's zero hesitation as I stalk across the floor. I don't even know if I shut the door behind me.

"Bro—" Duke tries to garner my attention, or at least I think he does. I couldn't tell you with any certainty with every atom in my body lasered in on Savvy and nothing else.

"Ja—" I cut off what might have been an unprompted use of my first name by snagging Savvy's wrist as her arm drops from pushing hair out of her face. With a jerk, I have her off the couch and stumbling into my side.

Clasping my fingers tight around her hand, I drag her with me to the powder room in the back corner of the den. Savvy's heels *click-clack-click-clack* across the tile as I swing her inside, slamming the door closed and throwing the lock an instant before caging her against the heavy mahogany.

One hand braced next to her face, I take our linked hands and stretch them above her head. Her breaths are coming fast, not in an asthmatic way, but enough to cause the section of hair obscuring part of her face to flutter.

Pushing my weight onto my hand, I lean forward until my face is directly in front of hers. Those deep purple pools inside her eyes suck me in and momentarily have me losing my train of thought, as does the way her sweet scent teases me. I've always had a thing for the way she smells, but there is *nothing* better than when that simple lime scent is mixed with my own sandalwood.

There's so much I want to say to her. I want to scream and shout, vent my frustrations, ask any number of questions swirling through my head.

We've found ourselves in a precarious situation with multiple parties trying to control us. The controlling aspect is one I'm used to, to the point that I'm practically immune. I've known from an early age that my lot in life was to take over a position at my father's company. It wasn't until I showed any real promise on the hockey rink that Dad relented to allow my life to take a slightly different path. Hockey first, then after retirement, I take my place by his side.

Though with the way he's tried to take over, the constant involvement—with Coach, Headmaster Woodbridge, and the scouts at both the collegiate and professional level—takes some of the joy away.

If I didn't know I was destined to be out on the ice pursuing a career in hockey, I would have quit years ago instead of putting up with Dad's demands.

Now he thinks he can threaten to take it all away?

Fuck that and fuck staying away from Savvy.

I tried. Really, truly, I did. But the sight of another man's ring on her finger broke me.

Speaking of which…

I lift my hand from the door and make a concerted effort to calm some of the fury rolling through me. Keeping my actions slow, I take a moment to brush the silky strands away and tuck them behind her ear, stroking down the shell in a lingering caress.

The mock turtleneck of her dress hits less than an inch below her jawline, and I curse at not being able to see the vein I can feel pulsing on the side of her neck when I skim my fingers down it. Continuing my downward trajectory, I follow each circle crocheted into the detailing along her collarbone, over the curve of her shoulder, and down her arm like they're spaces on a game board.

I keep expecting her to fight, but it's like she's frozen in place, trying to anticipate my next move.

When I finally reach her hand, her fingers contract as if to hold mine, but that's not my goal.

Instead, I feel around for her fourth finger, my own pinching the metal band encircling it when I do. In less than a blink, I have it ripped off her and tossed behind me, not giving one shit as it bounces across the floor.

Savvy gasps and shifts to look around me, but I block her by hammering my fist to the door again. "I need that." She tries to move away again, but I stretch the arm I have pinned higher above her head.

"No, you don't," I growl, barely resisting walking away from her to stomp the ring into something unrecognizable.

I only got a glimpse of it, and still, it feels seared into my memory, as is how I sat there like a chump as she received it without a thought to me.

"I don't like feeling ignored, Princess." I run the tip of my nose along her jaw, reveling in the tiny gasped moan she emits.

Above her head, her fingers flex in mine, but I don't let go. "What did you expect me to do?"

"Say no." Is it really such an unfair ask?

Her chin drops in defeat. "I couldn't."

That's where she's wrong. "Why the fuck not?" I snap. She's not the one whose future is at risk here.

"You wouldn't understand."

"Again"—I bend, nudging the fabric of her dress down and drag my piercing along the column of her throat—"why the *fuck* not?"

"Because…" She trembles. It's the tiniest vibration in her limbs, but I feel it regardless.

"Because why, Princess?" I nip her skin.

"Because Duke is my fiancé."

She did *not* just say that. My fingers curl, doing their best to dig into the door. No one, no-*fucking*-one gets to have any sort of claim on her but me.

"You know as well as I do that title is complete bullshit." I shove back and glare down at her.

"You're entitled to your opinion." The utter nonchalance she uses to tell me this sets fire to every one of my nerves.

"My opinion?" I grunt.

She flicks her gaze from my mouth to my eyes and nods. "Yeah…you know…a view or judgment formed about something, not necessarily based on fact or knowledge."

Is this bitch really trying to give me a vocabulary lesson right now?

"You want facts?" I ask, kicking her feet apart and stepping between them. "I'll give you fucking *facts*."

I abandon the door and curl my hand around her nape, lifting her until she's forced onto her toes, and I seal my mouth over hers in a punishing kiss, taking out all my frustrations on her.

Being told she's not mine when she is.

Being threatened to stay away.

Having the world think she belongs to my best friend when she's. Fucking. Mine.

Watching her accept Duke's ring.

Having her do a complete one-eighty on the whole engagement in the first place.

Every press of my lips, every stroke of my tongue, every

whirl of my piercing, every bite of my teeth doles out a punishment.

When I finally release her mouth, we're both breathing like we did blue line drills, chests heaving, the hard buds of her nipples poking me through our clothes.

"How's that for *fact*, Princess?" I challenge, taking in her flushed cheeks, her swollen lips, and the mild beard burn surrounding them from the stubble I'm sporting.

"Congratulations, Noble. You proved you know how to kiss, but I already knew that much."

I punch the door an inch from her head, but she doesn't so much as flinch. Her jaw is hard, her violet eyes watching me with disinterest despite the blown-out pupils.

"Will you chill? No need to get pretzeled," she tells me. "It was just a kiss."

Just a kiss? Is she for real?

"There was nothing *just* about that, Princess. That shit was straight fire."

Savvy doesn't say anything as she keeps her gaze locked on the space above my shoulder.

I skim my hand down her side, spreading my fingers as I take in the contours of her curves past the dip of her waist and the flare of her hips until I come to the hem of her skirt and slip underneath, only to groan when I'm met with bare skin.

Fuck me, she's wearing a thong.

Grabbing the thin strip of material bisecting the round globes of her ass cheeks, I give it a yank. It's a goddamn miracle the fabric doesn't rip from the force. I relish the hiss coming from Savvy's mouth as it tugs against her puckered hole and the way she instinctively rises onto her toes again to counter the pressure.

Releasing her panties, I smooth my hand over the curve of her ass, spreading her cheeks and thrusting a thumb into her asshole without warning or finesse.

I cup her from behind, her center slick when my fingers slide inside.

"Is this *just* finger fucking?" Savvy's whimper is music to my ears. "Is your pussy wet *just* because?"

"Noble." She bites back a cry, and I watch her start to fall, head falling back, eyes closing, lips parting as I work her.

"Your cunt isn't greedy for *just* anyone." I feel those telltale ripples, and instead of making her give in and say my name to get an orgasm, I scissor the fingers inside her pussy and circle the thumb inside her ass, pushing her over the edge.

I steal *just* another kiss to swallow down her screams of pleasure, and her body quakes from the strength of her release.

I slow my ministrations as she comes down but don't remove my fingers from inside her. My dick feels like it's about the break off it's so hard, but there's no time for him to get his. Besides, getting off wasn't the point. This was about proving something.

"Me," I say, pulling back once again. "It's *only* me your body wants. It doesn't matter whose ring you wear— that *fact* will *never* change." I thrust and pull back again. "And do you know why?"

I push deeper one more time before finally leaving the confines of her body and watch her sag back against the door. Her forehead wrinkles as she tries to marshal her thoughts.

"It's because you're *mine*, Savvy." Her eyes flare wide at the use of her name. "This"—I bring a hand to her mouth— "may lie to me." I drag my forefinger over her lip, smearing it with her pussy juices. "But the rest of your body can't."

I give her the chance to deny it, but the denial never comes.

"Make no mistake, Princess…" I lick her mouth, savoring the taste of all her flavors combining. "I will use it and anything else I have to until you can admit who you really belong to."

It's a bold claim, one I'm not exactly sure how I'll enact. More obstacles are standing in our way than ever before, but I'll be *damned* if they win.

CHAPTER 17

JESUS CHRIST. I can't believe I just let that happen. *How* did I let that happen? Why do I keep having sexual encounters with Jasper Noble in precarious places? I'm out of my flipping mind. *He* makes me lose my mind, and all common sense, apparently.

The sound of voices—voices as in *plural*—filter through the door, and I stiffen.

Oh shit! What did I do?

Who the hell knows how long Duke has had company. I thought we were safely left alone after all the moms followed his to look at wedding pictures from when she and the governor got married.

Gah! I hate thinking about that word, or really anything that would show up on a *Family Feud* board of top answers when it comes to weddings.

The sound is muffled, the words spoken indistinguishable through the heavy wood of the door. Does that mean they could or couldn't hear us?

Shit! Shit! Shit!

I can't get caught in here. I can't get caught with Jasper. And—

Oh my god! The ring.

I flatten my palms on Jasper's hard stomach and push. When I fail to move him even an inch, he chuckles, and I slap a hand over his mouth to smother the sound.

Are you insane? I mouth. Beneath my palm, his lips curl into a smile. Oh, look—Mr. Growly is feeling jovial now. I want to smack him.

Mind reeling, body still quaking with the aftershocks of that epic orgasm, I jump about a foot in the air when a heavy knock sounds.

"The coast is clear," Duke calls through the door. "You may begin your walk of shame."

I hate both of these assholes.

Jasper finally backs away from me, and I automatically start to scan the floor for the ring.

As I slide the antique piece on, I pause and wonder, *Why? Why the hell do I care so much?* The distance between Carter and me is really getting to me. That has to be it. Or maybe it's how Natalie constantly slips in her veiled threats. It's making my brain play tricks on me.

The hairs on the back of my neck stand on end. I don't need to turn around to know Jasper is watching me, probably studying me with that intensity that both pisses me off and makes my nipples hard.

Clearly, I have issues.

Duke leans against the arm of one of the couches, a shit-eating grin on his face, and it only grows in wattage as I step out of the bathroom and his baby blues rake over me. "Are we doing the bestie shuffle?"

"I don't even *wanna* know what you're talking about." I play dumb, purposely not turning around when I feel Jasper's body heat at my back.

Duke's gaze rises to peer behind me, that grin of his taking on an air of Joker-type mania.

My hands shake, and I tuck them into my armpits to hide it and the way my nipples are shouting *Look at me! Look at me!* at Jasper's proximity. Keeping my focus directed forward is essential if I'm going to keep my hands to myself.

How the hell am I supposed to make it through a whole meal after this? I really need to stop having orgasms as appetizers.

Ignoring the cloud of sexual tension now enveloping us, Duke makes a show of pushing up from the couch and drops one of his beefy arms around my shoulders.

I don't bother pushing it off because he'll only put it right back like he's been doing since the engagement became public knowledge.

"Why do you insist on constantly touching things that aren't yours?" Jasper's voice is gruff as he directs his question at Duke.

With Duke's body a physical barrier between us, I chance a glance at Jasper from over the curve of Duke's bicep. Oh, would you look at that? He's scowling, that dimple in his chin extra prominent with the pop of his jaw.

"Bruh." Duke chuckles—no surprise there—as he pulls me in a bit closer. Jasper is not a fan if the murderous edge his glare takes on is any indication. "You need to mellow. You'd think busting a nut would take your temper out of the danger zone." He starts to hum the melody from the popular song from *Top Gun* as he leads us down a wide hallway decorated with detailed crown molding and priceless artwork on the walls.

"If that's the cure for him being an asshole, he's probably at DEFCON 1 since he was left with blue balls," I can't help but add.

I fold my lips between my teeth to restrain my smile when

an animalistic sound fills the hall. I shouldn't play into Duke's antics, but I can't help it if it means taking a dig at Jasper.

Duke and I come to a halt when Jasper steps in front of us. "You got jokes, Princess?" He turns the full weight of his broody glare on me, promising all kinds of retribution.

"It's not my fault you can only dish it out and not take it." One would think he would know me better than this by now.

We stand there, him glaring, me tilting my head in that *You silly, silly clueless man* way. The silence wraps around us, heavy and thick, and I swear it revs like an engine when I start to twirl a section of hair around my fingers—the fingers of my *left* hand.

"As much as I do so enjoy watching your foreplay and all," Duke interrupts, moving in a way that forces Jasper to shift back after the step closer he took. "If we don't get in there"—he points to an open archway a few feet ahead—"in the next minute, somebody else might come looking for us, and I'm not sure how believable my excuses will be a second time."

Nobody addresses the foreplay comment as we head for the formal dining room. My jaw drops, and my feet come to a stop as soon as we cross the threshold. The room is stunning and not at all what I would have expected before tonight. Still, it manages to fit in perfectly with the few other rooms I've seen of the Delacourtes' mansion.

Rustic elegance is the best way to describe it. The dining room has the same vaulted beamed ceiling as the den, and a stone feature wall manages to be the perfect complement to the crystal chandelier hanging over the center of a polished oak butcher block table.

"Wow," I say breathily. My feet are still stationary, but my eyes continue bouncing, trying to take in every single detail.

"Not what you were expecting?" Duke asks, humor simmering in his words.

I shake my head while looking at the low flower arrangements set in small glass vases spaced out along the length of the dining table. The place settings are simple white porcelain, but the rose gold charger plates and matching flatware paired with them add a certain kind of understated elegance. It's lovely; truly it is.

Mrs. Noble perks up at the sight of her son, her husband a direct contrast with a less severe version of his son's scowl on his face as we move to take three of the four remaining vacant seats.

The table fits ten, seating the nine of us comfortably in padded Charlotte dining chairs. It feels slightly like a middle school dance with all the parents placed together on one side and at the end caps and the guys and me on the other, but it works.

Dinner starts off fine. The parents talk mostly amongst themselves, leaving us in peace to enjoy the braised duck and grilled asparagus.

It's about halfway through the meal when things shift.

It starts off with a question about what I think about my new ring and the history of the generations of Delacourtes who have worn it in the past. I do my best to breathe through the bubble of anxiety the prism of color reflecting off my left hand brings. The ring may be beautiful, but it feels more like a shackle than jewelry.

A part of me feels a prickle of guilt that such a significant piece is being wasted on me when I have zero intention of letting this engagement develop far enough for a wedding to actually take place.

"We should arrange for a photo shoot in the upcoming weeks." My hand tightens around the handle of my fork when Mr. Noble chimes in with that particular suggestion after Mrs. Delacourte finishes. "Personal anecdotes like that really resonates with voters."

"Oh, Walter"—Mrs. Noble playfully waves off her

husband—"can't you turn off the strategist brain for *one* night? You're taking the romance out of things."

Romance? Please. There's nothing romantic about an arranged marriage. Tragedy is more like it. I can't believe they want to use us in some twisted form of political propaganda. We're in flipping high school, people! I can't even legally vote yet!

"I'm just saying, they're young." Walter Noble bounces a finger between Duke and me. "The more they are *photographed*"—he cuts a glare at his son, who's statue-still beside me—"together, the more invested people will get in them, which should, in turn, hopefully translate to you and the polls." He finishes with his gaze locked on the governor.

I squirm in my seat, my knee knocking against Jasper's tense thigh. I wish I was anywhere but here. Annoyance stabs me between the ribs at Carter leaving me to handle this on my own. Yes, I know I'm always preaching how I don't need him to fight my battles, but backup in a situation like this couldn't hurt.

My throat grows tight, and I slip a finger inside the collar of my dress and tug it as if it were choking me. It's not; it's all…*this* that's strangling me with the unknown.

"Speaking of pictures." Mitchell shoots me a wink and pulls out his phone. "Did you all get to see this beauty Blackwell Public pulled off?"

Relief washes over me at his quick change of subject. He may have assumed I was uncomfortable about being the center of attention, but it doesn't matter. I was close to my breaking point, and how he was able to recognize that, I don't know, but I'm grateful nonetheless. When he takes the opportunity to tease Duke and Jasper about knowing the details about the prank, it amuses me profusely.

With the attention off me, I shift to lean against my seat, pressing my shoulders back until the chair's padded material digs into them. The movement helps loosen the restriction in my chest, but it doesn't stop an arc of disappointment from the lack of weight from a particular person's arm draped behind me.

Shaking *that* off, I tune back in to the conversation happening between the father figures. Walter Noble is a few years older than Mitchell and Frank Delacourte, but that's not stopping him from joining in as they start to compare notes on the pranks that happened during their tenures at BA.

Governor Delacourte is in the middle of a story involving the sprinkler system spewing out purple water one time when BP added dye to it when he stops mid-sentence and stares at me with wide eyes.

"Honey?" Mrs. Delacourte covers his hand with hers as her husband continues to bounce his gaze between Natalie and me.

"King was your surname before you married Mitchell?" the governor asks Natalie, who looks like she swallowed an egg but manages to nod.

"That means Jeremy King was your father?" This time the question is directed at me.

A sudden wave of emotion strangles me at the mention of Dad, and now I'm the one nodding. It's been years since he suddenly passed, but damn do I miss him.

"Shit." He slaps the table good-naturedly, causing the glassware to rattle as he falls back against his chair.

"You owe the swear jar a C-note, old man," Duke chortles.

Governor Delacourte brushes his snickering son off with a wave of his hand. "Your dad is the one who orchestrated the whole dye prank."

It's childish, but pride fills my chest. One of the reasons I got involved in the prank wars between the schools was to feel closer to my dad.

"Wait…" There's another weighted pause from the governor, his finger tapping some invisible button in the air as he pieces his thoughts together. "Is that why you seem so close to the mayor?"

A rumble emits from Jasper's chest at the mention of Chuck, and under the table, I slide a hand onto his knee. Wait…what? Not wanting to risk analyzing what that move means in front of an audience, I nod to Governor Delacourte.

"I can't believe I didn't piece it together sooner. Damn." When he smiles, it's the first time I've seen a real resemblance to his jokester son. "He was good friends with Anthony Falco, wasn't he?"

Natalie hisses through her teeth. Oh yes. There's no love lost between her and anyone in the Falco family, but Anthony is the most vocal about her failures as a parent.

"The best," I confirm. "Anthony is actually my godfather, as well as my brother's."

Like Carter with Leo and Wes, most of the generations gravitated toward forming close friendships with each other thanks to the nature of the founding families being so closely involved with the town.

"Oh this is great." The governor starts to laugh to himself, and when I slide a glance to Duke, he gives me an *I have no idea* headshake. "Mitchell, remember when we trapped them in the equipment cage?"

Mitchell's earlier spirited nature seems muted now, and I get hit with an unexpected pang of guilt, though I'm not quite sure why. "Yeah." He nods, but it almost feels resigned. "Wasn't it Falco who thought for them to use the air ducts?"

"Yup." The governor is all smiles and has even more stories—these featuring my dad and Uncle Anthony specifically—as he and Mitchell revisit their youth.

Through the years while attending Sunday dinners, I've heard more stories than I could possibly count about the trouble my dad and godfather used to get into. There's even one here and there about how they would sucker Chuck into their schemes before he knew better. Nonna Falco is a fan of those in particular.

"People often forget how young Chuck is because of his position in town," I add when there's a break in the conversation. "But he's only ten years older than my brother, so we grew up with him being more like our cousin than anything else." It's my turn to chuckle, and I glance at Duke from the corner of my eye, thinking how much he'll enjoy this next factoid. "Anthony has always been Uncle Anthony to us, but it freaks Chuck out when we call him Uncle Chuck."

"Why do I get the impression you do it a lot?" Duke asks, and I beam, another rumbly sound coming from my opposite side.

"Only because I do it all the time." Recent social events notwithstanding.

When the meal is over, the two servers Duke told me his parents hired along with a chef to help for the evening clear the plates. *Look at that—we made it through a* whole *meal this time.*

"Do you have a Pinterest account, sweetheart?" Mrs. Delacourte asks me as I take a sip of water.

"Yes?" I don't know why it comes out as more question than statement.

Duke cups a hand in front of his mouth to appear to hide behind it. "Mom's a social media addict," he stage-whispers.

"Am not."

"Mine too," Jasper adds, his grin catching me off guard, causing me to blink up at him, stunned stupid.

"How did we raise such disrespectful sons, Hillary?" Mrs. Noble asks, but the twinkle in her eyes as she looks at Jasper reveals how much she loves him.

"I have no clue, Buffy." The quick way Mrs. Delacourte joins in reminds me so much of Duke stirring the pot at school. "For Samantha's sake, I hope he learns to grow out of it." She winks at me in a way that is one hundred percent her son. She's a lovely woman—both women are—and has been beyond sweet in our interactions, but there's not a snowball's chance in hell that I will be marrying her son.

"Mom," Duke whines.

"*Pish.*" She waves him off and keeps her focus on me. "I know we have lots of time, dear, but we can make a collaborative board. This way, when we start to make wedding plans, I'll have an idea of your style and the things you like."

I damn near choke on my tongue. Everyone around the table freezes when I start to cough. It's my turn to wave a hand in the air as I reach for my water and take a healthy swallow. Shockingly enough, I'm not about to have an asthma attack, though I'm sure that memory is still fresh in their minds.

First the ring, now actual talk of the wedding—it's too much too soon. She may have said we have lots of time, but if I'm not careful, who's to say that won't change?

CHAPTER 18

THOUGH DINNER TONIGHT was enjoyable overall, there was still way more talk of wedding planning than I'm comfortable with, seeing as I'm supposed to have *years* before any nuptials occur.

The elevator ride up to the penthouse is silent and filled with a tension that makes my chest tight. I need to text Tessa to have her pick me up so I can get out of here and to my brother's ASAP.

The elevator dings, announcing our arrival. Mitchell immediately excuses himself and disappears down the hall that leads to his home office. I don't make it two feet toward the one that leads to my bedroom before Natalie is snagging my arm and pulling me to a stop. "I don't know what you think you're doing with that Noble boy, but it ends now, Samantha."

I do my best to school my features, both out of indifference to the scratch of her nails as I yank myself free from her hold and because I don't want to inadvertently give anything away before I figure out what exactly it is that she knows.

"What are you going on about, Natalie?" I live for the way she bristles every time I use her name instead of calling her Mom.

"I *told you* not to call me that." See what I mean? "And I'm talking about *this*," she hisses, stalking to close the distance I managed to put between us and thrusting her phone into my face.

It takes a few seconds for my eyes to focus on the image lighting the screen. Once they do, Natalie's thumb is swiping across it, revealing others of a similar nature.

Oh shit is my immediate response, following quickly by *Who the hell took these? How did they take them?* and finally *Why are they only coming out now?*

It's been a few weeks, but I don't remember anyone else being in the parking lot with us that day—though I can admit that might not be the best way to measure that statement's accuracy since I didn't realize Duke had left us. It's entirely possible I wouldn't have noticed someone joining us. Right?

Natalie flips back to the first picture, an image of Jasper kissing me against Duke's Mercedes. Both our eyes are closed, lost in the chaos brewing between us with Jasper's hand very clearly on my ass. I remember the way his fingers kneaded the muscle, tugging it until there was a delicious burn as he stretched it just past my limits.

The next is an image of Jasper tossing me inside the G Wagon, and thank Christ the tinting is too dark for whoever our mystery paparazzo is to have gotten a clear shot of what happened *inside*. Being the star of a sex tape is not a life achievement I need unlocked.

The last is Jasper caging me in against the school, our clothing obviously rumpled, my hair a tangled disaster I hadn't yet tamed.

"What do you think people would think if they saw these?"

"I don't care."

"What do you think the Delacourtes will say when they see their son's fiancée kissing someone who isn't *their son*?"

"As an elected official, I'm hoping our fair governor isn't homophobic and it wouldn't be 'At least she's not kissing a girl.'" I lift a hand to my mouth as if to say *Oh, the scandal.* "I mean, how Katy Perry, am I right?"

"This is *not* the time for jokes, young lady," Natalie snaps, her expression turning thunderous when I snort at her calling me *young lady*.

"As always, Natalie, you're treating your life like it's a telenovela." I shake my head. "And you tried calling Tessa the dramatic one."

I'm too busy wiping the tear my laughter brought on from my lash line to see the slap before it lands on my face. Fire blooms in my cheek, and the sting radiating from the center makes me suspect the bands of her wedding rings caught me just so.

"Don't test me, Samantha." Natalie moves until the space between us is eliminated, and I'm forced to tilt my head back to maintain eye contact thanks to the spiked heels she's wearing. "I'm not playing games with you."

I cup my cheek, hoping to soothe the worst of the pain. Damn, the woman knows how to slap. "When have you *not* played games?" I can't help but challenge her.

A sinister smile curls her scarlet lips. "Did you think I was playing when I threatened to have your brother arrested?"

My throat goes dry, the breath stilling in my lungs as panic strangles me, my body going cold. I see the moment Natalie realizes her threat hit its intended target, victory sparking in her devil eyes.

"That's what I thought," she coos. "There are any *number* of illegal activities I can turn him in for. I have the evidence."

The same evidence she's claimed to have that I've failed to find during the limited time I've spent in the penthouse.

Maybe I should hang around here this weekend to look for it.

"I'm not as stupid as you think I am." Her devil-hidden-behind-an-angel's-mask face dares me to deny the claim. "I saw the way he stormed out of the room tonight." She snatches my left hand up, bending my fingers down to show off my new bling. "Despite what your childish mind may think"—she shakes my hand in front of my face—"this is very much real."

"Oh-okay."

"I've worked *too* hard to set this all up to let you ruin things for me." She pinches my chin, the claws she calls nails digging into my skin, and I swallow down a wince. "If you think I'm going to let you go running around, allowing pictures to be taken of you in compromising positions with men who aren't your betrothed—"

Oh god, the urge to laugh is *so* not appropriate right now, but it's a struggle not to give in to it. I know we've made all sorts of betrothal jokes—more because if we hadn't laughed about it, I may have cried—but the way Natalie uses it is so *serious*. At least I can appreciate the moment of levity in the situation.

"—you better think long and hard before you go slutting around like a common whore."

Love you too, Mom.

If only she knew what she saw is the least "compromised" I've been with Jasper and that those pictures aren't even from the most recent event.

"Because if you *embarrass* me in *any* way, Samantha…" The threat looms heavy like a storm cloud. "I *promise* you it won't just be your brother I go after."

Goose bumps cover my skin, each word digging deep into my soul.

She releases her hold on me, strutting over to the bar and gathering the makings for a martini.

I watch as she scoops in the ice, pours out the appropriate amount of vermouth and gin, caps the shaker, and shakes. I dig the heel of my hand into my breastbone, a cough escaping despite how much I concentrate on breathing through it, and dig out my inhaler.

Once the martini is served and garnished with a metal skewer of three olives, Natalie spins to face me, leaning against the bar and balancing the delicate crystal on her fingertips.

"If you go against me in this, I'll bring down *all* of your *precious* Royals."

CHAPTER 19

WITH THE ADDED weight to Natalie's threat, I thought it best to keep a little bit of space between the Royals and me, which pisses me off to no end. So now, after one of the most frustrating weekends on record, I am most definitely not looking forward to school today.

Every now and then, sunlight glints off the shiny shackle on my ring finger as I compose text message after text message.

Carter is up to one hundred and thirty-seven unanswered text messages from me. If he doesn't text me back by the time I get out of school today, I will be forced to officially start stalking him.

Being the bestest best friend in existence, Tessa had zero qualms about altering our original weekend plans to help me strategize an action plan. We've concluded that I'm going to need assistance in making Natalie believe I'm toeing the line while I continue my hunt for this "evidence" she claims to have. It also means I'm going to have to start spending more time at the penthouse to do so. *Oh joy!*

It goes against every fiber of my being to enlist people outside of the Royals, but with my brother actively avoiding me, I don't feel like I have much of a choice.

Duke and Jasper are easy to find thanks to the small cluster of students vying for attention from their kings. It amazes me how easily others do what they want—then a sudden thought hits me.

There's no way Natalie had those pictures of Jasper and me before Saturday. The temptation to use them as a way to control me would have been too great for her to sit on them for weeks.

No. That means…whoever took them held them until it would benefit them most. But who? And why?

An ugly thought slithers its way into my thoughts, grabbing on and trying to take root. What if…

No. No way.

But…could it?

One would think that when the engagement announcement hit the papers, they would have been released. I'm sure something like that would have been a massive payday from one of the many trash rags of the world. More importantly, why would they go to Natalie and not the press?

I give a little finger wave to Arabella and her bitch brigade, upping the *Go fuck yourself* wattage on my grin as I pass them. I would love nothing more than to blame one of them, but the timing of the photos being sent to Natalie is suspect.

Obviously, Jasper was pissed about the whole engagement ring thing given how he stormed out and later ripped it off my person, but would it push him to be vindictive enough to incriminate himself with the photos?

I want to say no. A part of me needs to *believe* he couldn't be capable of such duplicity, but history proves otherwise.

That was before, I think when those pearly eyes land on me as I approach. I don't know why I bother arguing with myself. I need to keep my distance from him. I've already proved—time and time again—that I have no self-control when it comes to Jasper Noble. Maybe believing the worst about him will help keep my brother and those I care most about safe.

"I need to talk to you." I step in front of Duke. "Please tell me you aren't looking to *him* for permission." I ask when he side-eyes Jasper. "I'm pretty sure you're supposed to be engaged to me, not Noble." I wiggle my fingers in his face, ignoring the gasps and murmurs the sight of the ring sets off.

This conversation needs to happen now before I lose the rest of my mind, and the last thing I need is an audience.

Not giving Duke the chance to deny me, I wrap his tie around my fist and drag him with me to the first empty classroom I can find.

He chuckles—of course he does—as his feet trip over mine, the toes of his shoes pushing down the backs of mine as he stumbles behind me.

I fall against the door, my shoulders pressing into the wood as I lean against it, feeling around the knob for the lock and clicking it home. When I finally release my death grip on Duke, the silk of his tie is a wrinkled disaster.

I jump, my heart trying to escape my chest, when two heavy fists beat at the door, followed by Jasper's angry voice demanding I open it.

I…can't.

I've denied it at every turn, but it's no use now. I'm drawn to him like I am to nobody else. The fact that he might have… betrayed me doesn't factor in at all. I want Jasper Noble. Except…I can't have him.

It doesn't matter what I want. My family—Carter and the Royals—will *always* come first. Until I can do away with the evidence that could hurt them, I'll do everything else in my power to protect them. And right now? That means going along with Natalie's plans.

The classroom walls feel like they're closing in on me as Jasper continues to make his demands from the other side of the door.

Spinning, I meet his gaze through the long vertical window, and *holy shit*, the fire burning in his eyes comes from Hades himself.

I hold his gaze for a second longer, trying to telegraph how sorry I am before locking the guilty feeling in a box.

I debated well into the dark morning hours if this is the best plan, and I'm still not entirely sure.

Resting my hands on top of my head, I start to pace and sort through my conflicting thoughts.

As always, Duke seems to be without a care, making himself at home on top of the desk of whoever this classroom belongs to. I observe him out of the corner of my eye, casually leaning back with hands braced behind him, legs swinging, heels kicking out a steady staccato, goofy grin on his handsome face.

Ugh!

The tips of my fingers start to go numb, and I realize I've been holding my breath, actively triggering my symptoms to flare up. I don't bother to caution myself to calm down. Calm left the realm of possibility a long time ago. Instead of wasting time attempting to corral my emotions, I use my inhaler. I get the feeling this is only the beginning of the emotional maelstrom for the day.

There's no missing the change in Duke's demeanor. He shifts so his elbows rest on his spread knees, and his eyes are locked on the inhaler at my mouth. It strikes my notice how much more often I'm using it in front of others. Typically it's only the Royals and Tessa that I've allowed to see me with it.

Could the fact that I didn't hesitate to pull it out in front of Duke be a sign?

I…don't know.

That's my problem in a nutshell.

I'm in uncharted territory here, and I don't know if the path I'm thinking of taking will lead me to safety or straight off a cliff.

You'll never know unless you take a chance.

"Did you really need to talk? Or was dragging me in here just a new kind of foreplay between you two?" Duke bounces a finger from me to a scowling-through-the-window Jasper.

Another arrow of guilt lodges deep in my soul.

This…

This…*sucks*.

"I mean…" Duke holds his hands up, his ass dancing on the desktop with a pelvic thrust. "I'm down for a little sandwich action if it is."

A small laugh escapes me at his ridiculousness. Should I take it as a sign that maybe what I want to ask him—no, it's not to have a three-way with Jasper and me—isn't the worst idea I've ever had?

Instinct and experience tell me not to trust anyone outside of the Royals (I'm including Tessa in this).

What to do? What to do? What to do?

"Princess—"

"Don't." I throw a hand up to cut him off, softening my tone when I realize how harsh it is. "Don't call me that." That's Jasper's name for me. It hurts too much to hear it.

"You're my fiancée, though. Shouldn't I have a pet name for you?"

I dig my knuckles into my forehead, once again reevaluating my entire thought process. I haven't even broached the subject of my plan, and I'm already regretting it.

How can he be so nonchalant about all this?

I move until I'm standing in front of him, his knees butting up against my stomach, jovial expression back in full force as he shifts back to rest on his hands, legs spreading to invite me to step between them.

Just ask him already, Savvy.

"Look." I fold my arms over my chest, using the move to hide the unsteadiness of my hands. "Deadass. No cap. What do you think about…this whole engagement thing?"

Silence stretches between us, and I don't miss how Duke chances another glance toward the now silent door of the classroom. He licks his lips, and I can hear the joking comment before he says it, so I cut him off at the pass.

"Duke…*please*." I abhor the desperate plea in my tone. I can't help it though. I'm like a frayed rope, my threads unraveling one at a time, not sure which one snapping will be the cause of my demise.

"I could think of worse things than having you shackled to me as the old ball and chain." He waggles his eyebrows. "Mom's been playing matchmaker since I hit puberty. I could have ended up with someone fugly instead of a smokeshow."

His twisted attempt at a compliment has the first vestiges of a smile tugging at my lips. Still…if he can't be serious when I straight up asked him to be, asking him for help will be a pointless endeavor.

I should have known better and take a step to leave, only to be stopped by Duke jumping down from his perch and wrapping warm hands around my upper arms. Whatever he reads on my face has him revealing a side of him I've never seen before.

Gone is the cocky playboy jock who's always quick with a joke or a flirt. In his place is the version I'm sure he's been taught to be on the campaign trail. As his chest rises and falls, I will say there seems to be far more compassion in his baby blues than one would expect from a politician's son.

"How about you tell me this first…" Duke rocks back on his heels, his hands sweeping up and down my arms, soothing me while keeping me in place.

"Tell you what?" I shake my head. "And why should I answer your question when you still haven't answered mine?"

He studies me for a beat, happy grin closer to being back in place the longer he stares. "Why does the thought of marrying me upset you so much?"

No.

He didn't ask me that? Right?

Because if he's asking me…that, does it mean…

He doesn't actually *want* to marry me…

Right?

"Oh God, that look on your face." Duke's hands leave my body to slap one to his heart as he stumbles backward. "You're breaking my heart, Princess."

"I SAID DON'T CALL ME THAT!" I snap.

You know what? I'm done. This was pointless. Why did I think a few weeks of sort-of friendship and being…whatever I was to Jasper would mean I could *maybe* turn to Duke for help?

"Whoa." Arms band around me, and I'm tugged against a hard chest in a firm hug. "You're wiggin', and that makes it no fun to tease you, Pri—" He cuts himself off at my growl and corrects to not very smoothly finish with "Savvy."

"Forget it, Duke." I wiggle around, trying to remove myself from his hold without any success.

"Nah, I don't think so. This"—he circles a finger an inch from my nose—"is a side of you I haven't seen."

Yeah, that's because he's right. To quote my girl Cher in *Clueless*, I'm totally buggin'. There are too many moving parts I have zero control over, things that have the potential to rock my foundation at its core.

"Because of that, and because Jasper would kill me if I were somehow the one to make your asthma spaz out, I'll keep it one hundred with you."

"Is that possible?" I arch a brow.

"I have my moments," he says on a laugh before straightening, that earnestness from earlier returning. "Do I think our parents are cray for suggesting this while we're in high school?" He nods. "Hundo P. But…"

Panic seizes my throat, making it hard to breathe. It feels like there's a guillotine hanging over my head, and Duke is the one in control of the release lever.

"Jasper's my boy, and he's got dibs. That officially makes you a no-fly zone for any of the assholes at this school"—he gives an almost boyish shrug—"including me."

The statement should irk me, but for some reason, it doesn't. It also gives me the push to ask what I need to.

"I…" My head falls forward, my forehead landing to rest on his chest. "I…need your…help."

Duke hooks a finger under my chin, lifting my gaze to his. "That's music to my ears, sweet cheeks."

"Ugh." I thunk my head against him, somewhat wishing it were a wall. "We're *really* going to have to work on your nickname skills."

"You'll learn to love it." The surety in his voice is concerning. "Now, sugar lips"—he barks out a laugh at my nose scrunch—"tell Big Daddy what you need."

"Let's start with you *never* calling yourself *Big Daddy* again." The twinkle in his eyes does not bode well for my sanity.

The warning bell rings. I don't have a lot of time to start putting the pieces in motion.

"I make no promises, Boo Bear."

I glance to my left. I glance to my right.

"What are you doing, pookie?"

With Duke being my only option, I think I'm going to have to draw on over a decade's worth of experience with Tessa as my bestie if I'm going to have any hope of surviving…this.

"I'm looking for something sharp to stab you with," I grumble, which only causes him to laugh more.

"*Spicy.*" He touches a finger to my shoulder before shaking out his hand while hissing through his teeth. "I like this feisty side of you."

"Because this is any different from how I've always been, how?"

"Touché." He releases me to retake his spot on top of the desk. "All right, babycakes." He claps his hands together. "Hit me."

Oh, I'm tempted to hit him, all right.

"First, I need to make it clear that I have *no* intention of marrying you."

He mimes being stabbed in the heart. "Is the rock not big enough?" He lifts my arm by pinching the tip of my ring finger. "Didn't take you for one of those materialistic bimbos like we've got around here."

I don't dignify his comment with a response. "I need you to help me pretend we're planning to follow through on this insanity from our parents."

"And why…would I do that?" He hitches a leg up, crossing his legs by resting a foot on his knee.

If I didn't need him, I would strangle him. Yup, definitely would strangle him. "Because you're such a good guy?"

"*Ehnt.*" He imitates the sound of the world's most annoying buzzer. "Try again."

"What—would—you—want?" I ask through my teeth.

I regret asking the instant I do. The way he rubs his hands in glee really, really, *really* makes me want to slap him.

"No. Wait!" I hold up a hand before he can answer and push me over the violent edge. "How's this for incentive…"

He strokes his chin in an *I'm listening* manner.

"If you agree to play along, it means you'll be spending more time with me, which in turn"—*Tess, please don't kill me for making this offer*—"means you'll spend more time around Tessa."

Duke hops off the desk and lifts me up in a spinning hug. "You got yourself a deal, snookums."

He agreed.

This should be a good thing.

Why do I feel like this is going to bite me in the ass?

CHAPTER 20

BANG!

I shake out my hand, looking at the fist-shaped hole I punched into the locker.

What the fuck?

Did I all of a sudden turn invisible this morning?

Savvy looked right at me, but it was like she was looking through me.

Not one word was spoken to me. There was barely even an acknowledgment that she noticed I exist.

Every crack I've been able to make in her walls was sealed up tight, leaving behind an ice princess. Now she's locked in a room, away from me, with *my* best fucking friend.

He's her fiancé.

I punch the locker again, the divot in the metal deepening at the taunt from my internal voice. I don't care.

I.

DON'T.

FUCKING.

CARE.

Dad can threaten me all he likes; I'm done letting him keep me from claiming what I want. I've never been one to run scared. Why the hell am I starting now?

Acid boils in my gut and burns me from the inside out seeing the way Savvy defeatedly drops her head to Duke's chest. Watching my friend's hands comfort my girl— my *fucking* girl—feels like a betrayal of the highest order.

The warning bell for class rang a minute ago, but that hasn't stopped the handful or so of students from loitering in the hall. I get it; they aren't used to seeing one of their kings lose it, but that's precisely what I'm doing—losing it.

The door opens, and I spring across the hall, grabbing Savvy's wrist the second she steps out of the classroom. "We need to talk, Princess."

She glances first to where my fingers overlap around the fragile joint then slowly slides her eyes to mine. Ice fills my veins at the vacant glaze coating her gaze. "We have nothing to talk about."

"The fuck we don't." I yank her to me, her small body falling onto mine as I anchor her to me with an arm wrapped behind her back.

"Bro." Duke steps in close, jerking a chin at the crowd gathering around us. I don't give a shit about them or the phones I see pointed in our direction.

"Don't call me *bro* when you're nothing but a fucking traitor." I uncoil my arm from around Savvy to shove him away from us.

"That's rich." Duke barks out a laugh that grates on my nerves and has my already bruised knuckles screaming to meet his jaw.

"Tell me, *brother*…" He spits the word at me like an insult. "How is it I'm the traitor when *you're*"—he pokes my shoulder—"the *one*"—another poke—"with *his*"—one more poke—"hands on *my* fiancée?"

Red tinges my vision, and I grab his finger before it can

poke me again, twisting it until he has to bend forward to avoid me breaking his hand.

"Kind of hypocritical calling *me* the traitor, don't you think?" he taunts.

I wrench his arm higher, but he spins out of my hold and comes at me swinging. I turn my head, but his fist still manages to connect with my jaw, setting me off with renewed fury.

"Motherfucker." I lunge for him, but he sidesteps out of the way, forcing me to pivot in order to land a blow to the side of his ribs.

I expect him to come at me again, but instead, he drops down into a crouch with an "Oh shit!"

I brace for him to tackle me, but when I see him stretching out a hand to somebody on the ground, all the rage leaves me, and my heart drops to my toes when I realize it's Savvy.

Goddammit, I shouldn't have gone after Duke with her so close by. It's my fault she got caught in the crossfire.

I'm down by her other side, offering my hand to help her up only to have her smack it away with a glare so full of venom my balls shrivel up. "Don't fucking touch me."

My teeth grind, and it takes everything in me not to lunge at Duke again as he takes her hand to help her stand. She murmurs a soft thanks and steps out of reach from both of us.

"Can you two assholes keep your dick-measuring contests confined to the locker room and leave me out of it?" Her breathing is slightly rushed, and a prickly panic takes root when I recall her using her inhaler when she was with Duke.

She continues to glare, her cheeks flushed, the right one darker than the other, evidence of a cut in the center of the mark. *Fuck!* One of us did clip her; that's why she was on the ground. The need to reaffirm that she is okay and we didn't do any permanent damage surges inside me. She slaps me away again when I try to cup her cheek to inspect the mark.

All thoughts of why Duke and I were fighting in the first place mean nothing if the end result was Savvy being hurt.

Shit! I'm spiraling worse than I thought. First, I'm fighting with my best friend, my ride or die. Then I potentially accidentally hurt the one person who is coming to mean as much to me as him, if not more.

"I'm *so* over playing everybody's games." She sighs and runs a hand through her disheveled hair, tugging on the long ends. Her eyes bounce between mine before she shifts her attention to Duke, my spine lengthening as she sends a pleading, almost remorseful look his way.

None of us say a word as we stand in this weird three-way stare down. The silence is heavy with everything not being said.

"Move along," Savvy snaps at an overly ballsy underclassman who makes the mistake of trying to move in closer to our cluster.

Duke and I share our first smirk since Savvy arrived at school today as the kid partially wets himself, tucks tail, and runs away. Watching the way people react to and around Savvy is fascinating. Where people do what we say out of fear, it's easy to see they follow her orders out of a strange respect.

"I don't want to fight...with either of you," she admits, inhaling another deep, measured breath. "But if you push me into it, I won't hesitate in doing so."

Again she shares a look with Duke, and it's annoying as fuck that I can't decipher it.

"This isn't what I meant when I asked for your help, but remember this..." She moves in front of Duke, stepping in close and rising onto her toes to kiss his cheek while he watches me with guilt swimming in his gaze. "You're either on my side"—she lowers herself down and steps back—"by my side"—she takes the few steps needed until she's standing toe to toe with me—"or in my *fucking* way."

CHAPTER 21

I MAY HAVE BEEN LATE to the start of first period, but I didn't even make it to the end of it before my phone was blowing up with texts. My group chat with the Royals is filled with enough expletives to make Samuel L. Jackson blush, and if the death threats from Tessa were to be taken seriously, whatever FBI agents tasked with monitoring the texts of teenagers would already be en route.

Honestly, I didn't think anything of it—too focused on the lack of a text from the *one* person I was still waiting to hear back from—until Chuck, Kay, and Em started popping up in my notification banners.

It was lunchtime by the time I worked my way through all the messages and got a chance to watch the video that had those who love me ready to lay siege and storm the castle—or in this case, Blackwell Academy.

At first glance, it looked bad, but if you stopped and watched it closely, you could see it was an accident. I only fell because Duke bumped into me. I was in the wrong place at the wrong time and fell from losing my balance, *not* because

Duke or Jasper hit me. Though I guess some blame can be placed on me because I did *not* see Duke's method of playing along going *anything* like that.

The phrase "Boys are dumb" has *never* held more meaning to me. Granted, I'm happy the two of them made up, but Duke's approach of puckering up and tapping his lips so they could literally kiss and makeup…yeah, I still can't believe I'm entrusting him to help me.

Lunch was also when my luck ran out with Jasper, and he was able to corner me.

I swear I can still feel the warmth from when his palm cupped my cheek with a tenderness I didn't think him capable of, his calloused skin lightly brushing along the edge of the bruise Natalie left behind.

Even now, his pained voice haunts me. *"Fuck, Princess. Tell me I didn't do this."*

He didn't believe my first attempt at reassuring him that he didn't. It took Tinsley shoving her phone literally in his face, the screen bumping his nose, and him seeing it for himself for him to lose the haunted look in his eyes.

His reaction to what happened this morning confirmed two things for me. One, there's no way he was involved in the taking or sharing of the pictures of us. That is a problem we will have to address…at another time.

The other thing it made me realize was, while I asked Duke to play along as a dutiful fiancé to help protect me, and thereby Jasper, from people thinking there is still…*something* going on between us, I can't in good conscience have Jasper believe it's actually true. He *has* to know it's nothing more than a game that needs to be played.

A part of me tells me not to bother, to just throw caution to the wind and put an end to this whole charade with Duke. Thoughts like that are cray. I know what's at stake if I get caught with Jasper again.

This has been the Monday-est Monday *ever*, and I'm

beyond ready for another coffee from Espresso Patronum or a nap. Don't let it be said I'm not flexible.

"So…" Duke rushes toward Tinsley and me, dropping an arm around each of our shoulders. "I was wondering, pudding pie—"

"What the fuck did you just call her?" Jasper growls, coming up from behind us.

"Ignore him," I suggest. "Lord knows I do."

"Amen." Tinsley's quick agreement makes me smile.

Duke huffs as if put out from being ignored. "*Anyway…*" His stupid long arms make it easy for him to reach up and muss both my and Tinsley's hair without much effort.

"Hey!" Tinsley squeals.

"Asshole," I curse and jump out of reach, combing out the tangles he was able to form.

It's no surprise he's laughing, dropping a bent elbow to Jasper's shoulder, leaning on him in a half bend as he yucks it up like he's the funniest person on the planet.

With a roll of the eyes, I hook an arm with Tinsley's and make for the entrance doors, more than ready to escape this place for the next seventeen hours.

"Where you going, honey bunches?"

I fold my lips between my teeth to restrain my smile. If Duke gets even a whiff of amusement, he'll take his efforts to a level that will far surpass entertaining. He's the type where if you give him an inch, he's going to take a whole cross-country road trip.

"Seriously? What the fuck do you keep going on about?" Jasper asks Duke before turning the full weight of his broody glare on me. "Where the fuck do you think you're going?"

It amazes me how he still hasn't learned that he can't intimidate me into bending to his will. When will he learn I don't take orders? Hell, I barely take suggestions. I don't care how sexy he looks with his rolled cuffs showing off his muscular forearms and dark ink decorating them.

A head tilting shrug is all the answer I give as I stride for the door. Through the ornate detailing in the window, I spot a familiar and, given recent behavior, unexpected Corvette idling in front of the school. It's about damn time my brother showed his face.

"Savvy!" There's a familiar demand in Jasper's shout.

Halfway down the stone steps, I stop. Why am I not surprised he followed me outside?

The sound of a door opening has me glancing over my shoulder. Sure enough, Carter has gotten out of the Vette, elbows bent, forearms stretched across the low roof as he takes in the scene with narrowed eyes.

I don't know what Jasper wants to say to me, but the best thing I can do for him is hustle down the steps before Carter decides to storm up them. Jasper didn't do himself any favors spouting off at the hospital.

"Don't run," Carter scolds in his best dad voice.

I give him a *Stop overreacting* eye roll and slide into the passenger seat.

It takes another infuriatingly long minute before he stops trying to murder Jasper with his eyes, and I swear I hear him growl over the sound of Fall Out Boy playing through the speakers.

By the time Carter is seated beside me in the driver's seat, my frustration toward him is eclipsed by my amusement at his alpha posturing. All I'm able to think about is how Cisco claimed being growly must be in our DNA.

"What are you laughing at?" Carter's brow line is a harsh slash underneath his knitted beanie.

"Nothing." His eyes narrow to slits. "I just think it's funny when you go all *I'm big brother, hear me roar* at the world." I turn up the wattage on my smile, letting all my teeth show. "It's entertaining to watch…really."

The harsh edge to his expression melts away, and he shakes his head then shifts the car into gear.

I spend the entirety of the car ride from BA to Carter's without speaking. Given my brother's skill behind the wheel and his lead foot, it's not as impressive of a feat as I make it sound.

Still…

As he parks inside the garage and I head toward the residence, I wield my silence as a weapon. I'm pissed at him. I'm also hurt.

The first thing I do is go upstairs to my room to change. If I have to have an uncomfortable conversation, I'm at least going to be in comfortable clothes.

Dressed in leggings and a cropped sweatshirt, I tuck my legs under me, settle into a corner of the couch, and wait for Carter to join me from the kitchen.

He takes his damn sweet time pulling two bottles from the fridge—a blue Gatorade for him and a seltzer for me—before he finally makes his way over. Except instead of sitting down, the jerk stalls again by walking over to Merlin's glass enclosure.

I wait for him, something I've gotten a lot of practice doing these last few weeks. If he doesn't hurry this along, though, I can't promise I won't snap.

What the hell is he waiting for anyway? We're alone. We're not in public. There may be things I don't necessarily want to talk about, things I've been putting off myself for far too long, but *damn*, can we get this show on the road?

The click of a latch shifts my attention off picking at my nail polish and back to Carter in time to see him pulling Merlin out of his enclosure.

I straighten from my slouch, my back lifting away from the cushion, one of my legs unfurling to drop a foot to the ground as I brace myself. Either what Carter wants to talk about is more grave than I thought, or he's feeling guiltier than the selfish part of me hoped.

Carter sits on the opposite end of the couch, Merlin, his ghost morph boa constrictor, lifting his head, bobbing to and fro, tongue peeking out to scent the air as the muscles of his body move him closer toward me.

Holding out an arm, I leave the flat of my palm facing up toward the ceiling, allowing Merlin to come to me, the smooth bumps of his scales sliding across my skin.

"I know what you're doing," I state accusingly, keeping the volume of my voice pitched low as not to spook the Boidae coiling around my forearm.

"I have no idea what you're talking about."

I narrow my eyes at Carter's attempt at playing dumb. Unfortunately, his distraction technique is working, the calm that infuses my system any time Merlin settles himself on me instant. The deep chuckle from my brother tells me he knows it too. I blame Leo and his claims about Merlin being my emotional support animal despite how true it might be.

We lapse back into silence, and I have to make a conscious effort not to bite Carter's head off as he studies me as if he can determine my health status by sight alone. "You look good."

I stroke a hand down the length of Merlin's body. "I always look good."

Carter scoffs. "You're a brat." I beam. "You would take that as a compliment."

"You should too," I offer. "You raised me."

His grumpy facade fades, as I knew it would. I may feel guilty about the things he's done to take care of me, but not once has it stemmed from him. He takes as much pride in my achievements and "how I turned out" as Pops does with Tessa. No matter how ticked off I am with him, that fact will never change.

"For real, though…" Carter sips his Gatorade. "How are you doing?"

I'd make fun of him for saying the classic Joey line wrong, but I can't.

"You would know if you weren't avoiding me." Pain slices into me at the guilt that washes over his expression. However pissed I am, it still feels unfair for me to accuse him of keeping things from me when I've been keeping things from him.

But you haven't avoided him because of them.

My chest grows tight, and I focus on breathing through it. I'm a mess of conflicting emotions.

"I'm fine, Cart." I stretch a leg out to nudge him with my sock-covered foot.

These last few months have been challenging, to say the least. While I was the one thrust into a new world, a place we knew little about, and was without allies, Carter was the one left to deal with those facts.

My overprotective, used to people keeping him apprised of essential details, accustomed to people not daring to mess with those close to him brother had to sit back while the baby sister he altered his whole life to make sure was cared for was suddenly out of his realm of power.

Then to compound the issue—prior to the active avoidance—he also had to deal with not seeing me every day, not having me sleeping under the same roof, not being able to confirm with his own eyes that I was, in fact, fine.

It's a vicious cycle.

Carter's head falls forward, his chin tucking into his chest. "I'm sorry." He inhales deeply, his chest expanding with the action.

"I know." My forgiveness is instant. My brother is the *last* person I would hold a grudge against.

Plus, I'm sure, given everything, he's all kinds of worried about triggering an asthma attack.

With my cheek pillowing against the back of the couch, I glance back toward the breakfast bar and note the empty space at the end. "You still have to go furniture shopping, I see." I arch a brow, silently asking if he wants to expand on the topic.

"Gossiping assholes," he grumbles. "It shouldn't surprise me that you know the story behind"—he gestures to the empty space with his chin—"that."

I shrug, letting the good humor of his overreaction to the engagement announcement wash over us. This time the silence is a comfortable one I'm familiar with.

"Has—" Carter starts, only to stop. He clears his throat. "Has anyone tried anything now that they know"—he waves a hand between us—"we're…you know."

A big part of me wants to call him out for how he overreacted about people knowing we're related. I mean…it's not like we completely hid our connection to each other, but I know when to pick my battles, and this isn't one of them.

"Nothing crazy." I recall how it felt like most of the school was waiting for me the morning after the engagement announcement hit the internet, but that was it. "I think for most it was more of an aha moment as they figured that's why I wasn't scared to stand up to their own kings."

Carter's scowl is back. "Yeah…the douche with a death wish."

My lips twitch at the accurate descriptor for Jasper. I'll never admit it to Carter—lord knows that would be signing Jasper's death warrant—but it was how Jasper *wasn't* afraid to mess with me that was the biggest draw.

For as much as I despise people calling me Samantha—and yes, I can admit the bullying was annoying as fuck—it was…sorta freeing. I love my brother dearly, but after a while, it gets old being Carter King's sister.

Some people seem to forget that just because I'm a girl doesn't mean I don't know how to build an empire.

"I don't need people to fear me, or better yet, fear you,

Cart." This is the part his big brother side has a hard time grasping.

"It doesn't hurt," Carter challenges, and I call him out for sounding like a petulant child. His left eye twitches, but so do his lips. I love how I can crack his shell like no one else.

"You're right," I concede. "But I need respect too if I'm going to survive in the world on my own."

Fear isn't all it takes to rule; there's also respect. It's knowing how to leverage the two together that leads to the longevity of a kingdom.

"Take Gunderson, for example." I shouldn't smile at the scowl simply mentioning Scott Gunderson inspires. It may have happened more than a month ago, but the guys have told me Carter still bitches about me insisting he not intervene. "If he only feared me—feared you—he wouldn't have sought me out to apologize." It also would have taken more than one reminder to set things right for Tessa at BP.

Another tense silence settles between us. If there is one absolute in this world, it's that Carter hates to feel out of control. Ironic for a guy who made a name for himself driving his car at insane speeds. The fact that the things he feels unable to control directly correlate to what he considers my safety is pushing him to his breaking point. We're a lot alike in that way.

Which leads us to…

"Being MIA isn't the only thing I need to apologize to you for." Carter's statement is so unexpected I completely forget about what I need to say to him.

"Uh…" I sputter. "What else?"

He shifts forward, propping his arm along the back of the couch. "Cisco told me you were less than thrilled about our… suggestion on *how* you could play along with this engagement thing with Delacourte."

Accurate, but that isn't the big picture issue anymore. "It wasn't the plan I had an issue with, Carter."

"Had?" He eyes me skeptically. Not at all surprising he picked up on the past tense I used.

I nod. "My problem is how you and the guys *constantly* leave me out of the planning *process*."

"I'm sorry." The sincerity in his tone rings true. Too bad experience has taught me it's moot because it won't stop him from acting the same way again.

"It's fine." I tell him about my conversation with Duke and how I enlisted his help in selling us as a couple for Natalie's benefit. That Carter King mask grows stronger with every detail I give. "Ah…not as fun when the shoe is on the other foot?"

"Touché, brat. Tou-fucking-ché."

We spend the next few minutes trading barbs, and for the first time in weeks, it feels like it's us against the world again. Not many get to experience this side of Carter and most wouldn't believe me if I told them how corny my brother can be, but it's my favorite side of him.

Unfortunately, the side with shadows darkening his features, a clenched jaw, and a vein pulsing in his temple as he sobers is the one I've seen the most lately.

"You want to tell me *why* you agreed to play along with the Momster's master plan in the first place?"

Damn. There's no more avoiding the conversation when he gives me an opening like that.

I drop my attention to Merlin slithering over my shoulder to hide under my hair where it hangs down my back. Maybe we should have gone somewhere public. Being around potential witnesses might have helped keep Carter from epically losing his shit.

"Umm…" Oh, look how the light plays off of the white and gray in Merlin's scales. He's so shiny he must have shed recently.

"Savvy," Carter prods.

Suck it up, bitch.

Swallowing past the lump in my throat, I inhale a steadying breath and admit, "I'm doing it to protect you."

"Me?" Carter barks out a laugh. I know it's not because he thinks I can't protect him. He's the one who coined the Savage name for me; it's more the idea of him being the one in need of protection in general.

Still…there are times when it rankles.

"Natalie…" My words trail off as I try to think of the best way to phrase things. I'm not blind or stupid. Neither is Carter.

"Natalie what?" He keeps the volume of his voice low, but it doesn't make it any less dark or dangerous—goose bumps bloom across my skin.

"She told me if I don't do what she wants, she'll…"

"She'll what?"

I'm stalling. I know I am. Maybe a part of me wants to remain ignorant about his business dealings. Maybe a part of me is afraid knowing the details will ruin the illusion I have of my brother.

"She said she'll give the police enough evidence on you to have you arrested."

I have to look away when the gray of Carter's eyes starts to eclipse the purple in them.

"Arrested?"

I nod, bile rising in my throat at the mere mention of the possibility. I'd never survive it if that happened.

"That bitch." Carter turns and slams a fist onto the coffee table. The ferocity of the action makes me jump, and Merlin's body tightens around my arm. "I *knew* something didn't add up." He slams his fist down again and jumps to his feet.

As Carter starts to pace, I slip my phone from the side pocket of my leggings and thumb off a text to Cisco since he's the closest. My brother is a mass of barely banked rage. Tension radiates off him, his shoulders are up to his ears, and if it were physically possible, I think steam would be coming out of his head. His fingers are flying across his phone, and I can only imagine the typos the Royalty group chat will be filled with from him typing too fast. Guess there was no need for my text.

"*Sonofabitch!*" I jump as Carter punches a hole through the drywall.

The pressure inside my chest grows, squeezing me like Merlin around my arm from the sudden onslaught of sound. The mounting stress has me slumping into the corner of the couch. Stroking a hand over Merlin's smooth, bumpy skin, I keep a wary eye on Carter as he resumes pacing.

Halfway through his route toward the couch, he comes to an abrupt stop, realization and clarity blooming across his face seconds before he rushes me, my body jostled by the bounce of the cushions from the force.

"She's the one," he says cryptically, pulling out his phone again before I can ask who *the one* is. "It's Natalie," he says in lieu of a greeting. "It has to be."

What's Natalie? Who's he talking to? Why is he leaving me in the dark...again?

"It makes total sense. Our net was too big. We were looking outside when we should have concentrated our efforts closer to home." Carter's eyes rise to mine as he pauses to listen to his mystery caller. "Savvy said Natalie threatened to turn over evidence on us. What are the *odds* there would be two people looking into us?"

Air makes my eyes sting as they gape at my brother. My mind races as I blink away the uncomfortable sensation. Someone's been investigating him? Who? Why? When?

Holy shit! Maybe Natalie really does have evidence. An invisible hand wraps around my heart, crushing it in its grip as it dawns on me that maybe she *isn't* bluffing.

Lost in my mental spiral, I don't realize that Carter is off the phone and speaking to me when he asks, "She said this to you to get you to agree to marry Delacourte?"

"Yes." I shake my head. "Well…no." His blank expression says *Explain*, so I go on to tell him how the first time she made the threat was to force me into moving to the St. James.

"Is this why you wanted me to be a St. James at BA?" It's the only thing I can think of to explain why he didn't seem as upset about the name thing as me.

"Yeah." He nods. "I know it didn't make sense to you, but I figured it was one way to help distance you from the situation when we weren't clear on where the threat was coming from."

He's right. It doesn't make sense to me.

"Do you think I'm ashamed of you?" Incredulity makes my voice squeak.

"No." He's quick to answer, but I see the flash of doubt he wasn't able to snuff out. "I'll fix this, I promise." The way he says it makes it sound more like a threat.

When he jumps up to resume pacing, I long to go to him, to wrap my arms around him in the world's tightest hug. As much as instinct pulls me to offer comfort, self-preservation holds me back from intervening. Carter would *never* physically hurt me, but it's best to give him space when his hands flex like he's looking for something to choke the life out of.

"I hate that you felt like you needed to sacrifice for me," he admits, his stride lengthening, his heels coming down with an audible *stomp-stomp-stomp* with each hard step he takes.

His word choice reignites my own anger at him. "What about you?" I snap, my words clipped. "Isn't that what you did when we were growing up? To help me? To make sure I had my asthma medicine and money to pay for it?"

"What?!" Carter whips around with a dropped-jaw glare, his foot clipping the end of the couch, causing him to stumble.

"You sacrificed things you didn't even know about." I think about Em. He tries to hide it, but I see the way he looks at the senator's daughter.

It's only been in the last year or so that they've been around each other with more frequency, but he's yet to make a move.

Maybe finding whatever proof Natalie claims to have against him and destroying it can do more than merely keeping him from ending up in the big house. Maybe it will be enough for him to feel like he can take the leap with the person he wants.

Something has to give before one—or both—of them breaks beyond repair. Em and Carter bicker more than any two people I've ever met, and I'm including Jasper and myself in that equation.

Shit! I need to forget about Jasper and me. That can never happen. Not anymore. At least things ended before they got serious. It's not like feelings were involved...

CHAPTER 22

PRACTICE MAY BE GRUELING, but out here on the ice is where I belong. My focus needs to be singular to achieve my goal. Nothing else matters except getting the biscuit in the basket and ending up with a higher number on the scoreboard than our opponents.

So why is it that my gaze rises up to the stands, searching out my ultimate distraction?

The shrill of Coach's whistle has my attention breaking away from my biggest frustration and back to the ice.

Another face-off, and we're off again. Quads burning and chest heaving, I chase the puck down the ice. All practice, our line has been playing a man down as we work on our penalty kill skills. Coach is relentless, having us run the same play repeatedly until we not only stop them from scoring but can turn the other team's man advantage into a scoring opportunity for us.

My skates send a spray of snow at the boards as I stop, hooking the blade of my stick over the edge of the puck, and pass to Duke, who's waiting to send it sailing into the back of the net.

Coach nods his approval as we skate back to the bench, but I'm unable to bask in it because my attention is drawn to a bowing Duke. One arm folds across his stomach as he bends forward before repeating the process with the other arm. It's not his over-the-top antics that are pulling my and most of the team's focus, but the beauty applauding him from her perch high in the stands.

For the last week and a half, Savvy has watched our practices more often than not. At first, I couldn't believe Coach allowed it, but the only person her presence seems to affect is me.

"You good?" Duke asks as we skate out to the face-off circle near our goal.

"Fine," I mutter for what feels like the millionth time. It's not much of an exaggeration. Since Savvy propositioned him into playing into their engagement last week, he's made sure to check in a few times a day. If I wasn't such a selfish bastard, I would credit them to keeping us from having any new conversations with our fists, but I haven't found myself in much of a giving mood of late.

The self-serving side of me tells me I should be grateful for the out. With Duke playing the doting fiancé, it creates a barrier that will help keep me from acting in a way that could cost me my future.

Unfortunately, it's the selfish side of me that keeps taking issue with it. I want her, and keeping my distance is killing me.

The first time I tried to drape my arm behind her chair at lunch after she brokered her deal with Duke, the plea in her purple eyes gutted me. It would be so much easier if I could claim she was going back to playing games with me, using my jealousy against me to toy with me by flirting with guys in front of me. Except I can't. She was straight up with me, explaining that while her relationship with Duke might not be real, it needs to seem like it to the outside world.

It physically pains me to not touch her. It only gets worse every time Duke brushes the hair from her face, throws an arm around her shoulders, or just holds her hand. It's like I'm being prodded with a hot poker. Each one of his obnoxious nicknames grates like nails on a chalkboard.

"Noble," Coach barks.

I shake myself out of my mental musings and skate to my spot. Hands flexing around the carbon fiber shaft, I readjust my grip on my stick, knees bending, torso folding forward, and settle into position for a face-off.

The rubber puck hits the ice, and I use my stick's blade to smack my opponent's away and send it sailing back to a waiting Banks.

Like a carefully choreographed dance, I push to the right. At the same time, Banks goes left, splitting the opposition's line and skating into their territory.

Checks are exchanged, the sounds of bodies slamming into the boards reverberating through the empty stands inside the arena as players battle it out for possession.

Duke accepts a pass from Banks, dipping a shoulder to avoid a hit from an opposing defender while I get into position near the crease. He doesn't need to look up to know I'm there, passing me the puck to slip between the leg pads of our starting goalie to light the lamp.

My gaze automatically goes to the stands again, searching out Savvy. While she is still watching, there's no outward sign of approval or appreciation like Duke received for his goal. She's way too good at pretending nothing exists between us for my sanity.

My thoughts can't help but continue in a constant spiral. What could make her instigate a fake relationship with my best friend? What could push her into keeping her distance from me? Scared is the last adjective I would use to describe Savvy, but that's exactly how she's been acting.

Where is the girl who defied the kings on her first day? The same one who threatened guys she knew nothing about away from her friend? Where is that spark of attitude?

Sure, she still doesn't take any shit from anybody, but all our interactions seem…flat now. Where is that instinct to challenge me at every turn?

We're a week out from our first regular season game; I shouldn't be worrying about these things. I need to get my head out from between Savvy's legs and into the game. I've got enough things coming for my future. Why the hell am I letting her demons get in my way?

"Noble," Coach snaps.

Fuck! The first few days, I was able to function normally, but with each one that passes, it's getting harder to shut it all out.

"Come on, bro." Duke claps me on the back, his hockey gloves thumping against my pads. He casts his gaze north and gives a subtle shake of his head. He's right. Not the time.

We rejoin our line, and for the rest of practice, I'm able to successfully shut out all thoughts of Savvy. By the time we're done, my muscles are fatigued, and sweat causes my practice jersey to stick to my skin.

Banks and I hang back with Duke as the rest of the team filters off the ice, Savvy meeting us at the mouth of the tunnel that leads to the locker room.

"Hey there, snuggle bunny." Duke attempts to drop an arm around Savvy's shoulders, but the added height from our skates makes his already towering stature too much for it to be more than resting a hand on her.

"First off…" Savvy uses the tips of two fingers to pluck Duke's arm off of her, unceremoniously dropping it and drawing a grin from me. "Ew." The top of her lip crinkles in disgust. "And second…" She fiddles with the flap of her messenger bag, pulling out something pink and fluffy before slapping it against Duke's stomach with enough force to have an "oof" escape. "Don't *ever* use *bunny* in your nicknames for me again."

She starts to walk away, but I snag her wrist before she can get too far. Her gaze goes to the padded fingers wrapped around her then up to my face, one of her blonde brows arching in question. This is the most I've touched her in over a week, and I swear even through all the layers of material separating us, her skin burns mine.

Next to us, Duke juggles the offending object. "The fuck?" he asks, lifting a set of pink bunny ears once he gets a solid hold on it. "You trying to tell me you're a furry or something?"

Savvy sighs heavily and rolls her eyes. "Why am I not surprised your demented mind would instantly go to something sexual?"

"It's what I do best, kitten." Duke plants his skates into the rubber mat and thrusts his hips, channeling his inner Channing Tatum.

"I can't even with you." Savvy may complain, may seem like she's put out by my best friend's antics, but there's no missing the almost conspiratorial smirk the two share.

They've been bonding, and it irks the shit out of me, as does the way she gives a pointed glance at where I haven't released my hold on her. It takes another too-long moment before common sense pushes to the forefront and I do.

"If you're not trying to tell me you wanna get down with the kinky shit, what's with the Playboy accessory?" Savvy smacks Duke's hand away when he tries to plant the ears on her head. The scowl she levels him with has my dick pushing against my cup.

Something is seriously wrong with me that even when it's not directed my way, I'm affected just being in close proximity to her fire.

"You keep that shit up, and I'll be a widow, or whatever you call it before we get married."

Duke beams from ear to ear, hands—one still clutching the bunny ears—pressed to his heart. "And here I thought you had no intention of walking down the aisle. Are you saying you changed your mind, boo-boo?"

"Jesus." Savvy kneads the bridge of her brow.

It's probably wrong to derive pleasure from Duke's continued annoyance of Savvy, but I don't give a fuck. Being told their relationship isn't real only goes so far when forced to sit back and watch as they portray the exact opposite. It's its own brand of torture, mainly because it only emphasizes how little control I have over the situation.

It doesn't help that Savvy has completely shut me out, leaving me without an opportunity to glean any information on why she needs Duke to play into their parents' insanity. I can't exert my control without proper intel.

"Look"—her cheeks puff out as she exhales a controlled breath—"I'm not trying to pick a fight, but remember how you idiots tried to *prove*—"

The pointed glance she sends my way is filled with the familiar challenge that heats my blood and has me looking for the closest object to bend her over.

"—to me you were the reigning kings in this place?"

The three of us nod, and it's a struggle not to reach out and run my thumb across her mouth as it presses into a flat line.

"Well…you might want to remind Arabella and her minions what I did the *last* time someone left something attached to my locker."

"Arabella gave you this?" I snatch the ears from Duke, the thin plastic band bending in my grip thanks to the surge of protectiveness flooding my system.

Savvy nods. "Along with a note filled with all *kinds* of tips on how to *properly* be the team's new puck bunny."

"If that's not the pot calling the kettle black..." Banks murmurs.

Since Savvy's arrival, things have shifted at BA. Students noticed her and were curious to learn about the girl who openly challenged their leaders. She defied us and retaliated, but the balance of power remained intact. It wasn't until we started to broker a truce between us that the real change occurred. Then came the engagement announcement and the realization that Savvy is related to Carter King. With every bit of ground Savvy gained, The Unholy Trilogy lost some.

"Her hypocrisy isn't the issue here, nor is the weak attempt at threatening me she ended the note with." Savvy plucks the ears from me and tosses them into a nearby trash can. "But since we're"—she bounces a finger between herself and us—"supposed to be playing nice, I'll give you a chance to handle this before I do."

CHAPTER 23

HIGH SCHOOL FOOTBALL games are a teenage rite of passage, whether it's Friday night lights or a Saturday afternoon playoff game like today—though the games are infinitely more enjoyable when we get to watch from the stands instead of one of the few luxury boxes near the press box.

It's not at all uncommon for my family or Duke's to attend a BA Knights football game, but unlike any they've attended during the regular season, our presence has been requested to put in some face time with the 'rents.

This whole day would be better if I wasn't battling with myself over asking Duke for details of his "date" with Savvy last night. For the sake of our friendship, we've agreed to avoid the topic of the girl who should be mine but the world thinks is his. Intellectually, I know what they have isn't real, but I'm not feeling all that intellectual these days. Barbaric and controlled by my baser instincts is more like it.

Midas and the guys are driving downfield toward the end zone by the time Duke and I can no longer put off making an appearance. I shouldn't have come today. The more stairs we ascend, the clearer this becomes. I'm antsy and edgy, and if I don't find a way to expel some of this destructive energy, I'm at risk of doing something I can't take back.

We make it to the glossy gray door with the small gold plaque that tells us we've reached our destination. Duke reaches for the handle but pauses to glance my way before turning it. "You straight?"

I nod but don't say anything. I hate the guilt that coils in my gut at his need to check in. Bro is a better man than I. While he worries about me, all I can think about is the quickest way to get his fiancée naked and writhing under me.

We enter the box and are immediately enveloped in hugs from our moms. Unfortunately, Natalie St. James is with them, her disdain for me hidden beneath a sugary sweet smile.

"Really, Mom?" Duke rolls his eyes at the various pictures of floral arrangements and wedding ideas displayed on her phone's screen. "Addicted," he whispers, referring to her Pinterest page, then places a kiss on the crown of her head.

The sight of planning for a wedding that isn't supposed to happen until years from now has knots forming between my shoulder blades and shooting down my spine.

Before I say something I can't take back or that will expose me in front of my father, I jerk a chin toward where the man himself sits in one of the leather seats overlooking the football field below.

Handshakes are exchanged, and we settle in just as BA scores a touchdown. The crowd cheers and the fight song is played from the loudspeaker before the buoyant mood is wrecked with one comment from dear ol' Dad.

"It's too bad Savvy couldn't join us today. It would have been a great opportunity to get some candid shots to use of her and Duke for their social media."

Duke gives an Elvis lip curl as he shifts his phone side to side. He's bitched more than his fair share about the pressure to up his public profile to fall in line with the family-friendly storybook romance image Dad wants them to project.

"Does it earn us any points that she *is* at a football game too?" Duke asks, barely keeping his sarcasm in check.

Dad's mouth presses into a flat line, unimpressed. The answer is no; it *doesn't* earn any points that Savvy is at BP's playoff game. In his mind, her cheering for her old school is playing for the wrong team. If you were wondering who I inherited the control freak gene from, it was one Walter Noble. The fact that Savvy doesn't fall in line with his plans has to drive him crazy.

"I hope you stressed the importance of her attending *your* game next week," Dad comments.

A thrill rolls through me, followed quickly by a sense of dread at the idea of Savvy watching me play. The former stems from a basic caveman posturing of showing off exactly what I'm capable of doing. She may be friends with Lance Bennett, but hockey is the one area in my life I know her precious Royals can't touch me. Though I should probably heed the latter more given how poorly I've been performing in practice these last few days.

The majority of the game passes by in a blur. By the time it's over, it feels like I might permanently have a chunk of my cheek missing from biting it, but I had no other option. The one time I contributed to the conversation, Dad nearly ripped my head off. I get that he wants me to keep my distance from Savvy, but pretending we don't interact daily is unreasonable.

The moment the game is over—the Knights falling to the Chiefs by a field goal—I'm out of my seat and saying my goodbyes. I'm a mass of banked adrenaline from restraining myself and holding my tongue for hours. I need an outlet for this explosive energy, and I need it now.

Two days. I have to wait two fucking days before I see Savvy again, and the kicker is when I do, I have to pretend we're nothing more than friends, pretend I don't know what it feels like to be buried balls-deep inside her or how perfectly her pussy strangles my cock. I have to act like hearing her say Duke's name isn't like taking a dagger to the gut when she vehemently refuses to say mine.

The worst thing is, without being able to outright claim her as mine, it feels like my hands are tied when it comes to protecting her. She would probably scoff and tell me she doesn't need my protection, but that's the crux of it.

I love Duke dearly. He's my un-biological brother, my ride or die, but he's not seeing what I'm seeing. He may be the one spending most of his time with Savvy, but their interactions are surface level. He's not seeing beneath her tough-girl exterior.

Savvy isn't the type who needs saving. I saw it every day she challenged me at school but didn't truly understand it until the day I drove her to BP for Tessa. It wasn't until after learning of her Royal connection that other little things started to fall into place.

While Savvy's built tough, she's also been the treasured jewel of the Royalty Crew. I get the impression it's why she feels the need to prove she can handle the world on her own. I don't want to slay her dragons for her; I want to be by her side while she does. It's because she doesn't need me that I want her more.

That being said, it doesn't mean I won't help behind the scenes—especially knowing someone is attempting to threaten her.

The sight of long brown hair drives that point home, and I pick up my pace. As soon as I clear the bottom step leading to the bleachers, I yank Arabella beneath them and pin her to the scaffolding with a hand wrapped around her throat.

"I knew you missed me," she purrs, dragging a finger down the center of my chest.

Bitch is delusional and has zero sense of self-preservation. This isn't a lead-in to a kinky fuck. There's no want or desire as I glare down at her. Pure menace pulses off of me as I squeeze hard enough to cut off the last of her air supply. Finally, there's a widening of her eyes as panic starts to override the misplaced lust.

"You couldn't be more wrong if you tried." The only thing harder than my voice is my grip. "Now, let's get a few things straight."

I feel Duke move behind me so he's at my back, hovering should I need him but not interfering.

Arabella blinks rapidly, her eyelash extensions fluttering with the action. Her eyes rise to the space above my shoulder, and there's no missing the plea for help she directs at Duke. Too bad it's a wasted effort.

"You and I will *never* happen again, but you knew that already." She licks her lips, and beneath my hand, her throat works with a swallow. "Now for the important part." I push up on her jaw, forcing her head to fall to what is probably an uncomfortable angle, not that I care. "You *will* leave Savvy alone."

"Wh-why are you the one warning me off?" She coughs, hands coming up to clutch at my arm, but I don't loosen my hold.

The funny thing is if it weren't me, if I decided to sit back and let Savvy handle things, it would be a lot less pleasant for Arabella.

"Shouldn't it be her fiancé coming to her rescue?" She clucks her tongue, and red tinges the edges of my vision. "Or does the fact that she bounces on both your dicks mean the white knight treatment is interchangeable?"

"The fuck you just say to me?" I squeeze harder, Arabella's face flushing with color as her body starts to thrash against me. Gone is any sensible thought. It isn't until Duke lays his hand over mine that I let her go.

Arabella instantly falls to her knees, hand clutching at the front of her throat as she releases a series of hacking coughs. It doesn't faze me, nor do the tears streaming down her face, cutting wavy tracks in her makeup.

It's safe to say with Duke and Savvy being engaged, most people will assume they are having sex, but they haven't done more than kiss on the cheek, and even those are rare.

It's the assumption that I'm fucking Savvy that has blind rage making me step forward. The last time Arabella and I had any sort of a conversation, she commented about my *lack* of fucking Savvy. What has her thinking differently now? Unless…

Before I can move in and actually put Arabella down like the bitch she is, Duke steps between us, posture rigid.

"Those who live in glass houses shouldn't throw stones, Arabella." It's a canned proverb, but there's no missing the way she trembles at his dark tone.

"It's amazing what you can see when not hidden behind tinted glass though." She rises to stand, brushing off the dirt staining the knees of her designer jeans and leveling us with her Queen B icy glare. That just won't do.

Moving so I'm standing shoulder to shoulder with Duke, I fold my arms across my chest and glower until Arabella shrinks back, her own shoulders folding in.

"In case you haven't noticed…things have shifted at BA." She has, I know she has. I get that she doesn't like that it comes at the cost of her power, but that's not my problem. She's nothing more than basic. "Right now, you're still recognized in the social hierarchy…but if you keep coming for Savvy, I won't stop until you're nothing more than an inconsequential stain inside the BA yearbook."

She gasps, and again I see the how-dare-you swimming behind her eyes.

I don't have definitive proof yet, but Arabella has my suspicions raised based on a few things she's said. I'm done with people testing me and trying to have a say in my life. It's time they all learn just how ruthless I can be.

CHAPTER 24

THE REFLECTION STARING BACK at me is full of judgment I certainly don't need. It's not like I asked for this. I'm doing the only thing I know how to help mitigate Natalie's increased threats against Carter. Still, it doesn't stop me from feeling helpless in the situation.

"You better be on your best behavior later," Natalie cautions.

"Aye, aye." Her eyes turn to ice at my jaunty salute.

There are times she makes it too easy to get under her skin. Unfortunately, the same can be said about me. I've learned to live with a constant tightness in my chest. I'm starting to forget what it's like to go about my day without feeling like my body has taken a beating.

"Remember"—Natalie moves to the counter and lifts a bundle of fabric from it—"you're going to the game to root for your fiancé." She holds the bundle out for me to take, my hand annoyingly shaky as I do.

The smug satisfaction on her painted lips is imprinted in my memory even now as I worry the hem of the jersey between my fingers.

"But just in case you forget who *that is, this should help."* A *hand hooks over the top of the jersey I have stretched out to display, a scarlet nail tapping the nameplate.*

While football and cheerleading are my first loves when it comes to choosing sporting events to attend, hockey has been climbing the ranks since Lance has become friends with my brother. I'm not as well versed in sticks and pucks as I am in pigskins and basket tosses, but I know enough to enjoy a game without a tutor.

Worrying the black hem of the too-large jersey, my eyes narrow at the Knight taking up most of my torso. Ugh! It's just *wrong*.

Knock-knock.

I turn to see Mitchell looming in the doorway to my bedroom, an unexpected spark of enjoyment flickering at seeing him dressed down in a pair of dark jeans and a Blackwell Academy gray polo shirt. "Ready to go?"

I nod despite not feeling it. It's not like it matters anyway. If I tried to back out of going, who knows what Natalie would do to retaliate.

"You're riding with us to the arena, correct?"

"Yeah. Tessa and Tinsley agreed to meet us there." I walk to my bed and pull the strap of my overnight bag over my shoulder. At least I know this night will end with me sleeping at Carter's instead of this place. Small favors. "Thanks again for arranging for them to join us."

"Of course." It's weird how I believe the affectionate grin he sends my way. He's directly linked to a person I despise above all others, yet there's a core goodness in him that helps to ease the anxiety Natalie causes.

It doesn't matter how much time I've spent in the BA hockey arena these last couple of weeks; I don't think I'll ever not be impressed by it. There's an ambiance to it that is more reminiscent of a top-tier college like BTU than where a high school team would play. Perks of the obscenely wealthy.

Gray, white, and black banners and pennants hang from the rafters for all the conference and state championships the hockey team has won through the years, as well as names and numbers of alumni who have gone on to play professionally. BP has a similar setup in the main gym, but theirs boasts for all of the school's sports, while this is strictly for hockey. I can admit it's impressive.

Unlike when I would observe practice, tonight I'll be watching the action happening on the ice from one of the suites, and *oh my damn*. Sure, I've watched my fair share of BP football games in the founders' box, but that's nothing special. It's more an enclosed room to protect from the elements with heat for when the weather turns cold. This is…wow.

There are large leather chairs stacked in two stadium-style rows and a marble counter set up with chafing dishes and chilled beverages. It feels more like something you would find at a professional sporting event, though I honestly shouldn't expect anything less.

"You think if I send some pics to your Uncle Chuck, he'll renovate the founders' box?" Tessa's eyes are out on stalks as we walk arm in arm through the space.

"I wouldn't hold your breath." I snort, guiding the two of us and Tinsley to three seats tucked in the corner.

"*Ba-zing!*" Tessa mimes ringing a bell. "Breathing advice from the asthmatic."

Tinsley's mouth is agape when I side-eye Tess, but there's no offense given or taken in Tessa's joke. "Someone's in a mood tonight," I observe instead.

"Eh." Tessa shrugs, dropping into her seat with a flourish. "My inappropriate factor increases with heightened awkwardness. I suspect that's just the tip of the iceberg." She nudges me between the ribs with an elbow. "Get it? *Ice*berg?" She waggles her eyebrows, bouncing her gaze between me and the rink below.

"Corny…even for you." Though she met her objective because I'm laughing.

Below us, the stands are mostly full and continue to steadily fill with spectators. A part of me is surprised to see so many people with the puck drop happening at four in the afternoon. Then again, Mitchell rearranged his schedule to attend, as did Governor Delacourte and Mr. Noble, so I guess these things are a bigger deal than one would expect.

Because of the early start, there's thankfully not a whole lot of time for us to get pulled into a conversation with the adults before we need to stand for the obligatory singing of the national anthem and the game gets underway.

Having gone to a school without a hockey team, I know zilch when it comes to who is a contender and who's not. The only reason I know this game is more a gimme for the BA Knights is because the guys have talked nonstop about it all week.

Unlike with football, the action is a lot faster with hockey, and I quickly find myself sitting on the edge of my seat in an effort to keep track of the puck flying across the ice.

Hanging around after school to watch practice and then letting Duke bring me home afterward was a method I employed to make Natalie think I was playing along with her wedded-bliss dreams, though I can admit I learned enough to have me feeling more invested in today's game than I would have thought I'd be.

I know Jasper, Banks, and Duke all play on the Knights' starting line, with the former two as offensive players and my darling fiancé on defense. They've also all mentioned how they hope to play at the college level after graduation, and even a layman like me can tell they each possess the skill to do so.

Ooo, especially Jasper. Look at the way he flies down the ice.

Running my fingers through my hair, I use the move to hide how I glance back to check to see if Natalie is paying us any attention, as if her satanic personality could make it possible to hear my inner thoughts. Thankfully, she seems to be engrossed in conversation with Mrs. Delacourte and Mrs. Noble. Unfortunately, I'm pretty sure they are also talking about the wedding they claim isn't supposed to happen for many years. Even though I have no intention of following through on any of those plans, bile still churns in my gut at how I haven't found an out yet.

Ignoring the constriction of my ribcage, I bring my focus back to the game. And, yes, my mental musings were spot-on because Jasper is practically a blur as he weaves through the white and red jerseys of the other team's defense. The way he holds his stick slightly off the ice tells me he doesn't have the puck, but he's enough of a threat that they still cover him.

Banks takes a hard check in the corner that surprisingly has Tinsley wincing and Tessa and me sharing *Now that's interesting* eye contact. The next time Tess gets on my case about my *star-crossed*—oh, you heard my sarcasm, did you— love with Jasper, I need to remember to bring up the Tinsley and Banks show. I'll make sure to leave out how that partic- ular name comes from Jasper himself because that would defeat the purpose of the distraction technique.

The puck is passed between players, the Knights losing possession to the Wolves before they steal it back and so forth. Jasper manages to regain control of the puck and takes a nasty check to the boards. Unlike in the pros, fighting is not allowed at the high school level, but that doesn't stop Jasper from staring down the defender who hit him after he shakes him off.

I'm dozens of feet away, but the image projected on the screen hanging above center ice is enough to have my nipples tighten painfully against my bra and my panties turning damp. There is nothing like Jasper's dangerous glower.

A ref skates between them, breaking things up before they escalate to places that would require suspensions.

There's a face-off in one of the circles by the Wolves' net. Mr. Noble is on his feet, hands braced on the railing atop the half wall that makes up the balcony of the suite as Jasper wins the face-off, passing the puck to Banks the way I've seen him do in practice countless times.

Jasper feints left then skates right, sailing around the back of the net, his skates sending a spray of shaved ice into the air as he takes a position in front of the goalie and accepts a pass back from Banks before hitting it into the back of the net.

Absorbed in the action, I'm on my feet cheering as the red light attached to the net lights up with the scoring goal.

Mrs. Noble is clapping like Jasper scored the game-winning goal in the Olympics, with Mrs. Delacourte showing a little more decorum. Natalie—surprise, surprise—is doing the bare minimum needed to seem invested.

The dads of the bunch are all high-fiving and bro back-slapping like they were the ones who pulled off the play.

Jasper's line swarms on him in front of the goal, sticks raised high in the air, gloved hands patting him on the back in celebration. As they break away, Jasper lifts his gaze toward our box, and like a homing beacon, I swear it meets mine.

My heart rate picks up, and the way pride infuses my system tells me one thing: I'm in trouble. Big, big complicated trouble.

CHAPTER 25

THE PLUS SIDE to attending a weird late-afternoon/early-evening hockey game is it allowed enough time for Tessa, Tinsley, and me to get in a nap before the evening's festivities.

It's rare for one of Carter's poker nights to happen on a Friday given that Tessa is his Texas Hold' Em ringer and she typically has cheerleading practice on Saturday mornings. He made an exception this week since her brother, JT, is home from Kentucky, and the change allowed for both of them to hang out with the oldest Taylor sibling.

Now the basement at Carter's is close to capacity, both poker tables filled with ten players each and about a dozen or so of our other friends scattered amongst the couches, pool table, and bar.

I didn't realize how much I needed a night like this, a chance to experience a sense of normalcy in all the crazy my life has become.

Curses ring out from one of the tables, and based on the

way Tessa throws her arms in the air and dances around in her seat, I take it she's won another hand.

"For T's sake, I hope she dominates quick tonight," Kay comments, gaze trained in the same direction as mine. "Lack of sleep won't do her any favors tomorrow at practice if this goes all night."

"There's way too much evil packed into this pint-sized body of yours, Skittles," says Mase, Kay's hunky football-playing boyfriend, as he buries his face in her hair with a kiss to her head.

The stunting clinics Kay runs with JT when he's home are notorious in both their intensity and in the results they yield from her athletes.

"You love me anyway." She snuggles deeper into his embrace, her back leaning against his front with a sigh.

"For keeps."

I look away when the kiss they share escalates into something not appropriate for mixed company, and it's my turn to expel a sigh. *That's* what true love looks like. If anyone in the room should be wearing an engagement ring, it's Kay, *not* me. Wiggling the fingers of my left hand, I can't help but smirk at the notable absence of said ring. Natalie would shit a brick if she knew I take off the sparkly shackle every chance I get.

If only reclaiming control of my life was as easy as removing a piece of jewelry.

Thankfully before I can fall down the rabbit hole of all the things I told myself I wouldn't think about this weekend, my phone vibrates in my back pocket.

The sight of Gunderson's name flashing across the screen when I pull it free gives me pause, and I quickly bounce my gaze around the room—looking for what, I'm not sure.

Excusing myself, I push out of my seat and move toward a corner of the room where it's quieter then swipe to answer.

"Scott," I say in greeting.

"Savvy."

Shouts and other indistinguishable sounds have me plugging my opposite ear to hear him better. "What's going on?"

A chill of uncertainty has goose bumps breaking out across my skin. A phone call from Gunderson isn't normal to begin with. Calling with massive amounts of background noise? Yeah, no, something's not right here.

"Gunderson?" I try again, and this time the cacophony fades the slightest bit, enabling me to hear marginally better.

"You might want to have one of the Royals bring you to BP ASAP."

What? Why would I go to BP on a Friday night? That chill intensifies into full-on foreboding, and I lower my hand to cup the side of my ribcage, squeezing to counter the pressure beneath it. What the hell? I'm getting all triggery without any actual triggers.

"Why?" My voice is rougher than normal, my throat feeling rubbed raw.

"Because the guys and I caught ourselves a few of your BAssholes."

"What?"

Gunderson says something else I can't quite make out, and I tell him to hold on while I head for the door to the basement. Leo spots me as I open it and point to my phone then my ear, shaking my head to mime that I can't hear. He nods, but I wait for him to turn back to his game of pool before actually taking my leave.

"What were you saying?" I ask Gunderson once I'm alone in the empty garage.

"So the guys and I like to come sit in the bleachers the night before a game."

"I know I come to the games to cheer you on, but I don't really give a damn about your jock superstitions." I roll my eyes, walking over to the Camaro and lovingly stroking a hand along the rear wing.

"Why doesn't it surprise me that you found a way to give

me shit when I'm trying to do you a favor?" His tone takes on an incredulous edge.

I'm *so* over needing to coddle fragile male egos.

"Scott." I pause to take a breath, temper flaring, my chest growing tight. "I swear to *fucking* Christ."

"You know, King…you make it really fucking difficult to try to stay on your good side."

My next breath is slightly harder to take.

"Are you going to get to the point? Or am I going to have to get my *brother*?" I growl both to add weight to the threat and because it frustrates the absolute *hell* out of me that I need to do so in the first place when Scott. Called. Me. "Spoiler alert"—I drop my voice to a whisper because when I get annoyed, I get mildly vindictive—"that wouldn't be in your *best* interest since he hasn't been *your* biggest fan since you left bruises on me."

I swear I can hear him swallow through the phone.

Still…he makes me wait, my irritation growing as I run a nail up and down the razor-thin metallic purple lines bordering the black glossy racing stripes running down the center of the matte black paint job on the Camaro.

"Shit, woman, be easy." There's a garbled choking sound, and I can picture him smoothing a palm along his face and into his hair. It's his tell when he's nervous.

"*Gunderson.*"

Something in the way he clears his throat has me straightening from my lean against the Camaro's trunk. "When we got here, we caught a few of your new school *chums* in the midst of BA's latest prank attempt."

Jesus. I pinch the bridge of my nose, beyond exasperated. Is it really so much to ask to spend an entire weekend without having my new life encroach on my real life?

"And I'm supposed to care because…" I let my words trail off. It's obvious to anyone with half a brain what side of the rivalry line I fall on. Hello! I helped Gunderson and the BP football team *plan* the car prank. Without me, it would have been impossible.

"Look...we all know you're a dragon at heart, despite where you take class." *Thank you!* "That's not why I'm calling." I make a rolling motion with my hand despite him not being able to see me. "The reason I am is that *one* of the guys we caught is your...fiancé." The pause he took before saying Duke's "label" to me is telling.

It's nice to know while the people in my new world didn't bat an eye at the sudden betrothal, those who have known me most of my life find the coupling suspect.

Unable to stay still, I start to pace. Why am I not surprised Duke is involved in the pranks? I know I promised him access to Tessa if he played along with our engagement, but those two seriously should not be allowed to spend any amount of time alone. With her love for fiction and his perpetual Peter Pan personality, the chaos they could dream up together could set the world on fire.

"I could make a dumb jock joke if you'd like, but Gunderson, you and I both know you aren't stupid. There is *zero*—hell, less than zero—chance of you guys getting away with doing something to the *governor's* son. Just let him go."

"You don't think we *know* that?"

I really hope he can feel the *So then what's the problem?* glare I'm directing at him through the phone.

"Look...this was just a courtesy call since your fiancé is involved. He may be safe, but I gotta go because the beat-down of his friends is about to start."

His friends?

Does that mean...Jasper?

As if a switch flipped, my heart suddenly takes off in a gallop inside my chest, at risk of falling out of its cavity and into my stomach. What the hell?

Laying the flat of my palm over the racing beat, I wipe the

other on the side of my jeans to clear off the sweat breaking out across my skin.

No, no, no, no, no.

Shit!

Frantically I run my hands along my body, my movements disjointed and jerky as I shove them inside my pockets, feeling around for something that isn't there. *Goddammit!* Why did I leave my inhaler in my room?

I stumble a step before stopping and planting my feet on the painted concrete floor.

"Savvy?" Scott's voice echoes like it's coming from inside a tunnel.

Relax. Breathe, I coach myself.

I squeeze my eyes closed.

One.

Two.

Three.

Four.

I count off in my head while I take a purposeful breath in through my nose.

One.

Two.

Three.

Four.

I repeat the count and release a steady stream of air out my mouth.

It takes one more set before I'm able to get my body to cooperate enough to walk without falling. My legs are wobbly, but I manage to stay upright as I head for the door.

My hand shakes when I go to scan the key card that will unlock the door to the main residential area.

"Jus—" I cough and need to clear the frog that has jumped into my throat. "Just let them go."

"Can't do it."

I try to growl again, but this time it comes out more like a wimpy purr thanks to the ever-growing restriction of my throat. It's been six weeks since my last full-blown asthma attack. What the hell is triggering me now?

"The guys want their pound of flesh."

"Seems a bit dramatic." I curl my hand over the staircase banister in a death grip and trudge up the steps, each footfall loud as it lands.

"Some might say that, but if we hadn't shown up and interrupted these motherfuckers—"

A bolt of trepidation shoots down my spine as I crest the top of the staircase and causes me to clutch at the half wall that overlooks the downstairs.

"—there's a very *real*, very *serious* possibility the game could have been forced to change venues tomorrow, costing us home-field advantage."

I pause at the threshold in my room. What the hell could they have done that would have that kind of effect on tomorrow's playoff game?

"So…no. I'm sorry, Savvy, but I can't. Like I said, this was just a courtesy call."

Sonofabitch.

I sit on my bed to riffle through my purse for my inhaler and waste no time using it.

The relief is instantaneous, my attack stopped before it fully blooms. Good. That's a good thing.

I remain seated on the soft mattress with a leg tucked under me and focus on inhaling and exhaling for a few beats.

A fresh burst of shouts comes from the other end of the phone, and Scott is cursing when he comes back on the line. "*Fuck!*"

I wince from the shout and dig a knuckle into my abused eardrum before pressing the phone as tight to my ear as I can, trying to make out what's going on.

"This one guy can fight, I'll give him that."

The breath I only just managed to get back under control

stutters inside my lungs again at the idea of Jasper fighting. Is it an unfair fight?

I jump from the bed, flying around my room much more quickly than I should postasthmatic episode, but I don't give a damn. I'm moving on autopilot, a deep-seated instinct urging me along as I yank my leather jacket from its hanger inside my closet.

All I can think about is Jasper.

Images flash through my brain: him trying to take on the entire Blackwell Public offensive line by himself and not faring any better than a tackling dummy.

I blink them away. The whole scenario is unreasonable and highly illogical. He wouldn't be fighting alone. Right?

Yes, yes, I'm right.

I may have hated Jasper and his merry band of douchebags when I first started at BA, but they're loyal—at least Duke and Banks are—like the Royals.

Yes. They are ride or die. Why else would I have gravitated to them?

They would *never* let Jasper fight on his own.

Right?

Right?

Right?

Oh god!

Why can't I get rid of these vile images?

Why does it feel like someone is reaching inside my chest and squeezing my heart in their fist?

Wait…

Am I…

No.

I'm not. No way.

Or…

Am I?

Oh shit! I am…

"Scott." I swallow and do my best to adopt the tone—the

scary one—Carter uses when he's trying to make people pee their pants. "I'm on my way."

I disconnect the call without giving him a chance to respond. There's no time. This isn't up for debate.

Fuck it.

Decision made.

I'm about to do the riskiest thing I've *ever* done. And no... I'm not talking about how I went and fell in love with Jasper Noble.

CHAPTER 26

BAM!

"*Oof.*" My torso falls forward, but I manage to eat most of the punch to my gut. Shaking it off, I shuffle back, cursing and kicking out a foot when I stumble over one of the mouse traps littering the field.

When Midas and Brad came by with their plan to prank BP by covering their football field with a few thousand mouse traps, it seemed simple enough. Fuck were we wrong.

I throw up an arm to block the latest punch of this asshat in a BP football hoodie and get him with my own to his jaw. He stumbles back before righting himself and returning the favor, the familiar coppery taste of blood trickling into my mouth from the hit.

With a shove and a solid right hook, I finally manage to cause enough separation for there to be a break in the fighting.

I drag a hand across my mouth, a streak of crimson staining the skin of my knuckles, thanks to my busted lip. This shit is getting old.

Lacing my fingers together, I press forward and crack my knuckles. Shaking out my hands, I bring them up, ready for the next round. This fucker thinks he can make me bleed? Yeah, I don't think so. I was taking it easy on him. Not anymore. Time to bring the pain.

"Enough!" A voice booms when I'm about to lunge, but the person stepping into the middle of the fray does *nothing* to lower the simmering fury pumping through my bloodstream. This is the motherfucker who put his hands on Savvy.

"Gunny," the guy fighting with Midas complains.

"Don't start." Douche numero uno cuts him off with a wave of his hand. "These assholes are connected to Savvy. Do you really wanna piss off the Royals?"

My first instinct is to tell this asshole to keep my girl's name out of his mouth, but hearing it is enough to give me pause. Why would he bring her up?

"It'll be fine, Gunny," another one of his teammates chimes in, hooking a thumb back at Duke standing at the edge of our makeshift circle. "We didn't touch the *fiancé*." The eye roll he tacks on makes me suspect a teenage engagement isn't as believable outside the land of the rich and entitled.

"Your friend is right." Duke seizes the opportunity to step in front of me, slipping into the slick politician persona his dad exudes. "I think we need to take a beat before things escalate to a point none of us can come back from."

Duke maintains eye contact with those he's speaking to while I check those moving around us. The clenched jaws and flexing hands project how reluctant everyone is about the idea, but it's not enough to stop them from heeding my friend's advice.

The atmosphere remains volatile as a dozen guys choose their sides in battle. Chests heave, nostrils flare, and except for Duke, not one person relaxes their stance.

The temperature isn't quite chilly enough to see one's

breath, but it's low enough for there to be that noticeable tingle as it fills your lungs.

There are side glances on both sides of the divide, neither grouping wanting to admit that Duke may have a point. Through all the years of pranks, both schools may have skirted the line of legality, but there's never been direct student-on-student violence.

"You come into our house"—one of the BP jocks steps forward, pointing an aggressive finger our way—"fuck with *our* eligibility to play on *this*"—he directs his finger down—"field, and you think we're supposed to just let this shit go?"

Duke's body is angled so he's standing partially in front of me, but I'm still able to see the way his cheeks rise and his jaw stretches. The slightly dazed glaze overtaking those in front of us confirms my suspicion that he's employing his playboy smile. Most think it only works on the ladies, but the way the facial expression oozes charm can disarm anybody it's directed at.

"Puh-lease." Duke pushes his hands into the front pouch of his hoodie and shrugs. "You assholes seem to have *conveniently* forgotten how you *Grand Theft Auto*-ed my car for your little parking prank." He nods his chin toward where his G Wagon is parked near the entrance to the field.

"Hey, don't blame us for that one," comes from someone else. "This awesomeness was the brainchild of *your* girl." He holds out his phone, the aerial shot of the cars set as his screen's wallpaper.

Duke dips his chin to look at me from over the curve of his shoulder, smirking at the incorrect reference to who Savvy belongs to and the hint of amusement at her being the mastermind.

The throaty purr of a finely tuned engine revs as it approaches, cutting off whatever the next argument would have been, and we collectively turn to face the matte black Camaro driving right onto the football field.

"Well…damn."

"Oh shit."

"She had Wes bring her."

"Fuck, he's the more unpredictable of the two."

The comments continue to roll out of the BP players, the last one I assume referring to Prince and King.

The bright headlights cut through the dark of the night, blinding us enough in their intensity that most of us have to throw an arm up to block the worst of the glare.

Dust mites and such dance inside the beams of light with the gentle breeze as the car continues to idle. The low thrum of bass bumping from its speakers can be heard, the music muted with both doors remaining closed.

A hum builds at the base of my spine, and my feet shift a few steps closer of their own accord, drawn to the vehicle like a magnet.

I have no clue what Savvy could or would have said to Prince to get him to bring her here, but the way my blood buzzes beneath my skin leaves zero doubt that she *is* in the car with him. My body has always felt attuned to Savvy's, but the forced distance between us has only seemed to heighten the sensation.

The click of locks disengaging and the door unlatching sounds deafening as the group of us collectively hold our breath while the door is pushed open, the dark tint of the window preventing any of us from seeing the driver before they step out.

Beneath the door, I can make out the shadow of a foot. Other than that, there are no distinguishable features until the driver stands.

A driver a lot shorter than Wesley Prince.

A driver with hair not inky black but shiny silver.

A driver I know for a fact lacks a penis between her legs but who still might have bigger balls than any of us standing here.

Because who steps out of the Camaro?

Well, none other than Savvy King.

CHAPTER 27

"SAVVY?!" Multiple male voices call out her name.

There's a faint pleased curl to her once again black-painted lips as she rounds the open door and hip-checks it closed.

I couldn't tell you what has me more gobsmacked, her being here in the first place, her having driven herself here, or the way she looks—though it's definitely the latter that has my dick straining to wave hello.

Her long hair is tied back in an artfully messy high pony-tail, her makeup simple outside of that need-to-smear-it-now black lipstick. She has one of those black chokers around her neck, drawing my attention to the long line of her throat and making my fingers itch to wrap around it.

She has on that familiar leather jacket, her top loose and cropped beneath it, a sliver of pale toned stomach visible between it and the band of her light blue practically-painted-on jeans. More of her creamy skin peeks through the vari-ously sized rips running from the tops of her thighs and down over her knees before disappearing under those boots I'm well acquainted with.

The amount of swagger in the way one foot crosses in front of the other and the sway of her hips have my balls tightening until the moment she moves to stand in front of the OG douchebag. Thankfully for the sake of his life expectancy, the d-bag keeps his hands to himself this time as she gives him a nod and a short "Thanks."

Savvy only gives the others a cursory glance as she moves around them, pausing to share a *You good?* eyebrow raise with Duke then continuing to me like I was her mission all along.

Fire burns in her eyes as they bounce over the features of my face, the heat in them practically singeing my skin when they lock onto the cut in my puffy lip.

Her toes bump mine as she reaches an arm up to cup my cheek, her thumb stretching to ghost over the abused flesh with a gentleness that has my knees close to buckling.

What the fuck?

This is the first time she's initiated physical contact with me in weeks, and I can't resist the compulsion to reciprocate.

I slide a hand over the curve of her hip, two of my fingers threading into an empty belt loop, the others slipping into her back pocket while I trace the jut of her hip bone with my thumb. Her skin is silky smooth, if not mildly chilly to the touch.

Straight white teeth flash as she hisses through them, though I'm not sure if it's from the sight of my blood or the feel of my hands finally back on her.

Her eyes never leave mine, the purple hue dark and turbulent as she speaks. "*Who* hit you?"

I cast my gaze over her head, watching with satisfied amusement as most of the BP pricks shuffle uneasily on their feet. My mouth starts to curve upward, and the skin pulls with a sting as my split lip starts to bleed again. The pain is so insignificant it barely registers.

"You worried about me, Princess?" I can't help the tease, but even I can hear the softness in my voice.

The muscles in my back bunch as I brace myself for one of her cutting retorts, except it never comes. Instead, her teeth bite into the plump flesh of her lower lip, my dick jumping at the sight. It's such a simple move, but it's sexy as all hell.

"Did you drive?" Distracted by thoughts of all the things I would like to do to her mouth, it takes a second for her question and the concern in it to register. When it does, I shake my head. "Duke and Midas did."

"Okay." Savvy skims a hand down the back of my arm, and I've never wished I wasn't wearing a hoodie more than I do at this moment when it prevents me from feeling her touch on my bare skin. "We're leaving." She threads her fingers with mine and gives a gentle tug.

"He can't leave." The jock jerk who hit me steps forward, beefy arms folded across his chest.

"Yeah…oh-kay, Brian…whatever you say."

Brian, the moron, sidesteps into Savvy's path. I give her hand a squeeze and bury my face against my shoulder to smother a laugh.

Savvy dips her chin, mouth pressed into a flat line as she shoots me a *Like you were any better?* lip purse.

"That one can go." Brian jerks a chin at Duke. "The others stay."

"No." Savvy's tone leaves zero room for argument.

Again she starts forward only to stop because of Brian—again. "This isn't a Royal issue, Savvy."

The end of her ponytail falls over her shoulder as she tilts her head at him. I wish I could see her face because I would bet good money she's got one of her *Are you really trying to tell me what to do?* brow crinkles. I shift on my feet at how just the memory of her defiance gets to me.

"You're making it one by continuing to get in my way." She steps to the right. "Now move. We're leaving."

"No, you're not." The inflection in the way Brian speaks has me closing the small gap between Savvy and me until I'm standing behind her, having her back quite literally.

There's no missing the assessing confusion in how Brian narrows his eyes at me. He's trying to figure me, figure *us* out. *Good luck.*

"We already agreed governor boy can go—"

Duke mutters a few creative curses at Brian's choice of words.

"—why are you making a big deal about the others?"

Savvy doesn't dignify his question with a response. Instead, she spins, ponytail hitting my chest when she does, and searches the area behind us for Midas and the others. When she finds him, she tells them to go. The way Midas hesitates has me wondering if he drank the same idiot juice as Brian here, but eventually, he gestures for the others to follow.

Banks joins Duke, and together they move until they're standing beside us.

A vein of steel enters Savvy's eyes as she takes us all in at her side. She straightens her shoulders with a subtle nod, shifting marginally until her back is touching my front.

Her back expands with a measured breath. This is the feisty badass I've come to know and love.

Wait…

Love?

Whatever, you know what I mean. This is the side of Savvy that caught my attention and the reason I can't quit her.

It's fierce as fuck and hot as hell.

More than once, these fools made the mistake of thinking Savvy needed one of the other Royals with her. They failed to recognize the queen in their midst.

CHAPTER 28

YOU WOULD THINK BEING in the middle of a fistfight would be the most volatile situation I found myself in tonight, but you would be wrong.

Savvy staring down half a dozen guys with only the three of us at her back has the atmosphere so fraught with tension it's a damn miracle it's not something able to be seen with the naked eye.

She releases a sigh, and with our bodies touching how they are, I can make out a slight rattle inside her chest.

Fuck, her asthma.

A part of me wishes I didn't know about her asthma because, since the moment I learned about it, I've come to worry about Savvy in a way I haven't about anybody else before.

The most fucked-up thing about that realization is how she got *pissed* at me for doing so. I can still remember how she slapped me and called me a pussy when I let fear override my lust that day in the parking lot.

She'll have to learn to live with it, to deal with the fact that

I'm always going to worry about her, wanting to make sure she's managing it correctly because I care. It's not because I think she's weak or that her asthma makes her any less of an opponent.

No.

It's.

Because.

I.

Care.

And because I do, I reach around her side and feel around the pocket of her jacket, searching for her inhaler.

She stiffens when I find it, her blazing eyes meeting mine in a silent promise of all kinds of pain and retribution if I pull it out in front of all these people. I won't. I just needed to confirm it was in reach *should* she need it. The helplessness I felt the night she succumbed to her asthma attack is not something I *ever* wish to repeat.

Instead, I flatten my palm over the cylindrical object and press it against her side, purposely leaving my hand inside her pocket.

"Brian," Savvy says as she returns her attention to the group before us. "Is this some kind of power move? You saying who can and cannot go as a way to prove your own lineage?"

What the hell is she talking about? A quick glance at Duke tells me he's as clueless as I am.

Brian's face contorts, brows coming together, mouth turning down as an expression darker than the one he wore while we were fighting overtakes his features. This time, he makes the mistake of directing it at Savvy.

My adrenaline surges with my protective instincts. Reluctantly I pull my hand free from Savvy's pocket and slip the other from her hold. She's going to be pissed—surprise, surprise—but I step out from behind her until I'm standing partially in front of her. If this dumbass decides to act on his own poor instincts, he's going to have to go through me first.

"I shouldn't have to prove shit, Savvy." He beats a hand against his chest. "I'm from a founding family too." Another thump to his chest. "What makes *yours* more special than *mine*?"

"Nothing." It takes more than it should for me not to react to the implied *duh* she laces into the word. There are days I wonder if it's an impossibility for Savvy to resist sassing a person when she thinks they're being a dick. "But you have to stop holding it against *me* that my brother didn't ask you to roll with his crew. We're"—Savvy's arm brushes against mine as she bounces her hand between the two of them— "*five* years *younger* than Carter."

"You're still one of them," Brian says, but it comes out more accusation than anything else.

"Again…" Savvy modulates her voice like she's speaking to a child. "He's my *brother*. It's kind of hard *not* to be around the Royals when you *live* with them."

She used to live with Carter? Why wouldn't she live with her mom? Is that why she calls her mom by her name? Why is she living with Natalie and Mitchell now? What changed?

These thoughts continue to pop up in my mind like a game of Whac-A-Mole, but now is not the time or place.

Savvy's head falls back as she looks heavenward, mulling something over. I get distracted by how the move exposes the long line of her throat. It's all smooth, pale, unblemished skin begging me to mark her as mine.

For all this guy's bluster, he remains silent while Savvy thinks.

"How about this?" she asks, breaking the silence. "I'll race you for their freedom."

"What?" Brian barks out a laugh, and I whirl on Savvy like she's lost her damn mind. That's the only explanation I can think of. It's one thing for her to have managed to figure out how to drive herself the five minutes from her brother's place, but racing is not something an unlicensed driver can fake.

"Let Duke and Banks go now since you already said it was cool if Duke left." She hooks a thumb at them. "And I'll race you from here to BA for the right to finish your fight." She bounces a finger between Brian and me. "Because the way you're *really* digging your heels in on this makes me suspect you are the one responsible for Jasper's fat lip."

There are so many things happening at once that I don't even get the chance to bask in the fact that she said my name.

"I can't race you, Savvy."

"Why not?" Her voice is sugary sweet.

She does this thing where she cocks her hip out, tilts her head, and twirls the end of her ponytail like she's this innocent damsel. It's fascinating to watch when she's anything but. No...this is her luring a person who underestimated her into a false sense of security before she strikes.

"Afraid you'll lose to me?" Round and round, she twirls her hair. "I mean...it wouldn't be the first time."

"What?" Now I'm the one shouting, confused as all hell.

Savvy's smile widens until a full row of white teeth shows between her black-painted lips. "If the thought process behind it wasn't so brilliant, it would be *embarrassing* how *easily* you all believed the lie." She shakes her head as if she's the one in disbelief. "Think about it." She points to her temple then to the Camaro. "Carter's reputation as a racer started before he even had a license. Did you all *really* think he wouldn't make sure his baby sister knew how to drive?"

"But that's Wes's car," Brian counters.

"With purple under lighting, purple detailing in the paint, and a purple crown in the rear tint?" I swear the single eyebrow she arches asks, *Are you really that clueless?* "Tessa may have nicknamed him Prince Charming, but there's *no way* this—"

She struts away, not stopping until she gets to the Camaro, where she hoists herself up to sit on the hood. She eyes us from a distance, her eyes missing nothing as she takes in our dropped jaws, casually crosses one leg over the other, and braces herself with her hands flat on the hood behind her.

"—would be Wesley Prince's color scheme of choice."

Holy shit!

Savvy drives. Not only does she drive, she races.

Wait…

She said the Camaro is *her* car.

That means…

"Fuck me." My hands go to my head, my fingers curling over the ball cap covering my skull. "It was *you* driving in the races?"

The smug satisfaction on her gorgeous face has me close to coming in my pants. The only thing keeping me from going over there and kissing it off of her is the unknowns in the witness pool. The second I get her alone…

Savvy leans forward, forearms draped across her top thigh. "What's it gonna be, Brian?"

There's a lengthy pause while he debates; whether it's about racing or if he believes Savvy's claim is yet to be seen. "Let's do it."

"Perfect." Savvy claps her hands and hops off the car.

First, she instructs Duke to take Banks and go to her brother's. Then she lays out how the race will work without the aid of the typical GPS units.

Scott, the handsy one, is supposed to drive to BA with whoever else wants to go. Ten minutes after they leave, Savvy and Brian are to stick to the three main roads that lead from this side of town to the other. I'm to ride shotgun with Savvy, and if she wins, I'm free to go.

Brian and his teammate who will be riding with him head

for his Mustang in the parking lot while Savvy and I do the same with the Camaro.

Savvy never shut the car off when she arrived, so FINNEAS's "New Girl" fills the silence when I open the door.

Thankfully the passenger seat is already adjusted as far back as it can go, and I fold my legs under the dash and wait for Savvy to join me inside the car.

My eyes are locked on the way the denim of her jeans cups her ass as she stands at the open door, watching Brian walk away before she finally slips into the driver's seat. The second she does, I'm reaching across the center console, cupping her at the nape, and pulling her toward me to crush my mouth to hers.

She whimpers the moment our lips touch, and precum leaks onto my boxer briefs. Not even the sting from my cut is enough to deter me as my hold on her only tightens and I stroke my tongue inside her mouth.

Her hands come up between us and clutch the thick cotton of my hoodie. The tips of her chilly fingers brush against the hollow of my throat when they slip over the collar.

I palm the back of her head, changing the angle of our kiss and cursing our inability to take things further as weeks of pent-up lust, frustration, and longing spill out of us.

This is the moment where things officially change between us. There's no coming back from this. Fuck all the threats. I'll find a way to salvage the rest of my future. Because…Savvy not being a part of it is no longer an acceptable option. She's mine. It's time for the rest of the world to know it.

When the kiss finally breaks, we're both breathing heavily. I give a cursory check to make sure there's nothing abnormal about hers, but all seems to be fine on the asthmatic front. There's no missing the way Savvy narrows her eyes at me when she catches what I did.

"I'm fine," she huffs.

"I know." I slide a thumb over the apple of her cheek. "But

I'm not going to apologize for wanting to make sure you're okay, Princess."

Shockingly, her features visibly soften, and she nuzzles into the hand I have cupping the side of her face. This side of her is so rarely seen that I take a pointed moment to bask in it.

Her eyes fall to my mouth, and this time they narrow into slits. It's not at all typical of how she usually looks when my mouth is her focus. Even when she pretended to hate me, she could never disguise her want when locked onto the area south of my nose.

She cups my jaw and runs her thumb underneath my lip. "Of all the times to not have my gloves," she says as she stares at the blood gathered on the pad of her finger.

"It makes my dick hard when you get all feisty like that." I bring her hand back to my mouth and suck the tip of her finger into my mouth, cleaning off the blood and teasing her with an extra swirl of my tongue.

Her lips part with a gasp, her eyes flaring wide enough for me to see her dilated pupils. And because she's Savvy King, she trails a hand down the middle of my chest and palms my hard-on through my jeans, pushing the heel of her hand against my erection harder when I groan.

"Fuck, Princess."

"Not yet." Her breath is hot against my neck when she leans in and places a kiss on the underside of my jaw. "I have a race to win first."

She turns to click her seat belt home and shifts the car into reverse. She keeps slow as she backs the car off the football field and out through the large gates.

My gaze falls to how her fingers are curled confidently over the gearshift, her wrist flexing as she easily shifts into first and steers us toward the parking lot.

Her posture is relaxed, the way she's slightly slouched in the bucket seat portraying just how comfortable she is behind the wheel as she keeps her focus out the front windshield, her left hand draped over the top of the steering wheel.

"Where's your ring?" I ask when I notice the distinct lack of bling on her ring finger.

She folds her fingers down, her thumb pressing onto the naked area on the fourth one. "It has no place in my *real* life."

Satisfaction fills me with how easily she dismisses the engagement after spending weeks being subjected to watching her act like a picture-perfect fiancée.

"If the engagement isn't real, why did you come tonight?"

She pulls up along a cherry red Mustang, shifting into neutral before bringing her full attention to me. There's something unreadable in those purple pools as her eyes bounce between mine. "The engagement might not be real, but our… friendship is."

We are so much more than friends. Instead of arguing this fact, I let her have it for now. This is the first time she's admitted we are anything more than adversaries without being prompted. But make no mistake, I'll be coming for her soon. Really fucking soon.

Locked in each other's gaze, we both startle at the sound of a horn honking.

Savvy hits the button to lower the window but waits a second longer before finally turning away from me to look at the Mustang next to us.

"We're here," a voice says over the other car's Bluetooth.

"Okay…here's how we'll do this," Savvy says once the call disconnects. "You"—she points at Brian's passenger—"will honk the horn three times, and we go after the third. Got it?"

The window closes with a whirl, and Savvy shifts back, readying for the race. She hooks a thumb inside the steering wheel, her other fingers folding loosely over the top. The muscles of her thighs flex beneath the denim of her ripped jeans as she presses the clutch down and adjusts her foot on the brake to be able to quickly punch the gas when the time comes.

The transformation that overtakes her as she palms the gearshift is so complete that if I had any lingering doubts about her actually being the driver in all of her brother's races like she claimed, they would be obliterated.

Honk.

Honk.

Honk.

Tires spin until they grip the road, and then my back is slamming against my seat as Savvy tears out of the lot. She cuts the wheel to the right then jerks it to the left, kicking the clutch and executing a textbook-perfect drift onto the main road, overtaking the Mustang in a squeal of tires.

I've only ever been a driver in the street races I've partaken in, so being the passenger is a first for me. Experiencing one with Savvy as the driver sends all the blood surging to my cock in a painful fashion.

Again I find my gaze falling to the flex of her thighs, and I can no longer deny the compulsion to touch her.

I drop an arm over the console, slip my fingers inside one of the wide rips high up on her legs, and squeeze her thigh. Savvy's focus stays on the road as she drops a gear around another curve, but there is the smallest flicker to where my hand remains in an easy possessive grip.

"Your touch is very distracting."

My lips kick up, and by the way her eyelashes push closer together, I take it she's spotted my trademark smirk. "You seem to be managing just fine." The Camaro picks up more speed, and I can no longer see headlights as she makes another squealing turn.

"Years of experience with annoying passengers." The tip of her pink tongue peeks out playfully, taking any sting out of the words.

"Years?" My head lolls on the headrest as I take her in, my

thumb tracing figure eights between the frayed white strings inside the rip. "You're not even eighteen—that has you shy of the two-year mark from permit eligibility."

"I've been driving since I was fourteen and could properly reach the pedals."

I'm jolted, my gut jumping into my throat and my foot automatically pushing into the floorboard when Savvy suddenly brakes as we come upon a set of cars on the next road.

Tugging at the seat belt that locked across my chest, I smooth a finger under the Kevlar digging into me.

While my body's response was me grasping for control, Savvy remains almost unaffected as she effortlessly assesses the surrounding area before crossing the double yellow lines and maneuvering around them.

"Why doesn't that surprise me?" I ask, forcing myself to relax after her obvious display of skill.

"Because…" Her eyes slide to mine for an instant before the engine roars as she punches it into fifth gear. "Despite what you may think…you actually know me better than most."

This strange warmth blooms in my chest. Her shell has been harder to break through than vibranium. To hear her own admission that I—not Duke—could worm my way through it settles something I didn't know needed settling.

"If you've been driving that long, why does it always seem like others are driving you around?"

I'm impressed by her ability to carry on a conversation while driving when I typically can't manage more than a few grunts when I do. Racing has a way of forcing you to focus, but I guess if NASCAR and Formula 1 drivers talk to their crew chiefs, it makes sense.

When she suddenly goes silent, I pull my gaze from the scenery whizzing by to focus on the side of her face. Based on the passing landscape, we don't have long before we reach BA, and I wonder if she'll answer me before then or not.

"Carter learned to drive at about the same age as me, so by the time he got his license, he was instantly able to make a name for himself not only in the state's, but in the tri-state area's street-racing circuit."

Neither of these facts surprises me. "He does have quite a reputation."

"That he does." The light from the dash illuminates Savvy's face enough to make out the pride in how her cheeks rise. "But as you can imagine, not *everyone* was happy about some kid coming in and stealing all the glory."

Something I can't describe snakes it's way around my spine. "What happened?" The question comes out rough, my voice sounding like I've been swallowing gravel.

"A few guys saw his Corvette—a slightly older model than the one he drives now—while he was out somewhere—"

"He does have a distinct paint job," I muse.

"That we do." Her eyes rise to the rearview mirror, another smile, this one teasing with a hint of *Nice try there, buddy* in it at the sight of the fast-approaching headlights. "Anyway…luckily Wes and Leo were with him at the time, so he was fine, but he didn't want to risk the same ever happening to me."

I wholeheartedly agree.

"I get why you wouldn't openly drive the Camaro, but you don't drive at all." This is the part I can't work out in my head.

"The fact that I lived with my brother and that I could always be found with him or one of the other Royals made Carter worry people would assume I would follow in his footsteps." She shrugs.

She claimed I know her better than most, but it still feels like there's so much to unpack from this conversation. This is the second time she's mentioned that she lived with her brother, and I'm dying to find out why. Later though. Right now, I need answers about how the girl who handed me my own ass in the race was able to keep that kind of skill hidden from the outside world.

Why?

My hand spreads on her leg, my thumb slipping down the side of it to stroke the soft skin of her inner thigh, and I'm able to make out the indent left behind from the seam of her jeans. Her breathing hitches. I love that she is so responsive and that she can't hide how my touch affects her.

"To be fair…" Even her voice is huskier when she continues. "They weren't wrong."

No, they were not. Carter may still be *the* sought-after driver in the local-ish street-racing circuit, but the last two years, the Royal Camaro has quickly risen in the ranks when it comes to drawing new blood in.

"So Carter wanted to make sure they had no reason to suspect I had the skills to do so." The car slows as she downshifts, pulling into the main lot at BA and kicking the clutch again to spin us in a donut before engaging the parking brake. "There are *many* things I can accuse my brother of being overprotective about, but this isn't one of them."

While I can see the merit behind this particular issue, I can't help but wonder what other things Carter has been protective about…and just how much it affects the way Savvy lives her life.

CHAPTER 29

I'VE ALWAYS BEEN chatty when I'm behind the wheel, a condition I've tortured Wes with *a lot* given how he's always the one riding with me during races. It shouldn't really come as much of a shock that I essentially word-vomited my driving history to Jasper during the race.

What is a shock? The fact that I don't regret a single word I said.

I don't know if he believed my claim about him knowing me better than most, but again...I didn't lie. The only person I think can truly claim the top spot when it comes to all things *me* is Tessa, but that's different. The bestie bond can't be compared to the scale of a relationship. Not that Jasper and I have a relationship. Or didn't? I don't know. I'm all kinds of confused and *so* not in the place where I can or *should* be worrying about...that.

Still...

I can't help myself.

I want Jasper Noble.

I...

Oh my god. This is hard to admit, even just to myself. It makes me all kinds of triggery.

But…

I…

I… *Deep breath, Savvy.* I love Jasper Noble.

I'm *in* love with Jasper Noble.

When the fuck did that happen?

How the fuck did that happen?

Though as I watch him slap the dash, bellowing a "Fuck yeah!" as we pull to a screeching stop, clarity starts to set in.

I open my mouth to say…I don't know…*something*, but the hand clamped around my thigh tugs it until it knocks into the center console, and another grips my throat to drag me into a kiss that has my already damp panties completely ruined in an instant.

Kissing isn't something Jasper and I have done a lot of, despite all the *other* things we've done with each other—and in his case, all the things he's done *to* me—yet he somehow finds a way to make it carnal.

His teeth nip, his lips press and pillow, his mouth sucks, his tongue strokes, and his piercing whirls. One of these things can add to a good kiss, but the way he combines them all turns my brain off.

He has me in such a mess of hormones that the faint taste of blood from his cut barely registers until I see the trickle of it pooling in his chin dimple when we separate.

Like earlier, I catch the way his gaze flits down to my chest, except this time, my usual defensive impulse is absent. It might have to do with the way his kiss-swollen lips curl upward as he takes in the rise and fall of my cleavage peeking out of the scooped collar of my shirt. It's devilish.

But…

It's the subtle nod he gives as if telling himself, *Yes, that's arousal, not asthma.* It's how quickly he's learned to read the cues from my body that has my heart fluttering.

"Let's finish this." I unclip my seat belt and pat the dashboard affectionately, letting my palm slide over the surface. "Good job, Toothless."

Jasper's rumbly laughter has my nipples vibrating more than the torque of the engine. "What the fuck did you just call your car?"

I rotate in my seat, wedging myself between the door and steering wheel as much as I can, and hook a thumb at my seat back. "Toothless." I trace a nail over the green eyes stitched into the leather. "He's the dragon in *How to Train Your Dragon*."

Watching Jasper try to maneuver his large frame enough to see the matching detailing in his seat amuses me to no end. I'm also enjoying this playful, less broody side of him.

"BP Dragons, dragon name—I get it." His fingers trace along the curve of my Camaro's namesake, my core clenching at the way he caresses the leather, remembering what his touch is capable of. "You're kind of adorable for a badass."

My breath actually does stutter inside my lungs at his comment, and my cheeks heat. Holy crap, I'm blushing. I can't remember the last time I blushed, though to be fair, I don't think anyone has *ever* called me adorable before. If they did, they most certainly did not do so while also calling me a badass.

That flutter thing? Yeah, my heart is now doing it continuously.

Feeling unsteady and completely unsure of how I should respond, I open the door and step out of the car.

Behind me, I hear Jasper do the same but don't take my eyes off the half dozen awed, shocked, and some mildly aggressive jocks in front of me.

My body hums when Jasper positions himself beside me, the back of his hand brushing along mine as he leans against Toothless.

I've always found his relaxed, one ankle crossed over the

other, devil may care position infuriating but also annoyingly sexy.

"Things settled now?" I wave a hand through the air.

"Yeah." I run my tongue along the backs of my teeth at how reluctant the word sounds coming from Brian, as if it was physically yanked from his body.

"Respect." Scott hops down from his perch on his car's trunk and holds out a fist for me to bump as he rounds the vehicle for the driver's side.

Winning the race was an easy, quick fix to tonight's issue, but I can't let them leave without addressing the long-term one.

When I push off the car, Jasper straightens, his demeanor alert as I approach Brian's Mustang parked near the front of my Camaro.

Bending over, I brace my elbows inside the open driver's side window, clasping my hands together and locking eyes with Brian. Modulating my voice into the eerie calm I learned from my brother, I say, "In the future"—there's no stopping the sardonic edge from bleeding into my words—"it'll be best if you keep your hands to yourself where Jasper is involved."

"Oh *really*?" Both of Brian's brows wing up his forehead. "And *why's* that, King?"

Looks like I'm not the only one taking digs with their words. Too bad for him I'm proud as fuck about being a King.

"Because, *Salvatore*"—he's not the only one who can remind the other of their lineage; he's just the one who experiences a crisis of identity as a result—"Jasper is mine, and you *know* how I feel about my people being messed with."

Awareness flickers in his gaze because yes, yes he *does*, as he was one of the others who got the *Don't be an asshole* reminder with Gunderson.

I don't bother waiting for him to agree or respond. I don't need either. Instead, I straighten and step back from the

'Stang, watching as all my old classmates file out of the lot and through the BA iron gates.

I wait until the last of the taillights disappear into the night before turning around to face Jasper.

Holy fuckballs. Just give the man your panties because... well...fuck!

I'm rooted to the spot. The storm raging inside Jasper's pearly gaze looks ready to consume me like a hurricane as he rakes it over my body. There is such naked ownership and vulnerability in it that I don't know how to process either conflicting emotion.

Jasper doesn't wait for me to close the gap between us and reaches Toothless's front bumper the same moment I do.

A hand snags my wrist, and I'm spun, the front grill pressing into the backs of my legs.

Closer and closer, Jasper pushes in until I have no choice but to fall back onto the hood, the heat from the still-running engine warm even through the denim covering my ass.

My knees fall open in this position, and when Jasper steps between them, his massive frame looms over me. My neck arches in an effort to see him better, and I place my hands down behind me, palms flat to the hood, pressing the tips of my fingers against the mild vibration from the engine.

"You called me yours," he states simply.

I run my gaze over his face, trying to read him. I can't. It's annoying.

"I did." There's no point denying it when we both clearly heard what I said.

"You *claimed* me."

Again, it's a statement.

Again, I have no denial.

The tilt to his lips shouldn't come across with a boyish charm when they are still swollen from both our kisses and his fight tonight, but it does. It also shouldn't match with his backward hat bad-boy appeal, but it does—and neither of those things is helping the situation I have going on in my panties.

His chest brushes mine, my budded nipples poking the hardness of it as he lowers his head before burying his face in the side of my neck, inhaling deeply. "You said my name, Princess."

I nod, his lips skimming my skin. I did say his name, more than once if memory serves.

"Say it again."

Not even the demand behind the request can stop me from following through, and I expel a breathy "Jasper," my eyes falling closed when he latches onto that spot behind my ear.

He pulls back, cupping my face between his large hands like fragile glass, his thumb ghosting over the wet mark I expect he left behind with his hot mouth.

"Again."

"*Jasper.*"

His Adam's apple bobs with a concentrated swallow. Why is such a simple thing so damn hot?

"*Fuck*, Princess." The heels of his palms push into my cheeks until my lips purse, and he places a gentle kiss on them. "Do you have *any* idea what hearing you say that does to me?"

Lifting my legs, I wrap them around his waist, using the muscles in my thighs to tug his body closer, oscillating my hips against the erection straining inside his pants. "I have a *general* idea."

The way he seals his mouth over mine is almost savage in its intensity, but it's the emotion fueling it that has me whimpering with need. Need for the kiss. Need for more. Need to be closer. Need for him. Just him.

Unable to support myself against the onslaught of sensations and emotions bombarding me, I wind my arms around Jasper's neck and give myself over to him.

It should terrify me. Never have I ceded control to another, let alone willingly handed it over. It's pure insanity that Jasper is the one I choose to give it to. Here's a guy who once demanded my obedience yet has evolved into so much more than the bully he was.

Hands slip inside my leather jacket, rough palms gliding along my exposed skin, fingertips kneading the muscles of my back as they inch their way under the cropped hem of my shirt and the band of my bra.

I do a full-body roll as I undulate with the desire coursing through me.

"*Jasper.*" I speak his name in a broken whimper against his lips.

He's growling, biting along the cut of my jaw, dragging the ball of his piercing down the pulsing vein in my neck, sending an echoing beat between my legs.

"You're fucking *mine*, Princess."

"Yes," I agree on a moan.

My heart rate jumps into another gear, and I tilt my chin to breathe deeper. I didn't lie when I told Jasper physical exertions aren't my biggest triggers, but by the numbness forming in my fingertips, it's clear the emotional maelstrom I've found myself in is proving tonight is anything but typical.

Jasper's irises are like bruised pools when he pulls away, the fringe of his dark lashes lowering as his eyes narrow at the unsteady hitch to my breathing.

"When was the last time you used your inhaler?"

My mouth presses into a flat line, not wanting to answer. I hate that his mind can go there while mine is lost in a hazy fog. *Where the hell is your sense of self-preservation, Savvy?*

Jasper pinches my chin between his fingers and rotates my face around until we're making eye contact. "Answer the question, Savvy." His tone is harsh and brooks no room for argument.

"About an hour ago." *Right about the time I realized I'm in love with you.*

I choke, coughing at how clear that thought came through, *praying* he can't read it on my face.

"Are you able to use it again now?"

Removing a hand from around his neck, I use it to rub at my breastbone. "Why?" Sure, I'm triggery, but I'm still at the point where I can get myself under control without my inhaler. "I don't need it."

"Yet." His expression turns downright feral.

"What?" This time my breathing hitches for an entirely different reason.

"I said yet. Because…" He drags his thumb across my lower lip. "I'm going to fuck you."

"Here?" I squeak, casting my gaze at our surroundings.

We're parked in the back of the lot, far enough away from the road not to be seen by cars driving past and from security lights to be mostly in shadow, but…we're still in the parking lot of our school.

"Right fucking here, Savvy."

Maybe it's because I spent weeks having to hear him call me Samantha, but I love how my name rolls off his tongue.

"I've been forced to keep my distance for *too* long."

I'm hoisted up, my ass leaving Toothless a second before Jasper spins me, my back now flush to his front, officially pinned between him and my car. He anchors himself with a hand on my hip and pulls my inhaler free. He shakes it, thumbing off the cap, his action confident like it's muscle memory for him when it's not.

"The time it would take to get you to a bed is too long."

I scoff, the rolling motion in my throat making me cough. "You live on campus."

Teeth bite into my flank hard, and I hiss.

"Too far." He brings the inhaler to my mouth. "Now use

this so I don't have to worry about killing you when I fuck your brains out."

A bolt of heat shoots straight to my core, my panties officially disintegrated from lust.

I've had many people monitor when they thought I should use my inhaler, but never, *ever* has the reason been something so carnal.

I stretch forward. In my peripheral, I can make out the flare of heat that enters Jasper's eyes as they lock onto the way I bite down on the plastic lip and wrap my lips around it. *Holy shitballs.* Never in my life has medicating myself been an erotic experience. Can't say that anymore.

I lay my hand over his, holding his gaze as I depress the cylinder, inhaling deep enough to keep the chemical-tasting mist off my tongue and pause for a beat while it works its way through my system.

My eyes typically close when I go through the process so I couldn't say for sure, but the way the side of my face burns, I don't think Jasper blinks at all until he is certain I'm good.

With a small bob of his head, his arm stretches across the pristine glossy black paint of one of Toothless's rally stripes, setting the inhaler inside the divot where the hood meets the windshield. Once it's secured, a hand grips the back of my neck, and I'm shoved forward until I'm bent over my car, my cheek smooshed to the reverberating metal.

Warmth envelops me from behind as Jasper folds his body over mine, his hard-on digging into the curve of my ass.

His chest pins me in place, his hands running up my sides, over that spot in my armpits that makes me squirm to avoid the tickle. He chuckles darkly because it only makes me rub his erection more.

His hands continue their upward trajectory, stretching my arms overhead as hot breath blows across my ear. "I suggest you hold on." He bends my fingers to curl over the lip of the hood. "It's my turn to drive, Princess."

"*Jasper.*" My whisper is almost lost in the hum of the engine.

"*God* I love hearing you say that." His lips curve against my skin.

My scalp burns when he wraps my ponytail around his fist and tugs. I hiss, my neck arching from the force, and my elbows dig in as a mouth slams down onto mine.

The kiss ends as quickly as it started, our lips making a popping sound as they release.

"Get ready, baby."

The endearment makes my breath catch in a whole different way as I let my cheek rest against the hood again.

Fingertips skim my sides again until his palm flattens against me. Before I can blink, my shirt and bra are shoved to my chin, my breasts spilling free, the dueling temperatures of the chilly night air and the warm metal making my nipples bud painfully.

Large hands squeeze and knead my breasts before deft fingers pinch and tug my nipples, causing them to harden further.

I groan and attempt to squirm again but can't.

Next, leather falls like a blanket around me as Jasper flips the back of my jacket up, gooseflesh instantly coating the skin of my back but just as quickly chased away in the wake of heat shooting down my spine as he starts to kiss a path along the length of my tattoo.

My stomach caves in from the pressure of his hands working the button on my jeans open. One second my jeans are on; the next they're yanked down my thighs.

A hand splays on my lower back, and then Jasper is kneeling behind me, hooking a finger beneath the strip of my thong, the lace setting off new sparks as it traps my clit with a delicious abrasion when he pulls it to the side.

The cool air doesn't get the opportunity to chill my hot center because Jasper's burying his face in my pussy, the hand tugging my thong, splaying until his thumb breaches my ass at the same time his tongue spears my entrance.

He's not eating me—he's consuming me. Forget going zero to sixty in three seconds. No, this is him punching the gas and hitting the NOS injection simultaneously, dragging a guttural orgasm from me quicker than should be humanly possible.

I'm writhing, rising up onto my toes and dropping down in an uncoordinated pattern.

Pleasure ravages my body, but all Jasper does is continue to eat me, the barbell pierced through his tongue toying with the one in my clit.

His hand leaves my back and clutches the back of one thigh, the grip hard enough I'll probably be sporting finger-shaped bruises tomorrow.

He keeps going until I come again, my inner thighs coated in my juices. Only then does he rise to stand, one hand pinning me in place with that thumb shoved down to his bottom knuckle in my ass while he works his own jeans open. I feel his dick pop free from his boxer briefs, his hand brushing me as he rolls on a condom, then he thrusts inside me in one powerful, stretching, slightly painful go.

I cry out, the sound echoing into the dark.

Thank Christ Jasper told me to hold on because my body is pushed and dragged up and down the hood as he pounds into me even still.

"You're fucking *drenched*, Princess." A hand grips my throat, tilting my face to kiss. That situation only increases at the pleased, growly way he makes the declaration.

Pleasure dances in my clit as he yanks on my thong again, using the material to guide me into the rutting pumps of his hips.

"Ja—" I groan. "Jasper." I lick the seam of his lips. "I need —" My words break off as a guttural moan pulls from deep in my belly.

"I know, baby."

He swivels his hips, his dick hitting a spot I didn't know existed, and I detonate, the top of my head popping off and fireworks exploding behind my closed eyelids. A mini aftershock has me sagging boneless, body melting into the car beneath me when Jasper comes two hard thrusts later.

He holds himself still behind me, but I feel the faint tremble in the fingers around my throat. The fact that I'm not alone in this…intensity…this *insanity* has unexpected tears prickling in the backs of my eyes.

A hand smooths my ponytail off my face, and the gentleness of the action, as well as the featherlight kiss Jasper presses to my temple, is at complete odds with the animalistic way he fucked me and has me blinking my eyes like my lids are flipping hummingbird wings.

He pulls back, and both of us remain silent as we pull ourselves together, straightening our clothes. He smirks when I scowl at him for littering with the condom after he ties it off.

Unsure what to say with emotion choking me, I move to get back inside the car when two strong arms wrap around my middle.

Jasper pulls me into the cradle of his body, and the two of us stay like that, both leaning against the car I'll never be able to look at without remembering tonight.

He keeps his arms banded just beneath the swell of my breasts and props his chin on my shoulder.

"I meant what I said, baby."

I hum. There's that endearment again.

"I don't care what it'll cost me. I can't pretend anymore." What does he mean cost him? "You're mine, Princess."

I should say no, claim temporary insanity, and revert to keeping my distance again.

I haven't found the evidence Natalie has. Her threats are still very much real.

Yet…

The idea of staying away from Jasper hurts as much as the idea of Carter going to prison.

We have to be smart about this, though. If I learned anything from my brother, it is not to let the heat of the moment bring about an avoidable failure. We need a plan.

I run a hand along the sinew of Jasper's forearm and thread my fingers with his before stepping forward.

He easily moves with me, but one of his dark brows is raised to touch the edge of his hat in question.

Pushing onto my toes, I press a sweet kiss to his lips, pointedly giving another to the split in the bottom one before dropping back down.

"Will you come with me to my brother's?"

CHAPTER 30

THE RIDE to Carter's place was spent in silence. It wasn't necessarily an uncomfortable one, but it was charged none-theless.

Jasper's hand stayed on my thigh, his fingers threaded inside the strings of the frayed denim. I'd deny how much I liked it, but I don't want to. I like it...a lot.

I know why I was quiet, and let me tell you...it's quite a list.

First, I was in the midst of dealing with the aftermath that comes from a *major* realization—i.e., figuring out I'm in love.

Second, most of my brain cells are still currently melted from Jasper fucking me like an animal.

But the thing that has the few brain cells capable of working spinning is the barrage of fallout scenarios brought on by my actions tonight.

Carter is going to be…

Welp, honestly, I'm not sure I could even guess what he's going to be like.

Then there was Jasper…quiet, stoic, couldn't-stop-looking-at-me-while-I-drove,   oh-crap-I-love-you-how-am-I-supposed-to-tell-you Jasper. I wish I could read his thoughts. Maybe if I had that skill, I wouldn't be such a basket case worrying about how he feels about me.

Maybe you should write him a note. Do you love me? Check yes or no.

Gah! Look at me. When did I turn into this girl? The one who worries about if a boy likes her or not?

I ease off the gas when I pull onto my brother's property and take the long way around the cars parked in the large lot before finally hitting the button that will open the garage door.

The fluorescent lights connected to motion sensors click on as the door rolls back, and I pull into one of the empty spots amongst the rest of the Royal fleet.

My movements are robotic as I engage the parking brake and hit the button to turn off the ignition. The sudden silence that descends in the absence of music playing and an engine purring feels claustrophobic.

"Princess?" I turn at the sound of Jasper's voice, his astute eyes missing nothing as they take me in. "Unless you're planning for round two, we should probably get out. Though"—his chin dimple gets deeper—"if that *was* your plan, we *should have* parked somewhere that isn't owned by your brother."

While the two of us have proved we *excel* at car sex—both inside and out—he's got a point. Carter would straight-up murder him.

I did see Duke's G Wagon out in the lot when we drove through it, so while I'm happy to note the playboy can follow directions, it's more the fact that there aren't any bodies strewn across the floor waiting for us that pleases me most. That *should* be a good sign of what's to come.

Jasper takes my hand once we're both out of Toothless, and there's no missing the pointed way his thumb rubs the space of my missing ring.

He's so damn pleased with himself it's a fight not to have an outward reaction. There's no point encouraging his inner alphahole.

Except when he lifts my hand to place a gentle kiss to the spot, I give in and give him what I'm sure Tessa would describe as a moony smile. I'm not exactly sure what that looks like, but my face feels different than ever before.

I'd panic if it didn't seem like Jasper was suffering from the same affliction. Thankfully the softening around his eyes and the pinch to my knuckles as he squeezes them between his makes all those pesky symptoms wash away.

I stretch a thumb up to rub at the inside of his wrist, and with a lovesick smile still on my face, I take a step toward the basement door.

THWACK!

My arm is yanked and practically wrenched from its socket. Stumbling backward with the force, I lift my opposite arm to that one's shoulder and turn to ask Jasper, "What the fuck?" only to come face-to-face with my brother.

Oh fuck.

Nostrils flaring, mouth a nonexistent line, vein pulsing in his temple, eyeball twitching—he's *seething*.

He's shaking out his right hand when I finally get a peek at Jasper and see the blood that finally dried around his lip is once again flowing free as he grips his jaw, working it side to side.

Freeing my hand from his, I slide in front of him. "Stop!" I shout and slam my hands onto my brother's chest to keep him from going after Jasper a second time.

"What the fuck, Savvy?" Carter's voice is an echoing boom inside the garage, the harsh tone reverberating in the vast space.

Well…shit. Seething may be too tame of a word to describe him as his chest heaves and bumps me, his shoulders rolling back as he uses the full extent of his height to tower over me.

Jasper coils an arm around my middle and tries to pull me behind him, but I only dig my heels in and widen my stance. Sure, if he really wanted to move me, he could do so easily. He has proven as much a multitude of times—though thinking about how he manhandled me into Duke's G Wagon the first time he fucked me on school property is wholly inappropriate at this moment.

Carter pauses, his gaze taking in Jasper's protective move. It takes a beat, but eventually, his head tilts to the side as the pieces start to come together.

Natalie loves to call Carter "nothing but a common thug," but what she fails to see is how utterly brilliant he truly is. His ability to assess a situation and pivot if needed is unparalleled.

"You done?" I quirk a brow, my tone less than pleased.

"Don't"—a finger stops a millimeter from my nose, my eyes crossing to see it—"you even start, Samantha."

I hiss, my eyes narrowing demonically. It's the *worst* when he calls me that. "How about"—I smack the hand out of my face—"*you*"—I poke him—"don't, Carter Anthony."

"You're annoying," he complains, but I see the chink in his armor.

"And you're an overprotective ass, but I love you anyway." I pat him on the chest. Behind me, Jasper snorts. "Don't *you* start either, because you're just an ass."

That maddening smirk is quick to bloom on his stupidly handsome face, and it seems my recently discovered feelings haven't made that urge to smack him disappear. *Interesting.*

"You love me anyway." Jasper shrugs, throwing my own words back at me. Carter, proving his own assness, barks out a laugh.

"I do."

Er…say what now?

Did those words really just come out of my mouth?

Based on the way Carter's laughter has abruptly cut off and the *What the fuck?* slow blink he's giving me, I say yes... yes they did.

Holy shit!

A vise squeezes around my lungs and a cold sweat breaks out along my skin, and oh my god, oh my god, oh my god.

You gone and done it now, Savvy.

I didn't mean to say that. Why did I say that?

Holy crap, who is this person? Since when am I a neurotic mess? I'm Savvy King. I own my shit. I don't act like a chickenshit.

Except...

This is my first time experiencing love. Sure, I love Tessa, my brother, and the Royals...but that's different. This thing with Jasper? It's the first time I've really had to deal with feelings bigger than myself.

I'm just...not sure I'm capable enough or ready to handle something like this given all the other shit I'm currently dealing with.

Maybe I can play it off like it was just a figure of speech?

Yeah, yeah, that's a good plan.

But then I get a look at Jasper.

His smile is unrestrained, eyes lit up like it's the first time it's actually reaching them. I let out a gasp at the sight only to have it swallowed by his mouth when he snaps an arm out and snatches me by the nape.

Carter grumbles in the background, but I ignore it, not letting anything ruin this moment.

Jasper's fingers spear into my hair, probably destroying my ponytail more than he already did earlier, but again...I don't care.

I push up onto my toes, my body fusing with his, my arms locking tight around his neck, holding on for dear life as our kiss deepens. If I'm doing this, I'm going to do it with the savage intensity and vigor I'm famous for.

"Damn right you do, Princess," Jasper says against my lips, but I'm too dazed from that kiss to chastise his cocky ass.

Keeping with the theme of acting out of character—for both of us—Jasper tucks me against his side with an arm hooked over my shoulders while I wrap an arm behind his back before we give our attention over to Carter.

My brother runs a hand across his mouth then grabs at the back of his neck. A giddy zing zaps through me because I do so love catching the king off guard.

Huh? Guess that's something else I have in common with Jasper since he seems to live for knocking me off balance. *What a jerk.*

"You just had to go and complicate an already fucked-up situation, didn't you, Savvy?" Carter accuses.

I shrug beneath Jasper's heavy arm. It's not like it was a choice or anything. You can't help who you fall in love with. Well…shit. Guess I've absorbed more of Tessa's hopeless romanticism than I realized.

In one long stride, Carter gets in Jasper's face, the tip of one of his vintage Jordans stepping onto the pristine white of Jasper's Uptown without apology. "You hurt, fuck with, or *ever* disrespect my sister again…there won't be *any*where on this planet you could go that I wouldn't find you. You feel me?"

I hold my breath, both not to choke on all the testosterone clogging the air and because I'm not entirely sure how Jasper will react.

"I'm pretty sure if I ever did her wrong, Savvy would be more than capable of doling out her own punishment." *Damn right.* "Stop holding your breath," he chastises, cutting into my preening.

"And you'll do best to remember that particular detail

about our little savage." With that, Carter turns on his heel and calls for us to follow him into the basement.

"Booyah!" Tessa throws her arms in the air and dances in her seat as soon as we step inside the basement. "Suck it, Chuckie." She makes double finger guns, sound effects and all, before using both arms to rake in a massive pile of poker chips.

A quick glance shows that with Chuck's loss, they'll be able to combine both tables into one.

Chuck groans, burying his face in his hands. "It's already weird that I spend my poker nights with a minor, Tessa. Can you *not* make it worse by saying things like that?"

Used to the antics between these two, most of the room chuckles but doesn't comment. Key word there: most.

Duke, my dear, sweet, doesn't know how to heed a warning fake fiancé slides into the free chair next to Tessa and drops his arm around her, batting his baby blues with his hand propped on his fist. "I'll take you up on that offer."

Oh, stupid, *stupid* boy.

In a flurry of movement, bodies swarm around Tessa. Wes is the closest and shoves Duke clear out of his seat, while JT, two more Royals, and two star players for the U of J—one football, one basketball—glare down at the cocky playboy sprawled on the ground.

"I tried to warn you," I singsong as I pass him. "Should have listened, boo."

"Whoa, whoa, whoa, whoa." Wes snags my wrist, stopping me. "And where did you disappear to, *ma reine*?"

I chance a glance at Jasper, the amusement from Duke facing the metaphorical Tessa firing squad fading with a flattening of his mouth when he hears what Wes calls me.

"I had a Salvatore to straighten out." I slip myself free and finish closing the distance to the freezer to pull out one of the gel ice packs.

I wince when I make it back to Jasper; his lip is starting to resemble an open pomegranate after the latest hit to it courtesy of my brother.

Jasper hisses when I press the pack to his face and mouth "Sorry" as his hand comes up to cup the back of mine to help me hold it in place.

"Wait…" Duke calls out, still on the floor like a turtle stuck on its shell. "That asshat's last name is Salvatore?"

"Mmhmm," I answer but keep my eyes locked with Jasper's, enjoying the ball of warmth that forms in my gut as we silently communicate.

He's an idiot, his chin dip says.

He's your *friend*, the press of my lips returns.

He's your *fiancé*, the roll of his eyes volleys back.

Touché, asshole, the suck of my teeth answers, letting him have the final "word" as he blows me a kiss.

"I totally called it," Tessa screeches.

Yeah, I'm in for one hell of an *I told you so* conversation in the very near future.

"How does a person with Salvatore for a last name end up with *Brian* as a first name?" Duke muses, finally jumping to his feet, hands held out in front of him as he slowly backs away from the macho show of force glaring daggers at him.

"It's his maternal grandfather's name." Chuck is the one who answers.

A hand slipping over the curve of my waist brings my attention off those giving a small Blackwell history lesson and back to Jasper, dropping my forehead to rest against his chest.

Stomping footsteps have the majority of us looking toward the basement stairs, and I jerk upright at the sight of two uniformed police officers entering the room behind Leo.

What the hell?

Everyone from Blackwell—me, the Royals, Tessa and JT,

Kay, and on and on—whip around to the one person who should be able to shed some light on the new arrivals.

"Mr. King," says the one leading the charge as he approaches my brother, and more than one person in the room snorts at the formality.

I am *not* one of them.

Nope, instead, I'm freaking the fuck out.

I clutch the sides of Jasper's hoodie, using him as my anchor because it feels like I'm about to live out my worst nightmare.

"Johnson?" Chuck ambles over from his seat at the other poker table. "What seems the be the problem?"

"We got a report about a possible kidnapping, Mr. Mayor."

"What?" Jasper whispers, but I shush him, going as far as putting a finger across his lips while my heart trips at the word *kidnapping*.

"This is a joke, right?" Carter asks, his gaze jerking to Jasper. "Is BA pranking BP alumni now?"

"What?" Jasper stutters out a laugh only to cut it off when he gets hit with the full weight of the Carter King glare.

"I'm sorry, sir, this isn't a joke. We received a call from a Mrs. Natalie St. James that you're holding her daughter Samantha here against her will."

Oh my god.

No, no, no, no, no.

What is she doing? I've done *everything* she's asked. Why is she going after Carter now? And kidnapping? Fucking *kidnapping*? Is this bitch for real?

Jesus Christ, if I thought I was going to give myself an asthma attack worrying about Jasper before I even realized the depths of my feelings, this right here is a prime contender to flip that switch.

Jasper kneads his way up the length of my spine until he's gripping my nape, grounding me in the here and now while Carter, Chuck, and both officers confer with each other.

Releasing my hold on Jasper, I move to my brother's side. If ever we needed to present a united front, that time is now.

"I'm not here against my will. I *live* here," I inform the officer. Though it may not necessarily be *true*-true at the moment, I'm not really worried about semantics.

Officer Johnson takes note of Chuck's clear lack of concern about the accusations against my brother before turning almost regretful eyes my way. "I apologize, Miss St. James, but your mother was adamant she has sole custody of you and that you are still a minor."

Goddammit.

I had to go and have a late birthday.

I'm so over this woman messing with my life.

CHAPTER 31

AFTER AN ABRUPT *WHAT in the actual fuck?*-type ending to last night's festivities, I am no closer to figuring out what happened now than I was when I finally fell asleep sometime around four in the morning.

Thanks to the lack of sleep, my eyes feel like sandpaper and my head pounds like I went on a bender even though I didn't have a sip of alcohol.

Rolling over with a groan, I grab my pinging phone to shut off the incessant noise, only to smile at the messages filling the screen.

PRINCESS: The Momster is out running up Mitchell's credit card bill, so I'm taking advantage and granting myself parole.

PRINCESS: Before our night went to shit…

PRINCESS: Oh god! I'm going to KILL Tessa because this is ALL her fault.

PRINCESS: Word of advice…DON'T let your best friend infect you with her diabolical ways. Though with Duke, I guess you should be more worried about that fuckboy infecting you with something more venereal.

I may be tired as a motherfucker, but the rambling nature of Savvy's texting is so unlike her I can't help but laugh.

PRINCESS: Anyway…I know we both said some things last night and never really got to discuss what they might mean.

PRINCESS: Jesus! *GIF of a girl banging her head against a desk* I sound like such a girl right now.

That one has me full-on belly laughing, and I'm thumbing a response even while those three dots blink with yet another message being composed on her end.

ME: I happen to like that you're a girl. Your pussy is one of my favorite features on you.

PRINCESS: Oh I bet it is.

ME: Oh, Princess…you have NO idea. The way it squeezes my dick when you come is like it's trying to squeeze the life out of it.

PRINCESS: Are you trying to get me to sext you right now?

ME: I wouldn't be opposed to it.

If I needed proof of just how much I'm not, my aforementioned dick perks up further at the suggestion.

PRINCESS: Of course you wouldn't. *eggplant emoji* *donut emoji*

ME: Oh yeah, baby. Talk dirty to me. *tongue emoji* *cat emoji* *peach emoji*

PRINCESS: I'm not engaging.

ME: What if I told you that despite your pussy being sweet, sweet heaven, it's your mouth that's my favorite part about you?

I tap my fingers on the back of my phone, grinning to myself like a crazy person. I know *exactly* where her mind will go, and I'm twitchy anticipating my next chance to throw her off balance.

PRINCESS: I find that hard to believe, seeing as how, despite your best efforts, I've YET to kneel for you.

The image of her on her knees has me palming my growing morning wood through the cotton of my boxer briefs. There's no denying that is a visual I can't wait to experience in real life.

ME: You don't need to be on your knees to choke on my dick. I can be creative. But…no, that's not why I have a thing for your mouth.

Could I have told her the reason in the same text? Sure, but baiting her is half the fun.

PRINCESS: No? Okay…I'll bite. Why?

ME: *GIF of a man covering his junk* Mind the teeth, Princess.

PRINCESS: You're an asshole.

See what I mean? She's so fun when she's feisty.

ME: *guilty GIF*

PRINCESS: God, you're annoying, and I have places to be.

If she could see the way I'm grinning, she would probably smack me.

ME: You DO know YOU were the one who texted first, right?

I can't help myself. It's a sickness.

PRINCESS: A detail I'm severely regretting right now. But, anyway…the reason I did was to tell you I'll be here most of the day if you wanna roll through.

The next message is a web attachment for a place called The Barracks, and any other smartass comment I was about to make dies before it can finish forming. This is the first time Savvy has invited me somewhere. Going to her brother's yesterday doesn't count.

No, this moment is monumental. It's proof we really did turn a corner last night.

Scrolling back through the message thread, I see where she brought up the declarations we both made before the conversation took a turn. Not that I'm complaining.

The important thing to take from it is that she's acknowledging it. That means more than most when it comes to people like Savvy. Even I'm not dumb enough not to realize that.

It wasn't difficult to convince Duke and Banks to take a field trip with me. All I had to do was point out that if Savvy was spending her Saturday at a cheerleading gym, it was most likely the one Tessa and Tinsley cheer for. It was like shooting fish in a barrel.

Despite what I saw when I clicked on the link Savvy sent for the place, The Barracks is much more impressive in person. Mind you, this is coming from a guy who has gone to some of the nicest private schools in the country. Hell, the arena at BA rivals that of some of the top collegiate programs, yet this gigantic warehouse-style building still manages to have the three of us whistling in appreciation as we approach.

The parking lot is packed with cars of all shapes and sizes. Still, it's easy enough to spot the familiar matte black Camaro, would be even if it weren't parked between a light purple and a candy pink Jeep.

"Holy shit," Duke whisper-hisses when we step into a trophy-filled lobby.

Other people are milling about, but they are secondary compared to all the silver and gold megaphone-topped trophies in various heights and sizes featured on shelves adorning multiple walls.

"Can I help you?" asks the woman working the front desk.

Pulling my gaze off the plaque on one of the weird little glass-globed trophies—*who knew there were world championships for cheerleading?*—I close the distance and explain why we're here.

The way she seemed to know precisely who Savvy is without her being one of the cheerleaders has me remembering how often I've heard her talk about attending Tessa's practices. It's probably why she never seemed all that bored when she would watch our hockey practices.

We follow the directions past a huge pro shop, pictures of current and past NJA teams and staff, and a few closed doors until we come to the set of stairs we were told would take us to the family viewing areas. We bypass the lower one filled with parents and smaller children and head directly for the one on the top floor.

I look around the smattering of parents also in this one, searching for Savvy. She's easy to find; the silvery strands of her hair stand out under the gym's bright lights in the messy bun they are tied in.

She's über-casual in a pair of black leggings and a hooded sweatshirt. Her face is resting on her arms, which are folded on the ledge overlooking the gym below, but the way her lips are moving tells me she's still carrying on a conversation with those sitting around her.

A bunch of their faces are familiar from my short stint at Carter's yesterday—like the massive guy in the backward hat to Savvy's right, Mason Nova—but it's the U of J Athletics hoodies that make most of the others recognizable.

When she turns to backhand Travis McQueen on her other side, her eyes lock on mine, and that mouth of hers curls upward. She rises from her seat, mushing McQueen in the face and causing him to fall back in his seat dramatically, his back arching, arm splayed out wide, the other U of J athletes in the row behind them cheering and chortling.

"You came." Her hands go into the front pouch of her sweatshirt as she stops a few inches from me.

Not liking the distance, I hook an arm behind her back and hoist her to me, her front plastered to mine. She wiggles, attempting to create some space, but can't manage thanks to how I have her arms trapped by her sides with her hands still being in her pocket.

"I could get used to you being at my mercy, Princess." I steal a quick kiss because I can, grinning when she lets out a growl.

"I hate you."

My hold tightens as she struggles anew. "No you don't." I bring my free hand around to pinch her chin and lift that defiance-filled gaze to me. Fuck does her spark make my dick hard. "If I recall correctly…it's actually the opposite." I pull her lower lip down with my thumb, the urge to suck the soft flesh into my mouth strong.

"I don't know…" She attempts to shrug. "This morning's conversation might have me reevaluating that claim."

Lifting her up, her feet kicking my shins as they flail in the air, I walk us over to a back corner of the room and cage her in against the wall. She's glaring as I let her feet touch the ground, not that I care.

Gripping her throat, I tilt her chin and stretch my thumb up to staple her lips closed before she can argue.

"Now you see…" I keep my gaze trained on her mouth pillowed beneath my finger. "You distracted me earlier before I could tell you why this mouth"—I press against it—"is my favorite thing about you."

Beneath my fingers, her throat moves with a swallow. Releasing her lips, I run my thumb along the lower one, groaning when the tip of her tongue connects with my skin as she licks her lips.

"This mouth"—I bend until my eyes are directly in her line of sight—"is my favorite because of the way you can use it to put people in their place, even if one of them is me."

Savvy blinks. Then blinks again.

Her eyes flare wide enough for a full ring of white to be visible, and not gonna lie, I kind of love that I've surprised her.

A beat of silence passes, and then both her hands come up to cup the sides of my neck, and she's pulling me in for a kiss. It's sweet and so fueled by love I feel it in every beat of my heart. *Fuck!* Who the *hell* am I? Swear to god if you breathe a word of this to the guys, I'll slice your throat with my hockey skate.

I'm not sure how long our impromptu make-out sesh lasts, but it's long enough for her lips to be puffy and her breathing to be labored to the point that I pause to assess it.

That only gets me an eye roll before she links her hand with mine and leads me over to where she was sitting when I arrived.

She taps Travis McQueen to move to the other side of Mason Nova and goes back to watching the cheerleaders below like she never stopped.

I settle in next to Savvy, one eye on her, another on the ladies dancing and flipping across the blue floor.

"Short Stack is really putting them through the wringer today." I think it's Travis that speaks, but I'm not versed enough in what these people sound like to know for sure.

"This is nothing." Savvy's head falls to lean on my shoulder as she turns. "Just wait until Kay and JT get to the stunting clinics after the Admirals' practice."

A voice booms from below, and the way Mason chuckles makes me suspect I'm not the only one who thinks it's amusing that such a big sound can come from his tiny girlfriend.

It's not much longer before the practice comes to an end and Tessa and Tinsley are joining us, both collapsing on the floor in front of us.

"I love my brother…" Tessa's words come out choppy, all out of breath.

"But when he and Coach get together, it's like it's their mission to make sure we can't walk the next day?" Tinsley completes her thought.

"Ding-ding-ding." Tessa mimes ringing a bell then groans as she stretches out her legs.

"I have a question." Duke leans forward, pushing his way in closer from the row behind me, and raises his hand like he's in class.

"Why doesn't that surprise me?" Savvy says dryly.

"You wound me, pudding pop—OUCH! The fuck, Noble?" Duke rubs at his arm, trying to rid himself of the pain I delivered with a well-placed punch.

The ladies ignore Duke, carrying on like he isn't causing a dramatic scene.

Tessa weakly lifts a foot to nudge Savvy's leg. "I thought they called you Princess or something."

"I tried that," Duke explains, and Tessa gives him a *Go on* hand roll. "Only Jasper is allowed to call her that." He jerks a chin at me while Savvy gives him the hairy *Shut up* eyeball. *Interesting.*

"Something you're not telling me…" I pause, letting my mouth hitch, then finish, "Princess?"

One of those uncommon blushes blooms, and she buries her face in her hands, muffling her answer. After a second prodding, she whips her head around, that fire back to blazing in her eyes as she grits her teeth and mutters, "That's your name for me."

Fuck, this girl knows just where to cut so it slices to the deepest part of me. I tried to break her, but it becomes clearer and clearer every day that *I* was the one meant to fall to his knees.

Feeling…something, I give her an out by asking Duke what he wanted to ask in the first place.

"I was curious"—he circles a finger in the air to include everyone seated with us—"is this like an athlete exchange program?"

"Is it your mission in life to be the most ridiculous person ever?" Tinsley huffs. With each week that passes, the once shy, skittish Little Miss Scholarship fades more in light of the support of her friendship growing stronger with Savvy.

"I seriously question how I can like you given your choice of best friend." Shocker—Savvy is giving me shit.

"Guess it's a good thing you love me then, huh?"

Oh, listen—another one of those growls.

"WHAT?!" Tessa's ear-piercing screech has more than a few of us knuckling at our eardrums. "YOU DROPPED THE L-BOMB AND DIDN'T TELL ME?"

"Jesus, Tess."

Knowing the pain of having a dramatic, over-the-top person chosen as your closest friend, I wrap an arm around Savvy and tuck her against my side. I delight in the way she snuggles in deeper as Tessa gets distracted from her love crusade by answering Duke about why a chunk of the U of J football team's captains are at a cheerleading practice.

Unfortunately, our reprieve doesn't last long, and Tessa starts to lob question after question at Savvy. When that doesn't work, she tries her hand at me.

"If you two"—she Vs her fingers to point at both Savvy and me—"are making my heart all a-pitter-patter"—she flutters her hands over her heart—"by no *longer* denying your feelings…"

The emphasis and the pointed look she shares with Savvy makes me suspect this wasn't a one-time discussion. Nope, I take it I may have been the topic of conversation more than once. You're damn fucking right this pleases me to no end.

"What's this supposed to mean for the Momster's plans for your betrothal?"

"That bullshit is over." Now it's my voice that's thundering off the rafters. I don't care. Last night Savvy claimed me, and it's time for me to do the same. "Savvy is mine."

Tessa faints onto Tinsley like she's swooning from my statement. Savvy mutters something about her reading too much, and I'm in the best mood I've been in in a while. Until…

"What about your dad's threats?" Duke asks me, and when Savvy turns cunning eyes my way, it's an effort not to slap him.

Dad is an issue I'm going to have to deal with eventually, and I will. For now, solidifying my relationship with Savvy seems the most prudent because, without it, the upcoming battle ahead would be pointless.

"Threats? What threats?" Gone is the sleepy, relaxed girl

beside me; in her place is the badass who showed up to the BP football field last night.

I could lie, feign ignorance, but that'll only piss her off. Instead, I hold nothing back. I give her all the details, starting with the agreement Dad and I made that I would be allowed to pursue hockey as long as I returned to work alongside him afterward to carry on his business.

Except for slightly similar coloring, I haven't seen a considerable resemblance between Savvy and her brother, but when I get to the part about how Dad showed up at the dorm because somebody sent him pictures of the two of us, that sure as hell changes. That fierce-as-fuck full persona transformation must be a King trait.

"Someone…sent your dad pictures?" Each word is spoken slowly and with distinction. "Of you and me?" Savvy's finger bounces between us.

I nod. "After the engagement announcement hit the papers."

"Son of a bitch," she curses and slides her gaze to Tessa, who's doing her own nodding.

"Probably the same person," Tessa says out loud, as if finishing the thread of a silent conversation. "It was the same week your Momster got sent hers."

"Your parents were sent pictures too?" She nods. "Did yours?" I ask Duke, who shakes his head in the negative. This doesn't make sense. Too much doesn't add up. "And knowing we were…involved, your mom and Mitchell didn't want to call an end to the engagement?"

Savvy lets out a derisive snort. "Yeah right. I honestly wouldn't be surprised if you told me this whole thing was Natalie's idea to begin with."

Possibly, but I have a feeling my dad played a part in its conception as well.

"She'll do *anything* to be seen as the most important person. I have *no* clue why Mitchell married *her*, but

I *know* she married *him* for his money and his political aspirations. To be the *wife* of the possible future vice president of the United States is the ultimate feather in her cap. This"—she bounces a finger between her and Duke—"is just her attempt to give her even more of a connection. What better way to be connected to POTUS than having her daughter married to his son?"

Here's what I still don't get. Savvy has always been adamant that the engagement was nothing more than a joke to her. Hell, she even went as far as to make sure I knew she and Duke were only playing along and none of it was real. We made major strides last night, but we'll never fully be able to move forward until I understand all the reasons *why*.

"What would happen if you called off the engagement?"

"You mean besides her calling the cops with bogus kidnapping claims?"

I wondered what all that was about last night, but things happened too fast for us to get any details. After Savvy left with the cops, we didn't stick around to hang. With the hostile greeting I'd received from Carter when we showed up, I figured it was probably best for my self-preservation not to be around him without his sister around.

But to call the police and claim your son kidnapped your daughter when it's obvious to anyone with half a brain how close they are...who does that?

Savvy lets out a humorless chuckle when she catches sight of the expression contorting my face. "I have no idea what set her off, but last night was her way of proving to me that she's not making idle threats. I'm the puppet, and she's my puppeteer."

"You're *nobody's* puppet, Princess." My hands curl into fists thinking of that vile woman messing with what's mine.

Savvy's resigned sigh kills me. "Maybe not." She shrugs, but there's a defeated slope to her shoulders. "Still doesn't change the fact that I'm stuck playing her games until I find the evidence she claims to have against my brother."

"Carter?"

Fuck, this woman is her own brand of nasty. She's not threatening Savvy directly. No, because that wouldn't work. Instead, she's preying on my girl's innate sense of loyalty. If I didn't find what she was doing to her own *daughter* by threatening her *own* son deplorable, I'd be impressed by her ingenuity.

Savvy goes into more detail about Natalie's threats and her attempts at finding anything she could be hiding, only to yield nothing.

She threads her fingers with mine, but her expression grows more haunted the longer she speaks.

At one point, I have to reach over and rub my hand up and down her back in an attempt to calm her down when her breathing turns erratic. She's working herself into a panic over having to continue to hide our relationship now that we've steered into something more official, but things are different now.

For starters, we're not pushing each other away or denying our feelings anymore. And for real, shoot me now, because now I'm the one who sounds like a girl.

We also both know all the players involved, making it possible to come up with a proper game plan.

"I'll talk to my dad about putting an end to the engagement." Duke's offer has Savvy's jaw dropping. It shouldn't. The way he readily agreed to play along with her ask should have been enough proof for her to see how loyal he can be to those he cares about.

"You will?" Savvy's voice cracks at the end of the question.

"Yeah." He reaches up and runs a hand through his hair before jerking his chin in my direction. "The only way to keep J's dad from following through on his threats is if he believes it won't hurt him with voters. What better way to accomplish that than coming from the governor himself?"

"You think it would work?"

Duke teeter-totters his hand in the air. "Fifty-fifty."

Savvy doesn't seem to like those odds, but even if it were a zero percent chance, I still wouldn't give her up.

"Stop worrying." I reach up and cup the side of her face, curling my fingers around to her nape. "So what if my dad cuts me off?" I swallow down the panic the thought inspires. "Let him. I don't give a fuck." Lies, but I'll figure things out if that happens. Hockey is my endgame anyway. He can try, but he'll fail if he tries to keep a college from recruiting me. "You're mine, and I'm not giving you up now that you *finally* admitted it."

Savvy folds forward, pressing her forehead to my shoulder. "Even when you're saying sweet things, you still manage to let your inner asshole shine through."

I chuckle and crush her to me, going as far as pulling her from her seat and into my lap. "Really feeling the love, Princess." Her arms wrap around me in response. I'll take it.

"Not to break up this kinkfest you two have going on—" Duke interrupts.

"Kinkfest?" Tessa asks with a giggle.

"Yup." My best friend preens like a peacock, only to have one of the U of J guys tug him back by the hood of his sweatshirt. "These two"—he shakes off the warning about watching himself and waves his hands at Savvy and me like a game show host presenting a grand prize—"love to trade barbs as foreplay." He pretends to shield the side of his mouth and stage-whispers, "Kinky fuckers."

The *pop-pop-pop* of more than one set of knuckles cracking at Duke's constant flirting has him lowering the playboy charm a little bit and refocusing on Savvy. "You're going to have to find a way into your stepdad's safe. Chances are good that if Natalie has anything she's hiding from you and you haven't found it yet, it's because it's in there."

Good point. I've seen how Natalie is with Mitchell; it's like she's an entirely different person. I'm sure if she asked him to store something in his safe, he would do it without issue.

"How do you know he has a safe?" Savvy asks.

"Guys like our dads *always* have a safe," I confirm. "Now all you have to do is find it and get the combination."

"Because that's easy," she grumbles.

"Well buckle up, buttercup." Duke claps his hands together. "Time to come up with a plan."

CHAPTER 32

WHEN YOU LIVE in a place you consider more your personal prison than your home, having people over to hang out at it is a weird experience. The strangeness of it is not doing any favors for my already jumpy nerves.

Tessa, Tinsley, Duke, Jasper, Banks, and I have officially commandeered the penthouse's main living space. Natalie may have sneered and turned up her nose at our *juvenile* evening plans, but I caught the pleased gleam at how I'm finally (in her eyes) spending time with "appropriate" associations.

Cushions, pillows, and blankets have been rearranged to create a communal chill space in the once artfully arranged living room. Each of us are spread out in our own little cocoon of comfiness while we work our way through watching part of the *Fast and Furious* franchise. These boys think they're funny with their movie selections.

Off to the side, we set up a snack bar filled with enough sweets and treats to give a person a stomachache just by looking at it. And yes, before you ask, I've been self-medicating by eating my body weight in Swedish Fish.

Not Tessa. While I've used my inhaler more times than I would like to admit this week, my bestie has been living her best double agent life. She's embraced every plotting session with a zealousness that puts even some of her most extra moments to shame.

Remember how I said we shouldn't allow her and Duke to be in the same room as each other? Well, if there was *ever* any doubt regarding the validity of that statement, it was proven tenfold when the two of them tried to convince us to repel *Mission Impossible*–style from the ceiling into Mitchell's home office.

Today's snooping is just the next step in a plan we've been working on executing for the past week, though it's the one I'm struggling with the most.

Mitchell's home office was the one place I hadn't ventured into in my search for the evidence Natalie claims to have on Carter. For some reason, it felt fundamentally wrong to invade such a personal space. One of the things motivating my guilt about it is that it feels like it's a violation of his trust when he's been nothing but nice to me.

I've also been struggling with justifying *why* he would knowingly participate in Natalie scheming against her children. There's just too much to unpack there.

In the end, my love for my brother won out over any conflicting feelings toward my stepfather.

Despite Tessa's romantic suspense-loving heart, I am *not* a master spy or safecracker. Still, that didn't stop her from forcing us to watch *The Italian Job* as part of our "preparation". As hot as Charlize Theron is in that movie, I wasn't able to pick up any skills that would help us in this endeavor.

Thankfully, though I'll deny it if asked, Jasper's choice of a best friend came through in the clutch.

"Here." Duke hands me a long, skinny velvet box, the kind typically used for necklaces.

"What's this?" Instead of answering, he prompts me to open it. "Holy shit!" I whip my gaze back to his. He has to be joking, right? Nestled inside the cream-colored satin is an obscenely expensive diamond and sapphire necklace.

Even now, the memory of being in possession of such a valuable piece of jewelry makes me jittery.

Once I got over the shock of Duke carrying seven figures' worth of precious jewels around school like it was nothing more than a key chain, I got my wits about me enough to lay into him.

"Are you out of your fucking mind?" I snap the lid closed and thrust the box back at Duke, but he refuses to take it.

"It's debatable." He shrugs without a care in the world.

At one point, I made an offhanded comment to Jasper about how I wish I could channel Duke's carefree nature, to which he responded by dragging me into the nearest empty room with a lock and made me come until I forgot anybody's name but his.

My not-so-secret-but-not-quite-public boyfriend has a possessive, jealous streak longer than the Jersey Shore.

When I asked Duke where he got the necklace, he told me it was another heirloom passed down in his mother's family.

Carter and I grew up firmly in the upper middle class. Dad's position at Royal Enterprises made it so we never wanted for anything, and the same should have been true after his untimely death. That said, the draw of a multimillion dollar life insurance policy was too much for Natalie to resist, and thus began the downward spiral of our family.

The type of wealth Duke and Jasper come from is difficult for me to comprehend. Technically I'm now in that same faction with Natalie's marriage to Mitchell, but with how I've essentially been playing one role after another since I first walked through the penthouse doors, none of it has felt real to me.

Any time I've attempted to question Duke about the progress he'd been making with his dad concerning our engagement, I've been met with one of two responses.

One, Duke will tell me to focus on the issue I have to handle on my end.

Two, Jasper will take over and either kiss or fuck me stupid. Tessa accused him of trying to keep me dickmatized, and as soon as he learned the meaning of the word, it was like he took it as a personal challenge.

Neither of those things has helped me feel any better about what is about to go down once Natalie and Mitchell leave for the conveniently arranged dinner with the Delacourtes.

Five minutes after the elevator doors close with Natalie and Mitchell behind them, the timer Tessa set on her phone goes off, and the *Mission Impossible* theme song blares from the speaker. *Smartass.*

"All right, Bitchy." Tessa jumps, literally jumps in a spray of blankets from her spot on the floor. "Let's do this."

An unexpected laugh bubbles out of me watching her frog-march toward the entrance hall. Most days it's a miracle we paired ourselves up in our unconventional friendship over a decade ago. She always manages to bring light to my life, and right now? I desperately need that light.

"You ready for this, Princess?" Jasper runs a thumb across the backs of my knuckles.

With Natalie nearby, I couldn't snuggle with my boyfriend —that isn't proper when one is betrothed—but Jasper sat close enough that with each of our arms stretched out, we could hold hands beneath the blankets.

I swallow thickly. "No," I admit. "But let's do this anyway."

Jasper pushes up to stand and holds a hand out to help me as the rest of our group rises to their feet.

"Go team!" Tessa cheers, arms extended overhead, fingers wiggling in exaggerated spirit fingers.

"Have I told you yet today how much I like your friend, peaches?" Duke drops an arm around my shoulders and hooks a thumb back at Tessa. A second later, he's doubled over with a grunt from the elbow Jasper jabbed in his side with a *Hands off what's mine* growl.

I turn in Jasper's hold, my hands coming up to curl over the biceps straining the sleeve of his black T-shirt like I'm about to use his arm to do a chin-up. "You did." I walk backward to keep my eyes locked on Duke. "But you also *obviously* forgot about the warning you were issued last weekend."

After enduring listening to Duke's constant flirting at The Barracks, Tessa's "brother" contingent sat him down—rather forcefully, I might add—and told him in explicit detail what would happen to him should he play games with Tessa.

Surrounded by four hulking football players, a towering basketball star, and an overprotective male cheerleader used to tossing girls over his head on the daily, it finally started to sink in that I wasn't kidding when it came to Tessa, though in the end, I was still credited as the biggest threat.

"Nope. I'm good." I can't help but chuckle at the way Duke curls his hands into fists to hide the tips of his fingers. Mason may or may not have told him about my suggestion for how to handle Kay's ex-boyfriend.

"Battle stations, people." Tessa claps her hands, rallying the troops.

Jasper leans down to whisper as I turn around under his arm. "She's insane."

"I know." I beam with pride, which only has him shaking his head.

After recalling the elevator, Banks and Tinsley take it

down to the lobby. They will be our first set of eyes just in case any of the parents decide to leave dinner early.

Then Tessa will linger near the entrance foyer by the elevator with the hope to stall any early arrivals for as long as possible.

Duke will serve as our last line of defense, taking a post right outside of Mitchell's office.

With any luck, though, Jasper and I will be in and out of the office, the evidence finally in hand, before anyone returns to the penthouse.

Everyone assumes their position.

I pause, hand hovering over the brass doorknob.

You're doing this for Carter.

With a deep breath, I peer over my shoulder at Jasper and, at his nod, turn the handle and step inside.

This is only the second time I've been in Mitchell's home office, the first being the other day when I played my part to learn where he keeps his safe.

Here's the part I have to credit to Duke.

The necklace was our Trojan horse of sorts. It didn't take any acting on my end when I asked Mitchell if he had a safe place where we could store the necklace until the *hold on, let me clear my throat* wedding. The two hours the thing was in my possession were two of the most stressful hours of my life. I know it was unreasonable, but I swear I kept looking over my shoulder for potential muggers.

Natalie, as expected, lost her shit on sight. She *oohed* and *aahed*, gushing about how clearly right she was about suggesting Duke and I be paired together. Not gonna lie, it was weird as fuck for her to look at me with any kind of pride. Too bad it only came at the expense of me being traded like prized cattle.

"Princess?" Jasper's voice has me once again blinking back to the present, and my gaze automatically focuses on my reflection staring back at me in the large wall of windows across from the door.

Right. We're here on a mission—time to do this thing.

Shaking off my reservations, I move across the smooth gray tiles and over the plush lighter gray area rug in the center of the room. I remember thinking the other day how different Mitchell's office is than I would have expected. Still, the refined-but-homey vibes do a lot to help settle my nerves as I round the polished black desk and reach for the book that will open the hidden section of the built-in bookshelf behind it.

There's a soft click, and I wrap two hands around the edge of the shelf and pull to guide the case until it's fully perpendicular to the steel safe door.

Again a memory washes over me in a wave, this one of the almost boyish smile my stepdad gave me when I exclaimed a whispered "Whoa" as he did the grand reveal the other day.

"Cool, right?" Mitchell chuckles as I continue to gape at his Indiana Jones–esque setup.

"Please tell me you have a hidden passageway I haven't discovered yet."

"Unfortunately, no." A twinkle of mischief takes root in his gaze. "But maybe that's a deficiency we could look into rectifying." The moment would be sweet if it wasn't tainted by subterfuge as I move to stand at the proper angle to see the sequence of numbers Mitchell punches into the keypad.

Warmth meets my back as Jasper moves into place behind me. An arm comes around me before the anchoring weight of his hand splaying over my belly infuses me with the courage I need to carry on.

I curl then flex my fingers, hand suspended in the air, willing myself to plug in the code.

I close my eyes and lean back against him.

I need to push through the guilt.

I'm doing this for my brother. But more importantly, I'm doing it for *me*. I'm sick of Natalie coming in at the eleventh hour thinking she can control my life. No more.

"What if we don't find anything?" I voice my biggest fear.

"Then we pivot."

I wish it felt as simple as it sounds.

"I got you, Savvy." Jasper covers the back of my hand and guides it the rest of the way to the keypad. "Whatever is in there…we'll handle it…together. You're not alone in this." Lips ghost across my temple. "You've *never* been alone in this."

My eyes grow hot as tears burn at the backs of them. He's right. It's a fundamental truth I let the fear Natalie instilled cause me to forget.

I'm done.

Done letting her win without realizing it.

Done letting her try to rob me of the family who loved me when she failed to.

This is my moment.

I can do it.

My palm is sweaty, and I curl my fingers down, rubbing them against each other to wipe away the moisture before typing in the code that could lead to my freedom. Each beep of the six-digit combination feels heavy like the toll of a gong. I don't realize I was holding my breath until the air rushes from my lungs in relief when the electric whirl of the locks disengaging sounds.

Another glance over my shoulder at Jasper, and I turn the handle and step to the side to make room for the heavy door to swing open.

The safe is made up of four shelves. I ignore the bottom one with the gold bars and stacks of banded money and the top one with the necklace and other boxes filled with valuable jewelry and a selection of watches. This isn't a heist. Instead, after taking a picture to remember the proper placement, Jasper and I pull every piece of paper, document, and folder from the middle two shelves and set them in piles on the floor to go through.

The passports are easy to distinguish with their navy blue covers, as are the birth certificates and Social Security cards. There are also a handful of signed contracts, but they mean nothing to me.

The hope I had diminishes with each item we survey without finding anything useful.

I pick up the last manila folder from my pile and unwind the string coiled around the fasteners with a heavy heart.

Bracing myself to start over from square one, I pull the two pieces of paper tucked inside free.

Right away, I notice the logo for a genetics lab at the top of the page, and my first thought is, *Is Mitchell sick?* Does he have some kind of disease or disorder he'll need treatment for?

With weird frantic energy, I quickly scan the rest of the page only to come to a full stop at the bold words in the center of it.

PATERNITY TEST CERTIFICATE

What?

Mitchell has a kid? Where are they? Why haven't I met them? Or heard about them?

The sound of crinkling paper fills the silence when my grip tightens enough to wrinkle it inside my hold as I read more.

By order of Mitchell St. James, we were requested to perform a paternity test. The following individuals were examined.

There are sample numbers, and next to the column for *Alleged Father* is Mitchell's name, followed by his date of birth.

Wow. He really does have a kid. Or at least I'm assuming he does if he held on to the test results.

The idea of having a possible stepsibling sends an unexpected flurry of excitement through me.

Until…I get to the name in the column next to the one titled *Child*.

Samantha King

What?

Why is *my* name on this?

This has to be some kind of joke, right?

Except…

That's my birthday listed next to my name.

What the fuck?

"What is it?" It isn't until Jasper is crouched at my side that I realize I spoke out loud.

I don't respond. I don't think I'm capable as the words start to swim and blur in front of me.

What the hell?

What the hell?

What the hell?

My mind spins, trying to comprehend.

What does this mean?

Why would Mitchell run a paternity test on the two of us?

My chest grows tight, and I start to wheeze.

A hand grips the back of my neck and grounds me enough to see that there are no answers for me on this current page, and I throw it away. Where it lands, who the hell knows.

RESULTS

Yes, this is what I need. Except the first thing listed is a table of letters and numbers that might as well be hieroglyphics for all the clarity they provide.

My pulse starts to race to the point that I fear my heart might explode.

What does this mean?

What the hell does this mean?

I need answers.

I spear a hand into my hair and tug until the sting of pain brings my world back into focus.

CONCLUSION

I swallow, my throat tighter than it was a minute ago, and I read:

Based on our analysis, it is practically proven that Mr. Mitchell St. James is the biological father of the child Samantha King.

NO!

There's no way.

What?

Why?

How?

A coughing fit overtakes me, and the room starts to spin.

I think I'm going to be sick.

No…

Wait…

I *am* going to be sick.

Scrambling to my knees, the floor hard and unyielding as I crawl across it, I make it to the little garbage can just in time.

What the hell is happening to my life?

CHAPTER 33

"OH SHIT!" I hustle to follow Savvy, getting to her just as she starts to toss her cookies.

I take the time to gather her hair to hold it away from the danger zone before I reach into my pocket for her inhaler, sending up a silent thanks for having had the intuition to bring it with us. I have no clue if throwing up is a symptom of her asthma, but I'll be damned if I don't take the necessary precautions.

"Baby." I flop back onto my ass, pulling her to sit between my spread legs once her retching tapers off into dry heaves. "Tell me what to do."

I smooth more hair away from her face, her skin clammy and deathly pale. I can feel the rattle inside her lungs, and there's a slight tremble to her body as she curls into the fetal position against me.

Something is very, very wrong here.

"What happened, baby? What did you find?"

She shakes her head violently, eyes squeezed so tight only the tips of her eyelashes are visible.

I tug her closer, bending my knees, scooping her to sit in the deep V my legs form, and cradling her against me. She's floppy like a rag doll, as if all the fight has left her body. This is *not* my strong badass, and if I weren't panicked with the thought of her ending up in the hospital again, I would be out of this room hunting down those responsible for trying to break her, even if that person ends up being her mother. I don't give a fuck. You don't mess with what's mine without suffering the consequences.

Fuck! What did she find? Why didn't I read over her shoulder?

Nudging her with my free hand, I hold it up, palm extended, and offer her inhaler. She takes it and uses it without protest.

I lose my balance when I try to adjust my position, my hand slipping on a piece of paper discarded on the floor.

With one eye on Savvy, whose eyes are closed again, her breath tickling the skin of my throat with puffy exhalations, I pinch the paper between my fingers and turn it over. It takes a few seconds for the words to process, but when they do…

Holy fucking shit!

From Savvy's reaction, there's no way she knew this before today. Given what I know of her family, this type of information has to rock her down to her core.

Crumpling the paper into a ball, I toss it away as if it's to blame for my girl falling apart.

I have no idea what to do here. I want to rage, to punch something in defiance of the helplessness coursing through my system.

The possessive bastard inside me struggles with not being everything Savvy needs. But as a silent tear cuts across her ruddy cheek, my pride will have to take a back seat if there's somebody, *anybody* that can help ease her pain at this revelation.

Savvy needs Tessa, and then she needs her brother. She

needs to surround herself with all those who love her uncon-
ditionally while she's forced to wade through this unknown
territory.

With an arm around her back and another under her
knees, I stand, her arms weakly looping around my neck as I
carry her bridal style out of the room.

I don't bother putting the last of the safe's contents back,
nor do I even close it.

After what we discovered, I doubt us breaking into the
safe will be Mitchell's greatest concern.

CHAPTER 34

"PRINCESS?"

I jump when a warm, calloused hand cups my cheek.

I blink, the action painful like sandpaper against the puffiness I can feel around my eyes.

Slowly Jasper's concerned face comes into focus. His pouty lips are turned down, his chin dimple extra prominent in that way it gets when his jaw is clenched hard, and there's a deep furrow running between his brows. His typically pearly eyes have darkened closer to that charcoal hue, and his hair is disheveled in a way that makes me suspect he's been continually raking his hand through it.

With a bent knuckle, he wipes beneath my eye and frowns harder at the tear clinging to his skin. His eyes bounce between mine, and then with a heavy sigh, he unclicks his seat belt and unfolds himself from his Ferrari.

I don't remember getting in the car, let alone driving anywhere. I've been so lost inside my head.

While I'm sure it only takes seconds for him to round the

hood and open my door, it was long enough for that mental fog to take over again.

My door is open, and Jasper is crouched in front of me with his hand gripping my thigh by the time his voice brings me back. "Baby…you're scaring me."

The endearment and the admission cut through to my already bruised heart. Jasper Noble is the most formidable opponent I've ever encountered. He's the type of guy to come to…not necessarily enemy territory, but we'll call it that for simplicity's sake, and issue a challenge to its leaders. He doesn't *get* scared. *Right?*

In a daze, I lift my gaze to look over his shoulder, and… we're at my brother's?

Carter?

The tiny fissures in my heart crack all the way open, and it splits in two, anguish making me cry out and double over.

Distantly I make out the sound of someone cursing, and then I'm airborne. The familiar scent of sandalwood fills my nose, and comfort has the weak way my muscles tensed falling lax.

Completely drained, my eyes fall shut, and I bury my face into the skin bared above the collar of his T-shirt. *T-shirt? Where's his jacket? It's freezing outside.*

The telltale beeps of the outer door sound, and somebody must have used a key to let us in because I don't remember hearing the bell ring—though there is the distinct possibility that it did and I missed that as well because the next thing I know, there's another set of beeps and warm heat envelops us, chasing away the gooseflesh coating my body.

"Tessa? What are you—"

"Savvy?"

"THE FUCK IS WRONG WITH HER?"

Voices and shouting have the arms holding me tensing, and I squeeze my eyes closed tighter and turn inward as much as physically possible.

Again without being jostled once, I feel myself being lowered and realize Jasper must have sat on the couch.

Fingers brush the side of my face before curling around to cup the back of my head.

I squint against the light, and that furrow between Jasper's brows is even more profound than it was before, if that's possible.

"Wha—" My words cut off, my voice rough and husky like I've smoked two packs a day for twenty years, a feat in and of itself seeing as I don't smoke for obvious reasons and haven't even been alive for eighteen years, let alone two decades.

"I brought you to your brother's." The regard and compassion in Jasper's tone are almost enough to have me breaking down again. "If you need to talk to anyone about what we discovered, it's him."

"Not the bitch keeping secrets?" There's no keeping the contempt I feel from coating my words.

There's a minor twitch to Jasper's mouth, and the return of his good humor, however slight, has more of the fog dissolving. "No. Carter is your *family*. That's what you need right now." The way he says it tells me all I need to know. He gets it. He gets me.

When I finally move my gaze off Jasper, I see my brother is sitting on the coffee table, legs spread wide, elbows resting on his knees, and he's leaning in as close as he can get. Wes is on his right and Leo on his left. Swiveling my head around, I see Lance and Cisco standing behind the couch.

We're surrounded by Royals.

"*Oh my god.*" I choke on a sob. "I was right." The sudden realization is enough that if Jasper wasn't holding me in his arms, I would melt into a puddle of goo on the floor.

"Right about what, Princess?" Jasper coaxes while Carter's knee starts to bounce from holding himself back.

"I'm not a *real* Royal." Sobs rack my body, and tears fall in a steady stream down my face.

"What the fuck is she going on about?" Carter's voice booms.

The couch moves as Tessa plops down beside Jasper and me. "Do you think she needs the snake?" she asks someone.

"The *snake*?" I think that was Duke.

"No...well...maybe." I'm pretty sure that was Wes.

"It might not hurt." That came from Leo.

A box of tissues breaks into my field of vision, and I follow the arm holding it up to see Tinsley's face and give her a grateful but watery attempt at a smile.

"Somebody...*anybody* better explain why my sister is crying like someone died. Right. *Fucking*. Now." *Ooo*, the scary Carter King voice has made an appearance.

Guess that explains why I could never really pull it off. I'm not actually a King.

"I'm not a real Royal," I say again. "I'm a faux Royal."

"How many times do I have to tell you to knock it off with that shit?" Carter's dirty blond brows are a harsh line across his face as he levels me with *that* glare.

Will he love me half as much when he learns we're only half-siblings?

"How can I be a Royal if I'm not a King?" We'll pretend for a moment that Cisco and Lance aren't from outside families.

"What?" All the color drains from my brother's face. Oh my god, it's already happening. He's already starting to love me less.

"Dad isn't *my* dad," I explain, that knife from earlier spearing deeper, carving out another part of me.

My whole life has been a lie. *I'm* a lie.

"You know?" Carter breathes, his voice barely above a whisper.

I'm nodding before the words themselves register.

Wait…

Did he say…

No. He missed a few words. He meant to ask me *How* I know…right?

Because if not…that means…

"*You knew?*" I screech and jackknife up; the only thing keeping me from taking a header to the ground is Jasper's strong arms hugging me backward.

No.

No, no, no, no, no.

Just…no.

I misheard. The events from earlier have *clearly* caught up with me. I'm having a delayed adverse reaction to using my inhaler.

Yeah…

Yeah, that's it.

There's no way the person who taught me all about trust and loyalty, my *closest* confidant, my *brother* would keep something this *crucial* from me.

Nope. Not possible.

But the way his head falls forward and both hands come up to grip the back of his neck prove otherwise.

Oh my god.

He knew.

He knew, *and* he didn't *tell* me.

Oh my god.

An elephant sits on my chest, and razor blades slice into my lungs every time I inhale.

"When?" I mentally plead that Jasper, Tessa…*some*one called him on our way over and told him.

"The night you were hospitalized."

I suck in a startled breath, gagging on it. Every cough it sets off is like a blow to the ribs.

"Two months? You *knew* for almost *two* months and didn't *tell* me?" When a fresh wave of tears strikes, I don't bother to wipe them away. Instead, I clutch at Jasper's shirt, the cotton wrinkling and stretching out from my grip. He doesn't seem to care about how it's getting soaked and possibly covered in snot.

"Savvy—"

"Don't." I throw up a hand.

"I'm sorry," he finishes.

"I said don't," I whimper.

I…

I can't be here.

This place that's been my home, my sanctuary against the world, the home base I always come back to is tainted by betrayal.

Never…NEVER would I have expected something like this from Carter.

Sure, we both kept some stuff to ourselves recently, but they weren't anywhere near this scale of importance. And we came clean—

"Wait!" I flail about as I suddenly shout. "Is *this* why you were weird with me? For *weeks*? Why I felt like *you* were *avoiding* me?"

The sorrow filling his gaze as he lifts his eyes to mine would normally flay me alive, except I'm already drowning in agony.

Carter opens his mouth to speak, but I cut him off before he can. "You know what?" Physically I don't think I could handle what he has to say. "I don't want to hear it."

"Savvy," he tries.

"No. I can't."

My grip on Jasper tightens, but he doesn't flinch when my nails scratch at his skin. He's remained silent, but he's been fully present, helping keep me together even when it doesn't seem like it.

I tug and do my best to stretch closer to Jasper. "I want to go."

To where, I have no clue. Carter's is always where I go when I'm upset. This is my safe space. Was—it *was* my safe space. Not anymore. At least not right now.

"Princess…" Jasper's eyes shift to my brother as if he's unsure what to do.

"*Please?*" I'm not above begging. I need out.

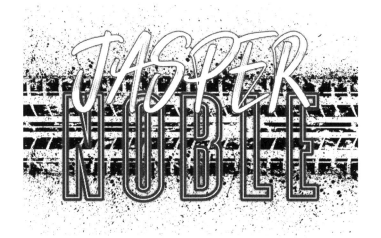

CHAPTER 35

BROKEN IS NOT a word I would ever have associated with Savvy, but the way she's shut down on me, stone silent, vacant stare, practically unmoving, I'm worried that is what has happened. What's worse is I'm not sure how to fix it.

She cried.

She begged. My girl *begged*.

I brought her to the one person who was supposed to make her better, and it backfired in spectacular fashion.

That's how we ended up outside my dormitory at BA. Bringing her here is most likely a mistake, but what else was I supposed to do? When I tried to put her in Tessa's Jeep, thinking being with her best friend would be best, she only clung to me like a baby koala.

The cold night air bites at my skin, but things like worrying about forgetting my jacket back at the St. James seem insignificant in comparison.

"Brother." Duke is at my side the second he's parked his G Wagon, eyes tracking to my Ferrari then back to me. He doesn't need to say it.

I shouldn't have brought her here.

We could be spotted together. Pictures could be taken. While we haven't gotten confirmation, we have a pretty good idea who's been sending photos to our parents. After the day at The Barracks, all the pieces started to come together. The timing of them is too suspect for it to be anybody else.

Do I give a fuck? Not a single one.

I move to go around Duke, but he puts a hand up to stop me. I give him the *bruh* eyebrow, his hesitation bringing me up short more than the physical barrier.

"Dad called."

I jolt backward, my back slamming against my Ferrari. "When?"

"Just now." Again his gaze goes to my car, or more importantly, the passenger still inside it.

"What did he say?"

"Well…" Duke rocks back on his heels. "He was surprised to find us gone given what I asked him to talk to Mitchell about."

Wow. With everything else that happened, I completely forgot that while we had our own mission to help Savvy against Natalie, Duke had sat down with his dad about the engagement.

A rock forms in my gut, and my muscles tense in preparation. The outcome of that dinner could very well render the threats on my end null and void. Why is it I'm more anxious about getting Savvy inside than I am about learning what happened?

"I didn't get a chance to ask how dinner went before Mitchell was taking the phone and demanding to know where Savvy was, if she was okay, and if she had her inhaler with her."

They must have gone into his office once they noticed we were gone. It would only take a few seconds for him to realize someone had been in there and *what* they learned. It was also an easy connection to *who* that someone was. My respect for Savvy's stepdad—well, I guess *dad*, biologically at least—goes up a few notches due to his concern for her health.

"What did *you* say?" I need to know if I'm going to have to shield Savvy from another family member tonight. While it's obvious Mitchell's heart is in the right place, I don't think Savvy is in the right headspace to be faced with the man himself so close on the heels of learning the truth about him.

"I told him the truth." His eyes meet mine, worried he did the wrong thing. I shake my head, because of course not. "I said she's with us, that you did make her use her inhaler but her asthma seems to be under control now, but I also thought it was best to give her the night away to not trigger her worse."

I'm nodding. Okay, this is good. At least I know we have until tomorrow to regroup. I still have no clue *how* to help, but I'll figure it out.

"For what it's worth—" Again, Duke reaches out for me to stop, and again I do. "It seems like Mitchell actually gives a shit about your girl."

Again...I nod but don't say anything. Things didn't go at all like I expected at Carter's. I'll reserve the right to pass judgment for now.

With a jerk of my chin, I give the order to move out.

I don't bother trying to coax Savvy out of my car. I just scoop her into my arms and carry her to where Duke and Banks wait to hold the door open for us.

Thankfully the dormitory seems quiet, and we don't pass any other students on our way up to our floor.

Once inside our suite, I bid a silent good night to my guys and head straight for my bedroom.

If I wasn't already aware how out of it Savvy is, her lack of comment about the fireplace and man cave–like setup of our common room would have done it.

I kick my door shut with my heel and reach back to turn

the lock before sitting on the edge of my bed with Savvy settled in my lap. I'm not the only one who forewent a jacket —hell, she doesn't even have shoes on, and her skin is chilly to the touch. Quickly toeing off my sneakers, I pull back the covers on the bed and slip us both beneath them.

Extending an arm behind Savvy's head, I maneuver her around so she's snuggled tight to my side, rubbing a hand back and forth over the clingy cotton of her long-sleeved shirt.

She molds herself to me more, the tip of her cold nose bumping my throat, her arm banding around my middle when I move on to rub at her back, my hand slipping beneath the cropped hem of her shirt as I do my best to share my body heat.

Even her toes have an icy edge to them inside her socks when her legs tangle with mine. It all adds up to yet another way I failed my girl tonight.

I'm not sure how much time has passed, but it's enough for a little cocoon of heat to have formed beneath the blankets when she finally whispers, "He knew." The small, broken way the statement comes out hits me like a crosscheck. "He knew, and he didn't *tell* me."

I band my arms around her like a vise, her body rocking into mine. "There had to be a reason, baby." I may not know...pretty much anything about Carter King outside of his reputation, but still, I know with complete certainty that he puts *no one* above his sister. If he held off telling Savvy about her bio dad, there most *certainly* was a reason for it.

"It hurts." She sobs, and another knife of pain slides between my ribs.

"We'll get through it," I promise. It's another in a long line of them I've been making to her, but fuck if I don't mean every single one.

Oh, how the mighty have fallen. At first, it was slow, so slow I didn't even realize it was happening, but the moment I decided Savvy was mine and *only* mine, something elemental changed inside me.

Fuck the consequences.

Fuck anyone who tries to break us apart.

We can face and conquer any obstacle that gets in our way because we have each other. I used to think caring for others was a weakness. It wasn't until I met Savvy that I saw that those same people, those same strings you tie yourself with could also be your greatest strength.

"Make me forget."

The unexpected plea causes my brain to stutter. "What?"

One of her legs comes up, a foot hooking over my hip, and tugs, shifting my weight enough to roll me onto my side and partially over her as Savvy falls to her back. "I…can't…" Her elbows dig into the tops of my shoulders, her forearms flattening to the back of my head, her hands spearing into my hair, tugging on the strands. "If I think about this any more, I'll go insane. Make me forget."

"Savvy…" She can't mean what I think she means, can she?

Lips press to the underside of my jaw, and a bolt of heat shoots down my spine, drawing my balls up tight. "*Jasper.*"

Fuck me. When she says my name…

Laying a forearm on the pillow beside her head, I balance myself while I shift my weight, her legs automatically falling open to create more space for me. The grind I do against her center is almost involuntary.

"Only you…" Both her legs wrap around my waist, her feet locking at the small of my back, and now it's her body undulating against mine. "…make me forget anything that's not *you* inside me."

That's it. I'm done. The last of my control disappears like it never even existed. A part of me feels like I'm taking advantage of her at what is probably her most vulnerable, but fuck if I can deny her. Besides…this is Savvy King we're talking about. If I'm taking advantage, who better to put me in my place than her?

Despite the animalistic urge to plunder and claim, I gently lay a hand on the side of her face, curling my fingers around her head and angling it before sealing my mouth over hers.

Our kiss is languid but ardent. The tip of my tongue traces the seam of her lips and slips inside when they open automatically for me. There's the slight saltiness from her tears, and I do everything in my power to replace it with the taste of me.

She may have asked me to help her forget, but my girl never has been, nor will she ever be a passive lover and gives as good as she gets.

Both her clothes and mine get discarded on the floor.

Her hands are back to yanking on my hair as her wet pussy glides along my bare cock.

"*Fuck*, Princess." I hiss, barely restraining myself from thrusting inside her as another roll of her hips has the ridge of my dick's head bumping along the swollen nub of her clit.

"Please, Jasper."

Smoothing a hand up the back of her thigh, I grab on and anchor her to me for another grind, gritting my teeth against the wet heat coating my length. "Are you sure?"

Her hair brushes my cheek with her nod. "I need you."

The automatic way she answered eases the last of my doubts, and I stretch an arm out to fumble inside my bedside drawer for a condom. Once that's taken care of, I return my hold to her leg, hiking it higher on my hip, and grip her at the nape with my other hand, bringing my forehead to hers.

I wait.

A deep inhalation brings that familiar scent of lime I've come to crave, and I wait for another beat until finally, her eyes meet mine. Then and only then do I ease my length inside her tight sheath.

For the first time ever, we take our time with each other.

Not one thing is hurried despite the emotional maelstrom that was the lead-up to it.

Our bodies are perfectly in sync.

Our breaths controlled and even, gradually building to a crescendo of panting gasps.

The rhythms of our hearts match from a steady beat to a thumping pulse.

Sweat slicks our skin as we cling to each other.

At one point, I pull one of her hands from my hair and link it with mine, my fingers threaded with hers as I extend her arm overhead and hold on.

One pump turns to two, which turns to three, and soon enough, what was once a smooth cadence evolves into us chasing release.

Over and over, I rock into Savvy, her legs squeezing around me at the same time as her pussy walls contract around my length.

In and out and in and out.

I bury my face in the curve of her neck and groan as her orgasm triggers mine.

I'm filling the condom close to bursting, licking up the vein pulsing at the side of her neck, dragging the ball of my piercing along it, grinning at her gasp before another clench of her cunt renders me too stupid to do anything but love her body the way she needs.

Her eyes are heavy when I pull out of her, already falling closed as she turns into my pillow when I get up to take care of the condom.

Tying off the latex, I dump it in the garbage can near my desk and pull on a pair of boxer briefs so I don't have to free-ball it to the bathroom for a wet washcloth.

Savvy barely stirs when I return and use the cloth to help clean her. Absentmindedly, I toss it aside and climb back in bed beside her. The way her body automatically molds to mine as she curls into me has a smile touching my lips, but not as much as the softly murmured "I love you" as she drifts off completely.

"I love you, too," I say into her hair before kissing the top of her head.

When I woke up this morning, I knew our relationship would change; I just never expected how much.

CHAPTER 36

A SOFT KNOCK on my bedroom door pulls me from the half awake, half asleep state I've been in for the last twenty minutes while listening to the steady rhythm of Savvy breathing.

Tucking my chin into my chest, I double-check that the sound didn't disturb her. Once I confirm she is still, in fact, blissfully asleep, I ease myself out from under her octopus-like hold and replace my body with my pillow for her to cuddle with instead.

Even closed in sleep, her eyes remain puffy and red from all the crying she did last night. *Fuck!* She cried. My girl broke down in a major way, and the only person she wanted was me.

I pull on a pair of gray sweatpants and am tugging a BA Hockey tee over my head when I open the door and slip out of the room before easing it closed behind me with a soft click.

I glance up and catch Duke's clenched jaw a second before my gaze tracks past him to Mitchell St. James standing in the middle of our common room. Well shit. Talk about a wake-up call.

Running a hand through my hair, I curse to myself. I had hoped I'd get the chance to talk to Savvy alone, to check in and see where her head is at before we needed to deal with anybody else. Guess that's not going to happen.

"How is she?" is the first thing out of Mitchell's mouth when we make eye contact. Again, my respect for him grows because Savvy and her well-being are his first and automatic concern.

I don't answer right away, pausing to take a beat and consider how best to answer his question. "Health-wise?" He nods. "She's fine." I pause again, yet Mitchell doesn't rush me. "Other than that, though...I don't know." I glance back at my closed bedroom door like I can see through it to the girl I left sleeping behind it.

"I didn't want her finding out this way." He slides his hands into his pockets, and it's then I notice how casually he's dressed in a pair of dark-washed jeans and a white polo.

I'm not sure if there would have been any way for Savvy to learn the truth about her paternity that wouldn't have set her off, and I tell him as much. The downturned corners of his eyes give away just how painful a realization that is for him, and there's a part of me that feels it's wrong that *I'm* the person he's having this conversation with.

Savvy already feels betrayed. The last thing she needs is to think—however mistakenly—that I'm also in cahoots against her.

I grip the back of my neck, forcing myself to take a breath, pause for a beat, and allow any anger I feel on behalf of my girl to level out. My temper has been known to get me in trouble—look at how I reacted the night Savvy was hospitalized if you need an example or two. Now, here with Mitchell, is not the time to let it win.

"To be honest..." I wasn't necessarily waiting for permission to speak, but I let Mitchell give a small nod regardless. "Your biggest challenge isn't going to be that you're her father or that you knew and didn't tell her." I move until I'm standing in front of him, my arms folded across my chest. "It's that you told *Carter…months* ago."

He runs a hand down his face, letting out a heavy sigh. Thanks to Mitchell's close relationship with Governor Delacourte, I've had many chances to be around him since Duke and I became friends. The man standing in front of me now? He's not the same as the one I knew before he became my girlfriend's stepdad—bio dad, or whatever you want to call him. No, this version looks like he has the weight of the world on his shoulders if the way they slope is any indication.

"That's not *exactly* how that played out," he admits.

Again…this feels like a betrayal. This conversation is quickly treading into dangerous territory for me. I chance a glance at Duke hovering at the counter that houses our Nespresso machine and indicate for him to make me a cup of coffee too. I'm going to need a hit of caffeine if I'm going to have any hope of surviving this day.

A bone-deep exhaustion is the only thing to which I can attribute me not sensing her before a raspy voice asks, "Then how did it play out?"

Three sets of eyes snap to where a sleepy, rumpled, hair tumbling in a mess around her shoulders Savvy stands leaning against the doorjamb to my bedroom. The swelling around her eyes seems worse now that they're open and watching us with an air of suspicion swimming in those purple irises.

My heart clenches at how she's pulled on one of my other hockey tees instead of her shirt. I tell myself now is not the time to notice how sexy that small sliver of skin visible between where she's knotted it and where her oversized joggers hang loose on her hips is.

Mitchell moves to take a step toward Savvy, and I counter

it with one of my own. He needs to keep his distance until she gives him the all-clear.

There's no missing the assessment in how Mitchell pauses to take me in, his eyes doing a full pass up and down my body. A knowing gleam slides behind his gaze, and if Governor Delacourte withheld the reasoning behind his son's request to nullify the betrothal, it's becoming more apparent the longer we stand here—especially when I hold out my hand to Savvy and she takes it, slipping into my hold automatically.

Beneath my arm, Savvy's body is rigid, her muscles tense and coiled tight despite allowing herself to lean on me.

"I take it *this*"—Mitchell glances from us to Duke, who's now leaning against the counter across the room—"is why you asked your dad to call off the engagement?"

Duke nods and takes a sip of his coffee. "She was never mine to have."

"Fuck that," Savvy counters. There she is. My girl may have been knocked down, but she's a fighter and is finally starting to rally. "It's the twenty-first century—I will *not* be bartered like some object. I am my own damn person, and the *only* person who will *decide* who I marry. Is. Me."

"You're forgetting one *little* detail, bugaboo." Savvy's gaze snaps to Duke. When he fails to smother a chuckle, her eyes narrow in that way that always makes my dick stand at attention. "J-Man would have to *ask* you first *before* you could *decide*."

"Do you *really* wanna argue with me about semantics right now?" That glare turns my way when I smirk at her frustrated growl. "DON'T. *You*. Start with me, Noble."

She pokes me in the nose, and I wrap my hand around her wrist and bring her hand down to nip at the tip of her finger. "Don't *you* start with that Noble shit again."

There's a challenge brewing behind her eyes. I can't wait

until we're alone so I can put it to the test. For now, I pull her closer and kiss the top of her head.

"Savvy." Mitchell's voice is soft. He goes to reach for her but lets his hand fall before it can connect.

Fingers slip under the hem of my T-shirt, brushing along the bare skin of my lower back as Savvy adjusts her hold on me when she squares off against her...Mitchell.

"How long?" Mitchell's brows scrunch together. "How long have...have you known...you're...my..." This time, when Savvy's voice breaks, she doesn't continue.

"Father?"

"*Yeah.*" Fuck me, there's that broken tone that gutted me last night.

"I found out about you this summer when I reconnected with your mother." The sound Savvy makes in the back of her throat is filled with so much derision I'm surprised we're not all choking on it. "I need you to know, Savvy, when I knew your mother back then, I didn't know she was married." This time when he reaches for her, he doesn't stop until he has her hand cupped between his. "It's important to me that you know that."

Savvy's mouth presses into a flat line. The stubborn hunch to her shoulders makes me think she doesn't want to believe him, but despite his terrible taste in spouses, he's a lot more genuine than most men in his position.

"Why *did* you marry Natalie?" She pulls her hand free.

I gotta admit, I've wondered this myself.

"Why do you call her Natalie?"

Savvy's nostrils flare, and she runs her tongue across the front of her teeth. She's told me how hard it's been to keep quiet about the true nature of her relationship—or lack thereof—with Natalie. Part of the reason for it was the threats Natalie has been holding over her head, threats we failed to put an end to last night because we turned up nothing on the evidence front. Though, based on seeing how these two interact with each other, I suspect she's also avoided divulging the information out of respect for the genuine feelings Mitchell seems to have for Natalie.

"Because…" She starts then stops. Another beat passes, and her chest rises and falls with one deep inhalation and exhalation. "Despite how *hard* she's pretended in front of you, she's never been much of a mother to me."

Savvy steps out from under my arm, and it's like she's waiting for Mitchell to challenge her. He doesn't.

"I'll admit she had to be…decent at some point, or I doubt my…*dad*"—she chokes on a sob then clears her throat—"would ever have married her or had two—" She goes stock-still as she realizes the inaccuracy of the statement. "Shit."

Shifting forward, I let my front press to her back, reminding her I'm here and I have her back while I angle my chin to keep watch from over her shoulder.

She squeezes her eyes shut, turning and giving me some of her weight. When they reopen, a sheen of moisture coats her lower lash line, and the floodgates open.

She purges detail after detail about how her life was with Natalie, though most of it occurred after her dad's (Jeremy King) death. She had told me some of it, like how she came to live with Carter and how he took care of her before that, but even I didn't know the full extent of it.

The longer she speaks, the paler Mitchell becomes. To be honest, by the time she gets to the part about Natalie's continued threats about having Carter thrown in jail, I think he might actually be looking a little green.

The worst part wasn't listening to the atrocities her mother is guilty of. No. Instead, it was how every time Savvy said her brother's name, her voice would hitch at the end, that small broken edge bringing tiny pinpricks of pain with it.

"So…" Savvy holds her arms out at her sides when she finally finishes. "I showed you mine. Now it's your turn."

CHAPTER 37

MY HEAD HURTS.

My eyes burn.

Razor blades attack every time I swallow.

My body feels like I let Wes use me for a sparring partner.

But…

It's my heart that has taken the worst beating of all.

Jasper is the only reason it's not shattered beyond all repair. He helped hold it, and me, together at my most broken, most vulnerable, even when I could tell he felt uncomfortable with some of my requests.

If there were any lingering doubts when it came to our feelings for each other, we banished them time and time again last night. Even now, he's like a silent sentry at my back, not moving away but not trying to insert himself into the situation. He does that a lot, letting me handle things on my own but staying close enough to back me up should I need him.

It's…different. Not at all like how it feels when I'm with the Royals, and that's telling.

It's also something I didn't think an alpha like him would be capable of, yet here we are.

My throat is dry from all the word vomit I spewed as I dragged every skeleton I could think of out of the King closet. How is it possible to feel lighter while simultaneously feeling like you're about to be crushed by your truth?

I can't believe I admitted…*all* of it. I told every-*fucking*-thing. It was a risk, one that very well might bite me in the ass, but I needed to take the chance. I'm done.

I'm done hiding.

Done playing along.

Done being used.

Done being kept in the dark.

Done being *lied* to.

Just…done.

I refuse to be controlled any longer.

I sway a bit, everything from the last twelve-plus hours catching up to me. The hand resting on my hip flexes then Jasper is there, flush against me, not letting me fall.

"I'll tell you," Mitchell agrees to my request. "But could we sit before you keel over?"

Jasper doesn't bother to wait for me to answer, instead guiding us to take one end of the large leather couch, me settled across his lap and leaving Mitchell to take the matching leather chair opposite us. Duke meanders over, passing a mug off to Jasper and taking the cushion beside us.

The sweet aroma of coffee hits my senses, and after taking a sip, Jasper hands the cup to me. It's more bitter than I usually take it. Still, caffeine is caffeine, and anything that can help me expel the sludge of yesterday from my brain is good enough for me.

I must make a face, though, because I can feel the faint reverberations of a restrained laugh everywhere my body touches Jasper's.

Again I notice the way Mitchell watches how we interact.

There isn't even a hint of disappointment or a trace of the disdain I'm used to from Natalie. Honestly, he seems…I don't know…almost like he's pleased? Like he enjoys the sight of me…well, I can't say happy at this particular moment, but I guess content could work.

Why isn't he more upset that I'm canoodling with a man who is most definitely not the man he arranged a betrothal to? Wasn't the whole thing meant to help foster his future political career?

"The only thing I ask before we begin…" He pauses and clears his throat. "Is that you reserve your judgment until I tell you everything." He doesn't actually say the word please, but the plea is there in his eyes. "I first met your moth— Natalie"—I appreciate the correction—"years ago."

"Roughly nineteen, give or take a few months," I supply. With my birthday closing in fast plus the nine months or so for pregnancy, it's simple enough math.

"Yes." Mitchell nods, shifting forward and resting his elbows on his knees.

My stomach rolls in anticipation, or more like trepidation, of what I'm about to hear.

An arm bands across the tops of my thighs, then a hand is gripping the side of the one furthest away before I feel the hypnotic back and forth pattern of a thumb tracing figure eights over the cotton of my sweats.

With Jasper's touch helping draw the stress from my body, I shift until my back is resting half against his chest and half against the arm of the couch and prepare myself to listen.

Mitchell tells the tale of how, as a young twentysome-thing, he was just starting to prove himself in the family busi-ness. He traveled all the time, visiting any St. James property he was tasked to handle projects for, until the flagship hotel— the one where we both currently reside—landed on his itinerary.

On his second night, he met a flirtatious Natalie at the bar at the St. James, and the two had an instant rapport unlike any he had experienced with anyone else before. As much as I wish I could, I can't blame him for falling for my Momster's charms. Her soul may be black and ugly—that's what happens when you sell it to the devil—but on the outside, she's a beautiful woman. For months now, I have experienced just how adept she is at pretending to be something she isn't.

Again he reiterates that he didn't know she was married, nor that she was pregnant when their affair—oh how that word applies in *so* many ways—ended when he left for his next St. James property.

"If—" He has to pause to clear his throat. "If I'd known about you, I would never have left."

I close my eyes and do my best to breathe through the emotions that simple confession invokes. While the Falcos love both Carter and me like one of their own, I haven't had a parent claim me since Dad died.

Oh my god!

Would he have even loved me if he knew I wasn't actually his?

Shit! Shit! Shit!

The seizing of my lungs is instantaneous as that thought slams home. I have my inhaler out of my pocket and at my mouth before I'm able to recognize how preposterous and outright wrong that thinking is. Jeremy King was a great man, an honorable man, a *loving* man. He wouldn't let the sins of my mother keep him from loving a child, from…loving me.

Leather groans as Mitchell shifts forward in the chair, worry flashing in his gaze at my need to use my inhaler. I wave him off, explaining that despite him learning about my asthma in one of the more traumatic ways he could, using it is common and not cause for concern.

I don't miss the way Jasper slides a hand along my back, leaving it to rest near the bottom of my lungs, or how he squeezes me just a bit tighter when I give him an *I know what you're doing* side-eye.

Still...

I have to know. If only for my peace of mind.

"Did—" It's my turn to clear my throat, swallowing to soothe the scratchiness. "Did my dad know?"

Mitchell doesn't flinch or balk at me referring to Jeremy as my dad. "From what your mo—Natalie has said...no, he didn't."

"Why tell you?" I snap, defensiveness on behalf of my dad creeping into my tone.

His expression remains neutral, not reacting to the sharpness in my voice. "It was a case of fortuitous timing on my part."

I arch a brow at the positive spin he put on that statement.

"Shortly after I moved back to town, there was a fundraising event—though for what, I'm not entirely sure—hosted at the St. James. I had just finished meeting with my bar manager when the event let out, when who should I spot but the same woman I carried this strange torch for, for almost two decades."

I could scroll through my memories to figure out the event, but there would be no use. Before the day Natalie called us to *her* house to tell us about her recent elopement, it had been *months* since the last time we'd seen her.

"She was easy to recognize," Mitchell states. I can believe it. Again, with the whole *sold her soul to the devil* thing, Natalie doesn't look much older than she did when she had me. There's also the plastic surgery she used part of Dad's life insurance money on, sooo...

I listen with a sense of detachment as he continues with his story, doing my best not to let on how it affects me when he relates that he overheard Natalie's casual brushoff when her friend asked if she needed to be home for me. Of course she didn't. I was living with Carter.

Thankfully, he glosses over most of the details of their reunion, sticking with an almost bullet point–type list.

He was sad for Natalie when he learned she was a widow but happy for himself because it meant she was available. It wasn't until he asked about the child he'd overheard she had that he did the math.

"This is the part I need you to not judge me for." He runs a hand across his mouth, and I do my best not to outwardly react. It wasn't the widow comment he was worried about?

"It was also around this time that I had been in talks with my good friend Frank"—he gestures to Duke, who nods in recognition of his father—"about my plans to transition into politics."

"Makes sense to seek out advice from a current elected official." Some of the tension leaves Mitchell at my statement, and his shoulders fall away from where they were hiked up near his ears.

"Yes, but this is where I'm afraid I might have put your current situation"—he bounces a finger between Jasper and me sitting together and Duke—"in motion, albeit unintentionally."

He explains how Governor Delacourte introduced him to Walter Noble. I pointedly ignore how my nipples perk up at the growl Jasper emits when his dad is mentioned. Aren't we a pair with all our parental baggage?

Thankfully, the sound was too low for Mitchell to hear. He continues with how he was told candidates who are married, especially those with children, statistically do better with voters than those who are single. Therefore he had already been in the mindset of looking for somebody to settle down with when he reconnected with "the one who got away." And, *bonus*, she came with a kid—one he could even biologically link back to himself if the story was spun correctly.

"Why didn't you tell me?" I ask.

"About being your dad?" I flinch. I try not to, but I do,

and then I give him a nod. "You were already going through so many other changes—your mom's new marriage, moving into a new home, changing schools—I didn't want to blind-side you with *this*."

"So much for that idea." Though, admittedly, that's my fault because I was the one who snooped her way into his safe.

Instead of calling me out on my underhanded sleuthing, he only gives me a sad smile. "When I realized the...delicate circumstances, I thought it would be best if we got to know each other first before dropping that kind of information on you. Because, Savvy—"

Gah! Why? Why did he have to call me Savvy right now? Natalie refuses to use it, but when he learned that's what I typically go by, he quickly switched over to using it.

"—I am proud as hell to be able to call you my daughter."

Emotion works its way up my throat, and I'm blinking back tears. I don't think I can *ever* recall Natalie saying those words to me.

It's too much. I need a minute.

"Why did you tell Carter before me?" I ask the one question that has been burning on the tip of my tongue since my brother confessed he knew.

"That's not *exactly* how it went down."

He explains that after the showdown between my brother and my currently-muttering-curses boyfriend at the hospital, Carter decided to go for round two with him. Mitchell had just learned about my asthma in a harrowing experience and was dealing with all the fallout that comes with it while making the necessary arrangements for bringing me home once I was released from the hospital.

Carter, who I'm sure was feeling guilty for not being at the dinner party, was most likely triggered into being all kinds of extra overprotective. He demanded I went home with him when I was released, and Mitchell pushed back. Carter demanded to know what right he thought he had to make that call, and a confession about me being his burst free without thought.

I can practically see how it all occurred in my head.

"After I realized what I did, I probably did the most selfish thing I could have done and asked him to let me be the one to tell you."

So many things are starting to make sense.

Carter's avoidance…he probably felt guilty as hell not being able to tell me.

I bet that's also why he all of a sudden seemed to be more comfortable when I decided to start sleeping at the penthouse more.

There's also…

"Is that why you never used the *step* title when you would introduce me to people?" Mitchell nods. "Wow." I slump against Jasper. Here I thought it was just a way for him to make me feel more…I don't know…accepted by him. Another thought slams into me and has me jackknifing up. "Did you enroll me here as St. James because you *want* me to change my name?" My pulse picks up speed, and a cold sweat breaks out across my neck.

"No." The quick, assertive way Mitchell delivers the answer has the worst of my panic ebbing. "I only did that because your—Natalie suggested it."

I pinch my lips together. I just bet she did.

"Can I ask you something now?" The intentional question has my back straightening with attention, and I dip my chin. "Why were you in my safe?"

Oh shit! I whip my gaze around to Jasper, my eyes wide, eyebrows flying up my face, not at all sure how I'm supposed to answer. Is this one of those times it's best to deny, deny, deny?

Jasper looks over my shoulder, keeping his gaze trained on Mitchell for a moment before reaching up to cup my cheek. "Princess." His pearly eyes hold me captive. "I think you should tell him. He might be able to help."

Help? Is he crazy? I know we're sitting here having a moment and shit, and yeah, sure, maybe we've decided Mitchell *is* a good guy.

But…

And, holy crap, it's a *huge* but.

He married Natalie. He flipping *asked* her to be his wife. I may have had my doubts that he was mixed up in her schemes, but why should I think he would go against her?

I'm just a girl he's only begun to get to know. They're the ones who have history. Sure, we share DNA…but the two of them shared vows. Which one of those holds more weight?

CHAPTER 38

RAIN DRUMS A STEADY BEAT, and wipers add a *swoosh-swoosh-swoosh-swoosh* to the cadence while I stare blindly out the windshield. The rain is heavy enough for the water to instantly distort the view in between each back and forth swish of the rubber blades, making the black building in front of me look like it's almost swaying.

I wish I could say my hesitation is because I'm waiting for a lull in the storm, but that is, unfortunately, a lie. All it would take is one text, and the garage door would open and allow us to enter without having to brave the elements.

Nope. The real reason I've sat here watching, waiting, debating is that I can't seem to find the nerve. It's embarrassing.

"Princess." Fingertips skim my cheek before tucking a piece of wayward hair behind my ear.

Sluggishly, I let the curve of my skull roll over the supple leather of the headrest and blink my frowning boyfriend into focus. A familiar wrinkle forms between his dark brows as he studies me, and like every time it's made an appearance this past week, I reach up to smooth it away.

With a hand cupping my nape, Jasper pulls me forward and rests his forehead against mine. I mirror his hold, letting my thumb run along the short hairs at the base of his hairline, simply breathing him in.

"I'm scared," I admit. The fear is irrational, but that doesn't stop me from feeling it.

Jasper's grip on me tightens before he slides his hand around until he's grasping me by the throat. His eyes scan my face, pausing on my mouth with a curl of his own.

My body sways in his hold, my hands falling to his muscular thigh.

A whimper escapes me when he licks his lips, and then they're brushing against mine when he leans in. "There's nothing for you to be scared of inside that building."

I try to turn to look out the window but am stopped with a gentle flexing of his fingers.

I want to believe him, so damn bad. Deep down, a part of me does, but it's buried under layers of doubt and insecurity.

"It's going to be fine." He gives me the tiniest peck, and I release a needy noise. "And if the impossible occurs and I'm wrong—"

I snort, and he nips at my lower lip in warning.

"If I'm wrong," he restarts, undeterred, "and this doesn't go the way I expect…you only need to remember one thing."

The smartass comment dies on my tongue at the pure certainty of his expression.

"If it's you and me against the world"—forehead to mine, tips of our noses touching, eyes crossed to maintain eye contact—"so be it." He punctuates the declaration by slamming his lips to mine.

By the time he breaks the kiss, I'm breathless, but the fear is…not gone, but it's no longer my prominent emotion.

Before I can lose my nerve, I pull out my phone and text Wes to open the garage.

Less than a minute later, Jasper has his Ferrari parked next to Cisco's Hellcat, and Wes is pulling me into a bone-breaking hug. My eyes fall closed as I settle into Wes's embrace, but I catch the half glare, half thankful look he sends Jasper over my shoulder. He yelps when I pinch him with my own warning.

Outside of my brother, Wes is the Royal I'm closest with. The way he holds me just a bit tighter and just a bit longer soothes the worst of my nerves. This feels the same.

"You doing okay, *ma reine*?"

Aww! Look who found his own growl. My lips twitch when I glance over at Jasper, my smile growing when he narrows his eyes. "Princess," he warns.

"You let him demote you?" Wes clucks his tongue. "I really should take his ass in the ring with me and teach him some respect."

I roll my eyes and jab Wes with a quick elbow to the gut. "Play nice." I step out of his hold, moving to Jasper and taking his outstretched hand.

"What?" Wes shrugs, turning to walk toward the door backward. "I'm just saying...all the Royals call you one variation of queen or another. Shouldn't your *boyfriend*?"

"Ignore him," I say to Jasper, coming to a halt when Wes beeps open the door to the residence.

Jasper pauses at the threshold, my arm outstretched between us, concern knitting his brow.

He doesn't rush me. He just gives my hand a squeeze, reminding me he's here should I need him.

"Bitchy, get your ass in here," Tessa shouts from inside, far less patient than my boyfriend. I should be surprised she's here, but then again, she's Tessa, and she takes her role as my ride or die *very* seriously.

The almost imperceptible bounce to Jasper's broad shoulders tells me he's doing his damnedest to restrain a laugh at my bestie's antics, but that slight glimpse into a human emotion is enough to get my feet moving.

My eyes find my brother the second I step inside. He's a mess. His short hair is disheveled like he's been constantly running his hands through it, and even from a distance, I can make out the dark circles under his eyes. I suspect he's been sleeping as shitty as I have this past week.

I don't know which one of us moves first, but I find my face smashed against his chest, the familiar scent of cinnamon and charcoal filling my lungs. Strong arms band around me, and as the weight of his chin falls to the crown of my head, I hear the relieved sigh he breathes against my hair.

"I'm so fucking sorry, Savs." His arms squeeze me tighter, and I can't help but find myself doing the same.

"I know," I admit. The betrayal I felt was gone before Mitchell ever explained the how and why Carter knew about my paternity so much sooner than me. Holding a grudge was not the reason behind our continued distance this last week.

"It *killed* me not to tell you."

"I know." I've spent the last several days picking apart every one of our interactions for the past couple of months. *All* the signs were there. I suspected something was going on. He had been acting too cagey to not think as much, but I had mistakenly chalked it up to the same stuff that made him think it was best for me to go by Samantha St. James at BA.

Oh, how that name has a whole new meaning now.

"Yo-you don't love me less now, do you?" My arms fall to my sides when Carter jerks back after I stutter out my biggest fear.

"The fuck, Savannah?"

A snicker comes from somewhere behind Carter, and I know without a doubt that it came from Tessa. She's generally the only person to use my not-real-name's full form with some sort of consistency. If Carter's slipping into it, it's a sure sign of how much we've caught him off guard.

I probably shouldn't be, but I can't help but be amused by it.

Besides Tessa, I spot each of the Royals spread out around the room, each silent, watching and waiting to see how this is going to play out. None of them move except Jasper, who takes one step closer before he stops at the end of the couch.

In front of me, Carter pinches the bridge of his nose. "Can you explain to me what in the *ever-loving hell* would make you ask me such a *goddamn* asinine question like that?"

I cast my gaze around the room, noting more than one befuddled expression staring back at me.

"Biologically, you're fifty percent less obligated to love me." I shrug, the up and down motion of my shoulder lackluster at best.

"*Obligated?*" Carter steps forward, his hands curling over the curves of my shoulders. The tension radiating from his hold gives away how much restraint he's using not to actually shake me. "You think I love you because I feel *obligated?*"

There's a vein pulsing at his temple, and his left eye is twitching the tiniest bit. I bite down on my lip hard enough to draw blood, squeeze my eyes shut, and nod.

"Jesus Christ."

Hands smack against denim as he releases his hold on me. When I peel one eyelid open, he has both of them folded on top of his head, elbows winged out to the side as he stares at me like I've lost my mind. To be fair, I feel like I might have.

"You listen to me right now, Savannah." He pokes a finger at me. "*Biology* has *nothing* to do with why I"—he smacks a hand to his chest—"love you." This time his finger actually pokes me. "Full siblings, half-siblings, fostered, adopted, born in a pod, or came from motherfucking outer space—I. *Love.* You."

Tears burn the backs of my eyes again, and I sniffle away the tickle inside my nose.

"Not fifty percent," Carter continues. "No *half* measures. You are one hundred percent *my* sister. My love for you is all in and *never* going to *fucking* change. You feel me?"

I nod, emotion choking me as the conviction and slight scold in his tone has it swelling inside me.

This time I'm the one throwing myself at him, wrapping my arms around him, and clinging to him like a lifeline.

A hand comes up to cradle the back of my head when I'm unable to swallow down my sob.

The shuffle of feet has me turning my head to the left, my wet cheek pillowing against the soft cotton of my brother's shirt as I look toward my wide-eyed boyfriend.

A grin forms almost on its own at the disbelieving way he watches how we interact. I get it. To most people, my brother is an unfeeling robot. They're wrong. He's just better at hiding his emotions than most.

With one more crushing embrace, Carter releases me, the compassion wiped off his face as he stares Jasper down with a *Hurt her and die* glare.

Boys. *insert eye roll*

Reunion and making up over, both couches, both Barca loungers, and even the coffee table fill up as everyone finds a seat.

Tessa is all smiles and wagging eyebrows at the hand Jasper threads into the rips of my jeans. I roll my lips between my teeth to restrain my own smile. Nobody else needs to know I've made it a point to work *all* of my ripped jeans into my regular rotation of clothes. What can I say? It's flipping hot how he latches onto any bare skin he can get his hands on.

"We missed you around here, Mini Royal," Leo tells me, holding out the side of his fist for me to knock mine against.

I grimace. "You guys should probably think of a new nickname for me," I say. Not because I hate it; I don't. It just feels like I don't have a right to it anymore.

"Why the hell would we do that?" comes from Cisco.

"It's one of my faves." *Me too*, I think, agreeing with Lance.

"Is that another one he's"—Wes wiggles a finger at Jasper —"going to get all growly about?"

"You going all shifter on us like *His Royal Highness*, too?" Tessa can't help but chime in too.

"Jesus," Carter mutters, running a hand over his face.

I do my best to let the chaos infuse me with joy, but then I remember why I started this conversation. I drop my gaze, focusing on one of the frayed threads of my jeans instead of the faces of the crew I've been proud as hell to call myself a part of.

"I'm not actually a King." I swallow. "So I'm really not a real Royal."

"Savvy." Carter puffs out a breath, but I keep my gaze trained on each individual string I'm adding into the rip closest to my knee.

It isn't until he grabs my chin gently and physically turns my head toward him that I lift my eyes to his. They narrow, and his Adam's apple bobs with a swallow. "How many more times are you going to force me to tell you to cut that shit out?" He arches a brow. "Being Jeremy King's daughter didn't make you a Royal."

"But I'm not actually from a founding family."

"And what about Cisco? Or Lance?" He waves a hand at where the two of them sit in the Barca loungers. "Are they not *real* Royals because they aren't from founding families either?"

Dammit! He had to go and use logic on me, didn't he? Every time my brain would remind me that, yes, there are Royals not from founding families, and in Lance's case, not even from Blackwell, I've ignored it. I hate losing an argument. I hate it even more when I know I'm *wrong,* and that's why I lost it. I shake my head.

"Name and blood relation don't make a Royal." Carter chucks my chin. "It's what's in here." He taps a spot above my heart. "And what you have in here?" Another tap. "Is the definition of being a Royal."

I will not cry.

I will not cry.

I will not cry.

I blink and look toward the ceiling.

Shit!

I'm totally going to cry.

"I know I step in and get involved in things you've told me time and time again I don't need to. I get it." I run a finger beneath my lashes and meet my brother's determined gaze. "I'm overprotective, and I won't apologize for it." His chest expands with a deep inhalation. "But *who's* the one leading us into battle later?"

My voice is small, barely above a whisper. "Me." I clear my throat and add a little force behind it when I repeat, "Me."

"Damn fucking right."

Jasper squeezes my thigh, Tessa cheers, and each of the Royals hits me with their own *Damn fucking right* nod. Each sign of encouragement reaches inside my chest and tugs until that insecurity is yanked from my subconscious.

A sense of rightness spreads through my veins, pulsing beneath my skin.

They're right. With a nod of my own, I admit it.

No more.

Time to go put an end to the Momster's evil reign.

CHAPTER 39

I HAVE BEEN in my fair share of offices for political figures, but none of them could have prepared me for Chuck Falco's.

Sure, there's the requisite American flag and state flag bracketing a large oak desk with an equally sizable padded leather chair behind it, but it's the homey, almost welcoming vibe of it I can't seem to wrap my head around.

The desk itself is positioned in front of a wall of glass draped in cream-colored curtains that coordinate perfectly with the cream and tan upholstered furniture and royal blue area rug arranged in the center of the room.

There's a signed Eric Dennings Baltimore Crabs jersey hanging on one wall, built-in bookshelves that match the wood of the desk on another, and a beautifully carved fire-place set into the wall opposite them.

While the football jersey is a cool touch, I couldn't tell you why I noticed any of the other details. I can only guess it was an attempt to distract myself from how utterly stressed Savvy seems.

She hasn't said a word in the ten minutes we've been here.

She came in, hoisted herself onto the edge of Chuck's desk, tucked her hands under her thighs, and has sat silent ever since.

Carter's been pacing the room like a caged lion while the other Royals settled in talking amongst themselves and Tessa.

Despite her current silence and how she's coming to terms with her own bombshells, Savvy has been a pillar of strength and the driving force in doing what needed to be done for today to protect those she cares about.

It's too early to tell how her relationship with Mitchell will shake out, but since he showed up at my dorm last weekend, he's been nothing if not a true partner to his biological daughter.

The heartbreak was clear to read on his face as Savvy told him about all the ways Carter, even at a young age, made sure she was cared for. The way Mitchell's expression transformed in anger at how Natalie was not only threatening *both* her children, but how she could so blatantly dismiss everything the one did to step up in the wake of her abandonment had me confident he would be our true ally.

Matching silver frames line the wide mantle above the fireplace. The heat from the healthy fire burning in the hearth warms my legs as I inspect each individual picture.

The largest frame, an eight-by-ten horizontal shot of what I can only assume is the entire Falco clan, sits front and center in the arrangement. A stout woman with curly white hair sits at the focal point, and the slightly younger Chuck and a man I guess is most likely his older brother Anthony given the strong resemblance stand just off-center from her, each with an arm around an adolescent version of a King sibling.

Another frame features a photo of Carter in a black cap and gown sandwiched between both Falco brothers, the three mugging it up for the camera.

Farther down the line is one of a little girl, and though the hair tied back into pigtails is blonde, not dyed silver, I'd recognize that taunting tilt to her lips anywhere. It shouldn't surprise me in the least that even as what is probably a six-year-old, Savvy managed to radiate her innate fierceness while clutching a familiar-looking black stuffed dragon in her arms and hanging upside down from a twentysomething Chuck's arms.

I've heard the stories and know the older Falco brother is their godfather. After I got over my irrational jealousy, I witnessed the familial way they interact with each other. Seeing Savvy and Carter featured so prominently in this display only drives that fact home.

"Is this where your obsession with Toothless began?" I tap the glass of the dragon picture, angling my body around to see Savvy where she's perched on Chuck's desk.

"Obsession." Wes snorts. "Yeah, that's an accurate description."

"Bite me, Wes." Savvy doesn't bother to look at him sprawled out in Chuck's chair, feet kicked up on the desk behind her. She just holds up a hand and flips him off, causing the others spread out around the room to laugh.

"Aww, don't be salty, *ma reine*."

My molars are at risk of cracking at the casual use of the endearment. The way he leans back farther in the chair and shoots me a wink tells me he knows it too and is going to keep doing it to mess with me. It might be safe to say I'll be dealing with delayed payback for how I treated Savvy when she first arrived at BA for some time to come.

"Plus, you're the one who still sleeps with that thing when you're at home, Savs" Cisco adds.

"*Really*, Princess?" My bad mood is gone in the wake of learning this shocking tidbit about my girlfriend.

"Not a word out of you about it, Noble," she threatens.

Undeterred, I close the distance between us, nudging her knees wide to move in close. Her long legs bracket my hips while I do the same with a balled fist on either side of hers. I feel as much as I hear her quick intake of breath when I bring my mouth down to her ear. "You know what you calling me Noble makes me want to do to you, Princess."

Hands coast up the length of my torso and grasp the strings hanging from my hoodie. "Promises, promises… Noble." She punctuates the taunt with a nip to my jaw.

I'm point two seconds away from saying *Fuck it.* Who gives a damn about all these people in the room or that one of them is her older brother. I even go as far as sliding a hand up to the middle of her back, readying myself to lay her down on the surface of the desk—

Knock, knock.

CHAPTER 40

THE SHARP RAP of knuckles knocking on the door has my head falling forward to rest on Jasper's chest. Breathing in his intoxicating sandalwood scent has me wishing we could stay in our own little bubble.

This past week has been exhausting in so many ways it's hard to believe we're in the home stretch.

Who would have thought the easiest obstacle we'd deal with would be putting an end to my engagement? I was prepared for a lot more pushback given that my proposed future father-in-law was a public figure, but Governor Delacourte surprised us all with his simple acceptance.

Even Jasper had a moment of shock at the lack of argument from his own father. I'm sure the governor's acquiescence helped smooth the way, but I think it was the open apology from my...Mitchell that helped the most.

Since hearing how he championed and defended me, I haven't been able to think of him as my stepdad any longer. I also haven't been able to think of him as my dad despite that being true, though the more time we spend together, the more

I've been growing toward being able to. For now, he's just Mitchell.

My feet kick against the side of the desk as my legs fall from Jasper stepping out from between them. I frown, but he doesn't go far. His shoulder brushes mine as he leans against the edge of the desk, his feet crossing at the ankles like they do when he posts up against my locker.

Wes mutters about someone having a death wish when the weight of Jasper's hand skims the curve of my ass as he flattens it on the desk's top, his thumb stretching up to play with the waistband of my jeans.

There's so much riding on the outcome of this meeting that I can already feel the tightness forming inside my chest, and I take a quick hit from my inhaler to help keep my asthma at bay.

Jasper pinches my ass as he watches me, reminding me he's here and to lean on him should I need to.

"Ready?" Chuck asks the room, hand poised on the door-knob. Collectively we nod, and he opens the door.

Mitchell's face is the first I see as the door swings open, and his eyes automatically scan the space until they lock on me. The moment he finds me, relief enters his gaze, and a warm fuzziness fills me. His mouth curves into a grin, and I feel mine mirroring the action.

What…is this?

This sudden surge of rightness? The confidence blooming in my gut and radiating out through the rest of my body?

It's familiar, but at the same time, it's not—that instinctive certainty that a person would put his life on the line to help save yours if needed. I know it from my brother, not from a parent.

I'm not entirely certain how I'm supposed to handle it, but I won't lie and say I'm not excited about getting the chance to figure it out.

When Mitchell steps to the side to allow Natalie to enter,

the icy chill emanating from her blue gaze sets me to rights. *That's* what I'm used to, that accusation for daring to be born. *Yeah, love you too, Mom.*

Natalie's haughty you-are-all-my-puppets-and-you-will-do-as-I-say air lessens the smallest smidge when she catches sight of not just me but Jasper sitting vigil with his arm around me, along with Carter and the rest of the Royals scattered about.

There's a clang then the slap of shoes hitting the floor as Wes straightens out of the chair, coming around the desk and taking the post on my other side while Carter moves in next to Jasper.

"What is all this?" With her shoulders rolled back, hands shoved in the pockets of her Burberry trench coat, one spiked heel planted in front of the other, Natalie does her best to look down her nose at us.

Verbally, no one says a word. Instead, like plates being added to a chest press bar, I feel the weight of each set of eyes as they land on me.

This is different—having the Royals look to me, not Carter, to take the lead.

Fingers spread up under my shirt, the press of their tips into my skin anchoring me and lending me their strength to see this thing through to the end.

"Well, Natalie…" I cross one leg over the other and lay my wrists on top of each other. "This is your chickens coming home to roost."

"Does she have to liken us to poultry?" Tessa whispers before she's hushed, Leo covering her mouth with a hand cupped over it.

"Mitchell." Natalie turns to him. "Why are we here?"

I need to bite my lip to keep from smiling at the way Natalie's micro-bladed brows knit when Mitchell doesn't reach for her like he would have a week ago.

"Why don't we sit?" He waves a hand toward the six-person table against the far wall.

"Go on, Natalie." Chuck makes a shooing motion with his hands when she hesitates. He might be enjoying this as much as I am. "Have a seat."

There's another scan of the room; this time, some of that holier-than-thou-ness slips a little. Her movements are stiff and robotic when she finally moves toward the table.

She's too busy huffing and puffing over nobody helping pull out her chair to see the slight nod Mitchell shares with me. He knows none of this would have been possible without him, but still, he's allowing me to have the control. That's all I ever wanted—to be the one in control of my own life.

It blows my mind that this man who grew up in a world of privilege, who could have so easily not helped me to foster his own goals, chose to put me first instead.

Trusting others outside the circle I grew up with is a new concept for me, yet each time I've chosen to do so in my bid to take back my life, I've learned something from it.

Scared is not an adjective I would have ever used to describe myself, so why is that exactly how I allowed Natalie to make me feel, make me act for months?

No more. It ends today.

Reaching a hand behind me, I feel around until I find the stack of folders I'm searching for.

With a quick kiss to Jasper's cheek, I jump down from my perch and cross the floor with long confident strides. Without giving Natalie a chance to levy a threat about my open association with Jasper, I slap the folders onto the polished tabletop with a resounding smack, each one fanning out from the force.

With a glance back over my shoulder, I see the *You got this* quirk to Jasper's lips before I direct Carter with a *Get over here* nod.

"You wanted to know why you're here, *hmm*, Natalie?" I

move until I'm standing on one side of Mitchell with Carter taking the other, the three of us a united force opposite where Natalie sits.

"What did I do to deserve such a disrespectful child?" Her carefully lined lips twist into a frown. The effortless way she can cast herself as the victim is something I don't think I'll ever be able to wrap my head around.

"Nothing." I run my tongue across the front of my teeth and share a look with my brother. "You've done absolutely *nothing*." A smug satisfaction starts to bloom on her face, but I shut that shit right down. "In fact...you've done so *little* you probably shouldn't be allowed to call me your child."

Panic flares swift in her eyes as her gaze jumps to Mitchell, who's sitting in almost bored stony silence.

"Hate to break it to you, Natalie—" A burst of laughter escapes me, cutting off my words. "Nobody is coming to your rescue. You're completely on your own here."

"You listen to me, you little brat." She stabs a finger to the table, her bloodred nail digging into the wood. Ah, there's the vitriol I'm used to. "Just because you *fail* to see how marriage is supposed to work by throwing away the engagement I so *painstakingly* arranged for you for *that* one"—she flicks a hand toward Jasper—"doesn't mean others do. Mitchell is my husband. He's not going to sit here and let you speak to me this way."

"Yes, he will," I say with complete confidence. "Just like he helped put an end to your antiquated attempt at a betrothal."

"What?" Natalie's eyes go wide, and her jaw unhinges. "I orchestrated that for *you*," she accuses Mitchell. "Why would you risk a possible path to the *White. House*?"

Mitchell only shrugs, one shoulder rising beneath his suit jacket. "Some things are more important."

"*What?*" Natalie's screech is enough to have everyone

wincing and a few of us covering our ears. "It's the White House, Mitchell. If we played our cards right, you might have been *president* one day. What could possibly be more important than a chance at the presidency?"

It's truly remarkable how the future was so clear in her mind, how sure she was that all these elements would just click into place because she willed it to be. To her, Mitchell eventually ascending to the country's highest office was a done deal as long as we fell in line. Delusional is the best descriptor to use.

"Oh...I don't know." I hold both hands out and shrug both my shoulders mockingly. "*Maaayybe* his only child's happiness?" I add in a head tilt for good measure. "Though I guess I shouldn't expect you to understand that since you have zero maternal instincts of your own."

A part of me is disappointed I shot down Tessa's offer to film this fiasco because Natalie's expression could have launched a thousand GIFs; it's *that* comical.

She gasps. "You know?"

"No thanks to you." A bone-deep satisfaction fills me. "It's a shame your hubris will be your downfall."

I spent so many years being neglected, followed by months of living under the weight of her threats. I honestly have a hard time remembering a time when I didn't wish she was gone from my life.

Finally, we found a way to make that happen, to put an end to all her lies and deceptions and excise the cancer from all our lives.

Bracing a hand on the table, I place a finger on the red folder and drag it from the fanned out pile before sliding it in front of a silent Natalie.

A half sneer, half smirk forms on my mouth as I slip a finger under a corner and flip the folder open. My birthday may be in a few weeks and will probably be here and gone before anything is processed, but still, Mitchell insisted on petitioning for full legal custody. "This was filed yesterday." I tap the papers inside before laying out another folder, this one with the paternity results I found in Mitchell's safe.

The color leeches from Natalie's face, but I'm not done.

Another folder, this one green and thicker than the others, is opened and set down to display the bound prenuptial agreement she signed before marrying Mitchell.

When I pick up the black and final folder, I extend it to Mitchell to see if he wants to do the honors on this one, but he motions for me to continue.

I won't lie—though my typical suggestion for getting retribution would have fallen along the lines of *Let's hold her down and pluck each of her eyelashes out*, knowing we're about to cut her off from everything she worked and schemed for fulfills my savage side.

Instead of gently placing this one down like I did the others, I let it drop with a plop, the color-tabbed papers inside fluttering from the force.

I fold my arms over my chest in an effort not to pump my fist in the air at how Natalie's eyes bug out when she reads the words *Petition for Divorce* typed in bold capital letters across the top of the page.

"Is this supposed to be some kind of joke?"

"I assure you it's not," Mitchell says. "While I can admit to some of the more self-serving motivations behind the quickness of our union, I did *not* enter this marriage on a foundation of lies like you."

"Wha—"

Mitchell holds up a hand to cut off whatever tirade Natalie was about to go on. "The tenure of our marriage was short enough that you actually aren't entitled to a thing from me—"

Any color remaining in Natalie's complexion is gone at the realization.

"—but if you sign these papers"—he circles a finger over

the whole pile—"before walking out the door, I'll cut you a check for a hundred thousand dollars as soon as the divorce is finalized with the courts."

Natalie opens her mouth again, but Mitchell stays her by extending one finger.

"Though there are a few strings that will be attached."

A war plays out on Natalie's features as she calculates how best to turn this around to her advantage. "What kind of strings?" she finally asks through gritted teeth.

The air shifts and crackles with new energy as Mitchell practically transforms in front of our eyes. Gone is the approachable man unashamed to show his vulnerability and eagerness to establish a relationship with his long-lost daughter. In his place is the formidable persona that aided him in becoming a revered hotelier.

"If you *ever* attempt to do anything that would hurt Savvy or Carter"—Natalie's eyes narrow at the inclusion of Mitchell's non-biological child—"I will have my legal team bury you in so many lawsuits you'll *never* be able to dig your way out."

"What do you care about Carter for? He's not yours."

My nose scrunches at her grasping at any straw she can in an attempt to hold on to the one thing she has in this situation, always resorting to threats even when she's clearly lost.

"He's Savvy's brother. That's good enough for me." Mitchell's answer is automatic. "Plus, he's done more for *my* daughter than I'll ever be able to repay—" Emotion has his voice wobbling, and he takes a beat to clear his throat. "Putting an end to your veiled threats is just one small step I can take to help show how much I appreciate everything he's done to care for Savvy when I wasn't able to."

This was the part I was most nervous about. There's no actual legal document we could present to garner Natalie's agreement on this. Not even an NDA could guarantee she wouldn't be able to turn over any evidence she claims to have

—though none of us could find proof it actually exists—to the authorities. We just have to hope our own financial and legal threats are enough to keep her in check.

A weight landing on my shoulders startles me, but I settle once I realize it's just Carter putting his arm around me. I reach for the hand hanging down my arm and link my fingers with his.

When I laid out the details of my plan, he was skeptical. Sure, we have the Falcos in our lives, but Carter has been operating on survival instinct for so long I understood the hesitancy. This all seemed too easy, too good to be true. Silly man. He should have trusted me enough to help handle our issues together instead of trying to shield me from them.

I get a whispered "Stop holding your breath" from him as we wait to see what Natalie will do.

After what feels like forever, the last of the fight seems to drain out of her, and she reaches for the pen Chuck was more than happy to offer her.

Once the last of the papers are signed, Mitchell pushes his chair back and rises to stand. He places a kiss on my cheek and tells me he'll see me tomorrow before he escorts Natalie out of the room. He already has movers at the St. James packing her belongings to expedite the extraction of her from our lives.

I'm not sure if I'll be returning to the penthouse or if I'll just go back to Carter's now that I'm not stuck living under Natalie's thumb.

It doesn't matter.

You know why?

Because when the time comes to choose, it'll be my decision—*mine*, and no one else's.

This year may have started entirely out of my control, but in the chaos, I've managed to create something for myself I never knew was possible.

EPILOGUE

THERE IS nothing hotter than seeing Savvy in full-on fierce boss bitch mode. She may not be ripping anyone's fingernails off like what I've learned is her go-to suggestion for payback, but I hundo P see how the Royals nicknamed her Savage. There's just this glow about her when she's plotting something that I can't explain outside of that it makes my dick harder than anything else. It has made getting through my morning classes extremely uncomfortable.

With winter fully upon us, the tables inside the cafeteria are filled to capacity. The pants-tightening issue I've had all morning is reaching problematic proportions as I follow the sway of Savvy's hips while she weaves through the tables until she comes to the one Arabella and The Unholy Trinity claim as their own.

Not sure what my girl has planned but trusting her enough to know she can handle herself in any situation, I stop on my way to our own table, close enough to overhear but not crowd Savvy while she does her thing.

Every eye in the lunchroom is on her, tracking her movements as she drags a chair around from another table and positions it at the head of theirs.

"Can we *help* you?" Arabella snarks.

Purple eyes flit up briefly to meet mine, a playful smirk curling at the corner of those still-puffy-from-my-last-kiss lips before she slowly crosses one leg over the other, the edges of her boots overlapping. That footwear should have been my first clue my girl was in a mood today: thigh high, leather, sky-high spiked heel.

"Well, you see…" Elbows slide across the wooden table-top, pushing deep and angling toward Arabella. Casually, Savvy rests her chin atop her folded knuckles, a waterfall of silver locks cascading over the curve of her shoulder as her head tilts to the side. The cacophony of conversation and cutlery moving across plates comes to a halt at how each of Savvy's measured movements are watched intently.

"Since my first day, I couldn't care less about the social hierarchy here"—Arabella lets out a *Whatever* snort, which Savvy pointedly ignores—"but *you* were the one hell-bent on asserting *your* place in it."

"Says the girl spreading her legs for the top king in this place when he wasn't hers to have in the *first place*." Usually, Arabella is the picture of calm, a poised ice queen. Except…in a single sentence, Savvy has managed to break that typical bitch facade of hers until her final words come out as an ear-splitting screech.

Again those eyes rise to mine, a familiar troublemaking twinkle in them before they slide back to Arabella, sparking with a dangerous edge.

"Is that why you decided to play creepy-psycho-bitch paparazzo?"

There's a slam of a foot hitting the floor as Savvy uncrosses her legs.

"You took pictures of us."

Savvy's spine snaps straight, her demeanor turning on a dime.

"You decided to play judge and jury, hoping that by sending our parents those pictures, they would play the role of the executioner."

"What in the *world* are you talking about?" Arabella's tone is confident, but the way her gaze keeps shifting to the side gives away her guilt.

"Playing dumb isn't going to help you now, Arabella. We know it was you." Savvy pushes up from her seat, setting her palms flat on the table and leaning in close. "Stay away from me and mine."

"How dar—"

"Don't." Savvy slashes a hand through the air, cutting off Arabella's attempt to assert her dominance before it can gain any traction. "It's Monday, and I'm *so* not in the mood for your bullshit, Arabitch."

A gleeful chuckle has me looking to my right, where Duke has the biggest shit-eating grin on his face, also watching the lunchtime entertainment. "I'm going to have to up my game to keep up with smoopsie-poo's insult creativity."

While I can one-hundred-percent agree with the accuracy of the statement, it doesn't stop me from throwing an elbow back until it connects with Duke's stomach. His soft *oof* is music to my ears. "What did I say about your pet names for *my* girlfriend?"

The wattage on his grin turns up impossibly higher, and my hand balls into a fist to prevent what I know will become the urge to punch him for whatever smartassery he's about to spew. "Savvy may have made you a *smidge*"—he puts his barely separated thumb and forefinger close enough to my face that his pinch is blurry—"less broody, but you're still just as much, if not more of, an alpha asshole."

My own lips start to tip up at the corners, but I'm quick to shush Duke's next quip so I can hear Savvy instead.

"We know what you did. But…" Savvy raises one arm, folding all the fingers on her hand down except for the middle one, which she uses to boop Arabella on the nose. "Try to keep this in mind…"

Even from here, I can make out the way Arabella's throat moves with a nervous swallow as she looks my way. If she's looking for my help, she'll be sorely disappointed. Honestly, she should know better. It's like she's forgotten how ruthless I can be.

Folding my arms over my chest, I rock back on my heels and continue to enjoy the experience of my savage queen going to work. Prince has taken great pleasure in regaling me with *all* the stories of how they came up with Savvy's…well… Savvy name. I'm pretty sure he did so to fuck with me, just like he makes sure to call Savvy *ma reine* every chance he gets. The fucker.

Not even Prince's razzing can take away from how hot Savvy is like this. The sex we had after the showdown with Natalie was the hottest we've *ever* had…and that's saying something.

"If you don't heed my warning about staying in your lane—"

Savvy straightens, stepping back from the table and sliding both her hands down the soft cashmere of her uniform blazer. Again her gaze rises to mine, and again we share another one of those wordless exchanges I didn't think I could share with anyone except Duke. Ours holds an entirely different kind of significance.

Savvy slides her gaze back to a now squirming Arabella. "—you might find your already tattered social status roadkill beneath my tires." A line of white flashes between her pink lips, the pure innocence in her smile causing all the ladies sitting around the table to fall back in their chairs. "We good?" She nods, not waiting for a response. "Toodles, bitches."

She punctuates her goodbye with an exaggerated finger wave and saunters back to me, stopping just out of my reach. Her eyes drop to my fly, her teeth pulling her bottom lip into her mouth when she spots the telltale bulge there. "You liked that, did you?" One of her brows arches high on her face.

"Immensely, Princess." Done with the distance, I step into her space, hooking a hand around her nape and tugging her close. "Why don't you come with me to the locker room or the parking lot, and I'll show you just how much."

Fingers walk their way up the buttons of my shirt like they're stepping stones before ending with one painted tip covering the dimple in my chin. "Did I ever tell you how much I like the way you think, Noble?"

I growl, and the twitch of her cheek gives her away. "Are you *purposely* baiting me, Princess?"

Arms loop around my neck. "What if I were?" Her lips brush mine as she speaks.

A face pushes its way between us. "It's *really* unfair how you two make me watch your foreplay when you refuse to let me have my own fun with Tessa."

Savvy smooshes Duke out of our personal space. With a shake of her head and a round of muttered curses, the three of us move to take our places at our own table.

With my arm draped across the back of Savvy's chair, we all settle into our new normal. The rest of the year should be interesting, that's for sure.

ANOTHER EPILOGUE

SOMETIME IN COLLEGE

The cool night air kisses my cheeks while the vibrations from my idling engine keep me warm as I wait for my boyfriend to get his sexy but slow self here.

I'm drumming my fingers on the hood behind me in sync with the sound of Kesha playing through the rolled-down windows when I finally hear the roar of Jasper's F8.

I squint my eyes against the glare of the headlights as they cut across where I'm perched on Toothless's hood. It may prevent me from being able to see through the windshield, but I can say with complete certainty he's giving me that smirk of his.

He pulls around until his front bumper aligns with mine, and sure enough, that maddening and nipple-hardening facial expression is firmly in place on his stupidly handsome face as he steps out of his Ferrari.

I match his with one of my own, running my tongue along

the backs of my teeth as he curls a hand over the top of my thigh and uncrosses my legs.

His hands slide up them, his fingers kneading the muscles along the way before slipping under the band of my jeans and caressing the naked skin beneath. "I've never taken you for a tease, Samantha."

Oh shit!

He hasn't called me Samantha much since he learned of my Savvy name, but when he does? Oh boy…the current method of teasing I chose is *all* the more noticeable right here, right now.

"It wasn't meant as a tease," I lie with a shrug of my shoulders.

"Oh yeah?" His fingers lower farther to fully cup my ass, using his new leverage to scoot me closer to him until my center is cradling the hard-on pressing against his fly. "Then what would you call leaving your panties"—he leans forward so his lips brush the shell of my ear, his hot breath blowing across my skin—"your *damp* panties, mind you, laid out across my center console?"

I raise my arms, running my fingers through the longer hairs on the top of his head to draw out the delay of my answer. His eyes go heavy under my touch, and when his pearly gaze connects with mine again, it's hazy with lust.

"How do you know they were damp?" I singsong to deflect. He's not wrong. I can't help it that I discovered watching him play hockey turns me on…*a lot*.

One of his hands leaves my body and disappears inside one of the back pockets of his jeans, only to reemerge with the purple lacy thong I wore to the BTU hockey game tonight.

They're hooked around one long finger, and my core clenches, knowing exactly how that finger feels inside my body, how the thumb now stroking along the interior of the front panel feels doing the same to my clit.

"Now…" He rolls his piercing along the shell of my ear, a

whimper escaping me as my head falls to the side. "You want to explain to me how these *aren't* a tease, Princess?"

The Royals give him all kinds of shit for choosing a nickname they consider a demotion, but I like it. It probably helps that it gives me all sorts of warm fuzzies I would *never* admit to out loud, but I can't deny experiencing them every time I recall how he challenges them back.

Let me tell you…

Jasper Noble staring down five guys and shamelessly telling them that while I am a queen, I'll *always* be his Princess…

Yeah…if I were still wearing those panties he's holding, they would one hundred percent be ruined.

"They were *an incentive*, Noble." I push forward and nip at his chin. My lips curl into a grin along his skin at the growl he emits in response to my use of his last name. I'll never stop calling him that when it so easily gets a rise out of him.

"You better fucking have your inhaler on you, baby, because I'm not going to hold back."

Yes please!

I swallow down that automatic enthusiastic response and twitch a finger in front of his nose. "Not so fast." I cluck my tongue. "There's only one way you get to ride me tonight."

Jasper pulls back, his dark brows dipping as he glares down at me. "Oh *really*?"

I love the almost exasperated doubt that laces his tone.

"Yup." I lay my hand over the BTU Titan logo covering his muscular chest and push until I'm able to slide off of Toothless. I step to the side once I'm on my feet, trailing my fingertips across the matte black paint as I move around the curve of the hood to the driver's side door. "And this time, the stakes will be fair because you'll know *who* you're *actually* racing."

"Are you trying to say if I can't beat you in a race"—he

makes his way to his own driver's side—"I won't find you naked in my bed tonight?"

"Of course not." I shake my head.

"Then why would I want to race when I could just bend you over Toothless right now and reenact one of my favorite nights of my life?" He gives a pointed glance around the empty lot we're parked in.

"Because…" I drawl. "If you win…I'll let you put it *anywhere*."

I don't think I've ever seen Jasper move faster in my life, and that man *flies* across the ice. I guess one should never underestimate the promise of anal.

Are you one of the cool people who writes reviews? Ruthless Noble can be found on Goodreads, BookBub, and Amazon.

Want a place you can talk all things Royal without worrying about spoiling things for those who haven't read it yet in The Coven? Join the Royalty Crew Spoiler Room HERE.

Randomness For My Readers

So…to say Jasper Noble was a difficult nut to crack would be an understatement. Every day when I sat down to write I would say, "Okay, I'm going to write, but I have no idea what I'm supposed to write."

When I first released book 1 of this duet I was beyond nervous. I wasn't sure how people would take to Savvy because of how strong willed she was. But, wow, oh wow, the fierce love this chick has gotten from readers makes my heart happy.

So now for a little bullet style fun facts:

- Savvy was first born in my brain when I had writers block back when I was writing *Puck Performance.* She was just something I played around with first for fun.
- Did you know when Savvy was first born in my brain her story was supposed to be an RH with Wes, Duke, and Jasper…with Jasper not even being the main guy.
- It wasn't until I was doing rewrites on my U of J

Series and I decided to add The Royals into that storyline that it had to change.

- Many of you have asked me about Tessa, but I have a feeling whenever I finally sit down to write her story she's going to be my most problematic child. She already has 3 potential suitors, and I already get the impression she might throw me for a curveball.
- We're not even going to talk about Carter and Em, oh-kay.
- Joey and Kennedy my cover models are a couple in real life.

If you don't want to miss out on anything new coming or when my crazy characters pop in with extra goodies make sure to sign up for my newsletter! If my rambling hasn't turned you off and you are like "This chick is my kind of crazy," feel free to reach out!

Lots of Love,

Alley

Acknowledgments

This is where I get to say thank you, hopefully I don't miss anyone. If I do I'm sorry and I still love you and blame mommy brain.

I'll start with the Hubs—who I can already hear giving me crap again that this book also isn't dedicated to him he's still the real MVP—he has to deal with my lack of sleep, putting off laundry *because… laundry* and helping to hold the fort down with our three crazy mini royals. You truly are my best friend. Also, I'm sure he would want me to make sure I say thanks for all the hero inspiration, but it is true (even if he has no ink *winking emoji*)

To Jenny my PA, the other half of my brain, the bestest best friend a girl could ask for. Why the hell do you live across the pond? I live for every shouty capital message you send me while you read my words 97398479 times.

To my group chats that give me life and help keep me sane: The OG Coven, The MINS, The Tacos, The Book Coven, and Procrastinors & Butt Stuff (hehe—still laugh at this name like a 13 year old boy).

To all my author besties that were okay with me forcing

my friendship on them and now are some of my favorite people to talk to on the inter webs.

I know I dedicated the book to them, but there needs to be an extra shout out to Laura and Julia, for without them I wouldn't have finished this book. I've lost count of how many times I texted "Help, this book sucks." Laura you've been stuck as my cross-country bestie for years but thanks for bringing Julia into my crazy!

For my beta readers and their shouty caps as I played around with the cliff and story.

To Maggie for being my asthma sensitivity reader and letting me ask her question after question as my inside source for Savvy and never thinking it was weird when I'd text her with "Question" at 2 a.m.

To Sarah and Claudia the most amazing graphics people ever in existence. Yeah I said it lol.

To Britt for helping Jenny keep my crazy self in line and making my Insta an absolute work of art.

To Jules my cover designer, for going above and beyond, then once more with designing these covers. I can't even handle the epicness of them.

To Jess my editor, who is always pushing me to make the story better and giving such evil inspiration that leads to shouty capitals from readers.

To Caitlin my other editor who helps clean up the mess I send her while at the same time totally getting my crazy.

To Gemma for going from my proofreader to fangirl and being so invested in my characters' stories to threaten my life *lovingly of course*.

To Dawn and Ellie for giving my books their final spit shine.

To my street team for being the best pimps ever. Seriously, you guys rock my socks.

To my ARC team for giving my books some early love and getting the word out there.

To Jen and Wildfire PR for taking on my crazy and helping me spread the word of my books and helping to take me to the next level.

To Wander and his team for being beyond amazing to work with and this custom shoot for Savvy and Jasper's books. And Joey and Kennedy for being the perfect models! Seriously I think the world can hear my fangirl squee whenever I get to message with you both on IG and I love that you guys are a real life couple!

To every blogger and bookstagrammer that takes a chance and reads my words and writes about them.

To my fellow Covenettes for making my reader group one of my happy places. Whenever you guys post things that you know belong there I squeal a little.

And, of course, to you my fabulous reader, for picking up my book and giving me a chance. Without you I wouldn't be able to live my dream of bringing to life the stories the voices in my head tell me.

Lots of Love,

Alley

For A Good Time Call

Do you want to stay up-to-date on releases, be the first to see cover reveals, excerpts from upcoming books, deleted scenes, sales, freebies, and all sorts of insider information you can't get anywhere else?

If you're like "Duh! Come on Alley." Make sure you sign up for my newsletter.

Ask yourself this:
    * Are you a Romance Junkie?
    * Do you like book boyfriends and book besties? (yes this is a thing)
    * Is your GIF game strong?
    * Want to get inside the crazy world of Alley Ciz?

If any of your answers are yes, maybe you should join my Facebook reader group, Romance Junkie's Coven

Join The Coven

Stalk Alley
    Master Blogger List
    Join The Coven
    Get the Newsletter

Like Alley on Facebook
Follow Alley on Instagram
Follow Alley on TikTok
Hang with Alley on Goodreads
Follow Alley on Amazon
Follow Alley on BookBub
Subscribe on YouTube for Book Trailers
Follow Alley's inspiration boards on Pinterest
All the Swag
Book Playlists
All Things Alley

Also by Alley Ciz

The Royalty Crew (A #UofJ Spin-Off)

Savage Queen

Ruthless Noble

#UofJ Series

Cut Above The Rest (Prequel) Freebie

Looking To Score

Game Changer

Playing For Keeps

Off The Bench- #UofJ4 Preorder, Releasing December 2021

BTU Alumni Series

Power Play (Jake and Jordan)

Musical Mayhem (Sammy and Jamie) BTU Novella

Tap Out (Gage and Rocky)

Sweet Victory (Vince and Holly)

Puck Performance (Jase and Melody)

Writing Dirty (Maddey and Dex)

Scoring Beauty- BTU6 Preorder, Releasing September 2021

About the Author

Alley Ciz is an internationally bestselling indie author of sassy heroines and the alpha men that fall on their knees for them. She is a romance junkie whose love for books turned into her telling the stories of the crazies who live in her head…even if they don't know how to stay in their lane.

This Potterhead can typically be found in the wild wearing a funny T-shirt, connected to an IV drip of coffee, stuffing her face with pizza and tacos, chasing behind her 3 minis, all while her 95lb yellow lab—the best behaved child—watches on in amusement.

facebook.com / AlleyCizAuthor
instagram.com / alley.ciz
pinterest.com / alleyciz
goodreads.com / alleyciz
bookbub.com / profile / alley-ciz
amazon.com / author / alleyciz

Printed in Great Britain
by Amazon